The
KEENING

ANNE EMERY

The KEENING

A MYSTERY OF GAELIC IRELAND

Published by ECW Press
665 Gerrard Street East
Toronto, Ontario, Canada M4M 1Y2
416-694-3348 / info@ecwpress.com

Cover design: Tania Craan
Map: Rhys Davies

LIBRARY AND ARCHIVES CANADA CATALOGUING IN
PUBLICATION

Title: The keening : a mystery of Gaelic Ireland /
Anne Emery.

Names: Emery, Anne, author.

Identifiers: Canadiana (print) 20210208899 |
Canadiana (ebook) 20210208902

ISBN 978-1-77041-584-3 (hardcover)
ISBN 978-1-77305-794-1 (ePub)
ISBN 978-1-77305-795-8 (PDF)
ISBN 978-1-77305-796-5 (Kindle)

Classification: LCC PS8609.M47 K44 2021 | DDC
C813/.6—dc23

We acknowledge the support of the Canada Council for the Arts. *Nous remercions le Conseil des arts du Canada de son
soutien.* This book is funded in part by the Government of Canada. *Ce livre est financé en partie par le gouvernement du
Canada.* We acknowledge the support of the Ontario Arts Council (OAC), an agency of the Government of Ontario,
which last year funded 1,965 individual artists and 1,152 organizations in 197 communities across Ontario for a total of
$51.9 million. We also acknowledge the support of the Government of Ontario through Ontario Creates.

ONTARIO
CREATES

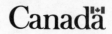

ONTARIO ARTS COUNCIL
CONSEIL DES ARTS DE L'ONTARIO
an Ontario government agency
un organisme du gouvernement de l'Ontario

Canada Council   Conseil des arts
for the Arts   du Canada

Canadä

PRINTED AND BOUND IN CANADA

PRINTING: FRIESENS   5   4   3   2   1

MIX
Paper from
responsible sources
FSC
www.fsc.org   FSC® C016245

In honour of my Fermanagh ancestors,
whose ships cast off from Irish shores
long before I was born.

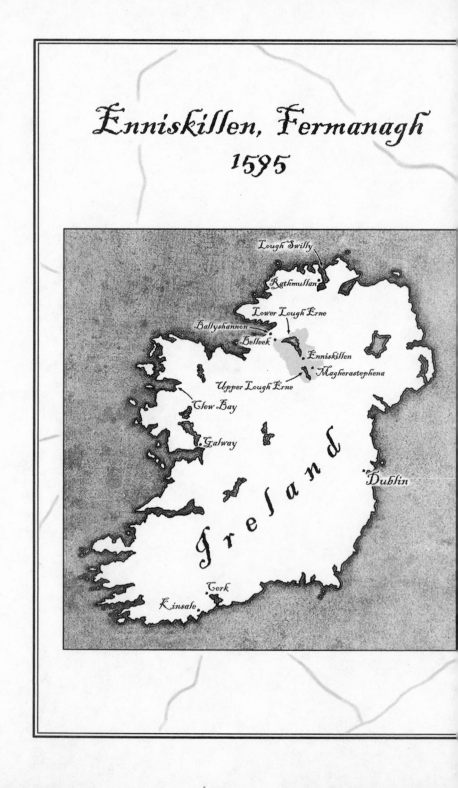

Enniskillen, Fermanagh 1595

Lough Swilly

Rathmullan

Lower Lough Erne

Ballyshannon

Belleek

Enniskillen

Magherastephena

Upper Lough Erne

Clew Bay

Galway

Ireland

Dublin

Cork

Kinsale

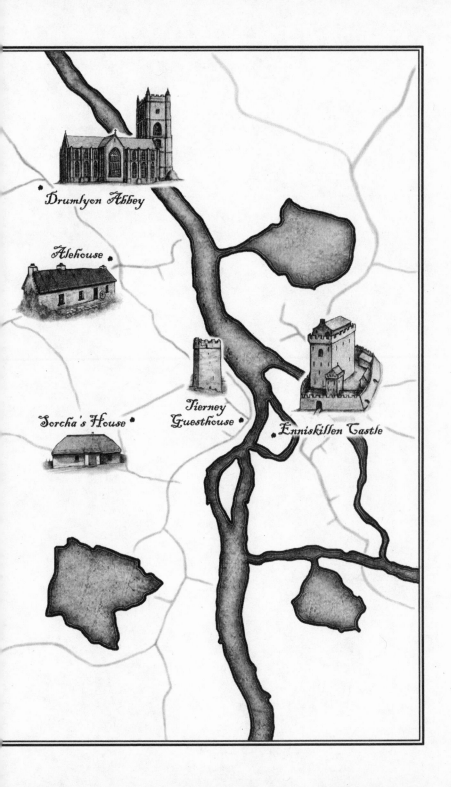

AUTHOR'S NOTE

A word about words: the Irish characters are, of course, speaking in the Irish language, so their parts of the story, written in English, are "translations" of the Irish. Even so, I have taken the liberty of inserting Irish-language words and phrases from time to time, to give a flavour of the richness of the language. On the other hand, I have used English-language versions of some personal names and place names, where the originals might prove difficult for the reader; for example, Owen for Eoghan and O'Hussey for Ó hEoghusa. A "hospitaller" is a person whose profession it is to provide hospitality: a guesthouse owner.

I have used quotations from various sources in my chapter epigraphs and in the text. Full credits for all quotations can be found in the notes at the end of the book. You will see other poems and recitals, which have sprung from the minds of my characters.

PROLOGUE

1595

"A never-dry cauldron, a dwelling on a public road, and a welcome for every face." Those were the requirements laid down in the eighth-century law text *Bretha Nemed Toísech* for a briugu, a hospitaller, like the ancestors of Brigid Tierney who had set up this house to welcome visitors nearly two hundred years ago. And although the formal designation of briugu or brughaidh had all but died out, the Tierneys' five-storey stone house was still known far and wide for its hospitality, and its rooms were often filled with guests. Of course, in Ireland every householder was under a duty to provide hospitality; a person who failed in this obligation could be required to pay compensation appropriate to the rank of the person refused. But with the Tierney family, this had been their profession, a calling that had given them an elevated rank in society equal to that of the nobility, equal even to a chief poet. Only a family of great wealth could take on such a responsibility, given that guests were not charged for their lodging, food, or drink. And Brigid's family were wealthy in lands and herds. The Tierney house overlooking the River Erne had been, and was now, open to anyone in need of hospitality.

And Brigid's cauldron — her cooking pot — was never dry. Her stores of ale and wine were never depleted, even after the excesses of last night. And her hearth was clean and warm — or would be, once the servants got it scrubbed and polished again.

PART I

CHAPTER I

*The boast of the Irish was hospitality, and even their
enemy . . . acknowledges that they were recklessly
hospitable.*

— John O'Donovan, *The Tribes of Ireland: A Satire
by Aenghus O'Daly with Poetical Translation by James
Clarence Mangan*

2017

"Top o' the mornin' to you, good sir!"

"Christ!" Mick Tierney muttered under his breath. He was
standing behind the reception desk of Tierney's Hotel, the family
business in County Fermanagh, and it wasn't morning at all, at least
not here in Ireland. It was late in the afternoon. The man who had
addressed him was an American clad in plaid short trousers and a
large floppy hat.

"And to you, sir," Mick responded, beaming all the sincerity
he could muster at this latest clump of tourists.

"We're later than planned," the man said. "One of the group
had to be taken off the bus and left in Drogheda." He pronounced
it Droh-GHEE-da, instead of DRAW-h'da. "Sick as a dog.

Something she ate; not used to the food over here." The food? "Hope you haven't cancelled our reservations!"

"Not at all."

"Okay, I'll bring the folks in."

The man turned and headed back outside. Mick followed him out and eyed the latest load of guests as they stumped out of their tour bus and gathered beside it in a flock. They all raised cameras, phones, and sundry other gadgets and snapped pictures of the three-storey Georgian house that was Tierney's Hotel. It was a hot day, early July, and the afternoon sun blazed upon the western end of the building, momentarily bleaching out the stains on the white façade, the crumbling masonry at the corners, the frames on the multipaned windows that were long overdue for a coat of white paint. The Victorian addition in the back needed even more work, but the visitors couldn't see that from here. The house faced east, overlooking Enniskillen town and the castle. The castle sat on the bank of the River Erne; in the past, it had been entirely surrounded by water-filled ditches, reinforcing its defensive position as an island fort. The tourists pivoted and trained their lenses on the castle and the river.

Mick took a deep breath and launched into his routine. "Céad míle mallacht!" he shouted at the group. "Sure, that's what we say in Ireland to welcome the likes of yous to the emerald isle!" As always, he marvelled at the clobber on them: garishly patterned short trousers, sandals with socks, baseball caps made of some kind of mesh with "one size fits all" plastic straps at the back of them, and something they called "fanny packs" (!) hanging below their bellies. The family jewels, he supposed. He continued with the blarney, and they beamed back at him. "Come in, come in. Don't be standin' out here in the blazin' sun. If it catches you enjoying it, it'll retreat to its usual place behind the clouds, and yous won't see it again till your plane lifts off at Shannon." Appreciative laughter greeted this little bon mot. He caught sight then of his pal Gerry, the driver of the bus, who was engaged in lifting the tourists' enormous travelling cases from the luggage compartment. Enough luggage for two months, even though Mick knew they were determined to "*do* Ireland" in seven days. He gave Gerry a wink and a jerk of his head, which meant, "See ye inside."

Mick shepherded his tourists into the lobby where Sharon, the receptionist, had taken up her post and was waiting for them with a friendly smile. Mick assured them that the lovely colleen behind the desk, and all the members of his staff, would cater to their every need. "Could we have stayed in business for six hundred years if we did not?"

Gerry came in then and waited until the latest mob had shuffled away out of earshot. Gerry was a Dublin man, and he was frequently at the wheel when a slew of tourists came to Tierney's.

Mick said to him, "How are things in the Free State, Gerry?"

"I see you've recovered your ability to speak, Michael," Gerry said. "I couldn't make out a word you were saying to that crowd. Thought you were possessed there for a minute. A fella from Cork had taken over your soul."

"Ah sure, that's what they expect to hear. They're from America."

"You didn't see the value in educating them to the way yous speak here in the North?"

"Nah. Give the punters what they want."

"'A hundred thousand curses' is how you greet them, and you say give them what they want?"

"There's not one of them would know the difference."

"Ah now, that's hardly the spirit set out in that charter you've posted on the wall." Gerry pointed to the poster Mick's daughter

Róisín had fastened to the wall beside the reception desk. The words had been written around three hundred years ago by a Mr. Dolan, a native of Fermanagh, who described the local nobility thus:

> The inhabitants are most commonly stout, high-minded, liberal, courteous, portly, and well-coloured; their nobility much given to recreations and pastimes as hunting, hawking, riding, drinking, feasting, and banqueting with each other, admirers of harp music and playing at chess or tables, lovers of science and comical pastimes. . . . Let them be poor or rich, all persons are welcome to what they have, either by night or day; they begrudge none, of what kind he be, and heartily give their best cheer (they can afford).

"Not a word in that about cursing your visitors, Mick."

"Ah now . . ."

"It's going to be a long, hot summer for you if you're annoyed with them already."

Róisín came in then, wearing a paint-spattered white smock over her summer-weight trousers and shirt. She had two small children in tow, a girl of four and a boy a year younger. All three of them were carrying art supplies, the markers and brushes hanging out of the boy's canvas bag at precarious angles. The wee lad, Rory, had a chubby little face, blue eyes, and black hair. His sister, Ciara, had hair of a rich red like her mother's, and her ma's hazel eyes as well. They both had hugs and kisses for Mick. Róisín said, "Welcome back, Gerry. You weren't stopped at the partition, I hope." A little jest about the fact that Ireland was still partitioned into two separate countries, despite the disappearance of the border checkpoints, and despite the peace agreement of 1998. She knew he was a lifelong republican, as, she suspected, was her dad.

"All right, to work now, lads," she said to the children. She pushed aside a large room divider that had been placed up against the wall, revealing two work-in-progress murals in the lobby. The small one, low to the ground, was the children's, and it featured brightly coloured donkeys, castles, puppies, and fish. A much larger tableau was being painted above it. "Remember how we do this now. I'm working on the left side today, so you work on the right." She held out her left hand and her right, and they staked out their ground and dumped their colouring implements on the floor.

Róisín's picture was a marvel. Armed with books full of images drawn in sixteenth-century Ireland, by John Derricke and Lucas de Heere and others of the period, she copied what she liked of them on her wall. She also had a colour photo of an intricate model constructed by a local man, Gordon Johnson, depicting a house party hosted by the Maguire family in 1586. At the centre of Róisín's mural was a banquet with the local chieftain — in this case, "The Maguire" — in the middle and other notable personages at the table. A man was standing and reciting a verse or telling a tale, while another was seated at a harp. Ladies wore elegant dresses in beautiful shades of rose, blue, green, and yellow, and some had elaborate head coverings made of white linen. There were golden goblets and platters of meat in front of the guests.

"This feast took place at the Maguires' table over four hundred years ago," she said, "but when I've finished here, there will be no doubt that my version of it took place at the original Tierney guesthouse. And no doubt either that we can pull the same thing off here any evening of the week."

"It's brilliant, Róisín," Gerry told her. "I can't imagine being able to draw like that."

"Ach, I'm only copying the pictures in this book."

"It's that simple, is it?" He rolled up his sleeves and walked towards the wall. "Would you like me to do some of the copying myself, help you out?"

"Ah well, no. Perhaps not, Gerry."

He laughed. "Exactly. It takes talent, and you have it and I have not."

"We'll leave yous to it," said Mick, and he led Gerry into the bar. Mick was pleased to see that more than half the tables were occupied. He had recently replaced the old scuffed barstools with chairs of dark wood, with comfortable backs, and had faced the inevitable slagging about keeping oul fellas comfortable for longer bouts of drinking. Mick and Gerry sat in two of the chairs, facing the gleaming array of bottles behind the bar. But it was the taps that interested the two of them, and they ordered pints of Guinness from Dinny, the barman. Dinny was slight and fair-haired, and he looked barely old enough to enter the place without showing proof of age, but he knew every stout and spirit in the place, and he provided service with humour and grace.

A few of the new guests came into the bar and seated themselves around a table, and one man, with a lopsided grin, struck up the tune "When Irish Eyes Are Smiling."

Gerry mouthed the words, "A fiver." But in fact they had long ago ceased betting on how soon "Irish Eyes" would come out of a tourist's mouth. A bunch of them swayed back and forth with their arms linked, trying to grin and sing at the same time, and took photos of one another while they were at it. Mick smiled at them and carried on a muttered conversation with Gerry about the latest goings-on — or, to be more accurate, goings-off — in relation to the shared government, shared between unionists / loyalists and nationalists / republicans, at Stormont in Belfast. The power-sharing arrangement had arisen out of the Good Friday Agreement of 1998 but in yet another instance of history repeating itself, the scheme had recently collapsed. Mick turned his mind away from the endless political travails of his country, just in time to hear an excited whisper as a woman emerged from the loo and encouraged her friend. "Go on in, Betty. It's so *modern!*"

"How long are we going to listen to this blather, Michael?" Gerry asked. "We should be with the lads down the pub. Sharon's got things in hand at reception."

"Abair é!" Say it! "Let's go before I lose the head with these people." The plan suited Mick. He'd never had a burning desire to be a hotelier; he'd had an earlier career selling football gear and other sports equipment. But when his father decided he'd worked the place long enough and it was time, according to family tradition, to hand it over to his eldest son, Mick didn't want to be ungracious, didn't want to buck tradition. His two brothers were far away, living in Australia, so he couldn't hand it off to them. But it became apparent early on who the genuine hospitaller was in the family; his daughter Róisín had loved the hotel from the time she was able to toddle round the place. Róisín's talent for drawing came not from Mick but from her mother, Mairead, and seeing Róisín with her brushes and her smock made his heart ache for his wife, gone seven years now. Mairead had been working as an assistant in an architectural firm where she did drafting by hand and on the computer. The firm designed new buildings and renovated older ones, and it was in one of the older ones that Mairead met her death. The structure was unsound, and she fell from a third-floor balcony. Died instantly. Mick and Róisín and her older sister, Bríd, were devastated and, of course, still grieved for Mairead. Bríd was now living in Canada, having married a man from Prince Edward Island. Mick considered it a blessing that Mairead's artistic abilities lived on in Róisín. And it was as if she had been born into the role of chatelaine; she was forever moving things about, recommending things Mick should install or remove, and it was Mick's plan to hand the business over to her whenever she felt ready to take it on. She had the two wee kids, and a husband who had done a runner, so she was not yet able to devote herself to the place full time.

Mick and Gerry finished off their pints and slipped out of the room. Mick signalled to the valet. "Give us a spin to Blake's, would you, Johnny?"

When they were seated in the car, Gerry said, "I've a busload of Germans coming to you next week, Mick. You're so busy at the hotel now, it'll only be the rare old times you'll be getting out to Blake's for a jar."

"So busy at the hotel, God willing. If ever a place was cursed! The downside of peace in the North of Ireland: there's a threat to our place now from a shower of property developers!"

"What? They want to buy it off you?"

"No, they've an option to buy the land just behind us, where the original guesthouse was back in the day. We've never been sure how extensive the grounds of the old tower house were, how far they went beyond the back garden of our hotel. Part of the old property is under our land, we know, but some of it might have been under land we don't now own. Well, they're after all that property there, and parcels to the side and almost to the front of us. Almost all around us, in other words."

"Who is it that's doing this to you?"

"A rich Yank, what d'ye expect? Him and his company."

"Don't be telling me it's for a golf course. Isn't that always the way of it?"

"Not a golf course. That would be bad enough, but at least we'd still be able to see over it. It wouldn't block our view of Lough Erne. No, they want to put up a pile of 'executive holiday homes' for the rich and infamous. And a clubhouse or a casino or some fucking thing, and that's what would be between us and our view of river and the castle."

"Jaysus, Mick."

The afternoon sun blazed down upon the blue waters of the River Erne, and the castle on its bank, as the car reached the low ground by the river. Mick twisted in his seat, pointed back towards the hotel. "Picture what we'll be looking at from here, Gerry, if the bloody things get built up there."

"God help us."

"I've a cousin over in America. Jimmy. We were like brothers growing up. He's in business in New Jersey, and he knows about this Prule."

"This what? What did you call it?"

"Prule. It's his name. He's not from New Jersey, but from one of their other states. I don't know which one. But he made a show of himself going to New York. New York because he wanted to 'get the Irish onside.' The Irish who live in that part of the U.S. He has big ideas about investing over here, now that 'the bullets have stopped flying.'"

"The bullets never stop flying where he comes from. They're all allowed to have guns, the Americans. How many mass shootings do they have in the run of a year?"

"Who can count that high? And I was after reading something in the news the other day: nobody over there can agree on how many people you have to shoot in order for your shooting to qualify as a 'mass' shooting. Four? Three? Anyway, back to this Prule. He has notions of tower blocks and shopping centres over there, and now these shagging holiday homes over here. He's considering opening places in Belfast, Derry, Omagh, and here in Enniskillen. And he has a two-year option to purchase the land here."

"Who owns the land now, Mick?"

"Family by the name of McCracken from Belfast. I don't know what they had in mind for the land; they never did anything with it. Now they're looking at selling it. So, anyway, this Prule fella showed up in New York and called some class of a meeting to entice investors."

Johnny glanced over at Mick and said, "That sounds like something right up my street, you know. That's what I'll do: invest in holiday homes, just outside your window, and make my fortune. And I'll keep my car and fetch the beaming new residents from the airport, deposit them right at their doors."

"You will in your hole, Johnny. Anyway, cousin Jimmy was curious and went to the meeting. He's always been of two minds about being over there, thinks about packing up the family and coming home here. His enthusiasm, at least for this venture, was short-lived. He sent me a video of the man's speech. Me and Roísín watched it on the computer. If you could have seen yer man! Prule is the owner of the company and he was so *excited* to be *sharing about* the project with all those lucky bog-trotters in New York. Enormous fucker with big hair, and the teeth on him. You know the great mouthful of teeth so many of the Yanks have, more in number than the rest of mankind, or so it appears, and the bright blue-white glare coming off them. And this fella never stopped grinning the whole time. I wanted to clatter the teeth down his throat."

"Who could blame you?"

"And he was on about these *executive homes* and their double garages, 'big enough for two Land Rovers!' Imagine all this going on around my hotel."

"Go séideadh an diabhal san aer iad!" May the Devil blow them into the air!

"Amen to that."

Out of long habit, all three men in the car made a quick sign of the cross as they passed St. Michael's Church in Enniskillen town. The Protestants were represented right across the street where another stone church was seated, St. Macartin's.

Gerry said, "Your guests will complain about the congestion and the noise, and no fine view."

"That's our biggest selling point, the spectacular view of the water and the castle."

"You'll be getting bad write-ups on the internet, and word will get around . . ."

"We'll be ruined. Róisín will have her heart broken."

"Fuck's sake, Mick. What are you going to do about it? I'm thinking some of the lads may have some materials left over from our recent Troubles, items that didn't quite make it to the decommissioning stage."

"Blow the fuck out of it, you're saying, Gerry. Sure it may come to that."

Mick had never taken up the gun during the Troubles, though there were many times when he had to steel himself against the temptation. But he had been more than willing, as a homeowner and then as a hotel owner, to provide shelter for fellas who were on the run from the alliance of loyalist paramilitaries and security forces that ran these six counties of Northern Ireland. Tierney's Hotel had at times been a safe house for those fighting the British-imposed partition of their country. The war, the Troubles, had been over for two decades now, but the partition was still in place.

Johnny stopped the car farther along on Church Street, in front of a building with a red-painted exterior bearing the name William Blake. Mick and Gerry thanked Johnny and headed for the pub.

"Place has been here since 1887, I see," said Gerry.

"Aye, and so have some of the punters," Mick replied as they went inside. The two of them exchanged the same remarks every time they came to the bar. "And this fella, for definite." He pointed to an elderly but vigorous man with a full head of iron-grey curls and lively dark-blue eyes. He was holding court at the bar, his curly head nodding in rhythm to the tale he was spinning. Mick stood by and waited for the story to end, for the appreciative laughter to die down. Then he greeted the storyteller. "'Bout ye, Da?"

"I'm stickin' out, thank ye, Michael," his father, Liam Tierney, said.

"And your mother, Liam?" asked Gerry.

"Ach, she's the same as ever. A wee bit frailer now but she's looking fine and healthy, and her past her ninetieth birthday."

"Good to hear."

"I've been doing a bit of patching and painting about the house. My room and hers, putting a bright yellow on the walls of both of them. Livens the place up, like."

"Sounds good. The tide's nearly out there," Mick said, pointing to his father's glass. "Kevin, refills for these gentlemen here and the same for myself and Gerry."

Mick sat next to his father, with Gerry on the other side. Gerry said, "Looks as if the hotel is doing a good trade, but Mick tells me the area may be getting a bit too popular. Attracting the attention of the wrong sort of people."

"Place is cursed, so it is," said Liam.

"Maybe the plan will fall through."

"Not if history has its way. There's a curse on it, I'm telling you. Has he never heard the whole story, Mick?"

Mick shook his head no.

"Come here till I tell ye," and Liam launched himself on the long, woeful tale of Tierney's Hotel. "The place was boycotted years back, and our family was still bearing the stigma up until very recently. It seems better now with the new generation."

"The stigma?"

"There has been a guesthouse of some kind or other on our land since the early 1400s, maybe even before that. Back in the old briugu days when being a hospitaller was a profession, and a high-ranking one at that. Oh, Tierneys were the quality in the olden times! Our branch of the family comes down from a woman named Brigid, who was legendary for her hospitality in the heyday of the Maguire chieftains. Now, she was a Tierney daughter, and she may have married but, if so, there is no record of his name. And the marriage may have been after her children came along. All we know is that she always used the name Tierney for herself and the children. And a line from an old history book stays with me. This was an Englishman commenting on our ways back in the 1600s, shocked about who could inherit property in Ireland: 'the bastards had their portions as well as the legitimate'! Isn't that a fine way to be talking about my ancestors! The house eventually became an inn where guests paid for their accommodation. In the 1920s, my great-grandfather took it back from another branch of the family who could never make a go of it, because of the boycott that had been going on for more than seventy years. But with the passage of more time, he started doing well with it.

"As shameful as it is in the telling, Gerry, some of the Tierneys did not behave admirably in Famine times. Or that's the story anyway. They had the inn, and they also had a farm with tenants on it in the usual way. And the Brits raised the rates they charged for the land. Then we had the Famine, which meant falling rents and landlords with increased expenses. So, people like Roderick Tierney booted their tenants off the land. And people around here remembered that, and many of them boycotted the inn."

"Yer man wouldn't have been held in high esteem, I can see that," Gerry agreed. They ordered another round, and when their pints were properly poured, they each enjoyed a sip.

"Speaking of the old place now, Da, Róisín is doing a mural. She's just getting started."

"Is she now? I haven't been in the place for a few days. I'll come by and take a gander at it."

"She's going to do pictures of the people who were here in Enniskillen when the old tower house was still standing. Right now, she's working on a mural of a banquet in the late 1500s, and she's going to put a wee girl and boy in it with the faces of her own weans, surprise them with it, like. Ah, she has great plans for the place."

"Róisín's a fine young lady. If anyone can do credit to that place," Gerry went on, "it's Róisín. Didn't she study hotel management or something like that?"

"Aye, she took correspondence courses in that after studying art and design here at the college. And her two weans came along in the middle of it and still she got it done. Tierney's Hotel is her vocation in life!"

"And," Liam put in, "that gurrier who left her on her own with those two wee cubs, he'll be sorry for what he lost."

"He's sorry already," Mick replied. "Saw how the business was improving and started regretting the divorce and coming around again. Róisín, bless her, will have nothing to do with him, except when he visits the kids."

"It's a wonder the gouger is still among the living, with you hating him so," the old fellow said.

"He's among the living, but if I had my way, he'd no longer reside among the citizenry of Enniskillen."

"Where would you be sending him, Mick?" asked Gerry. "Van Diemen's Land?"

"County Armagh, I'm thinking." Mick leaned in towards Gerry and said in the low, menacing voice he had used on his daughter's husband years before, "You know yourself, Gerry, what they used to call parts of County Armagh."

"Bandit country."

"That's right. And I know a number of lads there whose trigger fingers have been left idle and twitching since the peace agreement. So wouldn't I love to pack off young Brayden and send him there. But he has visiting rights to see the children, so . . ."

Liam nodded in sympathy. Unlike Mick, Liam Tierney had taken up the gun, after seeing a young woman friend shot and killed in a hail of bullets fired by a carload of loyalist paramilitaries who were aiming at somebody else entirely, a pair of well-known republicans emerging from a bar. Liam was wounded in the attack, and still walked with a limp, but that hadn't stopped him from taking up arms against the faction that had killed his friend, and so many others. Liam didn't talk much about those days, and Mick had never pressed him, even though as father and son they were very close. They were both widowers, Mick's mother, Fionnuala, having died of pneumonia twelve years earlier, at the age of sixty-one. Mick had had a couple of relationships since Mairead died, most recently with a Welsh woman, Lowri, who had visited Enniskillen as part of her research into the Celtic languages. He'd been over to Wales to see her, but there just wasn't that spark between them that had been there with Mairead. This wasn't love. Lowri knew it, too; they had said goodbye with half-hearted assurances that they would get together again, but they both knew it wasn't in the stars. As for Liam, if he had been squiring any ladies around, Mick had never heard about it.

If Liam was close-mouthed about his experiences as an IRA man, or as a man about town, he had a seemingly endless supply of conversation about other matters. Well oiled now and full of cheer, he made an offer: "Would yous like me to give you a recitation?"

That was greeted with enthusiasm by one and all, and Liam rose to his feet, pint in hand, and said, "Now I hope I won't be putting the frighteners on yous. One of our colonizers back around 1600, fella by the name of Fynes Moryson, had this to say about rhymers such as myself, and poor trembly folk like all yous in here today. He said that Irishmen are 'affecting extremely to be celebrated by their poets, or rather rhymers' — I guess he's making sure that the likes of me don't get notions above our station — 'and fearing more than death to have a rhyme made in their disgrace and infamy.' He refers to us rhymers as 'pestilent members' of the commonwealth and accuses us of encouraging folks to engage in 'licentious living' and 'lawless and rebellious actions.' I'll leave old Moryson now, and I'll get on to my recitation, before yous all go off to your licentious living and your rebellions."

"I don't have anybody lined up for licentious living till half ten tonight, Liam," one of the punters said, "and I know she won't let me out of the bed for the rebellion till well past noon tomorrow, so you go on with your rhyme now."

"I will." And so he launched into one of his party pieces. Mick's father had always nurtured a particular loathing for the English poet, and reviler of the Irish, Edmund Spenser, and he frequently adapted Spenser's words and delivered them to an appreciative audience.

"Now we're a well-educated, well-read pack of rabble here in Blake's, are we not?"

"We are, so!" came back the reply.

"And we've all read our Spenser, and his *View of the Present State of Ireland*, have we not?"

"Wouldn't have missed it!"

"And his lamentations over what befell the English who invaded here, or settled here, over the centuries, and how so many of them became, in the well-known phrase, more Irish than the Irish themselves. So pity poor Spenser, knowing that more and more of the Saxons were to be sent our way. And that's the subject of my rhyme today."

"Let's hear you, Liam!"

"Why did you send your gentlemen over here?
You haven't read your Spenser then, man dear.
Here's what old Edmund had to say
'Bout what happened to the Saxons of his day.

They invaded with the Normans back in time
And into bed with the Irish did they climb.
And like unto mere Irish did become,
Barb'rous and rude exactly like the scum.

More lawless and licentious were they then
Than the wild Irish themselves had ever been.
Idle and degenerate and lewd,
They lived amongst the savage and the rude.

How then does one subdue a stubborn nation?
Your Majesty, I say bring on starvation.
Let them eat grass until their mouths are green,
Then shall they revere our Faerie Queene."

His doggerel verse was met with great enthusiasm, and offers of drink, which Liam Tierney accepted with good grace.

"The old man still has it, Mick," Gerry remarked. "A dashing oul divil, and he has a way with words."

"He does."

When Liam had given them an encore, Mick allowed as how he should get back to his workplace, so he rang Johnny for a spin home. Mick and Gerry said their goodbyes and went outside to wait in the street. Mick said, "There may be one way to throw a fuck into that plan the developers have for my hill. Archaeology."

"How's that now?"

"We'll talk up the history of the old guesthouse, that the ruins of it are likely still there under the ground. And who knows what fascinating artifacts round the place as well? And we'll call in a crowd of archaeologists to commence digging. That often stops things in their tracks, or slows them down so much that the developer gives up."

"But, Mick, the Yank himself will have to apply for permission to build it, apply to the Department of the Environment, or whatever it is."

"Yeah, it's an agency of the Environment Department, the Planning Service."

"Well, there you are. You've looked into it. So you know the department is really strict about making sure nothing will hurt the environment or old buildings, archaeological sites and all that. From what I've heard over the years, there are all kinds of assessments and evaluations and God knows what else that can be ordered. The developer will be slowed down even without you getting involved."

"I don't want this hanging over our heads, Ger. I want to make sure this clown doesn't start the process, and get the momentum going, and me not knowing what's going to happen. I'm thinking there must be something under our land, walls of the old house, pottery, something. It's happened before. And then, when his option to purchase expires, I'll go to the bank, take out a loan, and buy as much of the land as I can to make future schemes like this impossible."

"You'll have to charge your guests more for their rooms. No more nights in the Big House for your middle-income bus tourist."

"We've always wanted to keep the place affordable; Liam was adamant on that point. Georgian splendour was not to be the preserve of the land-owning class any longer."

"You want to start the digging right away, forgetting that you yourself will have to wait and go through hoops of some kind to allow the archaeologists in."

"Yeah, the archaeologists need permission, too. A licence. I'll send my oul fella in to persuade the authorities."

"He won't have the, em, the same means of persuasion he used to carry in the troubled times."

"Maybe they'll be as terrified as the people back in the old times, terrified that if they don't fall into line, he'll condemn them to disgrace and infamy with his rhymes."

CHAPTER II

Strains of music from harpers, old stories with marvels,
drinking of wine and swift gaming — there are many
mead-assemblies in your royal palace; Ireland is one
like yourself, you are a fitting mate for her . . .

— Cú Choigcríche Ó Cléirigh, Maguire praise poem XX,
in *Duanaire Mhéig Uidhir*, ed. and trans. David Greene

1595

B rigid's servants had the Tierney house back to rights after
her latest guests departed. There were not as many servants
as there had been in her grandfather's day. It was Brigid who
greeted the guests and escorted them to their rooms, and who
usually served their drinks. But she had a cook, a maid for
personal services, and another to keep the house clean; there was
a horseboy and the men who worked the land and managed the
herds of cattle and sheep. It was a more modest operation than
it had been in the past, but Brigid was pleased with the way her
people kept things running. And was pleased with how the maids
kept a good eye on the children when Brigid was out of the house.

Right now it was the horseboy, Donal, whose services were required. Her daughter Eileen had lately fallen ill, and Brigid was taking her to see the banliaig, the woman physician. Brigid wrapped Eileen in her warm woollen cloak, and they went outside. It was late in the month of May, but the day was uncommonly cool. They headed towards the stable, but Donal saw them and waved. Brigid whispered words of reassurance to Eileen as they waited for him to lead Brigid's young black mare out of the stable.

"Is it still hurting you, Eileen, darling?"

"It is." The child looked up at her with eyes full of woe.

"Sorcha will make it all right for you."

"I don't know . . ."

"She will."

When Brigid was seated on the horse with Eileen in front of her, they started out on the short ride to the home of Sorcha, the physician. Eileen was eight years old now, but Brigid had never lost the joy she felt as a mother when her daughter was curled up against her. Eileen clung to her now, the cloak wrapped tight to keep out the chilly breeze. Brigid leaned over and kissed the top of her russet curls. "It won't be long now."

Sorcha's house was a modest one, with white lime-washed walls and a thatched roof. She had gardens of herbs and patches of blue and purple flowers; farther out from the house were an oak grove and other stands of trees. Brigid and Eileen walked into the house and sat by the fire, while the physician attended another person in the private curtained-off room at the back of her house. Lining the walls of the sitting room were flasks of herbs and medicines, alongside medical texts from Italy. Sorcha had had two husbands but, as was the custom, kept her own family name, Sorcha O'Cassidy. She was a descendant, on her father's side, of the O'Cassidys who had long been physicians to Fermanagh's leading family, the Maguires. Brigid heard someone at the door and turned to see the blacksmith stoop under the doorway and enter the room. "Domhnall, how are you?"

"I'm fine altogether, Brigid."

"Except that your arm is on fire." When he turned, she had seen a painful-looking gash of flaming red skin on his blackened arm.

"It was and it feels as if it still is. But Sorcha will set me right. You're waiting for her yourself?"

Brigid indicated Eileen with her head. "Stomach ache. Why don't you go ahead of us, Domhnall? We're in no hurry."

She got no argument from Eileen, whose compulsion to seek out the physician was in equal measure to her fear during these infrequent visits.

"Well, now, I wouldn't want to . . ."

Just then Sorcha emerged from her treatment room, with a heavily pregnant young woman ahead of her. The physician was saying, "This will have no bad effect on the baby. Don't be thinking about it at all."

The young woman left, relieved, and Sorcha turned to her next visitors. The physician looked like what she was: a strong, capable, professional woman. Her face was fairly broad, with high cheekbones and a wide mouth. Her eyes were so dark they were nearly black, and even though she was not at all an old woman, her shoulder-length hair was a light grey, nearly white.

Brigid brushed aside Domhnall's courteous insistence that she and Eileen go in first, and the smith disappeared behind the curtain with the physician.

He came out ten minutes later with a bandage on his arm. Brigid was about to address him but stopped cold when she saw the expression on his normally friendly face. The man appeared to have aged twenty years. Had he received bad news from Sorcha the banliaig? Or perhaps from Sorcha the ban-drui? The woman Druid. That was Sorcha's inheritance from her mother's side; the grandfather and those before him down through the ages had been Druids.

Brigid got up and went towards him. "Domhnall, your arm. It's serious then?"

He turned to her, but there was no recognition in his eyes. It took a few seconds before he registered who she was. "My arm is fine. I'm fine. I'm healthy. I must . . ." His voice trailed off and he walked out of the physician's house like an old, old man.

What had Sorcha told him? Brigid prayed to the Holy Mother of Mercy that Domhnall would continue in good health, and that Eileen would not emerge from their visit with a look of horror in her eyes.

Brigid took Eileen by the hand and drew her into the curtained room, which was bright with light from a fire and a dozen candles in sconces on the walls. There were more flasks and bottles in here, arranged on shelves. A bouquet of blue and yellow flowers in a jar added an element of cheer. Sorcha patted a cushioned stool, inviting Eileen to sit, and said to the child, "Eileen, what is troubling you today?"

Eileen put her hand on her stomach and moaned.

"Ah. Did you eat anything different from your usual meals?"

"I did not."

"Did you stand close to someone else who was feeling sick?"

"I did not."

The child looked puzzled, but Brigid knew from the brothers at the abbey that some physicians on the continent of Europe believed diseases were somehow transmitted from one person to another.

"When did it start?"

"Some days ago."

"Tell me, Eileen, how are things at the O'Boyle house?"

Brigid had decided against the common practice of fosterage for her two children and kept them home with her. But a couple of times a week, she took Eileen down the way to the O'Boyles' big farm, where two children were being fostered alongside the family's own four. Eileen liked to play with the girls there while her brother, Owny, was in school at the abbey.

"What do you mean?" Eileen asked.

"Are you enjoying your time with the O'Boyles? Who are the other girls there?"

"Mairsil and Catríona. Mairsil is better at dancing than me. But she's bigger! And she shouldn't boast about it and say I'm no good! She's always saying that!"

"Ach, she shouldn't. Now I'll make up a potion for your stomach, Eileen. Why don't you go out to the back of the house and see the little dog I have now."

Eileen's eyes brightened immediately. "What colour is he?"

"He's a golden brown colour, so his name is Goldie."

"I'll go see him!"

She trotted from the room, and Brigid asked the physician, "What are you making for her, Sorcha? Tell me how much to give her, so it's not too strong. She's so little."

"You'll have nothing to worry about, Brigid. I'm making it look medicinal, but there will be nothing in it with any power. I'll be adding ginger for flavour and sugar for sweetness. Children love these flavours."

Surprise must have been written across Brigid's face, because Sorcha laughed and said, "It won't matter what I mix up in my potion; it will cure her of her pains. That is, as long as you find out what is happening at the O'Boyles' place and get it sorted out."

"So there is nothing wrong with her stomach . . ."

"Nothing at all. Much of what we feel as illness starts here" — Sorcha pointed to her head — "and here." Her hand moved to her heart. "And makes itself known here." The stomach. "So, the O'Boyles?"

Brigid had recently confided to Sorcha that Eileen had sometimes come home unhappy from her time with the girls at O'Boyles'. "She comes home in tears some days," Brigid said now. "I'm thinking of keeping her home. Not that I want to insult the O'Boyles. They're a fine family. But the girl Eileen mentioned, Mairsil, taunts Eileen sometimes, and it's not just about dancing. Eileen is a bit timid, you know, about climbing on rocks or running across streams, and this girl makes her feel she's not as brave and as good at games as the other children. The other ones aren't as nasty, but they often ignore what the bigger one says. They are all a little afraid of her, or that's the way it looks to me."

"As you say, you may want to keep Eileen home more often, home where she knows she is just as good as everybody else. I predict that the stomach troubles will vanish like the dark of night!"

"That's what I'll do." Brigid smiled at Sorcha and thanked her. She collected Eileen and the two of them rode off home.

⊛

The next evening was a big night for Brigid and her children. Eileen was the younger of her two; big brother Owen, better known as Owny, was nine. They had been honoured with an invitation to a feast at Enniskillen Castle on its little island in the River Erne. That was the home of the Maguires, the Lords of Fermanagh. The current head of the clan was Hugh. After the death of his father in 1589, Hugh had been crowned at the traditional Maguire inauguration site, the Moat Ring ten or twelve miles from the castle. In that ceremony he became *the Maguire*. The occasion tonight was to celebrate Hugh's retaking of the castle from the English earlier in the month. There had been times over the years when the Tierney house was empty of visitors, times when men associated with the Maguires would be put up in the castle. But Brigid's house had often been filled with guests during the fifteen months that the island fortress was in English hands, between February of the previous year and May of this. The mood would be festive at Enniskillen tonight.

Brigid's maid, Gormlaith, filled the tub with heated water for the first of the evening's baths. After scrubbing the children and having her own bath, Brigid checked to see if her finest léine was dry from its washing. It was, so she donned the ankle-length linen shirt and put her pale-rose dress on over it. She brushed out her long coppery hair till it was nearly dry and wrapped rolls of white linen around the top of her head. She hung a large gold cross in the neckline of her dress, the neckline shaped like the English letter V. Her daughter's attire was much like her own, though Eileen's dress was a brighter rose. Owny affected as best he could the dress of a kern, the traditional Irish foot soldier, with tight-fitting trews, or britches, and a short jacket cinched in at the waist and the neck open wide at the top. It was a cool evening, so Brigid covered herself and the children with their woollen cloaks. Before they headed out, she said to the children, "And what will you not be doing at the castle?"

"We'll not be scratching our heads or spitting at the table!" shouted Owny.

"You certainly will not. And?"

"Making a loud noise by slurping up our soup!" That was Eileen. Then she turned to her brother and said, "And don't be picking your teeth with your knife!"

"I never do."

"You do. Are your fingernails clean? Mine are shining!"

"All right, children. You know your manners well." Table manners were a matter of great importance here in Fermanagh, not least at the castle, and her son and daughter had been well schooled in the particulars. "And don't be arguing, the pair of you." She put an arm around the shoulders of her little ones and squeezed. "It will be a lovely night for all of us."

They rode across their lands and down to the river's edge, where Maguire's men helped them into a cot, the shallow boat to take them across the short expanse of water to the castle.

Enniskillen Castle had been built by Hugh the Hospitable Maguire in the early 1400s and had been lost and regained, destroyed and rebuilt, by the family several times since then. The castle keep was a tall stone building, rectangular in shape, with crenellations surrounding a peaked roof. There were arrow loops, the small vertical openings at various places in the walls, from which soldiers fired upon attackers. A stone wall surrounded the courtyard, and Brigid and her children were welcomed at the entrance and led into the building. They entered and climbed the stairs to the great hall where the banquet was to take place.

The children were enthralled. "I'm going to build a castle someday," declared Owny. "And my warriors will guard it all day and night, with arrows and muskets."

A fire was blazing in the hearth, and candles flickered around the room, illuminating the brilliant blues and reds and saffron yellows of the people's clothing.

Eileen said, "I'm going to live in a castle, too. And I'll have dresses of all those beautiful colours! And my little girl will have those colours and so will her dolls."

Brigid could understand their excitement; she shared it. She had been to the castle many times over the years, but it always thrilled her to be standing with her children in the seat of Gaelic power in Fermanagh, in such elegant surroundings.

A smiling cup-bearer, Dualta, made the rounds offering tankards of ale and shining goblets of French wine. Dualta had been with the family for years, Brigid knew, and lived up to the requirements of his position as set out in the old laws: filling up, emptying, and self-control. The harper sat by the head table and played glorious music for the guests. His heavy brown hair moved up, down, and around in time with his tunes. He, too, had long been admired for living up to his responsibilities: to play music to bring on tears or joy or sleep. It was joy in the Maguire castle that evening; everyone was in high good humour. And Brigid, as she always did when visiting the castle, found the experience delightful.

Brigid was greeted by the Maguire himself. A man of about forty years, he was tall and muscular with glossy dark hair and a friendly, open face. He was wearing a luxuriously decorated leather jacket in colours of blue, brown, white, and red. Hugh was a man who inspired fear on the battlefield, but he was a gracious and good-humoured host to all who were guests in his castle home. He had always made Brigid feel as welcome as he himself would be if he were a guest at the Tierney house. Two years ago, he had gone into rebellion against Queen Elizabeth of England. A renowned cavalry man, he had achieved fame for his continuing defiance of the English government, which had ensconced itself in Dublin and the Pale, and for his resistance to England's continuing encroachment on the independence of

Irish Ulster. None of his warlike propensities were on display this evening as he smiled and chatted with Brigid and her children. But she knew that those qualities would be celebrated when the festivities got underway.

The Maguire excused himself and took his place at the centre of the head table. To his left was his wife, Margaret, dressed in dark blue, her head wrapped in folds of white linen. Also at the table were O'Hussey, Maguire's poet, and O'Breslin, his brehon or judge. Delicious scents rose from the tables. The feast consisted of a shield of boar with mustard, a boiled capon, a pig, a goose, a swan, a venison pastry, a spinach salad, and a custard. The wine had been imported from Bordeaux. Ale and mead were plentiful as well.

Father Fiach O'Moylan was sitting at the table next to Brigid's, dressed in the habit of the Cistercian order, a white tunic with a black scapular — a long sleeveless garment — over the front and back of the tunic. His dark reddish hair was cropped short, and his lively eyes were a light brown, almost the colour of amber. Beside him was another member of the order whom Brigid had seen at the abbey school and church, and had spoken to only briefly. He was the new abbot, a grey-haired man of middle age, and he had a stern look about him. Brigid knew that the old abbot had recently died of age. She turned to have a word with Fiach, and he took the opportunity to initiate a conversation.

"Brigid Tierney, have you been introduced to our new abbot? Father Marcus Valerius. He is from Rome, and he has studied and taught at the great college at Louvain, on the continent. It was there that I met him; he was the most illustrious of my teachers." The man rose and bowed to her. Fiach switched to Latin when he spoke to Father Valerius. Brigid's Latin was limited to what she knew from the Mass, but she caught a few of the words.

"Pardon me for the Latin," Fiach said then, "an old priestly habit! Father Valerius has an excellent command of our own language."

"You flatter me, Father O'Moylan. But," he said to Brigid, "I did start learning Irish under the tutelage of your esteemed priest here, when we were at Louvain." He spoke very good Irish, not perfect but comprehensible, even in the accent she assumed to be that of his native city.

"Marcus speaks French, Italian, and English, in addition to Latin, so it is no surprise that he excels at Irish."

There was a look of amusement in the Roman's dark brown eyes. "But it *would* be a surprise. Your language is very difficult. But wonderfully expressive and rich. After all that work, I had little choice but to eventually make my way to your lovely green island."

Brigid was not all that surprised that an educated man would speak some of the languages of continental Europe. But English? Where would he have heard that in the churches and monasteries of Europe? She decided it would not be courteous to ask.

"You are most welcome here in Fermanagh. If ever there is anything I can do or provide for you, or any of the other priests and brothers at the abbey, you only have to ask."

"Thank you. You are most kind."

The conversation continued in that vein, and then Brigid had a few words with Fiach about Owny and other students of Fiach's school at the abbey. "And my Eileen loves the pages of written work Owny brings home. Thank you for lending us the book on animals. I keep it safe on a shelf, and Eileen treats it as she would a newborn lamb." Brigid had taught her daughter to read and write; in her opinion — which she was not about to share with the priest or the abbot — her little girl had more the makings of a scholar than did her boy. She introduced her daughter to the abbot, and the little one blushed. The child greeted him, then said in a voice that was hardly more than a whisper, "Is it true, Father Abbot, that across the sea there is a 'Sweetheart Abbey'?"

Father Valerius smiled at her and said, "It is true. It's in Scotland and it's more than three hundred years old. Do you know why they call it that?"

Eileen shook her head.

"There was a powerful man there, a lord, and when he died, his wife was so sad that she kept his heart. And she, Lady Devorgilla, founded an abbey in his memory and was buried there with the heart. And the Latin name for the abbey is Dulce Cor. Sweet Heart."

"I wish I could see it. The abbey, I mean, not the heart!" She blushed scarlet again, and the abbot said that maybe she would see the place someday, and the monks would be happy to have her visit.

Fiach O'Moylan rose then to make a speech lauding the Maguire for driving the English out of the family stronghold, and thanking the Maguire family for supplying men and materials to maintain the buildings and carvings of Drumlyon Abbey and for supporting the abbey school, "even if we are not Franciscans!" This was met with laughter in the room; everyone knew that the Maguire family had long been supporters of the Augustinian order and had more recently come to favour the Franciscans. Drumlyon was neither: it was a Cistercian abbey founded over two hundred years before. "Without the strong faith and generosity of your noble family, our abbey would be falling apart from age, and we would be without the beautifully decorated vestments, the sacred vessels, the liturgical books, which — thanks be to God — have not been stolen from us as has happened in other places under the Tudor monarchs. You, my Lord, and your family, have made it possible for us to educate our children in the faith and in the knowledge all the people of Ireland should have."

The Maguire nodded in acknowledgement of the tribute; his family had always been known for its support of the faith and of learning. He thanked Fiach, and he greeted Father Marcus Valerius and spoke to him in Latin. The Roman priest bowed and responded in kind.

"Mammy," Eileen said, "there's the physician." The little girl pointed to a table in the middle of the room, and Brigid raised a hand in greeting.

"Oh, she doesn't see us," said Brigid. Then she laughed to herself; how strange to say that Sorcha didn't see someone. Sorcha's eyes saw things no other human eyes could see, hidden things, events yet to unfold in the future. But there was nothing unnatural in her sights this time. Her black eyes followed the man who had just walked into the room, Cúchonnacht Maguire, arriving late for his place at the head table. He was the half-brother of Hugh, and he was splendidly attired in his saffron-yellow léine, which came to his knees and was belted at the waist over his close-fitting trews. His short jacket was a brilliant red. He was, Brigid marvelled, in face and figure the most beautiful man she had ever seen. Smiling and jesting, he delighted the ladies and the men alike. But there was one whose delight outshone that of all others in the room. The physician, the white-robed seer, Sorcha stood at her table and beamed a gaze of such powerful love on Cúchonnacht Maguire that he appeared to be bathed in a glowing light. He took his place at the left of the head table and was greeted by his brother and the other members of the household.

Brigid had a man of comely appearance in her own life, too. Where was Shane? Back at their own house, she supposed. The house was full, with a party of merchants from Galway. Shane had his origins in Munster, in Cork, but Munster was increasingly under the yoke of the English. Shane had come north to Ulster in the previous decade to work for the powerful O'Neill clan in Tyrone. The O'Neills had accommodated themselves to the English, as had the Maguires at the time, but this part of Ireland still maintained its Gaelic culture and customs; it had not been "planted" with English settlers. The O'Neills were overlords to the Maguires, and so Shane had divided his time between Tyrone and Enniskillen Castle, where he started out as a watchman. He came into Brigid's life not long after his arrival in the north. Then Hugh was inaugurated as head of the clan and, a few years later, went to war against the English. Shane became one of the chieftain's marksmen. Here in Fermanagh, when not in battle, he had taken on the responsibility of managing the outdoor servants, the herdsmen and those who worked the large tracts of Tierney land. If ever there was a man born to provide hospitality, it was Shane O'Callaghan. And that's what he was doing right now, Brigid suspected, raising a tankard of ale with the men from Galway. He would arrive late as always, but he would not miss an evening such as this at the castle. She only hoped he'd be steady on his feet by the time he came in.

She walked over to greet Sorcha. "Do you foresee much drink taken tonight, oh great seer?" Their friendship was such that she could say things like this, confident that Sorcha would not take offence.

"I see so much drink taken that, before the night is done, the Maguire family will be left with nothing but empty casks and guests with their tongues hanging out and nothing for them to lap up. And Hugh will be disgraced throughout the land for his failure to provide hospitality to the people of Fermanagh. Or," she said then, giving Brigid a little nudge with her elbow, "perhaps we'll all go to the Tierney guesthouse and drink your own stock dry. How does that sound to you?"

"I'll do my best to be moderate here this evening and to urge moderation on all around me, so I won't be accused of over-shadowing the Maguire on this, his big night of celebration!" She heard a few preliminary notes from the harp and turned to watch. She herself played the harp — she loved the instrument — and she felt her fingers moving as if they were stroking the strings now. It was time to listen. To Sorcha she said, "We'll talk again later."

"We will." Sorcha smiled at her and sat at her place. Brigid returned to her children.

Hugh had been the chieftain for six years now, and his glorious deeds as lord and cavalry commander were sung and cheered. The harper sat at his instrument, its rich dark wood contrasting with the white of the walls and the cloth that draped the table. His fingers plucked the strings as he accompanied the reciter, who chanted the words of the praise poems composed by O'Hussey. The guests heard the history of three hundred years of Maguire rule in Fermanagh. Then it was the current lord's accomplish-ments, his provision of refuge for Red Hugh O'Donnell after his escape from Dublin Castle, the Maguire's incursions into Sligo, Roscommon, and later Monaghan, after which he was branded a traitor. A traitor to the English queen, but never a traitor to his own people. And the crowd revelled in the story of the time, not long after he became chieftain, when he was told by the Lord Deputy, Fitzwilliam, that he would have to allow the Queen's writ to run in Fermanagh. Hugh replied, "Your sheriff shall be welcome but let me know his éraic" — body fine — "that if my people cut his head off, I may levy it upon the country." There were roars of approval for this. Then there was a recounting of the day the castle had been taken by the English in February 1594 after a siege lasting several days. The Irish began a blockade of the castle in May of that year and regained it a year later.

The reciter paused for a drink of ale and then told the gathering that he would resume his recital with the big event of August 1594: the Battle of the Ford of the Biscuits.

"Biscuits!" Owny exclaimed, a big grin on his face.

Brigid leaned down and said, "Do you know the story?"

"I do!" said Owny.

"I don't," said his sister.

"Well," their mother explained, "the English forces took this castle, after half destroying it. And himself" — she nodded in the direction of the Maguire at his table — "was determined to get it back. He and his forces were aided by men sent by Red Hugh O'Donnell and they laid siege to the castle. The English garrison inside was running short of provisions. So the English and their allies obtained provisions and started back here to the castle with the things the men needed. Including a great supply of biscuits."

"Will there be biscuits here tonight?"

"There will, Owny."

"Then what happened?" Eileen asked.

"The Maguire and his men learned of the route the English were taking, and they were joined by forces lent them by O'Donnell and also by the brother of the Earl of Tyrone, and off they went. They stopped at a ford in the River Arney, a few miles away from here, where they knew the enemy was going to pass, and there was a fierce battle—"

"And Maguire's men filled them with lead! And ran them through with swords! I wish I'd been there! I'm going to fight in a battle someday!"

Brigid turned her mind away from the image of her young son in hand-to-hand combat and finished her story. "Hugh Maguire defeated the enemy. Many were killed, and there were weapons and horses left by the enemy. And there were all those biscuits floating in the river."

"The Maguire got the biscuits!"

"He did, he and his men. And so he changed the name of that place to the Ford of the Biscuits!"

"Let's go there!"

"We shall, but not tonight. We're going to enjoy our time here at this much-fought-over castle."

"Dervla makes lovely biscuits," Eileen said. Dervla was the Tierneys' cook and she was without question the maker of lovely biscuits and sweet cakes.

"She does. Now the pair of you have been given some small beer; drink it and stay quiet, and learn about your lord's great deeds!"

The praise poem resumed, with the famed battle and other achievements of the Maguire. But the succession of victories and defeats never seemed to end, never came to a clear resolution. And, Brigid wondered, how long would the Maguires hold Enniskillen, hold this castle? When would this island be able to relax its vigilance? When, if ever, would it settle into peace? But she was determined to shake off her pointless brooding and enjoy the festivities.

There was a break in the storytelling, and the harper played some lively tunes. Owny got up and started to dance, all by himself, until a few of the other children joined him. They moved joyfully to the rhythm of the music, and Brigid urged Eileen to leave the table and enjoy the dancing. But she shook her head. No. Too shy and, Brigid knew, afraid others would laugh. Then the little girl's blue eyes lit up, and her face creased in a smile. The children's father had arrived.

Shane O'Callaghan made his way through the great hall, with a greeting or a remark for everyone. He bowed to the nobility at the head table and accepted a goblet of wine; he raised it to Brigid when he caught sight of her. His face was mellowed with drink, but he walked with his usual grace. His eyes were blue like hers, but of a deeper shade. He was clean-shaven, and his face was framed by short black curls. Brigid remembered the suspicion and the jesting that had been directed his way when he first came north from Munster, for his deviation from the Irish style, the long, flowing hair and moustaches on the other men. But people were now well accustomed to Shane O'Callaghan and his independent ways.

He walked into the midst of the dancing children and did a few steps with Owny and the others, then came to the table, gave Brigid a kiss, and lifted Eileen from her chair. He led her by the hand and proceeded to dance her around the room. The little girl glowed with happiness; nobody would dare laugh at her dancing now.

Great quantities of drink were taken as the night went on, and there was singing and the telling of tales. When there was a moment of quiet, Shane stood with his goblet in hand and gave the assembly a poem, to the obvious displeasure of the court poet O'Hussey at the head table.

Shane said, "As was noted, my Lord, in the time of your illustrious father Cúchonnacht Maguire,

> Ships are not sufficient provision for the Maguires,
> they do not spare drink;
> the Maguires surpass in providing wine,
> they are not loath to dispense it."

Shane then turned to the subject of the Spanish Armada, the fleet of over a hundred ships sent out by the king of Spain in 1588 in an effort to overthrow England's Protestant queen and restore the country to Catholicism. England had long been a threat to Spain and its territories. But the plan failed terribly, and two dozen of the ships were wrecked on Ireland's northern and western shores, with great loss of life. Shane told the story of Brian O'Rourke, who had come to the aid of the poor sailors, shipwrecked so far from their home. Brigid gave her attention to the poem.

> "And then we have Brian O'Rourke in the tale
> Who came to the aid of our friends who set sail
> From Philip of Spain. They did come to our aid,
> Mighty fleet of great ships would old England invade.
>
> But foundered they did on our storm-battered strand
> And our lord and O'Rourke didst offer their hand.
> For that they were hounded by Liza's great horde
> We thank God Almighty for sparing our lord."

Everyone in the great hall knew that Hugh Maguire had worked with O'Rourke and members of the Burke clan in coming to the aid of the survivors of the wrecked Spanish fleet. The Lords of Ulster were now and would no doubt in the future be putting their hopes on a Spanish-Irish alliance to defeat the English invaders and drive them from Ireland.

> "Brian to Scotland did journey with hope
> Of being protected and spared of the rope.
> But he was arrested, and hanged he would be
> And yet still our Brian would not bend the knee.

Brian was asked, when refused he to bow,
Do you not bow to images greater than thou?
Said Brian there is a great difference seen
Between saints who are holy and your scurvy queen."

That went over well with the noble company assembled in Maguire's castle. Goblets were raised and toasts delivered to the saints of Ireland and the Holy Land. The bard wound up the story of Brian O'Rourke.

"They hanged him and quartered him, cut off his head,
For aiding poor sailors as they starved and they bled.
You English barbarians, be on your guard
For we will avenge him, so sweareth the bard!"

Brigid noticed how the brehon, O'Breslin, scowled at the savagery of the penalty. Those arrested for treason against England could have their bodies slit open and their intestines pulled out, their heads cut off and exhibited in public for all to see. And to be hanged, drawn, and quartered, you did not have to have taken up arms; you might simply have refused to acknowledge that the king or queen of England was the supreme head or governor of the Church. King Henry had sent two of his wives to the chopping block and had their heads cut off! In brehon law, the Irish system of laws handed down from ancient times, the remedy even for murder was a fine, and the payment of an honour price to make restitution to his family. And yet the English called the Irish *savages*!

Shane O'Callaghan's verses were not those of a file, one of the higher grades of poet who, some believed, had almost priestly power, the power to curse and engage in divination. Some even said they had the power to kill, to "rhyme to death." Shane was playing the role of a poet of the lesser class, a bard, a reciter, an attendant to the professional poets. His verses did not comply with the strict meters and complex structures required of a praise poem, but that was not his ambition here. He sought merely to entertain and amuse. And, of course, to make pointed barbs at the invading power. His recital met with roars of delight in the castle.

He struck a humble pose and said, "This lowly bard is most grateful to the Maguire and his clan for welcoming a stranger from the south. I have lived among you for a decade now, content to remain here for the rest of my days. How long might I have survived in those southern parts of our country? The English issued a proclamation nearly twenty-five years ago in Kildare: 'to punish by death or otherwise harpers, rhymers, and bards.'" He rose to his full height then and declaimed, "They are fearful of our power to curse and stir up rebellion. Let them remain afraid and trembling!" This was met with great applause, and Shane bowed and sat down.

Brigid knew that his rhyming had not always won him favour; Shane always said, in a jocular way, that his rhyming was one of the reasons he had left his native Cork. His satirical verses had not been popular with one of the powerful families there.

She watched now as the guests milled about, drinking and talking. Then she caught sight of her brother, Diarmait, who had just walked in. Diarmait was the true owner of the Tierney house; he had inherited the place following the death of their father when Diarmait and his sisters were barely out of childhood. Ardal Tierney had died of a fever after travelling to Galway to buy goods off a ship, and his wife, Clodagh, died a few years after that. Diarmait inherited the house and lands, but he was not a man for staying at home and entertaining guests, no matter how lordly those guests might be. Diarmait was a warrior, a musketeer in the service of the Maguire. He left the duties of hospitality to his sister. And here he was, back from the latest campaigns against the English. He came to her, and they embraced and asked about each other's well-being. Then Brigid was bumped aside by Owny, who gazed up at his uncle as if he were a god come down from Mount Olympus.

"Do you have your musket on you?" the bold child asked.

"I'm armed only with a knife to cut my dinner," his uncle replied, smiling down and ruffling the boy's hair.

"Tomorrow we'll go out on our horses, and you'll teach me to use the musket!"

"Not tomorrow. I have to go back out to work."

Brigid knew he and his fellow musketeers were posted a good few miles from the castle, watching for incursions by the enemy.

"What would the Maguire think of me," Diarmait said to his nephew, "if I stayed here all night drinking ale and fell asleep here at the castle? But I'll come back as soon as I can, and we'll go out on the horses then."

"That's what we'll do," Owny agreed, knowing it was the best he could hope for.

Diarmait looked up then and his gaze intensified. Brigid turned and saw Hugh Maguire standing beside Sorcha O'Cassidy in her long white dress. She was looking in the Tierneys' direction as she talked with the chieftain. Diarmait excused himself and strode over to the Maguire, greeting Sorcha and then drawing the chieftain aside. Brigid knew it must have been a rare opportunity, when a musketeer could exchange words with his commander at his home in the castle. Their father, Ardal, had been a good friend to Hugh, and Hugh a good friend to Ardal, which Brigid was sure made the encounter between the two even more gratifying for Diarmait. Owny stared at them in awe.

Sorcha turned her all-seeing dark eyes on Cúchonnacht Maguire, who was entertaining a group of women who listened avidly to his every word. Sorcha seemed barely aware of the man approaching her, the priest who had once been her husband, Fiach O'Moylan. He came to her with the offer of a goblet of wine and a piece of cake with honey. She shook off whatever had been preoccupying her and smiled at Fiach. They exchanged a few words and then were interrupted by an old man who obviously wanted to speak to Father O'Moylan in privacy. When the two men excused themselves, Brigid walked over to speak with Sorcha.

"Hugh the Hospitable would be proud of his great descendants tonight," she said. "The beauty of this place, and of the people in it. The warmth, the generosity of the Maguire, and the high time we're all having!"

"He'd be right to be proud," Sorcha agreed.

"We women never get to see, of course, Hugh's courage and his skill on the battlefield, but everything we hear tells us he is an exemplary cavalry commander."

"He is. Now, if only . . ." She stopped speaking when she noticed little Eileen coming towards her. "How are you feeling, Eileen? Any better?"

"Much better. That medicine works! I drank it all. May I have some more?" The child blushed then, at her boldness in asking for something so directly.

"Certainly, you may. Come to me tomorrow, and I'll have another bottle for you."

"Thank you!"

Eileen skipped away, back to where she had so recently triumphed on the dance floor.

"That concoction seems to have worked wonders for her, Sorcha, judging by her demeanour tonight."

"A drink flavoured with ginger and sugar. No wonder she enjoyed the workings of it. Her troubles are all up here." The physician pointed to her head and then watched as Eileen invited her father to dance again. She cast an eye on the other children to make sure they were watching.

"Now what was it you were saying earlier, Sorcha?" Brigid asked quietly. "You said, 'If only . . .'"

Sorcha looked her in the eye. "I have no doubt that the English have their dissensions and their rivalries at home. All men do, all countries. But when they invade our island, we must look upon them as one tremendous, united force. What about us, though? What are we when we face their incursions? Here in Ireland we have a history that goes back into the ages, the ancient times. There have been people on this island for thousands of years. Those who come here to Ulster, who come to us from the west of Ireland, the east and the south, all show us the same thing, that we all speak the same language, that we all follow the same ancient laws. And yet we are divided. And those alliances and divisions shift from year to year, from month to month. And the English stir us up, and make the most of our divisions, and contrive to create more of them. They set chieftain against chieftain, clan against clan. And we do that ourselves even without the intrigues of our invaders. Two brothers who have fallen out over their inheritance, or over who will be chosen as Tánaiste" — the man who will succeed the chief of his clan — "it is often that one such brother will side with the English queen and her minions here, and the other will remain loyal to his own people.

It leads to Irishmen turning on each other, killing each other. And it leaves the field to the English, who are determined to take over our island, to impose their foreign laws and religion on us." Sorcha was becoming more and more distressed as she spoke. "Our failure to achieve unity amongst ourselves has been a plague on us for generations. And it will destroy us!"

All around her, the Maguires and their guests drank and chatted and laughed. The harper played and the dancers in their luxurious fabrics swirled round the floor, as if the party would never end.

CHAPTER III

*There is, in their opinion, something sacred in the
female sex, and even the power of foreseeing future
events. Their advice is, therefore, always heard; they
are deemed oracular.*

— Tacitus, c. 98 AD

Father Marcus Valerius, abbot of Drumlyon Abbey, had
enjoyed last evening's banquet at the castle of the Lord of
Fermanagh. He was, however, suffering from a headache this
morning, even though he thought he had been moderate in his
consumption of the chieftain's wine. Small price to pay. The
castle was not as grand as some of the great castles and palaces
he had seen on the continent of Europe, but the tapestries on
the walls and the glistening silver wine cups added an elegance
to the surroundings. And he was struck by the brilliant colours
of the people's clothing, the deep blues, the vibrant reds, the
saffron yellows. Standing there, gazing around at the finely
dressed men and women, he had begun to wonder whether he
had dreamed or imagined that the English king, Henry VIII,

had enacted a law that prohibited the Irish from wearing the colour yellow! What was it? That yellow had associations with papists and foreigners, particularly the Irish, and that it was not a fit colour for the subjects of the Protestant king. This was just one of many foolish things Marcus had learned in the two years he had spent in England before coming to Ireland. He knew it was true, but it didn't bear thinking about.

Yes, the morning had come early following the night of celebration, but early mornings were nothing new for monks in an abbey. Marcus had dragged himself out of bed and washed and dressed himself for Prime, the prayers to be chanted and sung by the priests and brothers of Drumlyon Abbey at six o'clock in the morning. All the members of the order were present, including a pallid-looking Fiach O'Moylan, whose fine, mellifluous voice was subdued and shaky. And on this particular morning, Marcus had been called to the home of a man named Niall who, with his little boy of eight years, had fallen from one of the cots, the boats that plied the waters of Lough Erne and the river. Both were drowned. Niall was the young brother of the local blacksmith, Domhnall, and the family was devastated by the man's untimely death. Marcus had given the sacraments and offered what comfort he could, and then returned to Drumlyon.

He turned his mind once more to the feast at Hugh Maguire's castle. The hospitality there was second to none. The music of the harp, the exuberant dancing, the amusing verses of the poet — wonderful entertainment. And the drinking, well, he had been "warned" about that before setting forth for Ireland. At the banquet, Marcus had stayed with the wines which, it had to be said, were of the finest quality. They had, after all, been imported from France and Spain. But the other guests: how had they formed the capacity to stay on their feet and be able to sing and dance after imbibing so much ale and aqua vitae? That was what they called their strong drink: uisce beatha, the water of life. Marcus recalled the nasty remarks of some of the men he had met in England, that the "mere Irish" were much given to idleness, lechery, and excessive drinking. Marcus's decision to leave England for Ireland had been met with disbelief in some quarters. But Marcus had met many an Irish priest, monk, and student in his time teaching at Louvain, the Catholic college in Brabant on the continent. They were pious, well read, and scholarly; they were men who revered learning. He had heard that these fine qualities were possessed by members of the Maguire family, and now that he had met Hugh Maguire, and had heard all about the family's generosity to the monasteries in their territory, he knew he had not erred in coming here.

Of course, Father Fiach O'Moylan had been quite persuasive on the subject of Marcus coming to this country. And though that had never been the plan, Marcus had indeed washed up on the shore of Ireland. But first he had spent two years in England, where he saw first-hand the destruction that had been wrought by King Henry VIII and his minions in the course of Henry's Reformation. What Marcus hadn't seen with his own eyes had been described to him by others who had been present through all the upheavals. Nobody was more eloquent on the subject than Brother Aidan, an Irishman who had gone to England to teach, arriving there in the 1530s, not long before the Reformation began. It was Aidan more than Fiach who accounted for the fact that Marcus had come across the sea to Ireland. The old monk was ill — driven mad, it was said, by the horrors he had seen under the Tudor monarchs. Aidan wanted to come home to Fermanagh, and it was arranged that he would live and be cared for in Drumlyon Abbey. Marcus sent up a Te Deum thanking the Almighty God that the Tudors and their thieves and plunderers had not been as successful in suppressing the churches and monasteries here in the Gaelic stronghold in the northwest as they had been in Dublin and other places in the east of the country. Brother Aidan was placed under the care of Father Marcus, and so here they were. It had taken a while for Marcus to get accustomed to Aidan's ways; the old monk was outspoken, humorous sometimes when it would be better to be solemn, and he didn't always appear on time for his prayers in the chapel. But Marcus had grown very fond of the odd old brother, so he made it a point to keep an eye out for him. And Marcus had to be watchful indeed: Aidan loved to get up and wander off by himself through the fields and the woods. He could fall and hurt himself, and Marcus had to keep this in mind.

As for Fiach O'Moylan, he had arrived at Louvain a few years before Marcus's move to England. Fiach was an eager and talented student once he settled down. He was particularly adept at learning Greek and reading the classical epics. Marcus had no doubts about Fiach's strong faith and his high level of intelligence, even if he was a bit of a rake, to use the English term. He was fond of drinking and there was no question that he had an eye for the women. Like many of the priests in Ireland, he had once been married. His former wife was the physician here in Fermanagh, a woman by the name of Sorcha. Marcus had seen her at the banquet — a striking woman, it had to be said.

One of Marcus's ambitions here was to bring the clergy into line with the dictates of Rome, including fidelity to the vows of chastity for those in religious life. Now, Marcus understood the passions as well as did any man. And, if the truth be told, the women he had seen in Ireland would be a temptation to a saint. He was not the first to arrive on the shores of Ireland and be struck by the beauty of the women, with their ivory skin and clear blue eyes, their long lustrous hair, sometimes black as night, and sometimes a golden yellow. And occasionally he had seen a colour of hair here that he had not known anywhere else: a coppery shade that was most alluring. His admiration, of course, was like that of a man admiring the fine handiwork of the most holy God, not that of a man driven by uncontrollable lust. Marcus was in control of himself. But it was little wonder that Fiach had succumbed to the temptations of the flesh in the past and had sired more than one child over the course of his life, even, it was rumoured, during the course of his priesthood. But the man was coming around to the Roman virtues, Marcus knew; it was only a matter of time and prayer.

But what had Fiach been up to last night? Marcus had been excited by the music and the dancing, the bright colours and the high humour of the evening, and had not been able to fall asleep. Just when it seemed he might drift into a peaceful slumber, he heard the sound of a horse's hoofs approaching the abbey, followed soon afterwards by rapid footsteps outside the dormitory. It sounded as if someone tripped on his feet, got up, and carried on walking. As far as Marcus had been aware, all the monks were home and in their beds. Marcus rose from his bed and reached for a taper, then decided against lighting it; if the footsteps were those of an intruder, Marcus would be better off creeping around in darkness rather than lighting himself up as a target for possible mischief or worse. He stood for a moment, letting his eyes become accustomed to the dark, and then he left his room on silent feet and walked out into the corridor. Not a soul in sight. Trailing a hand along the stone walls to guide him, he made his way through the abbey. Nobody in the chapter house, where meetings were held. He turned towards the library then, made his way past the abbey's collection of books, some of them so valuable they were chained to the tables. He looked ahead and saw a candle flame at the far end of the room where there was a small scriptorium. A pair of desks faced one another, so two monks could work on manuscripts. Whoever was in there was not concerned about remaining unseen, perhaps thinking it unlikely that anyone else would be awake. Whatever the case, Marcus proceeded with caution. He stopped well before the niche containing the desks and stood silent in the shadows.

Father Fiach O'Moylan was hunched over his desk with a sheet of vellum and a quill in his hand. His candle flickered on the desk, the only light in the darkness surrounding him. The priest was usually orderly in his appearance and demeanour; now, his hair was dishevelled and his black scapular was flung off to the side. In contrast to his usual careful, deliberate style, he was writing swiftly and without correction. He was oblivious to the presence of Marcus watching him; his concentration was intense and complete. He filled one page, shoved it aside and picked up another, and continued his furious scribbling. The temptation to interrupt and demand to know what he was doing was almost overwhelming, but Marcus was a man well used to biding his time, waiting for his moment. Whatever this was, Marcus intended to read it. But not now, not when an interruption might throw the scribe off his course and bring his composition to a premature end. Fiach was unaware of him, and that suited Marcus. He backed away and made careful progress through the library, making sure he did not bump into anything that would betray his presence. He would find those pages in the morning, when Fiach was teaching his students. Marcus was the abbot of Drumlyon, and he intended to discover what had bedevilled his fellow priest, causing him to record his thoughts like a man possessed.

The evening at the castle had been filled with wine and song, marvellous stories and colourful personages. But that was small comfort to Brigid Tierney the following day. She had returned to an old worry, her worry about Owny, who was not doing all that well in the abbey school. So, that morning after Owny had gone off to his classes, she asked Donal to bring out her mare, Muirisc, so she could ride to the abbey. She greeted Muirisc and patted her head, then mounted the horse and set out at a leisurely pace with Donal as her escort. The Tierney house and outbuildings were on the high ground to the west of the island on which sat the Maguire castle. The house was five storeys high and faced east with a clear view down to the castle. Drumlyon Abbey was on the same side, farther north. There was a boggy area on the southern part of the Tierney land, and extensive pastures to the west and north for the grazing of their cattle. Brigid and Donal rode out onto a muddy, rocky path through the dense woodland that bordered the property. The mare's feet slipped from time to time, and the mile and a half journey took nearly half an hour. But it was a fine day, and Brigid enjoyed being out in the air.

Contrasting with the green richness of the farm and forest were the grey stone buildings of the abbey. Brigid had always loved the austere angular buildings, just as she loved the austerity of the chanted Latin prayers of the monks. On the north side of the cloister was the church, with its high square tower topped with pinnacles on each of its four corners. The refectory was across the cloister on the opposite side. There were guesthouses at the approach to the cloister, in addition to the dormitories for the monks and the lay brothers, who did much of the physical work. The brew house, the stables, the piggery, and various other outbuildings were scattered around the property. Brigid rode up to the gate, dismounted, and handed the horse over to Donal. She told him she would not be long inside the abbey. A monk appeared at the entrance, and she asked to speak with Father O'Moylan. He nodded to her and went inside. Fiach came out shortly afterwards and offered her a drink of ale, and he directed the young monk to take one outside for Donal. Fiach waited patiently for the purpose of her visit.

"I'm here about Owny, Fiach. He has me concerned."

"What has you concerned, Brigid?"

"He's been neglecting his studies, and I think it's because he finds them difficult."

Fiach nodded. "Would you like to come inside? Or we could go for a walk."

"There's no rain yet. Let's walk."

"We shall. Perhaps we'll find some wisdom in the oaks!"

"Oaks, is it? You old Druid!" She knew Fiach well, had known him for nearly her entire life, and his status as priest was not a barrier between him and the people in their part of Fermanagh. Oaks were sacred to the Druids, and there was a stand of oaks not far from the abbey.

Clouds were gathering and rain threatening as they started out. They strolled away from the complex of stone buildings and the monks' herb garden and pastures. Cattle and horses looked up from their grazing, as Brigid and Fiach walked between the field and the edge of the wood. They stopped under the shelter of the trees, and Brigid said, "Fiach, what should I be doing to help my boy with his reading? He turns away from me every time I mention the subject."

"It will come to him. He's a bright little lad."

"But Eileen learned her letters with me in a couple of days. She spends hours of her time reading the books you have lent us."

"Children are different from one another. I should know. I have three of them!"

"Three that you know of!"

"I shall expect you to confess that sinful slander and fall to your knees in penance, woman!"

She knew he had one daughter from his marriage to Sorcha, and the two others were the products of less formal unions.

He had taken no offence; he was laughing as he spoke. "We all know clerics who have far more than three. One in particular has fourteen at last count!"

"Poor Marcus has his work cut out for him, if his purpose is to bring you lot into line with Roman discipline!"

"Ah now, you know I've not been straying from the Church's teaching. Or, well, I do my best."

"We'll speak no more on the subject, Father."

"Owny, now, I've heard him recite verse upon verse of the old stories and poems, all from his memory, as our people did in the past. Not everyone has the talent to do that, as much as they might make the effort night after night in the alehouse."

"But he will be missing all the new stories, and the learning that is found in the books."

"I shall work with him, I promise you. And I can tell you he loves the numbers, loves the stars and the sciences. He will be fine."

"It seems to me that all he wants to do is be a warrior."

"Well, a boy living in these times . . ."

"These times or all times? I was speaking with Sorcha . . ."

There was a pause and then he said, "You were?" He was always interested in whatever might be the news about his former wife.

"She says that if our people don't put aside our own rivalries, which have always been exploited by our enemies, we will not be able to repel them, the English invaders. My son's dream of glory in battle will not be realized. Or if realized once, will not result in any conclusion for Fermanagh. Or for Ireland itself. It will be war into the future as long as we can see. I don't want my son, or Shane for that matter — but there's no stopping Shane."

"His course is set. Our chief will always need a marksman with a steady hand and eye, and an absolute absence of fear. But as for Owny, I shall try to stimulate his interest in science and mathematics, even if he shows little inclination for reading the great books of the sages. Perhaps we can make a priest of him!"

"I can't quite see that now, can you?"

"He's young yet."

"Thank you, Fiach."

"Em, when was it you heard this from Sorcha?"

"Last evening at the banquet. And now I shall let you return to your devotions. And your teaching, of course."

He didn't appear to be listening. But then he focused on her again and asked, "What was it that moved her to say that? Sorcha, I mean, about our people's rivalries and the English?"

"Well, of course, it was all the talk about the battles and the victories and the continuing threat from across the sea. I'm going to pay a visit to her. She asked me to come by."

"Oh?"

"She's going to give me a most pleasant-tasting potion for Eileen. Eileen thinks she has an illness, and if she thinks this potion has made her stronger, no harm done."

"Quite so."

They walked back to the abbey, Father Fiach lost in thoughts of his own.

CHAPTER IV

Would to God the day of doom were arrived,
Since Druids are arrived bringing the news of woe.

— Gwalchmai ap Meilyr, twelfth-century Welsh bard

After taking her leave of Fiach, Brigid set out with Donal on their horses towards Sorcha's house, which was on a little drumlin a short distance to the west of the Tierneys' place. The clouds broke and opened to display a sky of brilliant blue. But from somewhere a few drops of rain managed to fall. Nothing unusual about that. Brigid loved the patterns formed on the ground by the sun blazing around the branches and leaves of the oak trees. But . . .

"There's Peadar." Why was Sorcha's son standing there, rocking back and forth on his feet? Brigid pulled her horse to a sudden stop.

"What . . ." Donal followed her gaze.

Peadar was a young man of twenty years, the son Sorcha had with her first husband, Tomás MacMahon. The young fellow kept on making his repetitive motions, paying no attention to the new arrivals; his eyes were riveted upon the ground. Glistening in the sunlight was a white bundle of cloth on a bed of fallen leaves. Brigid asked herself, Didn't we see that white . . . "O God, bless us and save us!"

The white-clad body was in the sun; the head was in the shade. Brigid realized that she was looking at the remains of the woman she had known and loved so well. Two arrows were stuck in her, one in the chest and one in the throat, and blood spread out over her skin and her dress. There was no question that all the life had gone out of her. Her face was the colour of grey ash, and her large dark eyes were wide open, as if she were seeing, still seeing, whoever had visited this evil upon her. Donal made the sign of the cross with his right hand as he stared at the lifeless body. Brigid dismounted and fell to her knees and began to weep for her dear friend. Sorcha the physician, the wise woman, the woman who saw far into the future.

Peadar was short and reed-thin. His normally light skin was blanched to whiteness; his reddish freckles stood out like spots of blood. The poor young lad's eyes were red from crying, and his voice trembled as he told his story. "I was in my bed early last night. I awoke this morning and got myself dressed, and came downstairs and called out for her. I thought she must have gone out walking. A lovely day, I decided to join her. I came out and found her like this. Whatever man has done this will feel the point of my sword!"

Brigid tried to gather her wits about her, tried not to collapse in a fit of weeping. She expressed her deep sorrow to Peadar, who repeated his threat against the killer. "I'll be going out as a hunter, to find the man who took my mother from me, took her life from her!"

Brigid could not imagine the frail young son going into battle with a killer. She said, "Peadar, you must wait here. I'll go and get the brehon. The killer will be found and taken to judgment."

"I'll not wait for judgment. I shall make the judgment myself!"

"Please do not say that, Peadar. Donal will stay with you here until I return with the brehon."

She gave Donal the eye, and Donal quickly agreed to stay and watch over the body of Sorcha. And he would, she knew, restrain the grieving son from setting out on a pointless and dangerous search for the killer. Brigid got back on her horse and galloped home to alert Shane to the shocking news, and together they would go to the brehon.

⚮

She hoped Shane was back from wherever he had been carousing last night. He had not come in to their room after the banquet, which was by no means unusual, but she needed him home now. She needed his comfort, his strength. The reality of what had happened was now becoming clear to her. She had no idea how she was going to face the loss of Sorcha. Brigid had always relied on her as a friend, an older friend by around ten years; she had relied on her as a physician, as someone wise in the ways of the world. And in the ways of things beyond the world. Yet, despite her formidable talents, Sorcha had always been gentle and kind, and sometimes comical as well. Brigid began to tremble. If Shane wasn't here to help her . . . Ah, there he was at the far end of her property, practising shooting at an alder tree in the otherwise silent wood. He turned to her, startled, and put the muzzle of his gun against the ground. As he walked towards her, she noticed a thickness around his right knee, as if he had wrapped a strip of cloth over a wound. But he was walking normally, and a cut leg was of no consequence now.

"Shane! Come now! Sorcha! She—"

72

"What is it, a chroí?"

"Sorcha! She's . . . she's been murdered! Someone killed her with arrows!"

Normally the most voluble of men, Shane now stood silent as he took in the news.

"Please! Get your horse and come with me to O'Breslin."

"Of course, of course. I'll meet you at the house, and we'll go."

She turned her mare and rode to the house, where she waited for Shane. When he was mounted and ready to depart, they headed off to the home of the investigator and judge, the keeper of the ancient laws, O'Breslin.

O'Breslin and his family lived in a fine house of two levels, constructed of stone with a roof of thinly cut tiles and a chimney in the centre. The brehon's steward met Brigid and Shane at the door. They asked to speak to O'Breslin and were invited into the sitting room to wait. O'Breslin came in without delay and greeted them. The man was getting on in years, but his gaze and his gait were steady. He looked to Shane, but it was Brigid who spoke.

She took a deep shuddering breath and delivered the dreadful news. "Brehon, I made a most frightening discovery this morning. Well, it was not my discovery; her son was there. I'm sorry, I'm not telling this properly. I was on my way to see Sorcha the physician. I rode there with Donal, my horseboy. When we arrived at her property, we came upon her son, Peadar. He had found her lying on the ground at the edge of the oak wood by her house." Brigid could hear the tremor in her voice as she tried to describe the frightful scene. "There was no life in her, and there was an arrow in her heart and one in her throat, and there was a great amount of blood from her."

"This is terrible. I knew her family. Well, of course, we all did, or . . ." He looked at Shane, the man from Cork.

"I knew her, too, in my time here. A great loss to all of us."

"What time were you there, Brigid?"

"It would be less than an hour ago, Brehon. Donal and I were coming from the abbey. I was going to get a bottle of medicine for my daughter. As we approached Sorcha's house, I saw the son, and Sorcha lying near the trees. I rode home, found Shane, and we came here immediately."

"Thank you. Had the body been disturbed? I mean disturbed after death by animals? Or could you tell?"

"I saw no sign of that but, of course, I have no training, Brehon."

"We'll go there now. Once I have viewed the body, I shall arrange for it to be taken to the abbey."

So the three of them rode to the site of the murder, where Donal was sitting by his horse, keeping an eye on Peadar, who was crouched beside his mother. The young man's mouth was clamped shut as if he were afraid of what might come out of him if he opened it. O'Breslin signalled for Shane and Brigid to dismount some distance from the corpse, and Donal came with his horse to join them. O'Breslin walked over alone and gazed down at the white-clothed remains. He bent in close, gently pulled at Sorcha's clothing, and then took a walk around the area where she lay. He examined the ground and the nearby trees. He gently questioned the woman's son, who said he had no idea who had come for his mother; he had slept through the night and heard nothing of what had taken place outside the house. The brehon went into the house and came out again shortly after-wards. He then took a look around the property. There were hoofprints and cart tracks in all directions, as would be expected. It appeared to Brigid that the brehon had not noted anything that would help explain the outrage that had been committed the night before. Brigid could not stop her tears from flowing.

Every time Father Marcus Valerius had awakened during the night, his mind had returned instantly to the sight of his fellow priest furiously putting ink to the page in the scriptorium. Marcus would find those pages, but he would not be able to seize them until the afternoon, maybe between the prayers of Sext and None. Fiach had a group of students at two o'clock, so that is when Marcus would make his move.

The mysterious episode slipped his mind as he carried out his duties during the day, one of which was to stop by the bedside of Brother Aidan in the dormitory. Aidan, his long white hair fanned out on the pillow and his eyes closed, appeared to be exhausted. Marcus knew that he occasionally escaped his confines during the daylight hours and wandered off the grounds. He was a restless man, and little wonder; from the abbey he could see the countryside all about him, the river and the lough below. His illness seemed to be one of the mind rather than the body. Marcus had been told that Aidan had been deeply disturbed by what he had witnessed of the destruction of the churches and monasteries in England, and their sacred treasures. And by the people who had been left destitute as a result. Marcus had seen it himself during his time there. He knew that the money that had formerly come to the churches and monasteries had been used in part to relieve the poverty and illness of the common man and his family, the ordinary poor who lived within reach of the monasteries with their schools and hospitals. The dissolution of the monastic houses and the stopping of the flow of charity had led to enormous numbers of paupers in that rich country. What he and Aidan had seen was a land disfigured, a people impoverished.

So, if Aidan's mind compelled him to go out and about in his home country, Marcus couldn't see the harm in it. Sure, there was a worry that he would injure himself, but would that be any worse a fate than lying on a sick bed for his remaining time on earth?

Marcus said a prayer over the sleeping Aidan and then made his way to the classroom where he would meet his students for their one o'clock class in ancient history. Marcus enjoyed the class because almost always he had the students' attention. These boys, sons of a breed of warriors greatly celebrated in Ireland, thrilled to the accounts of battle and glory in the classical tales. They had travelled back in time with Homer and had acted out the part of Greek soldiers emerging from the Trojan horse to open the gates of Troy for the returning Greek army. They had instantly switched allegiance when they heard the resounding opening words of Virgil's *Aeneid*, "Arma virumque cano." I sing of arms and the man. They had competed with one another for the roles of Aeneas, his father, and son, as the great hero returned to the burning city of Troy and carried away his aged father on his back, his hand in that of his little boy as they escaped the ruined city.

This afternoon's lecture would bring the class to the death of classical civilization. Marcus told the boys to cast their minds back to the beginning of the fifth century Anno Domini. He described the great, fearsome barbaric hordes, hungry people with wild hair and grotesquely painted bodies, who crossed the frozen River Rhine in the year 406 AD and overran the settlements of the mighty Roman Empire. Thousands more came across the borders at various other times.

"These new people couldn't read. Couldn't write. So, think of what they missed. They didn't know Virgil from Homer from Augustus from Plato, Dido from Aphrodite. They sacked the great city of Rome — my city — in the year 410. They looted the artifacts and burned the books. But that was not the end of it. With the influence of these new tribes that had overrun the empire, many of the habits and customs of the Romans, including those who were the educated classes, declined over time. There was less reading, less demand for books, so fewer books were copied. There were many causes which, combined, led to this catastrophe: that many, many works representing over a thousand years of classical literature, art, law, philosophy, and the other marks of civilization were lost. The light of learning went out all over Europe. Many of our greatest treasures were gone."

The normally active boys were silent. They might prefer hurling to reading, but they understood the significance of what had been lost.

"Then how," one young fellow asked, "do we know about those warriors and Virgil and the old father and the little son, and all that? If all those men are dead and the books are all gone, how do we know?"

"In great part, it's because of your own people that we know. Irish monks spent years making copies of works of classical literature, any that they could find of the great works of civilization. You have seen some of the beautiful manuscripts we make here, with their elaborate and colourful decoration. You have made some of your own. Many monks from other lands fled the barbarians and came to the monasteries here and in other places like Scotland where Irishmen had built them. The men came to the Irish places because the Irish were known for their learning — as you yourselves will be! The Irish had their own written language more than a thousand years ago, long before many other countries did. There were books here in Ireland even before Saint Patrick came here. The learned Irishmen also wrote in Latin. And any of the great books that could be found were copied in the monasteries.

In the dark years after the sack of Rome, Irish monks set out across the continent of Europe and found and preserved some of the great works of classical civilization, inestimable treasures that might otherwise have been lost forever. There were Irishmen who became bishops in cities — or founded monasteries where cities would grow — all over Europe. The Irish played a very important role in preserving and teaching anew the great literature of the classical Roman world."

"It was our lads did that?" asked Owen Tierney.

Marcus nodded. "They had a big part in it." He gave the future men of Ireland a little bow. He then unfurled a large map and fixed it to the wall. The map showed the clusters of European cities that had grown up out of monastic communities founded by, or associated with, the monks of Ireland. He pointed to cities he particularly liked, including Fiesole and Lucca, Salzburg and Vienna. He was about to expound on the Irish satirist who had risen to become the archbishop of Salzburg, when he heard a commotion outside the classroom.

He walked out to the locutory, the area of the abbey where monks could converse with people from the outside, and he saw Brigid Tierney standing there with a man Marcus did not recognize.

"Forgive me, Father Abbot. I am here with Donal, my horseboy." The poor woman was distraught. "Donal, this is the abbot, Father Marcus Valerius. I am sorry, I . . . I have to see Father Fiach again. If I may. I . . ."

Marcus resisted the urge to ask her why she wanted to see O'Moylan. How was that his concern? He invited her to have a seat in the locutory and assured her that he would fetch the priest and bring him to her. He walked quickly to the classroom where O'Moylan was teaching. "Father," he said. O'Moylan looked up, startled. "Fiach, please come with me. The lady, Brigid Tierney, is here to see you."

"Ah." Fiach rose and followed.

When Brigid caught sight of Fiach, she got up and ran to him, threw her arms around him — well, Marcus knew they had been friends since childhood — and said, "Fiach, something terrible has happened!" Fiach gently disentangled himself and, with a hand on each of her arms, stood looking at her, waiting for the news. "It's Sorcha. Someone has killed her!"

It was the man, not the woman, who appeared ready to faint. Fiach stumbled back and reached out for something to support himself. He grabbed the edge of a table and stayed on his feet, staring at the woman in shock. Finally, he found words. "But I saw her—"

"She was at the banquet. We all saw her there, but . . . afterwards, sometime last night or perhaps this morning, I don't know, she was in the oak grove beside her house, and that's where we came upon her. It was after I left here with Donal, after I spoke with you this morning. Peadar was there by her body."

Marcus spoke to his fellow priest in Latin. "Sit down, Fiach, lest you fall. We shall all sit down, and hear this awful news."

When they were seated, Fiach said, "Tell me."

"It was horrid. After I left you, I rode with Donal to see Sorcha. She was going to give me a potion for Eileen. But Donal and I found Sorcha lying on the ground. There was no life in her. She had been killed by arrows shot into her."

Marcus made the sign of the cross and intoned a prayer for the dead woman. All the time, he was watching Fiach to gauge his reaction. It was as if the man had turned to stone. He did not move, did not speak, just stared at Brigid Tierney. Fiach had, of course, been married to the physician, the woman people considered a seer, and they had a child together, a daughter. Marcus remembered them exchanging a few words together at the banquet, but he had not noticed any passion or anger between them. If he hadn't known the history, he would have thought them old friends. After the feast, of course, much later, he had heard Fiach come running to the abbey, had seen him sitting alone in the scriptorium, madly filling the white vellum pages with words as yet unknown to Marcus. More than ever, it was imperative that the abbot see what the man had been so determined to commit to the page.

After Brigid Tierney had left and Fiach had returned, distracted and haunted, to the classroom, Marcus made a thorough search of the scriptorium. But he found nothing. Whatever was contained in those documents, Fiach O'Moylan did not want them seen by his fellow monks or his abbot. Marcus, of course, had the authority to enter the dormitory and search through a monk's sparse belongings, but he would prefer to address the problem openly, rather than go in like a thief in the night. He would speak to O'Moylan and make it clear to him that whatever was contained in those pages could no longer remain a secret.

CHAPTER V

*Shame is an ornament to the young, a disgrace to
the old.*

— Aristotle, d. 322 BC

2017

"My oul fella's all for it," Mick Tierney announced to his
daughter when he entered the hotel lobby and spotted
her perched at the edge of an armchair. His two grandchildren,
Ciara and Rory, were playing with a Lego set under the loving
eyes of their mother and the sullen gaze of their father. The young
guilpín lay slouched in his chair, looking exhausted. From another
late night in the clubs? Mick noticed that he'd taken to slicking
back his pale brown hair with grease of some kind. Following
some fad off the telly or the internet, no doubt. This was obviously one of the visiting days he had fought so tenaciously for in
the divorce proceedings; it said it all about the court's opinion
of Brayden Boyd Waring that any time he was to spend with his
children had to be spent on the premises of the Tierney family,
never on the home turf of Waring himself. Little wonder, given
the fact that Waring had been entertaining a crowd of stoned

and drunken arseholes when the children were last at his place. The man had passed out from the drink and drugs, so he failed to notice when his children left the flat on their own. They were found wandering the streets at two o'clock in the morning. The sleekit wee bastard. Mick ignored him, which was the kindest thing he could do, really. If Mick had his way, he'd give his daughter's ex-husband a kick up the arse and send him into orbit.

It was now the middle of July and Mick was after welcoming the latest busload of tourists, who had gone up to their rooms and were now flowing back down into the lobby. A fact not lost on Mick's former and not lamented son-in-law, who was eyeing the crowd. Employing his limited mathematical abilities to calculate just how much was going into the cash register. Right, pal: someday this could all have been yours, only now it won't.

But never mind that waster. Mick sat down opposite his daughter, and they proceeded to discuss their strategy for their hotel's survival. Its survival, Mick knew, was entirely dependent on the holiday homes and garages and the casino not making it off the drafting table. Mick had a bizarre dream last night; he dreamt that he couldn't get any archaeologists to dig beneath his property; he applied at state offices, one after another, and was told there weren't any archaeologists in the entire country. Nobody had ever heard of any. So he and Liam went out there with garden rakes, and little Rory, and Mick's old grandmother came roaring up in a big yellow mechanical digger, and they plunged the shovel into the earth and dug up the land and found something just as bad as the planned development. Under the Tierney land was a massive golf course, and the golfers all had big toothy grins and they kept whizzing by in golf carts with bright blazing headlamps. The foolish dream didn't afford him much amusement; he'd not been able to get back to sleep, and this didn't help his frame of mind. He couldn't let go of the fear that he would never see his plan realized, would never convince the planning authorities that there were significant historical sites and artifacts buried deep beneath the ground where the old guesthouse had been.

"Daddy! Daddy!" Mick looked over to see wee Rory trying to direct his father's attention to a pile of Lego blocks stuck together on the floor, but Daddy Waring was paying him little heed. Too busy eavesdropping on his ex-wife and father-in-law, Mick figured.

Róisín got down on her knees and admired Rory's handiwork. But she was still tuned in to the topic of the day. "You're right, Dad. That's a brilliant plan."

"Liam would be out there doing the job with a shovel himself. But we can't have diggers and archaeologists tearing up the place without warning our gran."

Cait Tierney was Mick's grandmother, Róisín's great-grandmother, but they had both always called her Gran.

"Let's go over there and talk to her now," Róisín said. She looked up at Brayden. "Can I rely on you to mind these two while we're gone?"

"It's not rocket science, is it?" came the less-than-Swiftian retort.

So Mick and Róisín left their Georgian hotel with its Victorian addition and traversed the grounds under which, they felt sure, lay parts of the structure of the much older inn. The house where Mick's father lived with Cait was of two storeys, white stucco with a black roof and two chimneys, one at each end. In front was a well-tended rose garden. Liam greeted them at the door, and Mick said, "Dia anseo isteach." God in here/God bless all in here.

"Home for a visit, are yous?" Liam came towards them with his awkward gait and a welcoming smile.

"A wee one, anyway," Mick replied.

"Good. I'll go into the town for a bit. Maisy will be coming over shortly." Maisy was the woman who came in to keep Cait company when Liam was out.

"We're here to warn her about the ruckus she'll be seeing from her garden."

"So you're going ahead with it?"

"Hope to."

"Brilliant. Wonder what they'll find buried under there."

"Doesn't matter. All we need is something that will pique the interest of the authorities and discourage any plan for a Las Vegas on the Erne."

"Ach, good name for it, Mick. Well, I'll be off."

Cait Tierney was sitting in the kitchen having a cup of tea when they walked in. She stared at them blankly for a long moment and then said, "Ah. Michael. And Róisín."

Róisín leaned over and gave her a hug and a kiss. "'Bout ye, Gran?"

"Fine, just fine, dear. Tea? The pot's full up."

"Sure. More for yourself?"

"Wouldn't turn it down."

So Róisín filled their cups, and they seated themselves at the table.

"Your wee girl and boy are looking fine these days, Róisín. I was delighted when you had them over here on Tuesday. Little Ciara's a dote. And Rory, he looks like my Liam. Long time ago that was, Liam as a little lad. He was an altar boy, you know! And he caused a sensation when he sang 'Panis Angelicus' at Father McDevitt's Mass."

"I'm sure he did," said Róisín. "I remember seeing a picture of him all dressed for Mass. And you're right. There is a resemblance there."

"Of course, Ciara is you all over."

"I'm glad!"

"Yes," the old lady nodded. Then she said, "That fella, do the children see him at all now?"

There was no need to ask who she meant. "Sure, he comes to visit them."

"Visit them!" In Cait's world, no doubt, a father's duties went far beyond *visiting* his children.

But Róisín showed no sign of being offended. "I know, Gran. He's over there now, in the lobby, with hardly a leg under him from partying last night."

"How ever did you take up with him in the first place, Róisín? A fine, lovely girl like yourself deserves so much better!"

"I was young and foolish, as the saying goes, Gran. I've no use for him now. But at the time, I think I was flattered. Here was this good-looking bloke, who everybody knew was in the clubs every night till all the hours God gives us, and him telling me I meant more to him than all that carry-on, that he would rather be with me than be off with his mates, than be off his head with the drink. He wanted nothing more in life than to settle down with me and be married and have a family. Now, he has all those same mates tormenting him, telling him I've put something over on him. I took his son and his wee girl away from him, I'll have the hotel business for my own, I've made him look like an eejit in front of everyone! Ah, Gran, I was young and stupid when I wedded myself to Brayden. But by the time my second wean came along, I was much older and wiser."

"Wise beyond your years now, I know, darling girl. You have your two dear children, and you're well rid of him that fathered them on ye. I'm surprised to hear he comes to see them at all."

"And he only does that to assert his rights of manhood, or whatever you might call it," Mick put in.

"Ah now, Dad. He loves them in—"

"Don't tell me. 'In his own way.' Enough breath wasted on him."

Mick then introduced the reason for their visit. "One of these days soon, Gran, we'll come and collect you and bring you over to the hotel. You'll not believe the fine art work Róisín is after putting up."

"Oh, is that so, Róisín? I'll want to see it for definite."

"I think you'll like it. I've created a mural, showing a banquet back in the time of the old tower house, and I have the Maguire presiding over it, and the gentlemen and ladies in their finery."

"Which Maguire would that be now?"

"It was Hugh who was Lord of Fermanagh at the time I'm portraying. I'm showing them at the Tierney guesthouse, instead of at the castle."

"I was at the castle myself. I wore a lovely gown, had my hair done up," Cait said, her eyes brightening at the memory.

"You must have looked like a fine lady, Gran!"

"I surely did. We're lords ourselves, are we not? I married into the Tierneys, which is just a simpler spelling of the old word for lords."

"Ah, we'll always be lords, Gran."

"Aye, we will. I can't remember now what the occasion was, when I was at the castle. But the news reporters were there."

Mick didn't know either, but it wasn't always good news when the news reporters turned up in Enniskillen. This, though, must have been a benign occasion.

"You love the old places, don't you, Gran?" he said. "The history, the old stories."

"Oh, aye."

"Well, we're going to be looking into some of that. We have reason to believe there are some important things buried around the tower house, maybe back as far as the time when our people were professional hospitallers. What's the Irish word for it, Róisín?"

"The old word was briugu, and I think it's brughaidh now. But even after the profession went out of fashion, the tower house continued to be a popular destination for visitors."

"Our ancestors must have been rich in cattle and fertile lands," Mick said, "since that's how wealth was measured in those days. Guests weren't charged for accommodation or for food or drink. Ah, those were the days. If you were a guest, that is! You'd best be careful what you put in those murals of yours, Rosie. Nothing about free accommodation, or we'll have to be going on the dole!"

"I'll leave that bit out, Dad. I'll paint in a big red arrow pointing to the cash register, just for you!"

"Child of my heart, you are! So, anyway, Gran, we've got some archaeologists coming in." He was getting ahead of himself; there were no archaeologists coming yet, but he judged it better to leave the impression that the project was well on its way. "They'll be digging around the old place. Machines and people working on the site."

"Oh?"

"And no doubt they'll find some fascinating objects there, and parts of the old building."

"No!" The old lady was spooked; she looked as if she had just heard the wailing of the banshee.

"What's the matter, Gran?"

"Your father would never stand for that."

Mick's father was fine with it. Liam couldn't wait to see the giant claws of a digger biting into the earth, signs up warning people off the grounds. All of it making the developers go mental with the waiting. What Cait meant was her long-deceased husband, Mick knew. But he played along. "Why's that, Gran?"

She turned her frightened eyes on Mick. "They'll know!"

"Who? Who will know what?"

"What this family has done!"

"Ah now, Gran. All that about the Famine times and Roderick Tierney evicting the tenants from the land, people know about it. They're not still blaming us for that."

"They will be if they get news of it all over again. Life was never easy even before the Famine. People were hungry between March and July of the year, as the old stock of spuds was gone and the new not available to them yet. You know yourself what the old people used to say: the praties were 'in for Paddy and up for Billy.'" Planted in March, the month of St. Patrick, and harvested in July, the month of King William of Orange. "And I take issue, Michael, with anyone who looks down on the lowly spud. Irishmen were strong and bursting with good health; they made fine labourers and soldiers. They were sought after by English military recruiters! Imagine that."

"Fine soldiers they were. And yet one of the early English kings, one of the Edwards I think it was, said, 'Use up the Irish. The dead cost nothing.'"

"Right, Dad. That was in *Braveheart*. I wonder if the king really said it."

"I wouldn't doubt it in the least," said Cait. "And as little as our people had, our 'peasants,' as they were called, had the reputation of being welcoming to one and all; they'd never deny you a plate of food if they had it. Not so Roddo Tierney. That's what the family always called him, Roddo. Not by reputation a hospitable man, never mind that he was in the business himself. He was from the other branch of the family, not our own, buíochas le Dia." Thank God.

"When the potato crops failed in the 1840s, of course, starvation was upon us. You hear about County Cork, Skibbereen and those places, being hit hard, and God knows they were. But we lost something like forty thousand people here in Fermanagh, to death, disease, or emigration. And you know yourself, the country was under the thumb of the English Victorians, who believed that poverty was the fault of the individual who just wasn't able for a better life. Didn't work hard enough!"

"But that's not right!" Róisín exclaimed. "How could they make that kind of judgment about an entire class of people?"

"That's exactly what they did, a chroí."

"I know, I know," Róisín acknowledged. "It was the whole laissez-faire philosophy."

"Aye," Mick agreed. "To help the poor by giving them food would bring prices down, affect the free market! The unfettered 'market' was why they wouldn't stop ships loaded with other food from sailing out of Ireland with the poor starving people standing on the shore, looking on. And it wasn't only the markets at work but God himself as interpreted by our English overlords. That oul bastard Trevelyan said the Famine was God's judgment on us here!"

It had all happened a hundred and seventy years ago, but Mick could still work up a head of steam about it, just as he could about the more recent Troubles here in the North. He was just a wee lad when that started up at the end of the 1960s. But it was still going full bore when he came of age. Should he have done more than provide safe houses for those fighting the British Army and its toadies amongst the local population? It was a debate he'd been having with himself for years. But it was the Famine that had him exercised now. He could picture a poor tenant and his family, living in their one-room cabin on the land, and when something good would happen, something bad would follow right on its heels. Any time an improvement was made to a wee cabin, the rent went up. And how could the man pay it, and him with his crops all blighted? Meanwhile up at the big house, the landlords were having an uproarious time for themselves. They'd not been spending their wealth to improve their lands. But then the English began charging them rates on the unimproved, low-value lands. Crop failures, falling rents, rising expenses. So, many of the landlords forced their tenants off their land and out of their cabins.

To his daughter and grandmother, he said, "You've heard the stories and seen the drawings of the tenant families who wouldn't leave their wee houses; they had nowhere to go. So, the sheriff and his ruffians came and dragged the people out, women and children and men and old grandparents, all of them barely able to stand, so weak were they from the hunger. And the sheriff's rabble burned or bashed in the thatched roofs of the houses, and this in the dead of winter. The tenants froze, or starved, or had to emigrate."

"That's another mural I should be doing! But I won't be able to see to work on it, won't be able to see for the tears. I mean, it's not as if I didn't know about the Famine and all that, and I've seen those pictures of the houses being destroyed. But when I think about it again, knowing that someone related to us . . ."

"Sure, you'll not be wanting a mural like that for people to see. People have long memories, and they'll know exactly who the villain should be in your picture. They'll know what that crowd of Tierneys was really like, no matter that old Roddo boasted he was better than that. He put it about that he paid the tenants' passage across the Atlantic Ocean to Saint John in New Brunswick. That's

Canada now, but it was a Brit colony back then. That's what he claimed. Nobody believed him."

"We don't know what he did, Gran," said Mick.

"People said worse about him." Cait looked about her and lowered her voice as if the spooks from one of the state's intelligence agencies had the place wired. "Worse than only evicting them. You know yourself what the other rumour was, that went round this place."

Mick knew. The rumour was that Roddo had actually *killed* some of his tenants to be rid of them. "Now, Gran, there's no proof of that."

"*Proof*, he says. What are you, a lawyer now, Michael?"

"Ach, the insults are flying in this house today!"

"Well, the Tierneys have acted like a shower of lawyers about this, this base accusation. Deny, deny, deny! We should be on our knees over at the Famine Memorial for what that man did!" The stone monument had been erected on the site of the old paupers' graveyard.

"People say a lot of things. They have overactive imaginations."

"If these people you're talking about, these nosy parkers . . ."

"They're archaeologists, Gran."

"If they root around beneath our land, God only knows what they might dig up! They might well find your *proof!*"

"Don't get yourself all wound up. It's not—"

"Scoff if you will, but how many people will come to our hotel? The Tierneys will be boycotted all over again."

Mick didn't give voice to the thought that occurred to him then, that there was a type of person who would come to the hotel precisely *because* there was a whiff of scandal or danger about the place. What he said was, "Nobody outside of County Fermanagh would know or care about any of that old bother. There is a real threat to our business now, and that is the new development they're trying to get going."

"What's that you're saying?"

"A new crowd coming in from America. They want to build holiday homes all round the hotel, with big garages attached to them. We'll be stuck in the middle of suburban hell. And then there'll be a casino, with the inevitable racket and people coming and going, and neon lights and bad music blasting from the place all hours. And, worst of all, our view will be obliterated."

His grandmother looked at him as if he had lost his senses. "And you believe them! Don't be so thick, Michael. You've been watching too many fillums. Nothing like that will be built up in this peaceful place. Go off and leave me now; you've got me worn out here with your foolishness."

"Gran, the only way we can stop the new development is to have archaeologists come onto the place, and do a dig, and that way the state will refuse or delay planning permission, and—"

The old lady lurched forward in her chair, and her eyes blazed at him. "Do not do this thing. Whatever is buried, let it stay buried!"

On the way home to the hotel, Róisín said, "We can't have this dig without her blessing, Dad. Can't do it to her."

"She remembers all this old guff. Why can't she be like so many of the other old dears who are away with the fairies?"

"Dad! You're not wishing senility on your gran!"

"No, no, of course I'm not, love." He made a hurried sign of the cross. "Sometimes I lose the run of myself when something has me vexed."

"Well, her mind is as sharp as yours or mine, and we can't have her gaping out her window and seeing all the digging going on and her fretting about it and having a spell of illness!"

"We'll all be having a spell if this casino and a load of shite-looking holiday homes are built all around us, and people stop coming to us because we've lost the view and the lovely walks and the peace and quiet we offer our guests. And we lose the business that's been in the family for centuries."

It came to Mick in a rush of sudden feeling then. He *did* care about the hotel, and the intensity of his attachment to the place surprised him. Sure, he made cynical cracks about the life of an innkeeper in the age of the bus tour, and the frequently uncultured tourists who were deposited at his door. But they weren't all like that. And he was proud of his family's long history, its tradition of hospitality going back hundreds of years, Roddo Tierney notwithstanding. Mick truly loved the beautiful Georgian building with its nineteenth-century addition and its spectacular view of the water and the castle. This was his ancestral home. He wanted it intact and thriving for the next generation, and the generations after that. And he wanted to keep on enjoying it himself, exactly as it was now. Allowing, of course, for the improvements Róisín would lovingly make to the place with her artwork, and that of her wee girl and boy. And Mick would do his part by repainting the exterior window frames and making repairs where needed to the walls. It was his legacy, too, after all.

"A dig," he said to Róisín now, "a bunch of archaeologists, and a refusal of planning permission, that is our only way to save Tierney's Hotel from extinction."

"But Gran says no! What will Liam say? He's always so good to her. She's his mum, and she says no."

CHAPTER VI

*The people are thus inclined: religious, frank, amorous,
ireful, sufferable of pain infinite, very glorious, many
sorcerers, excellent horsemen, delighted with wars,
great alms-givers, passing in hospitality. The lewder
sort, both clerks and laymen, are sensual and loose to
lechery above measure.*

— Edmund Campion, *A History of Ireland*, 1571

1595

For three nights the body of Sorcha O'Cassidy lay surrounded by candles in her home, and people gathered to sing and weep and tell stories about the beloved physician and friend who had been taken from them. The wake had been organized by Sorcha's sister Niamh, who had returned to Fermanagh upon hearing of Sorcha's death. Also present was a woman named Bronagh, a professional mourner whose keening lament was the most plaintive, most heartbreaking sound Brigid had ever heard. Heartbreaking but also somehow grand, as befitted the woman being mourned.

Now the Drumlyon Abbey church was packed with people grieving the death of Sorcha. Brigid could not imagine who would want to hurt her, let alone take her life. As she looked about her at the hundreds of mourners, she was sure that everyone present felt the same way. Tears flowed freely from the eyes of many of the women and young children. Brigid and Shane had decided to leave Eileen and Owny home with the maids; there would be plenty of time for grief later in their lives. A number of men appeared to be holding their emotions in check. Standing beside her, gripping her arm in support, Shane was the same way. Father O'Moylan, the priest who, of course, knew Sorcha best, was not on the altar with the other priests but in the front row of mourners. On a couple of occasions when he turned his head towards the congregation, Brigid could see the pallor of his face, an almost wild look in his eyes. It was as if he had awakened in a world he no longer understood. That was how Brigid herself felt, as she pictured her beloved friend lying in the oak leaves, her blood spilt and her eyes open but seeing nothing. Sorcha's son Peadar, up near the front of the church, was stooped over, his young frame no longer holding him straight. His father, Tomás, was not with him in the church. The rich aroma of the incense, the heavenly light blazing in through the coloured glass of the windows, the solemn dignity of the monks' chanting, all seemed to underscore the beauty of the life Sorcha had lost but also perhaps the beauty of what she might find in the life beyond.

Now, two days after the funeral, Brigid was sitting by the window in her room in the early evening. She could think of little else but the death of Sorcha. It was heart-scalding to remember their times together, listening to music or poetry, going for long walks and talking about their lives and their children, and their fears for the future of Ireland. She turned her attention from the window and picked up a book Fiach O'Moylan had lent her from the abbey, *Historia animalium* by a man called Gessner. This was only the first volume of several, Fiach had told her. He also said, with a mischievous look in his eyes, that Gessner was not of the faith, so Fiach wasn't sure whether he should even have it at the abbey. It was a wonderful book describing the four-footed animals of the world. It was written in Latin, with the names of the animals given in the languages of the Germans, the Italians, and the Gauls, so Brigid could not understand all of it, but there were illustrations of the creatures, which she and the children loved to look at.

Seeing the different languages and the references to other, remote parts of the world brought back conversations she and Sorcha had often enjoyed. They were both fascinated with the notion of boarding a ship someday and sailing to lands far from Ireland. Distant lands with lovely bright flowers in every colour known to man. And the flowers never died because there was no winter. And the sea was a pale green and it was so calm and so warm that people swam and played in it with their children all year round. And there would be very strange animals that could walk on land or swim in the sea or fly through the air. Brigid loved to imagine it. But it was the people she and Sorcha most wanted to see. What did the women wear in such warm countries? Short little dresses patterned after the flowers? And what of the men? Sorcha would stare ahead and point her hand to whatever she was seeing. Or pretending to see. "Look at *him*, Brigid. The tallest, most beautifully built man I have ever seen, and his skin is brown from the sun and his hair is cropped short and a shining black. Do you see? Oh, look now, there are two of them, and they are speaking such a musical language; it is just like music to hear them talk. They seem to be searching for something. For someone. Are they waiting for the pair of us, Brigid? Are they calling our names? We must get ourselves to the shore and board a ship right away before they give up all hope."

"Away with your foolish talk, Sorcha O'Cassidy," Brigid would say. And Sorcha would answer that Brigid had poured too generously from the bottle of wine that had come from France or Spain, and it was distorting her visions. And Brigid would pour them both more wine, and the conversation got even more outlandish, and they'd be laughing like fools.

What would life be like now without Sorcha in Fermanagh? Who would Brigid laugh with in that carefree way? Who would be their physician now? Who else would be so kind and understanding to a child like Eileen, understanding that her trouble did not originate in her stomach but giving her a sweet-tasting potion nonetheless?

So absorbed was she in her thoughts that it took a few moments to register the sound of horses outside. She turned and looked out: two horsemen were approaching the house. Ah! It was Diarmait with another man who looked familiar, another of the Maguire's musketeers. Cornelius O'Kelly, that was his name. They were in their short jackets with their long guns. They dismounted and walked towards the house. She descended the spiral stairs and greeted the two men.

"Welcome, Cornelius. And brother of mine. We'll have a meal prepared for you."

"Thank you, Brigid," O'Kelly said. "You are as always most kind to—"

He was interrupted by Diarmait. "Has the killer been found?" She shook her head no.

"I had hoped to come back to Fermanagh for the wake or the funeral. If the man who did this, if he showed himself amongst the mourners, I'm sure I would have seen something strange in his manner. Something that would reveal his guilt." O'Kelly was nodding his head in agreement. "But none of us were free to leave where we were posted. There had been sightings of the English."

"I hope to God they find the man soon," said O'Kelly, "so he can be brought to judgment."

"Or," said Diarmait, "so judgment can be brought to him!"

Brigid translated this as *so her family or others who loved her can take their revenge*. Brigid never doubted that, although her brother no longer lived near the guesthouse and did not have the opportunity to visit often, he would step up and defend the interests of his sister and his other family members any time the need arose. It was enough for him to know that a dear friend of Brigid had been killed; he was ready to go out, musket in hand, to avenge Sorcha's death. Brigid had to slow him down, as was sometimes the case.

"Diarmait, the brehon is investigating. We have to let him do his work."

"O'Breslin, God bless him, is too old to be tracking down a murderer."

"The brehon is not at all too old, Diarmait, and he is fully capable of doing his work, to investigate and then to judge." She put her hand on his arm in a calming gesture. "I imagine he has spoken to Fiach to see if Sorcha said anything to him at the banquet that night, if she mentioned anything or anyone she might have been worried about. And, of course, the brehon will talk to everyone who knew her well."

"Fiach," Diarmait said. "The lustful priest. One of the ruin-ations of a kingdom, the old law says, is a lustful priest."

"He is not a lustful priest, Diarmait. He was married to Sorcha, and she divorced him because he took Holy Orders, which was her right under the law. They still had great affection for one another. Father Fiach O'Moylan did not kill her. He wouldn't kill anyone, least of all Sorcha. She was the mother of his child."

"One of his children."

"Enough of this now. Let's leave tragedy aside for the moment. Cornelius, come inside. Donal will see to the horses. There he is now." Donal was standing by the stables, discreetly out of earshot, with his eyes on the animals. Diarmait turned and signalled to him, and he came and took the horses.

"Are you stopping with us for a while, Diarmait?"

"Just a brief visit. Two nights, that's all."

Diarmait took after their father, Ardal, with light brown hair, long and wavy, and eyes of a light green. He lived with his wife, Gráinne, several miles away in a large house surrounded by extensive fields. She had four children from her former husband, so she rarely if ever left home. Diarmait's marriage to Gráinne was not a marriage performed by a priest but a "union of a man on woman-property," whereby the man contributes little or nothing and the property comes from the woman's family. As a result, Diarmait was more than happy to leave the Tierney house and lands to his sister to run. He came by to visit when he could, but he was always on duty as a soldier.

"I'm glad you're here, both of you," Brigid said. She turned to lead them inside, when a small figure came flying out the door. "Mammy, is it my uncle Diarmait who's here?"

"Is it Diarmait?" his uncle chided young Owny. "Show me some deference or I'll drop you down the murder hole!" He pointed upwards.

"It's I'll be dropping *you* down it!"

They were referring to the hole in the ceiling of the main room on the ground floor, through which objects could be dropped from above onto unwelcome or threatening individuals who had entered the house. Brigid was gratified that the murder hole had long been covered over by the timber floor on the second level.

Diarmait swept his nephew off the ground, swung him around, and then deposited him at the foot of the staircase. Owny laughed with delight and fired questions at Diarmait as they all made their way up the spiral stairs to the main hall. The family had always used one end of the hall for eating and drinking. It had a long, heavy table with benches running along either side. The other end was for relaxing and entertaining, with comfortable chairs, tapestries on the walls, a fireplace, and Brigid's harp in the corner. And unlike the narrow vertical slits in the walls at ground level, the main hall had large mullioned windows, and the room was often awash with light. On the floor above were Brigid and Shane's room and those of the children. The upper two floors were divided into sleeping quarters for visitors. In Brigid's grandparents' time, the kitchen had been on the first floor next to the storage area, but a fire had put an end to the indoor kitchen; it was moved outside the main house. Even though in these times a hospitaller did not have the same formal recognition as in the past, most people still referred to the Tierney place as the Tierney guesthouse.

Now, while the cook was preparing the meal, the two soldiers began regaling Brigid and her children with hair-raising tales of the battles they had fought. Eileen, sensitive as she was, looked pale and shaky soon after the first shot had been fired. So Brigid took her by the hand and led her to her bedroom, where she set the child up with a wax tablet and a brass stylus for her favourite activity, drawing pictures of animals and flowers. When the images were to Eileen's liking after much practice on the tablet, she would switch to an inkhorn and quill and commit the final version to a piece of vellum.

"And when I do that, Mammy, guess what I'm going to do next?" The child was wide-eyed with excitement.

"What are you going to do?"

Eileen got up and fetched a bag and brought out several little pieces of fabric in varying colours. "Gormlaith gave me these! I'm going to cut them out in the shapes of the flowers and animals I draw!"

Eileen was particularly attached to Brigid's personal maid, Gormlaith, because Gormlaith had a talent for repairing and stitching clothes, and she occasionally passed on leftover scraps of fabric to Eileen.

"You've a great talent for pictures, a chroí. When you have them done, we'll put them up on your wall."

Eileen beamed at her mother with pleasure and then resumed her work.

When Brigid returned to her brother and O'Kelly, they had wound up Owny to even greater heights of excitement: Diarmait promised the boy that tomorrow morning, instead of going to the abbey for his lessons, he could go off with Diarmait and Cornelius and view the swords, shields, pikes, and muskets that the clan's fighting men had at their disposal.

"Not tomorrow," Brigid protested.

"I want it to be tomorrow!"

"You must not miss your classes."

"No difficulty there," his uncle assured him. "We'll do it after the school day ends."

"And then I'll see all the pikes. And I want to see muskets and calivers, and we'll make sure we have loads of gunpowder, and I'll fire them! And I'm going to get up on Flame — he's *my* horse — and follow you to the very next battle!"

"That would make you a camp follower, I guess, Owny," his uncle said, with a wink at Cornelius O'Kelly. "You're well familiar with camp followers, Cornelius. Do you have any advice for my young nephew? How to keep himself clean and healthy?"

"Enough of that," Brigid admonished the pair of them. She knew perfectly well who some of the camp followers were. And she knew of painful and mortifying conditions that afflicted some of the men who consorted with them. She turned the conversation in another direction. "Why don't you tell your uncle about some of the animals you've seen lately, Owny?"

"I've seen them all. Badgers and hedgehogs. And rabbits! I caught a rabbit myself!"

"Did you now?" his uncle asked. "And did you have it for your dinner?"

The little boy hesitated, then wove a tale that featured him as a remorseless hunter, killer and skinner of rabbits. The real story was that the child could not bring himself to kill the animal and had let it go. But Brigid was not about to ruin the moment for him in front of the warriors he so admired.

Seeing her brother and son having such an entertaining time together caused Brigid to ache with loneliness for her sister, Mary. There were just the three of them: Diarmait, Mary, and Brigid. Brigid was thirty now, Mary two years older, and Diarmait two years older again. Mary had been like Brigid in many ways, wanting to play music and learn from books, but Mary had skills with a needle and thread that Brigid most certainly did not. But that worked in with the way they played together. They had a group of little clay dolls their mother had been given as a child, and Mary made clothes for them. Brigid carved dogs and horses for them out of pieces of wood, and between the two sisters, they gave their dolls a good time indoors and out when the weather allowed.

When the sisters grew older, Mary was protective of Brigid, warning her of the dangers of too much drink and too much merriment in the company of men. You had to be careful around men; most were of a good, strong, and loving character, but there were a few who could hurt you if you didn't watch out. Brigid had learned many years ago that she was right about the need to be careful, but she forced herself to shut out those images from her mind. She had found a wonderful man in Shane, and once again she thanked God for her good fortune in meeting him. Her thoughts now, though, were with Mary and how much she missed her. She had not seen her since Mary was wed at a young age and moved across the country to Dublin with her husband, Cormac. Dublin was such a great distance away, Mary might as well have been in France!

Shane came in just as his son was rearing up in imitation of Flame the horse, and Brigid returned her attention to the present time. Shane gave a hearty welcome to the soldiers. Diarmait was courteous, even though Brigid knew that her brother — married within the traditions of the old Irish law — wished Brigid would insist that Shane marry her. But Shane still had a wife in Cork, whom he had never divorced and who had never divorced him. They had two children, she knew, two boys. Daniel and Eamon. According to Shane, he and his wife had married young, when she was pregnant with Daniel, and they had soon found them-selves at odds with each other. Things had not improved as the years went on. In fact, Shane said, there was another man in her life and had been from the time she was a young girl. And she, Daniel, and Eamon spent so much time at the home of that man's family that the two boys seemed confused as to which man was their father. Shane had once told Brigid, under the influence of a great quantity of ale, that the boys preferred their visits to the other man's richly adorned house and his horses to Shane's more modest property. Given what an exceptional father he was to Owny and Eileen, she knew he must miss his first children, but those reminiscences of his family life in Cork were rarely voiced in her presence.

Shane could, of course, have taken a second wife, but Brigid's outlook was in line with that of the Church, and Church law meant one husband, one wife. Like many Irish people, Brigid and Shane's approach to the divine was a combination of the old Celtic traditions and those of the Catholic Church. She had never pushed Shane to properly end his first marriage; the fact was that he and Brigid were perfectly happy with things the way they were.

Shane fetched goblets of ale for the men, and wine for Brigid, and toasted the warriors' return. Shane, being a man and a musketeer himself, made no protest over his son's enthusiasm for all things martial. "What is more natural for a boy?" he said to her later that night when they were in their bed.

"How about what is natural for a man and a woman lying together in the night?" she replied. And she was cheered to see that great quantities of ale had not diminished his natural abilities.

CHAPTER VII

Under Lionel Duke of Clarence, the then Lord
Lieutenant of Ireland, the Brehon law was formally
abolished, it being unanimously declared to be indeed
no law but a lewd custom . . . And yet, even in the
reign of Queen Elizabeth, the wild natives still kept
and preserved their Brehon law, which is described
to have been "a rule of right unwritten, but delivered
by tradition from one to another, in which oftentimes
there appeared great show of equity in determining
the right between party and party, but in many things
repugnant quite both to God's laws and man's."

— William Blackstone, *Commentary on the Laws*
of the Countries Subject to the Laws of England

A week and a half had passed since the discovery of Sorcha's murder, and it was a quiet evening at home; Brigid and Shane were inside with the two children. Eileen and Owny were enthralled as their father explained to them the rudiments of the game of chess. It had gone well until Owny decided that tossing the pieces around or setting them against one another in battle was more fun than listening to his father explain the rules of the game. Brigid was playing her harp, and she switched from a melancholy tune to a plinking sound which she made by holding the strings with one hand at the bottom and playing them higher up with her other hand. She meant it to sound like the chess pieces scattering to the floor, and the children both laughed. Then she struck a number of low notes all at once as she instructed her son, in an ominous voice to match the mood of the chord, "You bold child, pick up those chess pieces and play properly!" The children always enjoyed the humorous sounds she could make with her beautiful instrument.

After a few minutes, they returned to their chess game, and Brigid switched to a project she had been working on from time to time. It was a tapestry her mother had begun many years ago, shortly before her death. Brigid had little talent or inclination for sewing, but she had always wanted to finish the piece to honour her mother. The image on the cloth was of the guesthouse as seen from the lough below, with the setting sun blazing gold and vermillion in the costly glass windows of the house. Brigid was thankful that these artistic touches had been completed by her mother before her death, since she herself would be utterly incapable of such artistry. She would rather have been playing the harp, but she wanted to complete the project once and for all. A pattern around the edges of the cloth was all that Brigid had to do. She had decided on white lilies because of their beauty and their abundance around the guesthouse. So she worked away at her tapestry and enjoyed the quiet evening with her family.

She heard horses, and her first thought was regret that the four members of the family would be interrupted. She immediately chided herself for such a selfish thought, particularly inappropriate for someone descended from a long line of hospi-tallers! Well, Brigid would be happy to greet the guests and make them welcome. Have their baths prepared, and meals cooked and served. But when she went down the stairs, it was not a group of travellers at the door but the brehon, O'Breslin.

"Brehon," said Brigid, "it is an honour to have you here."

He acknowledged her greeting and followed her up the stairs. When he reached the main hall, he said, "I am not here to partake of your generous hospitality, Brigid, as sorry as I am to say it. I am here looking for Shane O'Callaghan." He then spotted Shane, who, when the chess game had been interrupted, had come forward with Eileen holding his right hand.

"Shane O'Callaghan," the brehon said, and Brigid felt a chill. Why would the judge be speaking in such a sombre tone unless there was something wrong?

"Brehon?" Shane asked, looking puzzled.

"The son of Sorcha O'Cassidy has come to me and made an assertion of duinetháide against you, that you did commit a secret killing, an unacknowledged killing of his mother, and did leave her body in the wilderness. You must appear before the court on judgment day, the twelfth of June."

Shane had gone as still as a tombstone. Little Eileen clutched her father's arm in her hands as if she feared he would be seized by the forces of the law and removed from the house. "Brehon, I did not kill Sorcha. I have been running thoughts over and over in my head, trying to understand who would do such a thing. It was not me." He turned to Brigid. "It was not me, Brigid, I swear to you."

"There is a witness who will give evidence against you."

"That is not possible. There can be no evidence. I did nothing wrong."

"You will want to hire an aigne to plead on your behalf." An advocate.

Whatever else he said was lost in the turmoil in Brigid's mind. The brehon took his leave, and Brigid fussed over the children, assuring them that the brehon had made a mistake. Their father would never commit a secret killing, and he would never have hurt Sorcha. She got the two of them settled in their beds and sang each of them a lullaby in the hope that it would reassure them and make them sleepy. After kissing them goodnight, she left their rooms and returned to Shane.

When she was alone with him, the words that left her mouth were not the words she had intended. "Where were you that night?"

"What do you mean, Brigid, where was I? Surely you don't think I had anything to do with Sorcha's death. You know me better than that."

"I do. I'm sorry. It's just that . . . the brehon says he has a witness!"

"And you sound as if you believe him!"

"A witness, Shane. Were you . . . were you with Sorcha that night after the feast? If you were with her, for some reason, perhaps that is what the witness saw, and—"

"The witness saw nothing! There was no witness. I did not see Sorcha after we were all at the castle."

But, Brigid reminded herself, she had not seen Shane after the feast either. She had said goodbye to him when she left the castle with the children. She had brought them home, got them settled for the night, and had gone to sleep without even wondering when or if Shane would come in. The house was quiet, and the stables closed, when she had arrived home, but she had not wondered whether her current crop of guests, the men from Galway, had gone to bed or gone out, perhaps to the alehouse. She knew Shane had been carousing with them before the banquet and she had assumed, to the extent that she gave it any thought at all, that he had met up with them again after leaving the castle. It was not unusual for him to sleep in other quarters in the house after a night of drinking; rather than awaken her with his arrival in the late hours, he simply found another bed and went to sleep there. It had never been a point of contention between them.

Now, with his movements crucial to his plea of innocence, he sought to reassure Brigid that he had not been with Sorcha O'Cassidy after the evening at the castle. "I did something foolish."

Go sábhála Dia sinn! God save us. What foolish thing had he done? "What was it, Shane?"

"When I left the castle and came back to the house, the crowd from Galway had settled in for the night, but I was restless, not ready to sleep. So I headed out, thinking of the alehouse, and I met some men on the way there, men camped out. And they were well supplied with drink, and I joined them."

She thought then of the cut on his right knee. She had asked him about it, and he told her he had fallen. "Drinking to the point where you were falling down!" She pointed to the knee.

"Ah, yes, I did stumble. And after the session of drinking, I fell asleep in their tent."

"Did you now. Well, you'll have some witnesses in your favour then."

"I will, indeed I will." Her man looked miserable, not at all like a man who had a pack of witnesses who would save him from a murder charge on judgment day.

Marcus Valerius was afraid that his planned evening away from the abbey would make him seem callous in light of the murder, and might also make his night terrors even more potent if he had too many glasses of ale. Drinking sometimes affected him that way. Images came to him of the jagged ruins of churches and monasteries he had seen in England, brutal punishments he had heard described. But his own city of Rome, one of the greatest cities of all time, had been sacked earlier in this century. Eleven hundred years after that first famous Sack of Rome. The more recent invasion was before his time, nearly seventy years ago, but it happened the year his mother was born, in 1527. Germanic invaders and Spaniards had stormed the city, murdering thousands of people. One of those killed was his great-aunt's husband, Erisman, a member of the Swiss Guard. When a mob of Spanish soldiers attacked the Vatican, Erisman was wounded. He escaped to his home, but the invaders followed him there and killed him as his wife looked on. Marcus had heard the story at the family table, told as the family tragedy that it was. Then there was the destruction: churches, abbeys, and palaces were looted and destroyed. But, Marcus always reminded himself, the popes had in recent years set out to renew the greatness of the Church and its tradition of art. Marcus had seen magnificent buildings, sculpture, and paintings that were marvels. Unequalled anywhere, he was sure. And the work was still going on. This in turn awakened in Marcus a longing to visit his home again, and to see his family.

He was hardly living the life of a monk these days, let alone an abbot! He had been to the sumptuous banquet at the castle, and now tonight it was the alehouse. Certainly, the monks made their own ale and, he had been surprised to learn when he arrived in Ireland, the allotment for members of the order was one and a half gallons a day! It had not been his custom to overindulge in wine when he was in Rome, or ale in England. So, he did not now require such a quantity in his daily life. Though Fiach O'Moylan had been heard to say that "On some days, it isn't enough!" And apparently it was not enough for O'Moylan now, in the wake of his former wife's death. Marcus often came upon a morose Fiach these days, his customary good nature nowhere to be seen. The man was drinking heavily, which made him more gloomy and distraught. The other evening, Marcus had come upon Fiach in the church, alone before the Blessed Sacrament in its tabernacle. But he was not kneeling as one would do in adoration; rather he was slumped over on his side. Marcus thought he must have fallen asleep but no, he was wide awake and staring at nothing in particular. Marcus could smell the ale off him. He did not remonstrate with him, merely helped him to his feet and walked him to his room. Even in spite of this, Marcus had agreed to accompany him to the home of Brian Magennis, who had been renowned for his hospitality and had used that quality to the advantage of one and all when, some years ago, he had turned his home into an alehouse. It was a place for Fiach to converse and raise a glass with travellers and with men he had grown up with in Fermanagh, and perhaps receive their condolences on the death of his former wife. Marcus saw no harm in having a few cups of ale. As long as it did not lead to a lowered resistance to other temptations.

Fiach was greeted with solemnity when he and Marcus walked into the large candlelit room. Men rose and expressed their sympathy to him as the former husband of the murdered woman, offering to help in any way they could. Marcus took this to mean that they would be happy to track down the killer and bring him to justice. Or perhaps mete out justice of their own. He and Fiach awaited their turn behind a young pregnant woman who had asked the landlord for a jug of beer to take away with her. Marcus raised an eyebrow at that, and Fiach whispered, "He's not permitted to refuse her. According to the ancient laws, it is forbidden to refuse a pregnant woman's request for beer." It was going to take a while for Marcus to accustom himself to the customs of this country. But it was not long before he and his fellow priest were seated with two tankards of ale on the table in front of them, gifts from a man and his wife at a nearby bench. Fiach introduced Marcus to the people there, and they were respectful in their greetings to the abbot of Drumlyon. Marcus could see the effort Fiach made to put on a pleasant aspect for the company in the alehouse.

And Marcus himself endeavoured to keep the conversation light. But when Fiach greeted a man and woman who were on their way out, the talk turned to marriage. That was because Fiach explained that the man was married to Fiach's cousin, and Marcus remarked upon how young the wife was — not that that was in any way unusual — and Fiach said, "That's not his wife. That's his, well, his concubine."

"But, Fiach, surely you understand that it is necessary for the people here to modify their behaviour, in order to live according the teachings of the Holy Church. Husbands casting off wives, wives casting off husbands, if indeed the marriages were valid in the first place—"

"Which you would say they were not."

"As would you, being a priest of the Church. And even when a man does stay married, he often has, as you say, a concubine. Allowing for that to continue, how must the wife feel when her husband takes a mistress or a second wife?"

"Well, now, our laws allow the wife some latitude there. A

chief wife will incur no fine if, during the first three days, she attacks a second wife, inflicting non-fatal injuries on her. And the second wife may retaliate, as long as she limits herself to scratching, pulling hair, and that sort of thing. At least, that's what the old laws say!" Fiach looked at Marcus and started to laugh. "Here, Father Abbot, you need another cup of ale. Or something stronger. Uisce beatha, perhaps?" The water of life. "This conversation has you looking pale and unwell."

"Thank you, I'll have a whiskey." Fiach got up and fetched a cup of uisce beatha for each of them and sat down. Marcus returned to the subject at hand. "This sort of thing, this marriage custom, is not unknown even among the chieftain's family here. I heard that one of the Maguires had twenty sons by eight different mothers, and fifty grandsons in the male line."

"Ah now, Marcus. That was long in the past. Philip Maguire, God rest him, died two hundred years ago."

"He'd be in need of God's rest. Exhausted, I should think."

"Perhaps so." Fiach smiled at him. "You were born too late to make the acquaintance of Port-Na-Dtrí-Namadh."

"That sounds odd," Marcus said.

"She was a daughter of the King of Connacht. That was her nickname, 'Meeting Place of Three Enemies,' because among her several husbands were three lords who were sworn enemies of one another!"

Marcus could not stifle a laugh at that one. But then he returned to his duties. "But truly, Fiach, the sexual . . . licentiousness of the Irish, that is not in accord with God's law."

"In accord with the natural law, though."

"You're having fun with me now, Father."

Fiach smiled again and finished his whiskey, and Marcus could see him trying to decide whether to go for another.

A young man came in then and spoke to the landlord Magennis, and Marcus saw him fixing a paper on the wall near the entrance. It was clear from the change of conversation in the room that this was a notice of something significant. It was in fact notice of a judgment day, sent out by the local judge, the brehon, and posted at such well-attended places as the alehouse and the church.

"Judgment day," Fiach said. "That is Cúan, the brehon's assistant."

"Does this mean the local people attend the judgments?" Marcus asked.

"Most do."

A man next to them called out to Cúan and asked the date. The brehon's assistant announced that it was June the twelfth.

The man said then, "I wonder if this means the brehon has identified the wretch who killed our physician."

"Perhaps so," Fiach replied.

Now that the subject had been raised, the night of the murder mentioned, Marcus decided to venture an inquiry. "Fiach, the night the woman was killed . . ."

He noticed an immediate tension in Fiach. How was Marcus to approach the matter? He did not want to admit that he had been spying on his fellow priest. "I heard sounds in the abbey that night," he began.

"Sounds?"

"And so I got out of my bed and walked through the abbey to see if anything was amiss."

"Was there anything out of place?"

"What I saw, Fiach, was you, writing frantically in the scriptorium. I could not stop myself from wondering, and I wonder now, what had you up so late in the night, writing in such a hurried manner."

Fiach looked down at his tankard. "Prophecies, uttered by Sorcha that night."

"What kind of prophecies? What did she see?"

Fiach put up his hands to ward off the questions. Marcus knew there was no point in trying to hurry the answers out of his usually talkative friend. But there was a question that had to be asked. "She was not uttering prophecies at the Maguire banquet. So, you saw her afterwards, later that night?"

"I did."

"You did." Marcus fixed him with a steady gaze.

"But you may be sure, Father Abbot, that I have nothing to confess. I did not kill her, did not hurt her."

"I want you to show me those pages, Fiach."

He nodded his head in resignation.

Terence Blake would not be crying this from the rooftops, or from the hilltop on judgment day, but he could not deny that he was pleased when Shane O'Callaghan arrived at the door of his house and asked for his assistance in the case of the murder of Sorcha, the seer and physician. Oh, never let it be doubted that Terence mourned the loss of Sorcha O'Cassidy and was horrified by her murder. But Terence, as an aigne, was a little weary of the sort of case that had taken up nearly an hour of his morning. What kind of a man hires an advocate to dispute a simple incidence of a dog fouling his neighbour's property? Everybody knows what the remedy is: first of all, pick up all the cac, the dung, then compensate the neighbour by giving him butter, curds, and dough equivalent to the volume of dog cac on the property. You didn't have to consult the Conslechta of the

Senchas Már, the dog sections of the Great Tradition, the ancient law texts. Terence had always thought those provisions suggested a convenient way of getting supplies in if you or your servants were too lazy, or disabled by a night's drinking, to milk the cows, churn the butter, harvest the grain, knead the dough. Just say to your children, "Come on, lads. Go out there to the boundary with Malachi's place and throw some sticks around and see if you can get Malachi's little Waggy-Tail over here." The dog shits on your property, and you get your compensation.

So Ulick, the man who had been taking up Terence's time this morning, should have admitted his fault, or that of his dog, and gathered up the required lumps of butter, curds, and dough and delivered them to his aggrieved neighbour. He should not have wasted the time of an aigne about so routine a matter. And it had to be said that Ulick had raised suspicions in Terence's mind during his prolonged stay. He asked Terence what the penalty was for someone who kills another man's dog. Terence didn't take this to mean that Ulick was considering killing his neighbour's dog in revenge. Rather, the lawyer suspected that someday in the not-too-distant future, Ulick's own dog would be found with a fatal wound. And the blame would be directed across the fence. The compensation coming the way of a man whose dog had been killed was five cows, a new dog of the same breed, and a replacement of any unprotected livestock killed by wild animals to the end of the year. Terence prophesied that if Ulick's dog were found dead, this would occur at a date early in the following year to take full advantage of the compensation on offer. Might not happen, of course, but all these years as an aigne had left Terence with a suspicious turn of mind.

He was in need of a serious case like the secret killing to keep his mind sharp, to justify the eighteen years he had spent studying at the Egan family's law school at Park Castle in County Galway. Terence had grown up in the town of Galway and had enrolled in the law school at Park as a young boy. He worked for a few years as an aigne in his hometown, but as an Irishman he was distressed by the English customs and mores that had taken over the place. In fact, Galway had been granted a special charter by King Richard III of England, giving the town the right to elect a mayor and corporation to run the place and make bylaws to that end. Some of the bylaws were strange, not to say outrageous. One such law was that the Anglo-Norman residents of the city were not to admit to their houses anyone by the name of Burke, McWilliam, or Kelly, or any members of the Gaelic septs that surrounded the city — in other words, the natives of the very country in which the town was located! It was written that "Neither O ne Mac shoulde strutte ne swagger throughe the streetes of Gallway." Particularly unwelcome were members of the O'Flaherty clan; there was a plaque on one of the city gates that read: "From the ferocious O'Flaherties Good Lord deliver us." Other bylaws provided that no boats or weapons were to be sold to any Irishman. This, in Ireland itself! And that "no man be made fre unless he can speke the English tonge and shave his upper lipe weekly, sub poena 20s." Outrageous.

A hundred years ago, an event occurred which still shocked those who heard the tale. A young man named Walter Lynch, who was the son of the mayor and magistrate of Galway, was believed to have killed another young man in a fit of jealousy. In fact, he surrendered himself to the law; he was filled with remorse. But his father, proud of his reputation as an upholder of law and order, ignored the pleas of many of the townsfolk, including the mayor's own wife (who, like Terence, was a Blake), ignored their pleas for mercy for the wretched young man. The mayor-magistrate presided over the trial, a latter-day Brutus, sitting in judgment of his own son, and condemned him to death. A large crowd of local people, enraged over the fate of young Walter, attempted to demolish the prison and the mayor's house, which adjoined it. But guards held the people off. The boy's mother rushed to her own family, the Blakes, who took up arms and marched to the prison to try to free their young relation. A parade of people joined them and cried out for mercy for Walter Lynch. But to no avail. Galway had a tradition of Roman and English law, and the penalty was death. In the end, the mayor hanged his son from an arched window above the crowded street.

If Walter had committed the offence in the parts of Ireland that were still Irish, where brehon law was the law of the land, Walter and his family would have been required to pay compensation to the victim's family, specifically a fine, which was based on the type of offence committed, and the honour price of the victim — the "price of his face" — which was based on a person's rank in society. These were heavy penalties and were very effective in assuring that the killer never committed such an offence again. In the Irish parts of Ireland, in a case like that of Walter Lynch, there would have been no second death; nobody would have been hanging at the end of a rope. There would have been no "lynching," as Terence had heard it called. If a killer or his family refused or failed to pay the fine and honour price, then it fell to the victim's family to step in and exact its own revenge, so there was a *very* strong incentive to pay the compensation to the family as required by law and have done with it. Pay up, and you may go on with your life. Whereas in England, a man could be hanged for stealing a hawk!

A few short years as a lawyer in Galway, and Terence Blake had had enough. He left the city of his birth and made his way north, and he had now spent nearly fifteen years working as an aigne here in Fermanagh.

He had taken a wife here, Aoife. She was the opposite to him in appearance: she had yellow hair and fair skin, in contrast to Terence's high colouring and dark hair. They had two daughters and a son. Terence and Aoife often had playful arguments in which provisions of the ancient laws came up, including the honour price assigned to women. A wife's honour price was, in most cases, half that of her husband. But not in a marriage like his, because he was, under the law, a husband who "followed his wife's arse over a border." That is, he had married a woman from another kingdom, that being Fermanagh, and had followed her to live here. Therefore, he would be paid the honour price of his wife. "Behave yourself now, Aoife," he'd say to her. "I don't want you losing your honour price!"

But it was time to shake off the foolish thoughts and direct his mind to the case in front of him. He now he had the rare opportunity to represent a man accused of a secret and unlawful killing. Terence's professional enthusiasm did not detract, though, from the remorse he felt for Sorcha O'Cassidy, to have died like that.

Shane O'Callaghan would not, of course, be facing a death penalty if he was judged to be the killer. He would have to pay compensation to Sorcha's family for her death. And the cost would be high for a killing, double for a secret killing, and he would also have to pay the honour price of a physician. In all, he would have to give Sorcha's family nearly four dozen milch cows, a great many animals to remove from a herd. And O'Callaghan did not own property in his own name in Fermanagh. The animals would presumably come from the Tierneys' herd; would the Tierneys be willing to pay such a price? Would Brigid still want Shane in her life after this?

Shane had told him very little when he sat down with Terence and spoke of the night of the banquet. His story was that he had left the castle and was still in the mood for drinking and enjoying a party. His guests, merchants from Galway, had settled for the night, so Shane left the house, apparently with the idea of going to the alehouse. On his way there, he met up with a group of men taking a break from a journey home to Tirconnell from Drogheda. He told them he would find space for them at the Tierney house but they declined, saying they had been sleeping in their tent and that was fine with them. They offered him a drink, and he had a few and fell asleep. This happened nowhere near the home of Sorcha the physician. He had not seen her again after exchanging a friendly greeting at the Maguire castle. O'Callaghan did not think he would be able to find the men from Tirconnell to give evidence on his behalf; he had paid scant attention to their names while they all drank and tried to outdo each other with improbable tales.

Terence wondered if this story was itself an improbable tale. But he set out to do his work. He spent the next couple of days visiting the houses of people who, he knew, would have seen Sorcha at the feast. He started at the Maguire castle. He had been to the castle on previous occasions, though not on the night of the banquet; he had been away that night and was sorry to have missed it. Now neither the Maguire himself, that being Hugh, nor his half-brother Cúchonnacht was present, but he spoke with a number of people who worked at and around the castle. Then he moved outwards from there, calling upon people he knew had been present at the feast. The story was pretty well the same everywhere: Sorcha had had short conversations with the other guests. Nobody had noticed anything amiss. She was quiet but friendly and did not appear to be concerned or upset. Several people saw her taking her leave, thanking the Maguire family for hosting such a sumptuous feast. A couple of people smiled when they spoke of Sorcha standing before Cúchonnacht Maguire at the end of the evening; they said her eyes "bathed him in love" or "shone upon him with great admiration." Terence was well aware that Cúchonnacht was a favourite with the ladies. But Sorcha had not acted in any way like a woman trying to entice a man to come away with her. Her behaviour, "as always, was irreproachable."

Terence accepted what he had heard from all those who saw her at the feast; he was not so sure about the account Shane gave of drinking with men neither he nor anyone else could identify.

CHAPTER VIII

She resided in the summit of a lofty tower. A near
relation, chosen for the purpose, conveyed to her
several questions, and from that sanctuary brought
back oracular responses, like a messenger who held
commerce with the gods.

— Tacitus, c. 98 AD

Father Fiach O'Moylan was bent over a manuscript when Marcus found him in the scriptorium the morning after their visit to the alehouse. Marcus peered over his shoulder at what he had completed so far. A psalm beginning with the word Animalia. Fiach was copying the psalm in Latin, and Marcus knew from experience that Fiach liked to add a little local colour, a little Irish flourish. And Fiach's local flourish was apparent in the opening capital letter, A. He had drawn it as a high stone house surrounded by cows, sheep, hounds, and birds in bright, vivid colours: blue and red, green and gold. One particular creature stood out, a cow done in a browny red, gazing up at the tower with a crafty look on her face. Fiach must have completed the A the day before because, already, there was a marginal note by one of the other monks. Marcus would have to have a word with these humorous scribes about their marginal comments! But he had to admit he enjoyed their remarks, some of which were sly comments on the work of the other scribes. One, he remembered, read, "This must be the work of Gregorius, his quill shaking from too much sacke wine the night before." Here, someone had written, "Bó Bheannaithe!" Blessed Cow.

"That cow looking upwards, she seems to have something on her mind."

Fiach gave a little start; he had been so absorbed in his work that he had not heard Marcus approach. "She's wondering why I'm so late coming down to chat with her. She was my favourite amongst my father's cows when I was a lad."

Cows. Marcus knew that here in Ireland wealth was measured in cattle. The O'Moylan family were craftsmen — wrights — Marcus had learned, but they had a good stock of animals as well.

"This cow I've portrayed here, she had a personality all her own, did Gorumplaith. Oh, she was a fine animal! And the look on her face when my father's pale old bull was brought to her. She was having none of it. It was the black bull for her, or nobody. I knew that if ever I saw that look in the eye of a girl I fancied, it would have reduced me to a soft, shrivelled — ach, well, enough of that now, Marcus. I'm sure you've no interest in hearing about my younger self, before I was consecrated to the Lord. I must put my mind only to God's work here."

"It was in fact another of your works that I am here to inquire about, Fiach."

"Ah, another of my works."

"I am here to see whatever you were writing the night the physician was killed. And you know that Shane O'Callaghan has been accused of her murder."

"I know. But I do not believe Shane would have killed her."

"Did you see him near her that night? Apart from seeing her at the castle, I mean."

"I did not."

"And where was it you saw her, heard her speaking?"

O'Moylan was clearly uncomfortable with the question. Or with the answer. "In the grove outside her house."

"You went to her house."

No answer.

"Did you see anyone else there?"

"I saw no one. Except Sorcha herself."

"You being there the night she was killed, in the place she was killed!"

There was a look of anguish on the face of his fellow priest. "I saw her but did not approach her. If I had, perhaps she would still be with us today."

"Why did you not approach her?"

"Because . . . because of what she was saying. She would not even have seen me. When she is like that, when she *was* like that, having her visions, she saw things not visible to the rest of us, and she had no eyes for her surroundings here in the present."

"Why did you go to her that night?"

"I saw her at the banquet, but there was not the opportunity for anything more than a short conversation."

"And you wanted more from her than a short conversation. More talking, I mean."

"I did."

"What was it you wanted to discuss with her? Your daughter perhaps?"

"That's right. Our daughter, Ónora," Fiach answered quickly. Marcus chastised himself. That was not the way to question someone, suggesting your own answer. That way, you never got the answer the person might have given otherwise. "Our child is in fosterage, as you know, with the O'Driscoll family. I have not heard news from her for a long while, so I wanted to speak with Sorcha."

That might be true or it might not; Marcus could not bring himself to suggest that it was not. He turned to the actions of the wise woman on that fateful night. "She appeared to be having one of her visions?"

"She did. And she was speaking to, well, speaking aloud. Standing in the oak grove and speaking to unseen ears."

The oak grove, sacred to the Druid ancestors of herself and of Father O'Moylan here.

"What did she say, Fiach?"

Fiach looked distressed. "She saw terrible things, Marcus. I felt as if I was bound by a spell; I couldn't stop listening. Finally she ceased speaking, but she continued to stand there, looking out at what the rest of us can never see. She never knew I was there. I . . . crept away so she wouldn't hear me, then got up on my horse and rode back here."

"And began writing down everything she had said."

"Not everything. I could not possibly remember it all."

"Let me see the pages, Fiach."

He hesitated, then said, "You'd not be able to make them out. I was writing so swiftly, my letters are unclear."

"You'll read them to me then."

He bowed his head in submission. "I'll fetch them and come to you."

When he returned, he held a few pages of vellum in his hand. They were small pages, about half the size the monks would normally use for recording verses of Holy Scripture. Vellum was valuable, made from the skin of calves, and sometimes the monks used half pages for less formal works.

Fiach spoke aloud the scribbled words of the manuscript. "She began with a verse from Scripture, the Gospel of Matthew: 'Every kingdom divided against itself is brought to desolation, and every city or house divided against itself will not stand.' I believed she was referring to our country, with the rivalries between clans, which have been encouraged and abetted by the English to their own advantage."

Marcus leaned forward and peered down at the page. The letters had indeed been hastily scribbled, but Marcus could decipher enough to be satisfied that Fiach had read exactly what was written there.

"Then she described what she saw for the future. 'I see the great harbour. I see a ship. Our men step off the land of Ireland for the last time. They climb aboard the ship and the ship sails out against the sky. Our beloved prince is upon it, the last of our princes. Our greatest men, the lords of Ireland, are away to sea. And I see women weeping and sons and daughters left behind. And we are without defences. They shall never, ever return. Our world has ended.'

"If you could have seen her face, Marcus, as she uttered these words, the look of desolation. It was as if she had aged thirty years."

"But, Fiach, it was just a trick of her mind."

"I hope with all my heart that you are right. But she has foreseen events before. And been proven correct."

"A ship, though? Taking all the chieftains? And what great harbour could she mean? On which part of our coast?"

"I know neither the ship nor the harbour."

Marcus could not help but think of the Gospel of Matthew: You know not the day nor the hour.

"Without the princes of our race we are, as she said, without defences."

"God save us!"

"And then she said, 'And a lonely lamp burns in the castle for Cúchonnacht Óg.'"

"But she was implying that the chieftains are going. That would be Hugh, not his brother. Half-brother. Her utterings were incoherent, Fiach."

"All I can do is repeat what she said. She loves Cúchonnacht Óg. I think she has always loved him. What woman would not?" This was said without rancour, or none that Marcus could detect. Marcus had always believed that Fiach still loved his wife — former wife — and would have stayed wedded to her even as a priest, as many in the old Irish tradition did. But in Irish law, a woman is entitled to a divorce if her husband becomes a priest, and divorce him she did. Marcus knew it was not the time to deliver another homily on the laws of marriage under the Church of Rome.

"But," Fiach was saying, "she never approached Cúchonnacht in that way. Sorcha is not, was not, a woman who would be a concubine in the home of a married man. That arrangement may work for others, but never for Sorcha."

"I understand," Marcus said, without further elaboration.

"And there was more." Fiach shuffled his pages and read, "Soon invaders will come and take for themselves the lands of the families of Ulster."

"They have been trying to do that as far back as anyone can remember."

"'Soon,' she said. And then 'A great heretic will come and claim that he is doing the work of God, and he will slaughter our warriors and our priests, our women and our innocents.'"

"God save us!" But then Marcus chided himself for his reaction. "These images, Fiach, surely they are preposterous. Whatever excites our minds late in the night, we cannot say, but our fears are surely not signs of future events to come."

"I know, but she has often been right in the past. I think I recorded her words as spoken, but it was all coming so fast I could not keep it all in my head. And then she said, 'After many more years have passed, our people will starve on the land.'"

"There she is speaking of what has already occurred, Fiach. We know that great numbers of people in Munster starved to death a dozen years ago."

"But hear this, Marcus: 'Our Holy Mass will be forbidden. Our sacraments will be given in secret, furtively, like sins. Our priests will be hunted down and expelled or battered to death.'" Fiach looked up from his pages and said, "God between us and all harm!"

Marcus felt a chill at the words and blessed himself, calling upon God for protection for the abbey, for the people of Ulster, for the island of Ireland.

"And that, Marcus, was all I could recall and write down."

"And you saw no one else on her property that night?"

"I saw no one. But there could have been someone hidden behind the trees. As I was myself."

"Someone who heard her prophecies."

"Or someone crept up on her afterwards. Someone got to her whilst she was still in the grove."

Marcus made ready to leave and said, "There was nothing else, nothing but these dismal prophecies for this country?"

Fiach squared the pages off in his hands and said, "Nothing."

⟲

Terence Blake finished his work at the house of O'Hussey, the poet, and mounted his horse for the ride back to his own place. This was Terence's first experience with a case of a man fasting at the door of a nemed, a member of the privileged class. If a nemed has committed a wrong against another person, that person may take himself to the front of the privileged man's house and fast there until he is given justice. Terence had heard of the practice being carried out in the past, often in the case of a complaint against a churchman. In that situation, the person with a grievance would fast against the cleric and give notice that the cleric was not to say a Pater or a Credo or go to Mass. O'Hussey, of course, was a file and was the court poet to the Maguires. His vocation was to compose praise poems for his patron, as well as to write satires and to keep and recite genealogies, histories, and family lore. But the claimed offence here was not that he had satirized a man named Gearalt to the point of dishonouring him, let alone to the point where satire raised blemishes on his face. This was instead a case of O'Hussey refusing hospitality to Gearalt and his family, refusing them food and shelter after a long and arduous journey through Fermanagh. With little prompting from Terence, O'Hussey had conceded justice to Gearalt. After all, what could be more dishonourable than allowing a man to go hungry by your front door to prove the rightness of his cause? No honourable man or woman would allow that to happen. And the law recognized this: a man who held out against a justified fast

129

lost his legal rights in the community. So O'Hussey had agreed to pay Gearalt his honour price to compensate him for the refusal of hospitality. And Terence walked away satisfied that all was well.

When he arrived home, there was someone waiting to see him. Standing at his door was a man he recognized as one of the Maguire's soldiers, a pikeman. He was tall and slender, as befitted a man required to be swift on the battlefield. After a short moment, Terence remembered his name, Murrough. There was a nervous look about him today. Terence greeted him and invited him inside.

"I saw something!" Murrough exclaimed. "Saw someone. The night she was killed, the wise woman. You'll not be pleased with what I say."

"Tell me."

"I don't know if it was him, but I saw the curls on his head!"

A curly-haired man. This did not bode well for the man Terence was representing, but he had to know. "Tell me what you saw, where you were, all of it, Murrough."

The pikeman took a ragged breath and said, "I had been away visiting my uncle, up towards Devenish, and I was coming back. I knew some of our men were camped out about halfway between there and the castle. I decided to stop there for the night."

"Who was at the camp?"

"Some cavalry, pikemen, musketeers. There had been talk of movement by the enemy, so they all gathered there. I had some food and drink, and I told the others I planned to ride home that night. And there was a message that had to be taken to the castle, but the other fellows, well . . ."

"What about them?"

"There was drink taken, and there were . . . there was somebody who had been cooking, and somebody else who had been doing the washing . . ."

"Women." Camp followers, who provided services beyond cooking and cleaning.

"So nobody wanted to leave, and they sent me out with the message."

"Who sent you?"

"I don't remember now who it was. Just that there was a message and I would ride to the castle and deliver it."

"Deliver it to whom?"

"One of the lookouts. Colm."

"One of the watchmen at the castle."

"Right."

"So, you got on your horse and left the camp."

"I did. And, as I often do, I cut through the woods and came out by her place, the wise woman's. But I did not see her lying there, I swear! What I did see was the tall figure of a man, and that curly hair on him. Short curls. He was running from the oak grove outside her house, turning his head and looking all about him, and running. I could not see his face well, but . . . I cannot say certainly that it was your . . . was O'Callaghan, and I know you do not want to hear this, but that is what I saw."

The short dark curls on the head of Shane O'Callaghan were unique in this part of the world where men wore their hair long with strands of it in front down to their eyes. Terence had not wanted to think of O'Callaghan as the kind of man who would kill a woman, and he did not want to think of how difficult it would be to defend him on judgment day with this piece of evidence now against him. But he had no right to lay blame on an honest witness who had come forward with what he had seen.

"You were right in telling me this, Murrough. You will, of course, have to testify as to what you saw when we all gather for judgment day. All evidence must be presented to the court."

Murrough nodded his head, turned, and left the house.

&

It was early the next evening when Terence entered the cloister of Drumlyon Abbey, and he could hear the beautiful chanting of the monks. Terence recognized the Canticle of Mary, the Magnificat, always sung at Vespers: Magnificat anima mea Dominum. My soul doth magnify the Lord.

Terence went inside and slipped into the chapel to take in the rest of the evening service. The robed monks at their devotions, the sublime chanting, the warm yellow glow of the candles, and the jewel-like reds, blues, yellows, and greens of the stained-glass windows gave rise to a feeling of unexpected joy. It was his understanding that when the Cistercian order had been founded centuries before, their buildings were very austere with a minimum of decoration. That had changed over the years, and Terence was appreciating the beauty around him now. He would have been content to stay on in this holy place all night, rather than attend to the mundane purpose of his visit. Even after the monks processed out of the chapel, he stayed on to absorb the beauty that surrounded him.

But soon enough he was in the locutory with Abbot Marcus Valerius, who had sent a messenger to Terence summoning him to the abbey. Or it was not a summons exactly; it was an invitation for Terence to come and hear something that might bear upon the Sorcha O'Cassidy murder. The abbot was accompanied by Father Fiach O'Moylan, and it was Fiach who had the story to tell. And it was chilling: Fiach had gone to Sorcha's house in the hope of a private conversation about their daughter but heard instead a litany of horrors that Sorcha had foretold for Ireland.

After hearing of the dire prophecies of his country's future, Terence felt he had no choice but to visit the castle once again. He had to be careful in what he said. He could not let slip any suggestion that one of the Maguires might have been cowering in the bushes and then killed the woman to shut down any further prognostications about the chieftains leaving the field, abandoning their people, losing their lands to the enemy. The thought inevitably occurred to him, but Terence blamed his long years as an aigne for the suspicions that cropped up in his mind. His work had taught him that even the most unlikely human behaviour was not all that unlikely.

When he arrived at the island castle the following morning, he was escorted up to the great hall and came upon two men working under the direction of Hugh Maguire himself. They were bent over a large sheet of vellum, and Terence saw that it was a drawing of a church, partially in ruins. This was obviously a plan to repair and restore the building. Well, the Maguire was well known for his support and devotion to the Catholic Church. When Maguire caught sight of Terence, he beckoned him over to a pair of comfortable seats and signalled to his cup-bearer to bring ale for himself, for Terence, and for the two men at work on the chapel.

Terence had to decide how best to approach the subject of his visit. He said, "My Lord, as you know, I shall be representing Shane O'Callaghan when the matter of Sorcha O'Cassidy's death comes up for judgment before the brehon."

"He will be in good hands with you, Terence."

"I thank you for those kind words. I have received some information from the abbot and from Father O'Moylan about a strange occurrence that very night."

"What would that be now?"

"Father O'Moylan, after enjoying your most generous hospitality that evening, had ridden to her place, Sorcha's, to speak to her. He had spoken with her briefly here at the castle but was hoping to continue his conversation, perhaps receive some news of their daughter, Ónora. But before he could approach Sorcha, he saw her outside the house, out in one of her groves of trees, and she was" — he could not say uttering prophecies of doom for the Maguires and their fellow princes of Ulster — "she was giving voice to her worries about rebellions against the enemy and how the enemy might react, might become even more ferocious in their efforts to impose their tyranny on us here in Ulster. Father O'Moylan did not know if there was someone else out there, a man hidden on the other side of the grove, in the bushes. He was not sure if she was speaking to some person there. Or whether she was alone and just giving expression to her thoughts."

The Lord of Fermanagh listened to this in silence.

Choosing his words carefully, Terence asked him, "I am wondering whether there might be someone who, out of loyalty, would be offended by the very notion of doubts being expressed. Doubts about the abilities of our warriors to keep the enemy at bay. And such a man, loyal to a fault perhaps, might lash out in anger."

"What man would not be offended by such doubts?" Hugh Maguire responded. "But I can think of no one who would strike out at a woman for saying those things. Sorcha O'Cassidy came from a long line of noble and loyal persons in this country. She was highly esteemed and always welcome here in our home. She was an able physician, and she was known as a wise woman. Many times her predictions came true, and she was respected for this." Maguire paused, and then said, "And, I suppose, feared. The things she said, as you have reported them to me, sound like expressions of her

134

worries, her nighttime terrors, that are no doubt the result of the savage treatment our people have suffered at the hands of those who have been trying, for centuries, to subdue and conquer us. They will not succeed. Ulster will forever be Irish. But a woman giving voice to her fears is not to be despised. Or punished. I am tempted to send my men out to find who did this and have him destroyed. But I have always abided by the ancient laws of our country, and those laws require that the matter be heard and decided by the brehon on judgment day."

The Maguire rose then, and Terence did the same. "And I can also tell you this, Terence. I do not know who killed Sorcha O'Cassidy, but I do not for one minute believe it was Shane O'Callaghan."

CHAPTER IX

Chains of gold and wealth profuse
The children of the low display;
That gold shall not escape ill luck,
Blame me not, O God, for that!

— Unknown poet, "Mallacht ort, a
Shuaitheantais" ("Curse on you, Emblem")

2018

"Come on now, lads. Time to go." That was Róisín, urging her father and grandfather to vacate their seats at the bar and follow her to an event that the two men were loath to attend. And they didn't even have to attend in person. The event was taking place in New York, and they were going to be watching it on Skype.

"I'd rather wrap myself in an orange sash," Liam grumbled, "and dance round the room in the arms of a resurrected Ian Paisley than watch . . . What is it, Róisín?"

"It's a 'team-building exercise,' Grandda."

"But we're not on their team."

"Of course we're not."

"You don't hold 'team-building exercises' for your staff here at the hotel, do you, my dear?"

"Of course we don't."

"Well, then, what possible reason could we have to leave our own warm and friendly and well-stocked bar and sit in the conference room staring at the computer screen, watching this crowd of gobshites in New York?"

"You know why, Grandda. To find out what they're planning to build here. Cousin Jimmy is there, and he's setting it up so we can see it."

"I'm not sure I'll survive finding out what they're planning to build. All round our family's property and business, the gall of them!"

"Shower of shites," Mick mumbled into his pint.

"I know, Dad, that's what they are. But it's not going to do us any good to be in denial, as they say, about what might happen here. I've already been on Skype with Jimmy. They've organized this information session for potential investors, and they plan to introduce the 'team' who are going to be working on the projects in the North of Ireland."

His daughter was right, of course. The Tierneys, of all people, had to know.

So they downed their pints. Mick poured two more to take with them, and then they headed for the conference room. Róisín got Jimmy on Skype again, and this time their cousin was in the ballroom of a hotel in New York City. Jimmy directed his device to a large table in the centre of the room.

"Go sábhála Dia sinn!" Liam exclaimed — God save us! — when he saw what was displayed on the table. It was a scale model of the new development. Mick glanced over at his daughter: Róisín looked ready to boke all over the computer screen. Each one of the holiday homes was got up to look like the watergate — a feature added to Enniskillen Castle in the early seventeenth century — with a raised turret at each end. But the proportions were all wrong; each of the tiny houses was fronted by two over-sized turrets. And, no surprise here, they were cladded — as the real houses would be cladded — with fake stone. Each of them had an improbably shiny roof in tiles of silver.

"Disney on crack!" Mick said to his father.

Dwarfing the phony castles was an immense hotel and casino. This time there was no pastiche of the older architecture. It looked like one of the tower blocks you'd see in a no-hope council estate in Belfast or Dublin, the kind of concrete slab that shut out all light from the crowds of young gurriers huddled outside, waiting to jump you for your wallet or your pack of fags. The only bright thing about this building was the name of the developer, PRULE, in huge blinding gold letters along the top storey.

"The glare off that would burn the eyeballs out of your head," said Liam.

The building brought to mind the phrase "Abandon hope, all ye who enter here." Appropriate, Mick noted, given that the place was to be home to a casino, a place devoted to making sure the house won, and you lost. And indeed his beloved daughter looked as if she had abandoned all hope of a future running a successful family guesthouse overlooking the River Erne in County Fermanagh.

"Well, I've had enough team-building for one day," Liam groused.

"It hasn't even begun yet, Grandda," Róisín told him. "But it's about to, by the look of things. Oh my God, would you look at yer man!"

Mick and his father peered at the screen, and Mick could scarcely believe what his eyes were seeing. Here was Prule himself with a big toothy grin. His massive girth was barely contained in his . . . costume. He had tarted himself up as one of the Gaelic chieftains, kitted out in a multicoloured leather jacket. Each patch of colour was separated from the next by threads of gold. The garment stretched across his bulging stomach, and his skintight britches looked as if any minute they'd split open across his arse. On his head was a tall, conical hat of a kind Mick had heard described as a Phrygian cap. Like the jacket, it had sections of different colours, and it had gold piping around the base and up the middle. Mick could hear giggles and snickers from some of the people on hand, but Prule was oblivious.

"Hey, folks! Happy New Year! Are we having fun?" The response was muted, so he tried again, "I said, are we having fun?"

A few good sports shouted, "Yeah!" And this seemed to be all he required.

"Hi, everybody, I'm Jebb Prule. You've seen our great ideas for Belfast and Londonderry!"

"*London*derry, yer arse," Liam groused.

"Now, thanks for coming out and seeing what we are hoping to bring to County Fermanick." That was how he said it. He had a harsh American accent; Mick had no idea what part of the United States of America it represented but, whatever it was, it grated on his nerves. "Wherever we go in the world, we being Jebb Prule Properties, we bring wealth, we bring opportunity, we bring jobs! But what are we bringing today, troops?" He turned to a rabble of people running into the room, dressed in foolish costumes. Like Prule, they were obviously trying to represent the old Gaelic nobility with their brightly coloured garments. Except these facsimiles were made of plastic and looked like garishly coloured bin liners. The crowd-exciters shouted — with an air of desperation, Mick thought — "Fun, fun, fun!"

And these eejits proceeded to hand out the bin bags to be donned by one and all, urging everyone to "take one for the team!" Then somebody wheeled in a huge plastic mock-up of Enniskillen Castle, the kind of bouncy castle the children loved — fair play to them — but it didn't end there. Next to come were plastic swords, and rules for some kind of ridiculous game. Jimmy stuck his face into view; he gave his relations a broad wink and jerked his head towards the pageantry behind him. Mick and his father and daughter looked on as otherwise-rational people wrapped themselves in plastic and began leaping about, thrusting swords into the air, and making grunts and war cries as they engaged in mock warfare.

Not everyone was smiling and shouting "Arrrghh!" There were sensible, unimpressed people quietly making their way out of the room. Jimmy's camera caught Jebb Prule in an unguarded moment. Prule looked across the room at those who had refused to be jollied, refused to join the team in its idiotic cavorting. The expression on the man's face was anything but jolly as he regarded those who were not team players, those who were pooping on his party.

Back in the sane confines of Tierney's Hotel, a subdued Róisín looked over at Liam. "Grandda, I know she's your mum, and I love her dearly and don't want to hurt her, but . . ."

"But it's time to dig up the past. We have to go all out to get this stopped or delayed so long that Prule is an old relic himself deserving of archaeological attention. If our Cait doesn't like it, she can throw me down into the hole with whatever other skeletons are buried there."

CHAPTER X

*How many kinds of court are there in Irish law? Not
difficult, five: the back court and the side court and the
waiting court and the court apart and the court itself.*

— *Airecht* text, appendix 1, no. 71, in Fergus Kelly,
A Guide to Early Irish Law

1595

Terence Blake arrived at the court well ahead of the time
when the murder case would be heard; a few less serious
matters would be decided first. The court was, as always, a hilltop
overlooking Lough Erne, and it looked as though the morning
clouds would clear away, leaving a fine day for the proceedings.
It was not long before the hilltop was packed with people from
all over Fermanagh, high-born and low. People were curious, no
question about that.

But there was another reason they were attracted to the court
on judgment day: respect for the law was fundamental to the
character of the Irish people. And even kings were not above
the law. Kings and lords could lose their honour price for a
number of reasons: for example, refusing hospitality, sheltering

a fugitive from the law, eating stolen food, or tolerating satire. In the back court today were the chieftain, he being the Maguire, and the chief poet, O'Hussey. Terence saw the bishop there as well. The three of them were regarded as the "cliff which is behind the courts," meaning it was they who controlled the courts. Also present was Hugh's half-brother Cúchonnacht. Over in the side court were the historians; the court relied upon the traditional lore of Ireland — traditions going back to the distant ages — and the clarification provided by the historians. Terence sat in the waiting court with Shane O'Callaghan. Near them was Peadar MacMahon, the son Sorcha O'Cassidy had had with her first husband, Tomás MacMahon. No sign of Tomás, but Terence thought that perhaps any tie between Sorcha and her former husband had been severed long before her death. Peadar was representing his mother's family; with him was the family's advocate, the woman lawyer Úna O'Hanlon. On the other side of the open space was the court apart, where witnesses and sureties were to sit until called upon to "go with clear memories into the midst of the court." And at the centre of it all were the brehons, the judges, three on this occasion where the case of a killing was to be heard.

It was Brehon O'Breslin who opened the proceedings and spoke for the court. He first dealt with the case of a man who had been attacked and lost one of his front teeth. This was, of course, a serious matter, as it exposed the person to ridicule in public. O'Breslin swiftly cited the law on the six classes of tooth injury and assessed the compensation to be paid to the victim. The next case was that of a mer, a person confused and deranged. The usual situation was that offences committed by a person of unsound mind were the responsibility of the person's guardian, generally a close member of his family. Members of the kin group were obliged to care for people in the family who were insane or physically disabled. But in this case, the offences arose out of a ruckus in the alehouse. The law was clear: a mer was permitted to be in the alehouse, and his guardian would not be held responsible for offences committed there as long as the mer had not been a person of known criminality. Terence turned his attention from the alehouse chaos to his own case, going over the law and arguments in his mind until O'Breslin finished with the other matter and called the Sorcha O'Cassidy case.

"On the morning of May the twenty-sixth of this year, the physician Sorcha O'Cassidy was found lifeless by a grove of trees near her house. She was killed by two arrows, one in her throat and one in her chest. No man has come forward to acknowledge responsibility for this offence. Shane O'Callaghan has now been accused of the secret and unlawful killing of Sorcha O'Cassidy. Úna O'Hanlon is the aigne who will represent the O'Cassidy family, and Terence Blake will represent the accused man." O'Breslin called upon O'Hanlon to plead her case, after which Terence would make his arguments for O'Callaghan. And the advocates would be held to a strict standard. Irish law recognized sixteen signs of bad pleading. These included praising oneself, speaking either in an undertone or speaking too loudly, opposing a fact that was known to be true, and inciting the crowd. An advocate who exhibited any of these failings could be fined.

O'Hanlon rose to speak, and she addressed the chieftain and other notable persons and the judges. "My Lord Judge," and, looking to the Maguire, "my Lord, on the night of May the twenty-fifth, there was a secret and unlawful killing of a most illustrious person in Fermanagh: the physician Sorcha O'Cassidy. She is descended from the O'Cassidy family of physicians, who have served this kingdom for generations. In all her time practising her profession, she was known for doing her best to live up to the standards expected of her status, those standards being: a complete cure, which she achieved very often; leaving no blemish, again something she achieved whenever possible; and a painless examination. As often as she could, she caused little or no pain to those who came to her with illness or injury. She was the mother of two children, the oldest being her son, Peadar, who is here to represent the family today.

"It was Peadar who discovered his mother's body on the morning of the twenty-sixth. The body had been left in the wilderness beyond her home, left where animals could have despoiled it. The killer has not acknowledged his deed. This is therefore an act of duinetháide, a secret killing; if such a killing is proven against a man by another's oath, the killer must pay to the victim's kin twice the fine that would be payable for an acknowledged killing. The fixed fine for a killing is seven cumals, so twice that amount is fourteen cumals. And the lóg n-enech, the price of her face, is seven séts, her being a physician."

A cumal equalled three milch cows, a sét half a cow, not that Terence had ever seen a half, at least not alive. So, the total O'Callaghan would have to pay if guilty would be forty-five or forty-six of the animals. The Tierneys had a large herd certainly, but it was by law the property of Brigid's brother, not Brigid herself, and certainly not O'Callaghan. Would Brigid and her brother be willing to see such a large fine taken out of their property, for a man who had killed Brigid's friend Sorcha? Or would she believe him to be innocent and want to spare him the fate that would befall him if the fine was not paid? In default of a fine, a man found guilty of murder was turned over to the family of the victim to do with as they pleased. Which often, of course, meant killing him.

Úna O'Hanlon then told the court about the witnesses who would be giving evidence, namely Sorcha's son and Murrough, the pikeman, who said he saw a man with short curly hair running from the direction of Sorcha's house in the middle of the night of May twenty-fifth. Then it was Terence's turn to plead, and he did the best he could with the little he had, that being Shane's denial of the offence. He would be calling Shane to testify to his innocence, and Father Fiach O'Moylan to describe what he saw and heard that night, and to emphasize that he did not see Shane O'Callaghan at or near the O'Cassidy home.

And now came the witnesses. Peadar MacMahon came forward to give his evidence: he had retired to his bed early, had slept all night, and heard nothing. He had risen in the morning and gone out to walk about the property, and found his mother dead of her wounds. He described his horror and anguish, and he told the court he had no idea who would have wanted to hurt or kill his mother. Terence did not question the grieving son; there was nothing the young man could say that would assist O'Callaghan.

Murrough the pikeman got up then, and O'Hanlon asked him to describe the events of that night.

"I had been visiting my uncle at his place up towards Devenish, and on my way back home I stopped in where some of our men were encamped. They knew I was planning to continue back this way, so I was asked to deliver a message to someone."

"Who was the message for?"

"One of the lookouts at the castle. His name is Colm."

"So, what did you do?"

"I agreed to take the message. I rode from there and took the most direct way, which meant going by the physician's lands. I heard the sound of a man running, the sounds of his feet. And I looked ahead and saw a tall man, with wide shoulders and short curls on his head. He was running from just beyond the oak grove outside the physician's place, going I guess east. Or going to his horse, I don't know."

It was clear to Terence and, he was sure, to the judges and all the crowd assembled that the tall man with a head of curls on him was, or was meant to be, Shane O'Callaghan.

Úna O'Hanlon asked him, "Do you see that man here today?"

The pikeman's eyes went to O'Callaghan and then away again. "When he was running, all I saw was the back of his head. I did not see his face. But the hair and the size of him look the same."

That was one of the shortest bits of testimony Terence had ever heard. Murrough did not have much to say, but what he said was devastating. If the witness had described seeing a man with long hair and a glib — the common style of locks of hair on the forehead — Murrough's identification evidence would have been worthless. His description would have fit practically every man in Fermanagh. But O'Callaghan's short curls were unusual here. Terence would have to make the best of it. He stood to question the witness.

"What time of the night was this, Murrough?"

"Em, it was late."

"What time did you leave the camp?"

"Some time before eleven, I suppose it was."

"And how long a ride is it to the O'Cassidy house?"

"An hour? Hour and a half maybe."

"You don't know?"

"I wasn't thinking about it. I was thinking about other things."

"Who was it who asked you to deliver the message?"

"I don't remember who it was."

"I see. Did that man, whoever he was, tell you why the message had not been delivered until you came along?"

Murrough looked as if he didn't understand the question.

Terence tried again. "There was a message that was supposed to go to somebody, and nobody had made the effort to deliver it until you, unexpectedly, happened along. Why was that?"

"I don't know."

Terence knew that if Murrough's story was true, or partly true, the men in the camp were having too good a time drinking and carrying on with the women, the camp followers, to leave and ride back to Enniskillen Castle with a message. But there was nothing to be gained by causing embarrassment to the Maguire's warriors camped out while fighting for their chieftain.

"Who was it you were to meet when you were sent from the camp?"

"It was Colm."

"And he was waiting for you in the middle of the night?"

"He was not."

"He was not?"

"He did not know I would be coming."

"Well, did you deliver your message?"

"I did. The next morning, after the sun was up."

"And what was that message?"

The pikeman's eyes shot up to where the Maguire was seated, then down again. "I should not . . . cannot say. It was about our movements, ours and those of our enemies."

"And you waited until morning to deliver it." No reply to that. "Where did you stay during the hours between arriving in this area and seeing Colm?"

"I went to my own house. It was late so I did not disturb him."

"Not a well-planned mission, by the sound of it."

No reply to that.

"Did Colm come with you to the court today?"

Murrough made a big show of twisting his head around and looking for the man he knew was not in the crowd. "I don't see him."

"That is unfortunate. For you, I mean. He could have confirmed your story. Strange that he is not here."

"He is a man with many duties."

It was Terence Blake's turn to make a show of looking around. "Our Lord Hugh Maguire is here. The three judges are here. The bishop is here. Are they not men with important duties?"

That brought a flush of embarrassment to the witness's face. Terence decided to end it there. The man's story was thin, but Terence did not know why he would make up a tale about O'Callaghan and place him at the scene of the killing. O'Callaghan had told Terence he knew the man, but not well, and said there had never been any conflict between them.

And now it was Terence's turn to present evidence. All he had was Shane himself, to deny the killing, and Father O'Moylan to say he was at Sorcha's place and did not see Shane there. Two witnesses taking that weakest of all positions: trying to make a point on the strength of what they had not seen. Just because you don't see someone doesn't mean he isn't there. But Terence had nobody who could make a positive identification of O'Callaghan in some other place at the likely time of the killing. So he had to make do with what he had.

He called Father O'Moylan to rise and give his evidence. He asked the priest to identify himself and then asked him about the night of the banquet at the Maguire castle. Father O'Moylan told the court that he had enjoyed the banquet, that he had spoken to Sorcha briefly there, but that there was no opportunity for a private conversation. He therefore decided to go to her house, and when he got there, she was outside in a trance-like state talking about — Fiach and Terence had agreed to tone down what the seer had foretold — her fears of what the English were doing to the people of Ireland. And fears that they might do worse. Fiach had decided that it was not the time to engage his former wife in a conversation about family matters, so he left without speaking to her.

"Father O'Moylan, did you see anyone on Sorcha O'Cassidy's property, aside from Sorcha herself?"

"I did not."

"Had you seen anyone while you were on your way there, or anyone when you were leaving?"

"No one."

This may have been the feeblest evidence Terence had ever put before the court on a judgment day, but it was all he had, aside from the testimony of the accused man himself. He indicated to the judges that he was through with this witness, and the O'Cassidy family's lawyer moved forward to question him.

"Father O'Moylan, where were you when you were listening to your former wife speaking about her fears?"

"Behind a stand of trees."

"Hidden like a guilty man," the aigne said.

"Not a guilty man, but a craven man, I suppose I was."

"Why were you there, spying on your former wife?"

Fiach looked down at his hands and then up at the brehon. "I was not spying on her at all. I had hoped to talk to her after the banquet."

"About what?" asked the lawyer.

"We have a child together, Ónora, in fosterage like so many children in this country, in fosterage with the O'Driscoll family, and I just . . ."

"You just what?"

"The O'Driscolls are a fine family. There is no question about that. And no question of the value of fosterage for forging strong ties between families. But the last couple of times I have seen Ónora, I have wondered whether she is getting . . ."

"Getting what?"

"As I say, the O'Driscolls are a fine family."

"You already told us that. What were you concerned about?"

"Our daughter is nearly twelve years old now, and she hopes to follow the profession of her mother. She wants to become a physician like Sorcha. And I had been thinking it was time to move her out of the foster family, bring her back home, and have her start training with her mother. And there were fees to be discussed if we ended the fosterage contract early. Of course, that's not going to happen now—" O'Moylan's voice faltered, and he looked down at his hands.

Úna O'Hanlon knew there was nothing to be gained by intruding on the priest's genuine grief, so she held off for a minute or so before asking in a gentle tone, "Could you not have spoken to her about the child while you were both at the banquet?"

"A family related to the O'Driscolls was there. I didn't want to bring it up in case any of them might hear. I wanted a private conversation with Sorcha."

"Which she refused?"

"I did not bring up the subject at all while we were still at the castle. But I had the impression from previous conversations with her that she was thinking the same way I was. I antici-pated a pleasant conversation, in the comfort of Sorcha's house. I thought—" The priest's voice failed him again, and he waited for a couple of seconds. "I simply thought I'd go see her afterwards, as I have done before."

"All right. Now, Father, you say Sorcha was giving voice to images or ideas that were in her mind, that she was in a trance of sorts."

"She was. And I knew that whenever she was like that, she was not to be interrupted. I'd never had to be told that; I just knew from long experience. No one was to stop the flow of her . . . the information that was coming through her. And if I did interrupt, she would be unsettled, would not be able to direct her mind to whatever I might have brought to her attention."

"Tell us again what kinds of things she was saying."

Fiach went through it once more, making sure again to avoid telling the chieftain, the judges, and the people of Fermanagh that the wise woman had foreseen abandonment and conquest, subjugation and banishment. Again, he referred only to her distress about England's efforts to take control of Ireland and her fears that things might get worse as time went on.

"Thank you, Father O'Moylan. Where was she looking while she uttered these words?"

"She seemed to be looking in the direction of another stand of trees on her land, not in my direction. Her face was partly turned away from where I was."

"Did you have the impression that she was talking to herself or talking to some other person?"

That was a question Fiach might not be qualified to answer; how could he know what she was seeing in the trees, if anything? But Terence did not object. As long as Fiach didn't say "*I thought she was talking to Shane O'Callaghan,*" there was little harm in it.

Fiach simply responded, "I don't know."

"Now," said the lawyer, "was there anything else she said, apart from her worries about our difficulties with the English, anything more specific or personal?"

Fiach had a wary look about him then, and Terence didn't like it. Fiach said, "What do you mean?"

"I mean, did she say anything about any particular person?"

The answer was a hasty "Nothing."

The lawyer eyed him for a few seconds and then said, "I have no more questions."

Fiach returned to his place in the court, and Terence called Shane O'Callaghan to give his testimony. Once the witness — the accused man — was duly identified, Terence got to the point.

"Did you kill Sorcha O'Cassidy?"

"I did not. That man Murrough's testimony is false. I was not there at any time during that night. So either that witness saw someone else and mistook that man for me, or the witness is lying. I did not, and would not, hurt the physician, the wise woman we all loved and respected."

Terence then had to ask the question that the judges and everyone in the assembly wanted answered. "Well, then, Shane O'Callaghan, where were you that night?"

Terence had not been satisfied with O'Callaghan's answer when he'd heard it, and he doubted the judges would be satisfied either. O'Callaghan said, "I was at the castle early in the night, enjoying with others the generous hospitality of the Maguire and his family, and after that I left the island. I was still in a merry sort of mood. I started to ride to the alehouse, but I met up with some fellows travelling through on their way to Tirconnell, and I spoke to them and they had some casks of ale, and we set to drinking. I had already had a fair amount of wine at the castle, and I fell into a deep sleep a mile or so from the alehouse, and it was past sunrise when I returned home."

The brehon intervened then. O'Breslin asked, "Where are

these men now? Are they here to speak in your defence, Shane O'Callaghan?"

"Brehon, they are not. When I awoke, they had already departed."

O'Breslin and the two other judges stared at the accused man, hoping perhaps that he would produce a better excuse. But he had nothing more to say.

To Terence, and he suspected, to the court, this sounded no better than Murrough's story of being on the road that night. Terence did his best to ask a few more questions to make his client appear credible, but Úna O'Hanlon questioned O'Callaghan in much the same way as Terence had questioned Murrough. Instead of looking credible, O'Callaghan gave the appearance of one who was unreliable. A man who had something to hide.

Terence thought the aigne had come to the end of her questions. Not so. She looked at O'Callaghan for a moment and then said, "This is not the first time you have been brought to judgment for a serious offence, is it?"

What was this?! O'Callaghan's eyes flew to Terence and then to O'Breslin. He had the look of a guilty man.

"Shane O'Callaghan?" the lawyer prompted. No reply. "Was there not an incident with a man named Cairbre MacSweeney? And did you not flee Cork soon after the judgment against you?"

Terence made an effort to control his breathing and the expression on his face. His client had left him in the dark about this, whatever it was. He went forward and spoke on his client's behalf. "Is lawyer O'Hanlon giving evidence here today, my Lord Judge? Is she a witness now?"

But O'Breslin gave permission for her to proceed; the judges would decide how much weight to accord to the evidence, if evidence it was.

To O'Callaghan, she said, "Is it not true that there was a judgment against you for your offence against MacSweeney and that you disputed the honour price owed to him?"

O'Callaghan didn't look at O'Hanlon, didn't look at Terence. He stared into the distance, and the silence dragged on for a long, long moment. There was no chattering amongst the people gathered on the hilltop. But finally the accused man took a deep breath and began to speak. "Here is what happened in Cork. I was a friend of the MacSweeney family there, a great family as many here may know. But there was one member of the clan who puffed himself up as the most loyal son of Ireland, and most loyal to the MacSweeneys, but who in fact showed no concern about dishonouring the family name. He pretended to greatness but he was nothing but an insect, scurrying off to meet with the English usurpers in the night. Telling them where this or that man could be found, letting the Saxons know when a certain man was away from his house, and his family and his lands not adequately defended. One night I saw him in the alehouse with some of his cousins who did not suspect him of treachery. He was playacting as the most loyal and loving of cousins, pretending to mourn a member of the clan who had been slain by the invaders. I had enjoyed a few cups of ale that night, and the presence of this fellow inspired me to compose a few lines of poetry.

"I was found guilty of the offence of unjustified satire, specifically of coining a nickname that sticks. In my case I coined the nickname 'the Saxons' Dung Beetle' for him." Terence heard some stifled laughter in the crowd over this. "And the name did stick to him, like, well . . ." O'Callaghan then recited a part of his verse:

"He is but a beetle who's happy to roll
In the stuff which comes out of the Saxon's hole.
He sucks at the stuff not by any means sparse
Spewing in gobs from an Englishman's arse.

He asks not for silver, he asks not for gold,
He asks only this, on which to grab hold
With his spindly wee legs, his lips, and his tongue.
He laps it all up, lumps of foul English dung."

What good this might have done for O'Callaghan was questionable, but he had won over the crowd, if their smiles and muted laughter were a measure of his acceptance. The judges' faces were unreadable.

O'Callaghan had not finished. "I did at first refuse to pay his honour price, because he was a man without honour. And then I disputed the amount owed. MacSweeney was a silversmith, with an honour price of seven séts. But I made the argument that he was merely a comb-maker, with a price of only half a sét. This fit in with my satire, because comb-makers are said to find their working material — bones and antlers — by digging for animal parts in the dunghills. I also made the point that my satire had not raised any blisters on MacSweeney's face."

There was a belief, held by some, that a satirist could raise blisters on the face of the one who is satirized and could even bring about a person's death by satire.

"The brehon dismissed that argument of mine," O'Callaghan said, "and I did in the end pay the full honour price of a silversmith. I will state here truthfully that I felt no remorse over my offence against MacSweeney. I saved my regrets for the great number of our people, some say thousands, who died of starvation in the years 1582 to 1583 in Munster. These people died as a result of the actions of the foreigners the Dung Beetle assisted. The invaders made it a point to kill us off by destroying our supply of food: they burned our crops and killed our cattle. People were reduced to such a state that they were eating the rotting corpses of animals. I saw people, women and children, whose mouths were green from eating grass. I saw a woman whose body had been torn apart by wolves. Those deaths I mourn with all my heart; the embarrassment to the Saxons' Dung Beetle, the murderers' ally, I do not."

O'Callaghan's testimony caused a stir amongst the crowd gathered for judgment day. But his evidence relating to the more recent offence, here in Fermanagh, was not so enjoyable. Terence thought that if he, Terence Blake, were sitting in the judgment seat, he would have trouble believing either man's evidence, Murrough's or O'Callaghan's. But while O'Callaghan clearly had a reason to lie, there was no reason before the court to explain why Murrough the pikeman would make up his story. Terence watched as the three judges conferred with one another, casting glances at O'Callaghan as they did so. It was time for the counter-pleadings by the two advocates. But Terence's mind leapt ahead to a finding of guilt, and the enormous price O'Callaghan would have to pay for the secret and unlawful killing of the prophetess and physician. And if he could not pay, or if the Tierney family refused to turn over the requisite number of animals from their herd, O'Callaghan could pay with his life.

And then there was a clamour at the far end of the assembly. People parted and looked astonished as a young man pushed his way through the crowd and came to stand facing the judges. His wavy black hair was dishevelled, and his eyes had a wild look about them. Terence glanced around and saw the alarm in Shane

O'Callaghan's face. O'Callaghan moved to the new arrival and grasped his arm. "No! Don't do this! We can—"

O'Breslin rose in his place and said to O'Callaghan, "Take your hand off that young man and move away."

The young fellow spoke up then. "He will not hurt me, your Lordship . . . Brehon. He is protecting me, but I will tell where he was that night. He was with me."

Terence turned to Brigid and saw the shock in her face, as she looked from the lad to O'Callaghan and back. O'Callaghan stepped away and stood at a distance from the person who now had the attention of the entire assembly.

"May I speak, Brehon?" the young stranger asked.

O'Breslin and the other two judges put their heads together and consulted with one another. The decision was quickly made. Their words were "You may," but their faces said, "We'll hear you, but there is no guarantee we'll believe you."

The boy looked nervous, as well he might. "My name is Daniel O'Callaghan."

There were gasps of surprise all over the hill. Again, Terence glanced over at Brigid. She was staring at Shane; she looked as if she was terrified of what she might hear next. She was doubtlessly aware, as was Terence, that Shane had a family in Cork. But as far as Terence knew from his conversations with Shane, there had been no contact between them for many years.

"My father left us, left Cork, when I was a lad of only six years. I'm seventeen now."

Terence could see Shane making an effort to look unshaken.

"It wasn't all his fault, the leaving. He was taken to law for something, an offence he caused to a man, and that man's family were friends of my mother, and . . ." He fell silent then, as if he had no idea how to go on.

"Explain," said the brehon.

"But that was long ago. And now I have done something. I didn't intend to cause him lasting harm, the fellow in—"

O'Breslin interrupted him then and said, "Keep still for a moment, Daniel O'Callaghan." O'Breslin conferred with the other two judges, then addressed the court. "This is what we are going to do. I am going to instruct Daniel O'Callaghan to depart from the hilltop."

"But I—" Daniel started to object.

The brehon cut him off. "He will be brought back up, but not until we have heard from the accused man. Not until we have heard what Shane O'Callaghan has to tell us about the sudden and unannounced appearance of this young man before the court. When we have heard what he has to say, we will bring the younger O'Callaghan back before us and hear his story. Does this meet with the approval of the two advocates?"

Úna O'Hanlon protested. "With all respect to you, Lord Judges, this has all the appearance of a trick devised by the accused man and his son in league with one another."

O'Breslin did not seem offended by her words. "I understand your objection, but to have Daniel O'Callaghan tell his story in front of Shane O'Callaghan would—" He did not want to say, "It would ensure that their stories are identical." What the brehon said was, "It might mean that one will rely on the other to give evidence, and we may not get the full flavour of what happened."

"Again, with respect, Brehon, if Shane O'Callaghan and his son have . . . worked together to paint a certain picture for us, their versions of events will be the same even if they do not hear each other's testimony."

The brehon leaned forward and said, "That is where your skill, yours and Terence Blake's, your skill as advocates comes into play. We shall allow you each a thorough examination of the evidence."

Terence saw O'Breslin send an inquiring look in the direction of Hugh Maguire, who immediately gestured to one of his men to escort Daniel from the court. The man walked towards the surprise witness, took him by the arm, and led him away.

Terence rose then and asked the brehons for permission to speak with his client for a moment before the testimony resumed. Permission was granted and he moved closer to O'Callaghan. "What in the name of God are you doing, Shane? Surprising the court, and me, your advocate here."

"He wasn't supposed to come to the court! I instructed him to stay away."

"Is anyone going to believe that?"

"I can see why they would not, but it's the truth. And the tale he was about to tell, that's the truth, too. It explains my own actions, and my reason for taking my chances on this judgment day, taking my chances and hoping our judges would be able to discern my innocence. If not, then I would have to make every effort possible to gather together the wealth to pay the fine for the killing, and the honour price of the physician. And then go in search of the man who really killed Sorcha, and—"

"Shane, what reason could possibly justify—"

"Let me speak to the court."

It was clear to the lawyer that his client intended to have his way; Terence merely shook his head and announced, "My Lord Judges, Shane O'Callaghan will address you now."

"I did not kill Sorcha O'Cassidy, and my hope has always been that the court will see that I am innocent. If the witness Murrough's testimony is believed, it suggests that I was on Sorcha's property that night, but I was not. I do not know why Murrough made up that story. But if the court rules against me, I shall have to do whatever I can to raise the payment to be made to Sorcha's family. That will be very difficult for me to do, but that hardship pales in comparison with what is awaiting my son if his trouble is not sorted out.

"Daniel decided to search for me. And who could blame him for that, wanting to find the father who left the family home all those years ago. It took him quite some time to learn that I had settled in Fermanagh and had become one of the Maguire's soldiers. And so Daniel undertook the long journey north to find me. It's a long and complex story, Brehons, and I shall condense it for you. Daniel got himself onto a ship sailing to Clew Bay, and then worked for a man on his property not far from the monastery at Mayo, tending the landowner's animals and doing other work, with a view to earning the right to possess one of the man's older horses for the long overland journey here to Fermanagh. But while Daniel was there, he took up with a young lady, and he began courting her. It turned out, though, that another man had it in mind to make this young lady his wife, as Daniel learned one night in the alehouse. Words were exchanged. Daniel and the man went outside. They got into a fight, and it ended up with Daniel wounding the man in his face. A few days after this, Daniel was told that the wound would leave a disfiguring mark on the other man's lip and the side of his face."

This brought a reaction from the crowd gathered on the hill; people looked at each other and muttered comments. And little wonder, given how seriously a facial disfigurement was regarded in Irish society.

"This, of course, merits a large fine. The more so since the man is an aigne. As your Lordships well know" — he nodded to them with respect — "a man who causes a disfigurement to the face of another must pay the initial penalty, and then a fine for each and every time that man has to appear, disfigured, in a public assembly. An advocate, of course, frequently appears in such an assembly. Daniel does not have the means to compensate the lawyer for the wound, let alone to keep compensating him over and over into the future. And, of course, if one does not make restitution, he is at risk of being killed by the victim or his family. And so here we are. Daniel maintains that his actions were in self-defence. But he took the horse and fled from that place and made his way here to Fermanagh, where he hoped he would eventually find me and prevail upon me to assist him."

There wasn't a sound on the hilltop, as the people listened to O'Callaghan's dramatic tale.

"If I am unable to help Daniel, he could be hunted down and killed. Or perhaps enslaved. He is my son, and as a father I would do anything for him. I admit in the presence of everyone here that I have not been a father to him until now. I left Cork for the reasons I gave you earlier. There was also trouble between me and my wife, long-standing trouble. And it got much worse after my dispute with the MacSweeneys, who were friends of her family. It all ended with me leaving Cork. I am determined not to abandon Daniel again. I urged him not to come here today, because his whereabouts will now be known. The word may get back to Mayo, and he will be in danger. But it is obvious from his arrival here today that he is determined to save me from being found guilty of an unacknowledged killing."

The people on the hill stared at O'Callaghan in astonishment, none more so than Brigid. Terence could also read anger and hurt in her face. It was obvious that Shane had kept this from her, kept from her the fact that there was an obligation so pressing to him that he was willing to take the chance of a conviction for a secret killing rather than reveal what had befallen a member of his first family.

"And this, my Lord Judges, is where my own behaviour yet again comes into question. Daniel found me one day when I was leaving the castle; this was a few weeks before the banquet. It was a painful reunion for the two of us, as you might imagine. But he told me of the trouble he was in, and he asked me to hide him here in Fermanagh, which I did. There is a ruin of an old house a few miles from the Tierney guesthouse. Only three of the four stone walls are still standing, and those are crumbling and covered with moss. Most of the thatch is still there for a roof, but many of the reeds are falling in. Such as it is, and with trees having grown up around it, we made it Daniel's hiding place. We patched it up as best we could. Daniel has been staying there. I provided him with a spear for hunting, so he could have an occasional piece of meat." A little smile here. "I don't think he got much of that. But I" — here he looked down at the ground, afraid, perhaps of meeting Brigid's eyes — "regularly took provisions from the guesthouse. Biscuits, butter, a bit of wine and ale from our supply and brought them to Daniel.

"And we tried to come up with a plan. A way to obtain enough wealth to pay off the man in Mayo. Daniel thought I could . . . once he saw the Tierney guesthouse and the herds and the extent of the lands . . ."

Shane could not bring himself to say it: that the son from his first family thought the second family was rich enough to provide the quantity of animals or valuable objects to erase his debt to the man he had injured. It was, Terence knew, Tierney property, not O'Callaghan property.

"I told him I could not deprive . . . There was nothing I myself could provide to meet his obligation. So, I tried to come up with

162

a way he could get hold of items of sufficient worth to cover the payment. Payment to buy back his life. How was I going to do this? I could hardly engage in a series of cattle raids! Daniel asked about the goods imported into this country from places like France and Spain, how things like jewels, silver and gold, wine and silk, are transported inland to us here."

So he could make a raid, Terence wondered, against the next load of imported luxuries coming into Fermanagh?

"And the reference to jewellery put me in mind of something I knew from my conversations in the alehouse. There is a man I see from time to time there, and we are on friendly terms. He has spoken to me on several occasions about a valuable collection of jewels and elaborately carved silver goblets and other such items. These had been given to his daughter by her husband early in their courtship and marriage. But after a few years with her, the husband left to marry another, younger, woman. And he took back the things he had given to his first wife and presented them to his second. The first wife and her father were, and still are, enraged by this. I came up with an idea, and I made a couple of trips to the alehouse until I saw the father there, and I sat down and got him onto the subject of the stolen treasures. As he got worked up all over again, I said, 'What would you be willing to pay if someone could get those things back and return them to your daughter?' He stared at me and then said that one or two of her least-favourite — but valuable — silver pieces could be given to any man who retrieved the gifts.

"And I told him I knew of someone who needed silver to pay a debt, and he would be willing to retrieve the daughter's things. The father did some thinking and told me that the husband and wife number two would be attending the banquet put on by the gracious Maguire family on the twenty-fifth of May. The couple had only two servants in the house, a man who would be escorting them to the castle that night and a maidservant. The maidservant, everyone knew, went off with the man she loved whenever her mistress was away for an evening. In short, Daniel was to enter the house the evening of the banquet and take the items and return them to the first wife who, not unreasonably, considered these treasures her own."

O'Callaghan stopped to take a deep breath, and people on the hilltop turned to one another and exchanged remarks, debating perhaps the question of ownership between two wives of the same man when valuable items were at stake.

"On the evening of May the twenty-fifth, I took Daniel to the house where the gifts now resided. And the first wife's father came along with us. His identity will be known sooner or later, so I will name him now: Ceallach Lunny. And his daughter's former husband's name is Dowd." Whispers of recognition went around the court. "Lunny's thinking was that if he and his daughter never got the articles back, they would eventually take Dowd to law over it. And if someone stepped in and retrieved the articles for their rightful owner, and Dowd made an accusation against Lunny, he would defend himself and his daughter on some future judgment day. Either way, the story would become public.

"So, the three of us lurked outside the house, in the shelter of the trees, and waited for the Dowds to leave home for the castle. And waited. Their preparations were taking a long time. Getting themselves bathed and dressed in their finery or whatever they were doing. I finally had to leave and make my own visit to the castle. I wouldn't have missed that splendid banquet for anything!"

Terence stole a glance at Hugh Maguire in the back court and noticed a rueful little smile on his face.

"Dowd and his new wife did finally appear at the banquet. I kept an eye on them whilst I enjoyed myself at the feast. Then I left the castle when they were still taking part in the festivities. I had told Daniel to wait for me in the wood beyond the house. I wanted to join him there in case anything went wrong. Which, of course, it did. I tied my horse some distance away, and looked about for Daniel and Lunny. No sign of them, so I walked in darkness towards the house, keeping to the edge of the wood. And I saw a lamp burning in the window. I was peering at the window as I crept along, trying to see if anyone was there. And all of a sudden, I crashed into something. It was an old wine cask in the wood twenty yards or so from the house. Why was it out there? Secret drinking by somebody, perhaps. I tried to veer around it but ended up knocking it over, and I lost my balance and fell. Cut my knee on something sharp. There were a couple of drinking vessels on the ground; at least I think that's what I saw. I looked up at the house and saw two people coming out the door, a man and a woman. The man shouted but I started running, with the blood coming out of my knee."

He pointed to his right knee, covered by his britches.

"I found Daniel and Lunny waiting farther away from the house. With no silver. They told me that the maidservant had left as predicted, but then she and her man returned, perhaps to enjoy themselves alone in the house. And so, the silver recovery plan was a dismal failure! A failure of a desperate plan to save my son. The only good thing to come out of this, if I may call it good, is that I have witnesses who saw me tripping and falling and running from the house like an amadán." A fool.

After this strange and rambling recitation, O'Breslin said, "I have one question. For now."

"Yes, Brehon?"

"What time were you seen by the maid and her man at the house?"

"It would have been half past midnight or one o'clock. I'm sorry but I cannot be precise."

That would correspond with the time given by the witness Murrough, the time he claimed to have seen a man looking like Shane O'Callaghan. But, Terence reflected, it would, given that Shane had heard the pikeman's testimony.

O'Breslin then asked that the younger O'Callaghan be brought back to the court. Another of the Maguire's men rose and went off to fetch Daniel, who returned to the hilltop. Daniel cast a nervous glance at his father, whose face was without expression. O'Breslin instructed the young man to tell the court what had brought him here. Daniel's description of the events was much the same as that given by his father. This was to be expected. But, to Terence, the story told by the father and son had the ring of truth. Strange and convoluted stories were not uncommon on judgment day, or on any day, come to think of it.

The brehons, understandably, wanted to make sure they had not been subjected to an elaborate set of lies designed to get Shane O'Callaghan off the hook for the killing of Sorcha. O'Breslin said, "The court would be remiss if we did not view the evidence offered on behalf of this man, who has been accused of the killing. What we are going to do is go to the house where these events were said to have occurred and examine the scene for ourselves. In order to see what is there now, and not have the scene altered or damaged in any way, it will be the brehons, the two advocates, the accused man, and the representative of Sorcha O'Cassidy's family who will go to the Dowds' house. I hereby instruct all those gathered here today not to travel to that property. We will have our viewing today, and we will resume the proceedings tomorrow at ten o'clock in the morning."

And with that, Shane O'Callaghan's fate hung in the air.

⁂

Brigid told herself she had never really doubted Shane's innocence. He would never kill any woman, least of all Sorcha O'Cassidy. And Brigid's own disappointment about being kept in the dark about Daniel's presence in Fermanagh was a very small matter compared to the charge that Shane had killed Sorcha. Brigid wished Shane had confided in her, and she would have made Daniel welcome in the guesthouse. But this was not the time to berate him over the course he had taken. Shane told her when he got home that Daniel did not want to meet Shane's second family, did not want to see Shane being a father to his other children, after leaving Daniel and his brother. The pain was written in Shane's face as he told her this. He said very little about the brehons' visit to the Dowd house — she attributed his reticence to embarrassment over the planned robbery — but he insisted that the brehons were sure to find in his favour when the judgment resumed tomorrow. He and Brigid offered the same reassurance to Eileen and Owny, without going into the sordid details. Then Shane took the children out into the garden to play games, and Brigid retired early to her bed.

But there was something else: the court hearing with its images of an unknown man concealed in the shadows outside Sorcha's house, waiting to kill her, brought back to Brigid an event that had occurred many years before, an event that had never gone to court. It was something she always tried to push out of her mind when it was time to sleep. And she should have been able to drift off to a peaceful sleep on this night, with Shane lying there beside her, Shane with a good chance of being declared innocent of the killing. Yet she was still awake after lying for hours in the silent house. The house was silent but the forest was not, and it was the forest that haunted Brigid's mind at that dread hour which she knew must have been three in the morning. She heard the eerie howling of wolves in the night. What had excited them at such a late hour? She knew the sheep were well protected, so she needn't worry about them, or any of the other animals on the property. But it was not a four-legged creature whose image haunted her this night. It was the two-legged savage who had attacked her in the wood all those years ago. Ten years ago now, late summer. She had gone out in the wood in the evening as she often did when the meal was over and she had a break from catering to her guests. She loved to sit at the foot of a tree and gaze up at the sky through the canopy of leaves; it was a peaceful time for her to collect her thoughts, or memorize a poem or a song she had recently heard. It was warm and quiet, and she was in no hurry to return to the house even after the sun had gone down.

On that particular evening, she had let her thoughts drift back to another night in this wood, a week before. She knew that this part of the wood was private; nobody ever came in here. When she had taken Shane for a walk through here, and they talked and joked with one another, and she looked at his fine, strong form and his dark curls and deep blue eyes, what could have been more natural than to find a soft place in the undergrowth and lie down with him there? He had recently come into her life, and she had quickly fallen in love, as he had done himself. Her love for him was even stronger after lying with him that evening in this soft place, and it was that encounter she was remembering as she sat against the tree a week later. When she heard the sudden snapping of twigs and the sound of footsteps, her first thought was Shane. He had come to find her in their cherished private space. But Shane had a more measured step than the trampling of the ground she was hearing now. She felt a stab of fear; was it an animal? A wolf, having scented her presence and . . . She rose to her feet and turned towards the sound. And leapt back in fright. It was a man, one of the monks, in his long robe and the cowl, or hood, over his head. Despite the mildness of the evening, he wore heavy leather gloves.

With his head bent down and obscured by his hood, she couldn't recognize him, but she accorded him a friendly greeting. "Good evening, Brother. You startled me, but—" She stumbled backwards and tried to get her footing. The man's entire face was hidden in a black mask. There were small holes cut out for his eyes and mouth; there was nothing she could identify. He grabbed her with both hands and, before she knew what was happening, he had her on the ground. She could feel rocks cutting into the backs of her hands. She struggled but to no avail; she was no match for his strength. She was terrified; her heart was racing. But she didn't dare cry out. If someone heard her and came by, would they save her or would they think she was . . . ? The man tore at her clothing and forced himself upon her. She cried out with the pain, and he slammed a gloved hand over her mouth. Her teeth pressed sharp against her lips. All she could do was pray that it would be over soon. When he had satisfied himself, he got up, shoved her over onto her stomach, and ran back through the trees in the direction whence he had come. She lay there weeping from the pain, and the rage, and the shame. The darkness around her deepened and finally she pushed herself up, adjusted her clothing, and attempted to make herself presentable before going back to her home.

No one was stirring in the house when she returned. She didn't know how she could face anyone, or how her mind was going to cope with the terrifying ordeal she had endured. She was in pain, she was outraged, and she felt herself to be filthy. She was longing for a hot bath, but that would have to wait till morning, when her maid would heat the water for her. She didn't have the strength to do it herself after what she had been through. Shane came to their bed in his usual good cheer and took her in his arms, but she made excuses to him, pleading her monthly inconvenience, and he withdrew without rancour. He gave her a quick kiss and was snoring lightly beside her two minutes later.

Of course, there was no rest for her that night. She was the victim of the offence of forcor, forcible rape. There was no one she could turn to. Her father was long dead, her brother away fighting in Connacht. More than ever, she longed for the support and comfort of her sister. Mary had warned her that there were men like this, and that women sometimes fell victim to their brutal assaults. Had Mary herself been a victim of something like this? Brigid had started to form the question as they stood together outside their home, but Mary had embraced her and merely said, "Always be careful." Perhaps she thought Brigid was too young at the time to hear any more about such a horrifying subject. By the time Brigid endured this violation, her sister had already left Fermanagh. She had married and was far away on the other side of the country.

Brigid could not bear the thought of Shane knowing what had been done to her in the very spot where they had lain together. But what recourse did she have in law, even if she could track down her attacker? Over the years she had attended judgment days, as most people did, and in her years serving guests at home, she had heard discussions of the laws of her country. She had talked about these particular things with other women of her status, women who were learned and wise. From what Brigid knew, she would not get very far by making known her shame and exposing it to the brehon and the entire community on judgment day. A man who had committed rape had to pay the honour price of the woman's husband or son, father or guardian. And the man had to pay the full éraic, the body fine, for a victim who was a virgin, a nun, or a principal wife. Well, Brigid was not a nun, a wife, or a virgin. She had no father, husband, or guardian. Anyway, she could not go through with such a humiliating public spectacle.

And there was more: she had heard the talk around the dining table, had heard the laughs. She knew that there were some women who had no right to take a man to law for rape, depending on the woman's past behaviour. Well, Brigid had not been a woman leaping from bed to bed, but she was not about to consult an aigne to ask whether she was a worthy victim or not. One other class of unworthy victim she remembered, though: a woman who has a tryst with a man in the woods. Did this mean not the offence committed upon her in the woods, but the loving embraces she had shared with Shane? Did this make her the sort of woman who had lost her right to complain? She didn't know and could not imagine asking such a question. A thought struck her then: did someone know about her time with Shane in the woods? The man who had raped her: had he been watching her? Had he seen her with Shane? Would he be able to use this against her if she brought him to judgment day? But she knew in her heart that none of this mattered. Because she would never be able to bear the shame of revealing what had befallen her.

That all changed, though, when she discovered that she was pregnant. She could hardly bear the memory of trying to summon the courage to admit to Shane what had happened. But one quiet evening when there were no guests in the house, the truth came out. And if she had loved Shane before that moment, her love was immeasurably greater afterwards, because he took her in his arms, whispered words of love to her, and vowed to take revenge on whoever had committed such an outrage against her. As for the child she was carrying, Shane was able to summon up a light-hearted remark: "The child you are carrying is mine. *My* seed would have been powerful enough the first time!" Shane offered marriage then, but Brigid knew about his wife still living in Cork. Brigid was inclined towards the Church's laws on marriage rather than the old Irish ways; if there was another wife out there, even though Shane had not seen her for more than a year at that time, Brigid would hold off on the idea of marriage. Their life together was just fine as it was. And it did appear, with the passing of the years, that Owny looked like Shane with his dark curly hair, fair skin, and blue eyes. But then again, thousands of men in Ireland had that same colouring.

Thinking back to the night of her revelation to Shane, she recalled the rage he expressed against the man who had defiled her. "I'll go over to that abbey and take every one of those priests and brothers by the throat, beginning with the abbot, until one of them confesses what he did! And I won't wait for judgment day to punish the blackguard who did this to you!"

"Shane, it would not have been one of the monks or the priests there. I have met, or at least seen, them all. Not one of them is the kind of man who could do this."

He emitted a bitter laugh at that. "We are all men, and any one of us could do this. Most of us control ourselves and don't fall upon an innocent woman. They are shut up in that place, day after day, night after night, without women. It is no surprise that one of them breaks loose and acts out his lusts on the first woman he sees."

"They are shut up in that place, it is true, but you and I know that many of them are no stranger to the flesh of women. Some of them had wives, some still have women of their own, some have children. The new, strict regime from Rome — the rule of chastity — has not been adopted by all of the monks in this country."

"Brigid, a stór, the man was in the robe and cowl of the Cistercian order."

"And he was also wearing a mask to disguise himself. That is not part of the habit of a monk. It was a man who wanted to disguise himself. He must have stolen the robe to direct the blame to the brothers."

"Why would he have to do that? Why not just wear a mask and regular clothes? Most of us wear the same type of clothing here, the léine, the trews, the mantle. And you understand, of course, that his wearing of the mask means he set out to do exactly what he did. And it also means—"

"He was afraid I would know him."

❧

Now, ten years later, Shane and Brigid were back on the hill for the judgment respecting the murder of Sorcha O'Cassidy. It did not take long. Before a great assembly of the people of Fermanagh, Brehon O'Breslin spoke in a voice that carried across the throng.

"I and my fellow brehons travelled to the Dowds' house yesterday in the company of the accused man, along with Sorcha O'Cassidy's son and their advocates. We, the brehons, spoke to

Dowd, his wife, and the maidservant. The maid confirmed that she was present when the attempt was made to enter the house on the night of May the twenty-fifth of this year, or the very early hours of May the twenty-sixth. She heard the sounds of someone entering the house, and she and 'a companion' saw two men fleeing the house. Later on, she heard a noise outside. She and her companion went to the door and saw a man get up off the ground and run away. She saw him from behind and could offer no description. She was asked whether there was anything she could say about him, his clothing, his hair, but she said could offer no description, apart from saying it was a tall man. She was flustered at the time, which is understandable, given the two incidents that night. And she was nervous again with our questioning. Her estimate of the time of the second occurrence was close to one o'clock. We also walked round the property and saw a wine cask broken on the ground and two glazed jugs, one of them broken and jagged. In light of these findings, both of the advocates agree that there is no need for further testimony or questioning.

"Having considered all the evidence gathered at the house, and the testimony given to the court, I find that Shane O'Callaghan did indeed attempt to execute the plan he devised to obtain the silver for his son, and that he was on the Dowds' property between half twelve and one o'clock in the morning, May the twenty-sixth. This means that he was not present at the home of Sorcha O'Cassidy when Murrough the pikeman claims he saw him there. The pikeman's testimony was the only evidence offered in support of the accusation that it was Shane O'Callaghan who killed the prophetess. I therefore find that he did not commit the secret and unlawful killing of Sorcha O'Cassidy. The killing remains unsolved. I implore whoever did this to come forward and acknowledge his deed, and pay the compensation that he owes to the O'Cassidy family."

No one came forward.

But the hilltop assembly came alive. Everyone had heard Daniel's story, and the brehon had backed it up, so all those gathered knew that Shane O'Callaghan had not killed the physician. The reaction ranged from women smiling at Shane to men shouting their approval of the verdict. It did Brigid's heart the world of good to see how the people supported her man. She knew he was well liked, and here in public was more affirmation when he needed it most.

The brehon then had another announcement to make. "I also declare that Murrough the pikeman gave false evidence to this court, and as a result he loses his honour price. Murrough, if you are here, come forward." He was nowhere to be seen. "That will be dealt with on another day. Shane O'Callaghan, too, gave false evidence but that was to protect his son, Daniel. And no one was injured by the story he first gave us. I can also state here that Shane O'Callaghan has agreed to compensate the Dowds for the offences committed on their property." And with that, the brehon formally closed the proceedings. The people walked away, all of them — except perhaps the guilty man if he was amongst them — wondering who had so cruelly murdered the wise woman, the physician, and left her body to the creatures of the night.

CHAPTER XI

*Cúchonnacht Maguire: an intelligent, comely,
courageous, magnanimous, rapid-marching,
adventurous man, endowed with wisdom and personal
beauty, and all the other good qualifications.*

— trans. John O'Donovan, *Annals of the Kingdom of
Ireland, by the Four Masters*

Two days after the judgment, Terence was spending the
evening in the alehouse, sitting at one of the long, rough-
hewn tables and well on his way to feeling merry. He was delighted
that Shane O'Callaghan had been vindicated on judgment day.
He and Shane had had a friendly conversation afterwards, during
which Terence refused to even consider taking his regular fee for
his services. As he said to Shane, "It was not me, but Daniel,
Lunny, and the Dowds' maidservant who provided you with a
defence!" But Shane was grateful for Terence's work, and they
settled on a portion of the normal fee. The finding of innocence
was, of course, an enormous relief for Shane, but he had sorrow
to contend with as well. Young Daniel had never told the men

in Mayo that he, Daniel, was from Cork, so Shane had reasoned that Cork was the safest place for Daniel to be. There was no hurry for the boy to leave Fermanagh, though Daniel had not seen it that way. He announced to his father that he was leaving immediately; he would travel to Ballyshannon and work to earn his passage on a ship from there to Cork. Shane promised his son that he would visit him there, and Daniel agreed with that. Then, as Shane recounted to Terence, he had stood there in front of the old crumbling house that had been Daniel's hiding place and watched his son disappear into the distance.

Terence tried to shake off the picture of the father and son saying goodbye without any certainty that they would ever meet again. Now, in the alehouse, Terence was surrounded by joyful faces shining in the warm yellow glow of the candles; there were some lewd-looking fellows there as well, some who had obviously been generous to themselves with servings of ale. A piper sat in the corner and accompanied the singing of raucous songs celebrating the legendary drinking and legendary couplings of Irish heroes down through the ages.

The merriment was interrupted — to be more accurate, the merriment was enhanced — by the entrance of a man dressed in a tightly fitted doublet with baggy sleeves; it was made of black satin with colourful embroidered figures on it. This garment was enough to single the man out for laughter and roars of disapproval, enough to show that he had come to them from Dublin.

Terence, having lived for a short time in that English-dominated city himself, in the heart of the English Pale, knew that regulations had been enacted to forbid the ordinary man and woman from dressing above their status and station! The Irish man or woman who was not blessed with wealth was not to be blessed with silk or luxurious fashions, but was limited to good, plain Irish cloth. As pretentious as this newcomer seemed to be, Terence felt compelled to rise to his defence. His mind lubricated and his tongue loosened by drink, Terence declaimed with metrical negligence:

"If we perceive a man to be
Dressed up in the latest finery,
Would we join in with the English queen
In stating he should not be seen
In clothing reserved to the rich and the hale?
And those licking their arses in the Pale?
Would we be bound in fashion fetters
And not be permitted the cloth of our 'betters'?"

Once again in his long illustrious time as a lawyer, Terence Blake had saved a man from death and from a fate much worse, deadly satire, at the hands of his fellow men. The mood in the room changed from mockery and rejection to good-humoured acceptance, and the stranger was plied with drink and foolish tales. The voices got louder, so the piper was forced to compete to be heard. The music became more boisterous, and the ale flowed more copiously as the evening went on.

Once again, Terence felt called upon to speak. He rose with goblet in hand and proclaimed, "Now, men, let us not fall below the standard of comportment set out for our chieftains in the ancient times. It was said that a chief was not to be greasy in the house of the mead-circuit, which all will agree would be best for the tribe! Let us all be as lords and chieftains in this house tonight!"

The crowd raised mugs and goblets and cheered his words, and he drank deep of the golden liquid and asked for more. This was met with another wise saying from the older times, as a man rose, unsteady on his feet, and said, "Be not a flea who spoils the ale in the house of your king! Do not be greedy and devour all the beer your host has provided!"

This was met by laughter, and Terence joined in. "I shall not devour it all, but shall leave much to be sucked up by the rest of yous here."

The good times were interrupted yet again, but this time there would be no beery poem, no roars of laughter. A young farmer named Dúnlang came flying in the door and announced to the room at large: "There's been a murder! I saw the body myself. Murrough the pikeman is lying dead in the woods with a sword stuck into his heart!" The music stopped as if the piper himself had been struck dead. Then there was a clamour of drink-fuelled voices.

Terence placed his goblet on the table and tried to compose his thoughts. The brehon would have to be told, and it would be best if he saw the man's body before it was moved. There was a wealth of evidence to be seen on a body and its surroundings, if things were not disturbed before the viewing. But if the news was told far and wide, how long would the body remain undisturbed? He made an effort to clear his head, not an easy task with all the ale he had in him. "Dúnlang, can you take me there?"

"I can. We'll both go on my horse."

Terence followed him out on wobbly feet. It was cold for the month of June with a brisk wind. It made him shiver. He took long, deep breaths of the chilly air, hoping it might blow away the fog of the drink. A horde of men stumbled out of the alehouse and looked about them, wondering no doubt how they could be conveyed to the place of death.

Terence and Dúnlang mounted Dúnlang's mare, and the bright moon lit the way as they rode off to the murder scene. Strands of

Dúnlang's long yellow hair whipped Terence in the face as they galloped along. They came into a clearing where the shadows of tree branches had the appearance of witches' hands pointing their fingers at the dreadful sight. Murrough was lying on his back, the sword stuck into his chest. The guard, or cross piece, and the black handle rose above his body like a grave marker. His face was distorted by the terror of the final moments of his life. Terence said a prayer over the dead man and then tried to determine the best course of action. He knew that others who had heard the news in the alehouse would find their way here. He had to preserve whatever might be helpful in identifying the killer, and that would be next to impossible if the clearing were soon crowded with drunken men stomping around and gaping at the body.

"Dúnlang, ride to the house of O'Breslin, the brehon, and escort him back here. I'll stay with Murrough until you return."

The farmer nodded his head in agreement, mounted his horse, and rode off into the night, leaving Terence to stand guard. The dead man's jacket was torn open, and blood had spread from his heart all over his pale yellow léine. Terence wondered, of course, whether the pikeman's death was related to his testimony on judgment day. He knew nothing of Murrough's life apart from his role as one of the Maguire's pikeman, knew nothing of his family. The only thing that came to the aigne's mind was Murrough's testimony against Shane O'Callaghan. Terence wasn't going to get the answers here tonight. He looked down upon the dead soldier, whose eyes were open to the cold, starry heavens above.

&

No one was in the main hall of the Tierney house on this brilliant moonlit night except Brigid and her two children. Eileen asked for a tune on the harp, so Brigid sat down to the instrument. The flickering light of the candles accentuated the warm tones of the wood of the harp and of the tapestry hanging on the wall across from her, a tapestry Shane had arranged to be made for her, and which she treasured above all her possessions. It depicted a red-haired woman at a harp and these words:

Blessings on your head in a glowing heap forever,
beloved, as you grip the great wooden carrying-harp.
With a stream of polished playing, profound and sweet,
you have banished the spiders' webs out of all our ears.

Brigid's musical skills were far below that of the professional harper who played for the Maguire at his castle, but she loved the sound of the instrument and knew some of the simpler tunes. And she was improving; she could hear the difference herself as time went on. She had in fact composed a few pieces of her own, and she played them over and over to commit them to memory. Shane encouraged her, and one night at the Maguire castle he had boasted to the Maguire's harper about her playing. Brigid had always known the man by the nickname Thumbs, which was not seriously meant. He was a most skillful musician. Much to Brigid's relief, Thumbs did not dismiss her with a laugh but actually invited her to sit at his harp and play. She was a little shaky at first but, after a few sips of wine, she eased into the music, played a couple of her own pieces, and was delighted when Thumbs said he would like to learn them. He promised to name her as the composer whenever he played them for the Lord of Fermanagh and his family. Brigid later learned that he did exactly that, and her music was well received at Enniskillen Castle!

Right now, though, her audience was her two young children, so she turned to her comical repertoire. She knocked on the wood of the harp, making the sound of heavy footsteps. "Oh, no," she cried out, "villains approaching!" Eileen began stomping around the room, chasing Owny, who went along with the jest. She gave him a shove, and he did a dramatic fall to the floor with a cry of anguish. His mother played along with a glissando down the strings with her fingernails, the musical equivalent of someone falling. This went on for a while until the children went their separate ways to enjoy their toys, and Brigid returned to more dignified selections.

What was it about music that could fill you with joy and send you dancing round the room, or make your heart ache with a grief that you had not seen coming? She recalled those feelings from her earliest years as a little girl when her mother sang a lullaby or her father played a lament on the pipes. He called them the elbow pipes, because you squeezed them with that part of your arm. Was there any sound in the world more sorrowful than that of a lament played on the pipes? Well, it was the harp this night. And now only the sad pieces came to Brigid, as she thought of her parents, gone all these years, and recalled the times she had spent with Sorcha, and thought of Shane and his first son parting after such a short and disheartening time in Fermanagh. So that is what she played as her fingers stroked the strings. She sang a lament, in a voice only she could hear.

Shane burst into the room then. The intense look in his eyes made Brigid freeze in place. What was she going to hear now?

"Brigid, acushla, that man who gave false evidence against me, he's dead!"

It came as a shock. Brigid did not know what to think. Murrough was a pikeman, a warrior. Was he killed in battle or by an unseen enemy? Or . . . This was the man who had lied about Shane, who would have had him guilty of murder. Now he was dead himself. She looked at her man and wondered . . .

"Somebody drove a sword into his heart. The news came into the alehouse, and I met some of the lads who had been there. They went to see the body."

How should she ask this question without hurting him if he had nothing to do with it? She was nearly certain that Shane would not commit such an act when his name would be on the lips of everyone in Fermanagh because of what Murrough had done to him. But she thought back to the painful revelation about Shane's son Daniel. Shane had kept secret from her the arrival of the son from his marriage in Cork; he had not asked for her assistance when he had to provide a hiding place for the boy, and provisions to keep him alive. She could have sheltered Daniel, provided food and drink for him, welcomed him into Shane's second home. And yet she was kept in the dark. Was Shane keeping something from her again?

"Shane, will suspicion fall on you?"

"It will not. I was at the castle. The Maguire himself was there! I was with some other men, sorting through some weapons that have been captured from the enemy. I had just come from there when I met the fellows who had seen Murrough lying dead. I listened to their news and returned here now."

Brigid felt as if an enormous weight had come over her and had now been lifted. She got up from the harp and took Shane in her embrace. He laughed. "You thought it was me, didn't you?"

She had her answer ready: "I thought that *others* would think it was you."

"They'll not be thinking it for long. I have the Maguire himself as my witness."

"Who killed the man, I wonder?"

"Someone else who was a victim of his lies, perhaps."

"Shane, what did you make of those terrible prophecies Sorcha uttered that night? That we will suffer even more grievously under the English than we have already done for all these years?"

"Do you know what struck me more than what Fiach said in his evidence? The look on his face. I've always thought of Father Fiach as an honest man, and I had the feeling looking at him that he was — not lying, not that at all. But I thought he was uneasy giving evidence about the prophecies. Any one of us could predict that the English will do us more harm in their determination to take our country for themselves, so for Fiach to look the way he did, I got the feeling that there was more to it. Whatever Sorcha said that night may have been much worse than what he testified to on judgment day. I just felt there was probably more to it, and he was not going to reveal it. And he felt guilty himself for keeping secrets from the court. And from the people of Fermanagh."

"That was my impression as well. I've known Fiach all my life. It was written all over his face that he knew more about Sorcha's prophecies than he was telling the court. And if he was keeping it hidden, you can be sure it was something worse, not better, that he was keeping from us all."

⚬

Father Marcus Valerius had just shepherded his students in for their first class of the day, and he stood outside the room talking with Brigid Tierney and her daughter, Eileen. Eileen had an armload of books to take home with her. The child loved to read, was a very skilled reader, and why not? Marcus had heard that

Brigid had been taught the great books at a young age by her own mother, and she was doing the same for Eileen. In fact, the girl was learning Latin and, if the truth be told, was much quicker to learn than her brother Owny. But Owny would catch up, Marcus was sure. The boy had other interests, and those lay in the fields of battle; he had no trouble reading when war was the subject under discussion! Brigid had just told Marcus about the pikeman who had been killed. He hoped his face did not betray the first thought that came to his mind: that the man who had a reason to kill Murrough was Shane O'Callaghan. Brigid did not have to read his mind, did not have to possess the skills of Sorcha O'Cassidy, God rest her, to know that Shane's name would come to mind. She said, "Shane was at the castle when it happened, Father Abbot. We don't know who killed the man . . ."

"You may be certain that we will find out who killed the man."

Marcus turned to see who had spoken. Well! Here was a most illustrious visitor. Cúchonnacht Maguire, half-brother of the Lord of Fermanagh, had come into the abbey with a couple of his men. Marcus greeted them and then stood back so Brigid could do the same. Her face shone with the delight that all the women displayed at the sight of Maguire. It had been quite a while since any woman had favoured Marcus with such an admiring glance!

"I am here, Father Abbot, to ask that you say a Mass for our pikeman who was killed last night. Murrough. My family and my men will be in attendance."

"We shall, of course. At a time of your choosing."

"Thank you, Father. Let us say this evening, after Vespers."

Marcus bowed his head in agreement.

Just then Brigid's son came flying in the door.

"Where were you, Owny?" his mother asked. "I thought you were with the class."

"There was a badger! When I came upon him, he stood up on his back legs and showed his teeth and his claws. And then he started running and I chased after him but couldn't catch him." The boy realized then who was in his presence. "Oh!" He stared up at the man from the castle. "Why are you here?"

"Owen!" His mother was mortified.

But Maguire laughed. "I'm here to give you lads a lesson."

"What kind of a lesson?"

"What would you like to learn?"

"Tell us about a battle!"

His little sister sought to apologize for her talkative brother. "Please forgive him, my . . . Lord? He's a boy so he likes to hear about fighting."

"How about you, little girl? Do you not like to hear about fighting?"

Her eyes shot over to her mother. Had she said something wrong? She tried to make amends. "We are thankful to you and your family and your warriors for fighting off our enemies!"

"Did you know that one of our greatest warriors is a woman?"

"Girls can't be soldiers," said Owny.

His mother put a warning hand on his shoulder and squeezed. "Don't be bold to Cúchonnacht Maguire."

Maguire spoke to the boy's sister. "Maybe you'll command a fleet of ships someday, Eileen." Owny laughed at that, and Maguire ignored him. "Do you know about Granuaile, Eileen?"

"Who is she?"

"She is the chieftain of the O'Malleys on the western coast of Ireland."

"A lady can't be a chieftain!"

"Woe to the young scoundrel who says that to the face of Grace O'Malley! She'd have you thrown overboard, Owny, my lad."

"Tell me, please," said Eileen.

"Why don't I tell you and all the boys in the class as well? Would you like to take a rest and let another man teach your class this morning, Father?"

"I would be honoured. We all would."

So that's what happened. Marcus sat in the room with his students, with Brigid and her daughter as guests. Cúchonnacht Maguire clapped his hands together and promised to weave a tale, a true tale Marcus knew, of adventure on the seas. The boys were nearly beside themselves with excitement. Most of them knew the brother of the Maguire on sight; those who did not were soon put in the know by their fellow students.

"I'm here to tell of Granuaile. Her English enemies know her as Grace O'Malley. She lives in Mayo, in the area of Clew Bay. And she commands a fleet of ships called galleys, and she also commands two hundred sailors."

This caused a stir, and one of the boys blurted out, "Is that true?"

"It certainly is, my lad. Not only is she a sea captain, she is also a *pirate*!"

Even Owny was riveted by this time.

"She is known, and feared, as the pirate queen."

"She must be a strange big woman!" one of the boys said.

"Not so strange. She has four children. The last child, a Bourke, was born on one of Grace's ships whilst it was at sea."

Eileen looked concerned. "A baby on a ship? Was he scared?"

"Nothing frightens the O'Malleys. Do you know what their family motto is? Terra marique potens. I'm sure your students know what that means, Father."

The keen faces on a few of the boys signalled that they knew; others were not as skilled at Latin. It was also clear that Eileen understood the motto.

"Well, lads? Let's hear you," Maguire urged them, in a manner recalled from his own school days.

A couple of the boys said it aloud, and Eileen mouthed the words silently along with them. "Powerful on land and sea!"

"Even the baby knows no fear. His name is Tibbot-na-Long, Toby of the Ships."

"I like that name!" Owny conceded.

"She has a son-in-law with another fine name: he was one of the Bourkes, and he was known as the Devil's Hook!"

This brought on the reaction one might have expected from a class of boys in a land where war and the threat of conquest were ever present. It took a few minutes for them to settle down.

"So," Maguire continued, "back to the ship. Here is Granuaile below decks with her little baby boy." Maguire, with his manly face and form, pretended to be the new mother. He grabbed a chair and sat down, then reached over to a desk and snatched up a heavy book. He clasped it to his breast and rocked back and forth to comfort the infant. "Good boy, sweet child," he murmured to the delight of the real-life children looking on. Then his face showed sudden alarm. His eyes darted upwards, and he cried, "What's that?" He stamped his feet and shouted and made Granuaile look up again. He then switched personas, got up, and walked quickly across the floor. He shouted, "We're under attack! Algerian pirates!"

"Pirates!" Owny was delighted. "But what does Algerian mean?"

"It means they came from a faraway land called Algeria, in Africa."

"I read about Africa in a book," said Eileen. "It was about Saint Augustine. Africa is very far away."

"That's right. That's how far away these pirates had sailed from." Grabbing the book, he was the mother again. As Granuaile, he made a face that bespoke impatience.

What was going to happen now? It was the sailor again. "Please, your Grace, come up on deck and order our men to fight!"

The tender new mother emitted a short, impatient sigh and placed her baby gently in his cot — Maguire placed the book on the chair — and Marcus watched with amusement as Brigid Tierney nodded her head, seemingly in agreement with Maguire's portrayal. Marcus remembered his own childhood, and the many times his mother had sighed and said, "Can't you people manage anything without me?"

Granuaile pushed the trembling mariner ahead of her and stomped up to the deck. She took hold of a musket and faced the Algerian marauders, and she bellowed a curse that must have shaken every timber in the ship. Eileen covered her mouth and giggled; Owny let out a roar of laughter. The pirate queen lifted her musket and fired it and sent the interlopers scrambling. She put down her gun, looked around at her crew, and then went below decks to tend to her newborn child. Applause broke out in the abbey school as Granuaile sat down placidly and rocked her baby.

Marcus looked about him and saw that a couple of other monks had come in and caught part of the performance. Father Fiach O'Moylan had come in as well. He looked delighted.

"You made up that story!" Owny said, when his laughter had died down.

"Owen!" his mother admonished him again.

But Maguire took it in good humour. "I did not."

"It's the truth," Father O'Moylan said.

"And that was not the end of it," said Maguire. "Granuaile and her fleet sailed to Munster to do some plundering in the territory of the Earl of Desmond. That was a rich country."

"What did she get there?" asked Owny.

"She got captured by the earl and locked up in Askeaton Castle."

"Ach!" Eileen cried. "Poor Granuaile!"

"And then the earl put her in Limerick jail."

"A jail!" one of the lads exclaimed.

"Be careful if ever you're in Limerick, boys; they have a jail there."

"We should have a jail here."

"We should not. So. Granuaile was held captive in the west for over a year. And then—"

"And then," Eileen prayed, "they let her go home to her children and her ships!"

"They did not. They put her in chains and took her all the way across Ireland and locked her up in Dublin Castle. Only the most important enemies of the English get thrown in there. And are yous wondering what became of Tibbot-na-Long?"

"What became of him?" the class demanded to know.

"He was captured by the English and locked up in Ballymote Castle."

"Let's go and march on the castle, right now!" insisted Brigid Tierney's militant young lad.

"Oh, Granuaile did better than that. I'll skip ahead here. Granuaile began writing to the queen of England!"

"You can do that?" Eileen asked.

"Well, it takes someone with, ah, nerves of iron. It takes someone like Granuaile, Grace O'Malley, to be brave and bold enough to directly petition the English queen. Granuaile's writing was in the English language and, from what I hear, her arguments were clever and wise and full of cunning. We are now in the year 1593."

"That's only — I can count them — two years ago."

"Right enough, Owny, the year Hugh Maguire went into rebellion."

"Your own brother!" one of the boys called out.

"My own brother, that's right. So, Granuaile gathered up her fighting men, boarded one of her galley ships, and set a perilous course for England!"

"It still astounds me every time I hear tell of it." That was Fiach, every bit as captivated by the tale as were the children.

"Sailed all the way to England, and met face to face with the queen. They were both at least sixty years old when they met. It is believed that they spoke in Latin. There are many tales and legends about that visit, and they remain to be written into the books, but I did hear that their queen is smaller than our queen — and I do call her a queen, her being Granuaile — and so the English queen had to look up to ours! And the English queen ordered her men to release Tibbot-na-Long!"

The children clapped and cheered.

Marcus turned to Fiach O'Moylan to have a word about the next class, but a young voice overrode what he was going to say.

"I want to sail in a ship and hunt for pirates!" This was Owny again. "I'll be Owny of the Ships! Would you like to go to sea in a ship, Cúchonnacht Maguire?"

He smiled at the boy. "I would indeed."

A shadow seemed to pass over the face of Fiach O'Moylan, whose eyes were fixed on Maguire. But Maguire didn't notice; he began saying his goodbyes, and the boys pleaded with him to return soon with another adventure for them.

He was about to depart when two more men arrived, nearly out of breath from running. They were dressed as bodyguards, perhaps, or watchmen.

Maguire turned to them. "What is the trouble?"

"Colm the lookout, he's been run through with a sword! A woman washing clothes in the river a mile or so from the castle, down river, she saw him lying there, and her husband came to us. He recognized Colm and knew he was one of the watchmen at the castle. We brought him here to the infirmary. He's in there now on a bed."

"What? Colm?" Maguire stared at the man.

"I've heard that name," Brigid said.

"You'd have heard it on judgment day," Maguire replied, with a composure Marcus attributed to his breeding and long experience with calamities of one kind or another. "His name was given during the proceedings along with that of Murrough, our pikeman. Murrough told the court that he had been sent to deliver a message to Colm, which he said he delivered the morning after the wise woman was killed. We'll see him now." He turned and headed for the infirmary, his two bodyguards at his side, and Marcus and Brigid close behind them.

Marcus reflected on the news of the pikeman's death and now the wounding of the watchman. The brothers in the abbey and the people of this part of Fermanagh were still reeling from the murder of their beloved physician, and then they had the shock of hearing that one of the Maguire's warriors had been slain. Now it was another of the Maguire's men. Murrough and Colm were both involved in the story told against Shane O'Callaghan at his trial. Marcus had been of the opinion all along that Shane was not the kind of man who would kill Sorcha. Whoever did that had either a secret personal motive or a sudden feeling of rage or fear at hearing her prophecies about the future facing Ireland, a future that was to unfold apparently without the support and military might of her leading men. Apparently, Shane had been at the castle at the time Murrough met his death.

But was it possible that he had arranged for someone else to take out his revenge on Murrough? And here was Colm at the abbey, fighting for his life.

⛢

Thank God and his Blessed Mother that Shane was at the castle last night, Brigid thought as she followed the others outside and across to the infirmary. She asked herself whether she had any right to be there, but this was a man who had been part of a conspiracy to blame Shane for a secret and unlawful killing. Whether Colm had come into the scheme wittingly or unwittingly, she had no idea, but if he was in a fit-enough condition to be questioned, the castle watchman would be questioned by the chieftain's brother. And Brigid was anxious to hear what the man had to say.

When they arrived at the infirmary building, Brother Dominic, the abbey physician, was tending to the injured man. Windows lined the infirmary walls, and a table and shelves at one end held various instruments and vials of medicine. There were several beds but, on this day, only one was occupied. A half-dozen monks were gathered in prayer a short distance from Colm the lookout. Brigid recognized him; she had seen him at the castle.

An old phrase came into her mind: "exempt fists." Some men employed by a king or lord were exempt from liability if they committed acts of violence whilst carrying out their duties. A lookout was one; a charioteer was another. Who else? For some reason she thought, *Buffoon*. Could one of the buffoons be among the "exempt fists"? Surely not. She chided herself for allowing her mind to wander while a man might be in his last moments of earthly life. The ends of Colm's ginger moustache rested on a face as white as milk, and his small brown eyes stared up at the ceiling. Brigid would not have known whether he was alive or dead. But the physician was pressing his hands on the bleeding wound in the man's side, so it seemed he was still of this world.

Cúchonnacht Maguire moved in close to the doctor and said, "Colm, may God bless you and keep you at His right hand."

Colm's body seemed to jolt at the sound of the voice, and his eyes fastened on Maguire. There was no mistaking the fear in those eyes. And little wonder, he was losing blood from the wound in his side.

"Colm, who did this?"

No answer, nothing but terror. Did he feel that death was imminent? Or was it fear of Maguire? Fear that he, Colm, would have to identify his attacker and be in jeopardy of further violence for revealing the man's name? For Brigid, it was almost as if she could feel the fear herself. She looked at him lying there on the bed, him not knowing whether he would live to walk out on his own two feet. And would he still be in danger if he did? Who was out there, killing and wounding all these people in Fermanagh? Who might be next?

The abbot spoke up then. He turned to the gathered monks and instructed them to bring a vial of holy oil for the sacrament of Extreme Unction, the last rites for the dying. Marcus turned back to Colm then and said, "My son, you will be in the everlasting love and protection of the loving God. This is no time for evasions, no time for prevarication. You are going to your Lord and Saviour. If you have something to say about the man who did this, tell us now. God is your witness." Colm opened his mouth, but nothing came out. Marcus then said, "I will confess you." And he switched to Latin and began the words of the Confiteor, and one of the monks arrived with the oil for the final rite.

But the abbey physician again examined his patient and said, "He will survive this. The wound will heal. Nothing vital has been damaged. He is weak from loss of blood and from the shock of it. I shall treat the wound, and then we should leave him to rest."

As the gathering broke up, Brigid noticed an ancient monk who had been hovering near the end of the bed. She knew who he was, the sick old brother whom Marcus had brought over to Ireland so the man could spend his final years amongst his own people. Brother Aidan, that was it. He was thin with long white hair. His face was deeply lined, and his prominent nose had the look of a beak. She watched as Aidan walked over to Cúchonnacht Maguire, Aidan being quick and spry for a man of his age. He looked up at Maguire and said, "It's a blessing that you were able to be here for him. Your presence will inspire him to recover and return to your family's service."

Maguire acknowledged the remark with a nod of his head. Aidan placed a gentle hand on Maguire's right arm and said, "Your arm was quick in healing, thanks be to God."

"My arm?"

"It was crooked and bound up when I saw you with him." With Colm, he meant. "That was when? A few weeks ago? I don't keep track of time these days; so many days are the very same. But it's good to see that the Lord worked his cures on you yourself, and I have faith that he will do the same for this poor man."

Cúchonnacht spoke sharply. "What was it you saw, Brother?"

"Ach, they tell me I'll fall and hurt myself someday, and me wandering off the way I do. But I'm a man who loves to walk the woods and the pastures and the shore of the river and the loughs, and if the Lord takes me off during one of my rambles, well then, let His will be done."

It was obvious that Cúchonnacht was calling on favours from a higher power, namely the grace of patience, and he said, "On your walks, Brother, you saw Colm with . . ."

"Yourself when your arm was hurt. You must have had him keeping watch way out in the woods that day. And well you should. You never know where the enemy will creep up. There will be Saxons with their faces at our windows if we're not vigilant."

The old man kept up his gabbling but Cúchonnacht Maguire had turned away, distracted. It was clear that he had something on his mind.

When Brigid got home and Shane had come in, she told him about Cúchonnacht Maguire's visit to the abbey and about the wounded man who was brought to the infirmary.

"The old monk there, Aidan, said he'd seen Cúchonnacht with an injured arm. This was a few weeks ago, it seems. Had he hurt his arm?"

"That would have been Connor Óg! I know he banged up his arm. Probably broke it by falling too quickly to his knees in the presence of the latest Lord Deputy sent to rule over us. Russell, it is this time. Or maybe he flung his arms around Russell in an embrace and smashed his arm against that foppish ruff they wear round their necks. The old fellow at the abbey must have mistaken Connor Óg Maguire for Cúchonnacht. Imagine what Cúchonnacht would think of that!"

Brigid well knew that this Connor Óg, son of Connor Roe (Rua) Maguire, was known as "the English Maguire" or "the Queen's Maguire." He was working with the English in opposition to Hugh Maguire's branch of the family. "Connor Óg, was it?

That would explain the expression on Cúchonnacht's face when Brother Aidan made the remark to him. Because what Aidan said was that he had seen Colm with the man he thought was Cúchonnacht but was really Connor Óg. What on earth was a watchman for Enniskillen Castle doing meeting in the woods with the English Maguire?"

CHAPTER XII

None shall wear in his apparel:
Cloth of gold, silver, tinseled satin, silk, or cloth
mixed or embroidered with any gold or silver: except
all degrees above viscounts, and viscounts, barons,
and other persons of like degree . . . no sort of people
have so much exceeded, or do daily more exceed in
the excess of apparel, contrary to the said statutes,
than such as be of the meaner sort . . .

— *Statutes of Apparel* (6 May 1562) 4 Elizabeth I
and (June 15, 1574) 16 Elizabeth I

2018

Mick Tierney was saying goodbye to a group of Belgian tourists when the telephone rang. The receptionist, Sharon, answered and called over to him. "For you, Mick." He gave the tourists a farewell wave and took the call.

"Hello, Mr. Tierney. This is Aisling." He drew in a quick breath. Could this be the news he'd been waiting for all these months? Aisling was an archaeologist and, yes, she had news.

"We have our licence to do the work on your land. We should be able to start excavating in a couple of weeks' time."

Yes! "Thank you, Aisling, thank you! Can't wait to see ye here."

"Be warned, now, we make a bit of a mess!"

"You'll be welcome to do all the messing you like!"

When they ended the call, Mick walked out into the lobby to give the news to Róisín.

She had completed her mural showing a sixteenth-century banquet at the old Tierney guesthouse, and it was meeting with great admiration from guests and also local people, who had made a point of coming to see it. Now she had another mural on the go, and Mick found her sitting up against the wall with papers spread all about her on the floor. "It's on," he announced. "The archaeologists have their licence, and in a couple of weeks they'll be starting the dig!"

She leapt up, and a grin spread across her face. "This is brilliant!" She threw her arms around Mick, and they hugged each other and talked about what the project would be like. Then he said, "So what have you got going here?" He pointed to the items she had spread out on the floor. Journal articles, drawings of people attired in the garb of the sixteenth century. Women in long elaborate dresses with fitted tops and billowing skirts; men in short, cinched jackets and tight-fighting leggings; others in long mantles with fringed collars.

"Look at this, Dad! The *Wilde Irish Man* and *Woman*! Drawn by a fella named Speed in the 1600s." She handed him the pictures of the wild Irish in their long, fringed cloaks. "Maybe we'll find some of this stuff when they start the dig."

"Sure we'll find trunk loads of stuff, all laundered and pressed and ready to wear."

"And here," Róisín said, "we have a *Civil Irish Man* and *Woman* and *Gentleman of Ireland* and *Gentlewoman*."

Mick took a gander at the picture. The Irish gentleman looked so veddy, veddy English in his turned-up moustache and high-crowned, wide-brimmed hat.

"I hope you're not planning to go out tonight, Dad, at least not in the elaborate clothing you usually wear. I hate to say it, but you may be dressing above your class. You know there were regulations in place to prevent the lower sort of person, like me and you, from dressing above our station."

"The likes of me would never want to offend in that way. People might think I have notions!"

"Good man. So, here's some advice for you. Do not go out in public ever again in any silk of the colour purple, cloth of gold tissue, nor fur of sables."

"But I've nothing else to put on me!"

"I'm sorry, but it is against the law for anyone but the royal family to be seen in those items. There is some leeway for dukes, marquises, and earls, who may wear those fabrics in some garments, such as doublets or jerkins. Are you by any chance a knight of the garter?"

"I haven't checked the honours list lately."

"No? Well, you can't even wear purple in a mantle then. But you're not alone in this, you lowly little man. I, as a woman, am not permitted to wear any velvet in gowns, furs of leopards, or embroidery of silk. Unless I marry a knight or the son of a baron. What are the chances of that?"

"You'd better change what drinking holes you patronize."

"I shall. And hope I'll have better luck than I had last time."

Her grandfather Liam walked in then, favouring his injured right leg while, as always, doing his best to hide the fact. "Better luck of what sort, angel?"

"Better husband than I had last time round."

"Be it not for me to state the obvious!"

"No need to state it, Grandda. You're thinking I could hardly do worse."

"Ah now . . ." He gazed at the materials displayed on the floor. "What's all this in aid of?"

"We're reviewing the sumptuary laws that were in place in the sixteenth century. You know, to make sure we don't put a foot wrong, so to speak."

Mick tugged his forelock and said, "The likes of us wouldn't want to dress like our betters, sir."

"Fuckers," Liam muttered, almost under his breath.

"To return to the subject of my former life's partner, he'll be coming over later to see the kids."

"I hope they don't pay him any mind, God be good to them."

"He's fairly well behaved around them, Grandda. I'm fine with him being here as long as he comes by himself. Did you happen to see on the news last night, two fellas lifted on drugs charges?"

"Don't be telling us that!"

"No, no, it wasn't Brayden. Not yet, at least. But those two are mates of his. They belong to this gang that's dealing drugs in the clubs."

"What kinds of drugs?" Mick asked.

"Every kind, Dad. Cocaine and ecstasy, and some of these fellas are even selling heroin. Not sure if Brayden's pals have any of that on hand. But I do know they're making a whack of money selling drugs that need a prescription."

"People are dying of that stuff," said Liam. "You read about it every week now. I never thought the day would come when I'd have to say my oul man was right."

"Right about what, Grandda?"

"I'd be over visiting and he'd be roaring about the young people. This was in the late 1960s, early '70s. Girls would have to be careful, make sure nobody put something in their drinks. And boys were cracked if they were swallowing pills and putting stuff up their noses just because their pals were doing it. 'Read the papers. Look at the crime that's going on now. It's all because of the drugs!' And I'd be ignoring him. I was young then, in my twenties, but drugs were the last thing I was concerned about. I was more worried about getting a bullet in the head! But look around you now! Young lads and even girls dying of overdoses. And gurriers out there enriching themselves by selling the stuff to them! And robberies and people attacking each other over the money that's in it."

"You're not trying to tell us that the 1970s here in Ireland would have been all sweetness and light if it weren't for the dope dealers, are you, Da?" Mick asked.

"That was different. We were at war. What am I just after telling ye? I was in danger of taking a bullet."

"So, if the occasional bank was raided . . ."

"It costs money to fight a war." Liam affected not to notice when his son directed a wink his way. Mick well knew that Liam had been a party to at least one bank raid. All in the name of the cause, of course.

"And things are out of control in the Free State as well," Liam said. "I was down in Dublin a couple of weeks ago and met up with an old friend of mine. Retired now, but he'd been in the Gardaí."

"You have friends amongst the peelers?"

"There were guards who were friendly to us, Michael." There was no need to ask the old rebel who he meant by *us*. "And this fella was one of them. We got on this very subject, given his time as a copper. He told me there'd been very little serious crime in Ireland until the late 1960s. He's a great man for the numbers, so he rattled off some figures to me. All I remember of it was that there was no murder or manslaughter or armed robbery in the Dublin area in the year 1960. And in 1963 and '64, he said, there was hardly a problem with serious crime in the Free State at all. But that started to change in the late '60s. And, to quote my father, rest his soul, it was 'the drugs!' So here we are throughout history with the Brits killing us and starving us to death, and we had all the deaths during the Troubles up here in the North. And now we have the peace agreement, and what's happening now? We've our own people killing each other with pills!"

"Ah, speak of the devil," said Róisín, looking down at her phone. "Or his associates. Brayden is on his way here to see the kids."

"Shame I won't be able to stay and visit," her grandfather replied. "I've been asked to do my party piece down the pub."

"Your party piece?"

"He has many to his name," said Mick.

"It's my bit on Spenser they're looking for today."

"Oh, right. Spenser, the poet."

"Your grandda does a fine recitation based on that old bastard."

"We did him in school, but I don't remember much of it. I'll google him." She turned again to her phone and typed in her search request. "Here he is. Edmund Spenser and the *Faerie Queene*."

"Find what he had to say on the subject of our country."

She tapped in her request and then, "He wrote something called *A View of the Present State of Ireland*. In 1596. He was sent over here as some kind of bureaucrat."

"On Her Majesty's Service he was. Elizabeth, the beloved Faerie Queene herself."

Róisín scrolled through Spenser's abhorrent remarks on the Irish and exclaimed, "Listen to this! He goes on and on about the *mere Irish* and the *wild Irish*! Maybe I'll fit him into my mural, have him looking on in horror. And, oh my God, is he saying what I think he's saying? It's sixteenth-century English but . . ."

"Yes, I suspect you're reading it correctly. Let me have a look." She turned the phone so Liam could read. "He is indeed advocating a policy of famine, advocating that the Irish be kept from 'manurance,' that is cultivation of their lands. It's a scorched-earth policy he's recommending, which would have the happy result that the people — our people — would 'quickly consume themselves and devour one another.' And he says he saw for himself how this would succeed, because during the wars in Munster he saw people brought to such wretchedness that they 'came creeping forth upon their hands, for their legs could not bear them; they . . . spake like ghosts crying out of their graves. They did eat the dead carrions, happy where they could find them, yea, and one another soon after . . . And if they found a plot of watercresses or shamrocks, there they flocked as to a feast.' There you have old Spenser, reporting on how well the scorched-earth policy worked in Munster, with our people dying of starvation."

"Imagine," Róisín cried, "writing that — advocating that — for any people, anywhere in the world, in any age!"

"Not only did they advocate it, they fuckin' boasted about it after they accomplished it. Excuse my language, love."

"It's not *your* language that needs excusing, Grandda!"

The expression on her face made Mick want to take his daughter in a consoling embrace and assure her that it wasn't real, hadn't happened, that human beings were basically good. But she knew it was all too real, and there was nothing her da could do to change it.

"The point has been made, on more than one occasion," said Liam, "that the wars of Queen Elizabeth the First were wars of extermination."

He placed his left hand over his heart and flung the right hand out, in the pose of a ham actor, and declaimed, "Great Queene of glory bright, Mirrour of grace and Majestie Divine, great lady of the greatest Isle!"

"He praised her to the skies," Róisín exclaimed, "and he's one of the most revered poets in the English language! Imagine!"

"Little wonder he wrote so many fawning lines about her. She'd already given him a castle to live in here in Ireland, and three thousand acres of land with it, during his fondly remembered time in this country. During Elizabeth's plantation of Munster. And then after he'd written the thing and presented it to her, she awarded him a lifelong pension of fifty pounds a year. Big money in those days."

Róisín shook her head in disgust.

"Come here to me," said Liam then. "D'ye know what Karl Marx had to say about the great Renaissance poet?"

"No," Róisín replied. "What did he say?"

"Marx called Spenser 'Elizabeth's arse-kissing poet'!"

"Well said, Karl!" Mick exclaimed, thumping the table with his fists.

"And with that, I'm off to Blake's to do my recital and enjoy a pint or two."

They bade farewell to Liam, and Róisín returned to the research for her new mural. "So I know enough now not to do a portrait of you, Dad, in clothing above your station. I'll dress you as a typical example of the meaner sort. But here's a bit of good news. In the mid 1600s, King Charles the First repealed an old law that said Irish people in Meath could be *killed* if they weren't wearing, or accompanied by someone wearing, proper clothes in the English style! The death penalty for not following the fashions of the invading country."

"I hope the penalty for that was not the same as for treason. For that, we'd be dragged through the streets, have our bodies sliced open and our innards ripped out, then have our heads cut off. And they wanted to civilize *us*?!"

"And this was going on not when people were living in caves, Dad, but when Shakespeare was writing some of the greatest works ever penned in the English language, when — who's the fellow that wrote the beautiful music we heard in that concert last year?"

"William Byrd. Him and Thomas Tallis. Two of the greatest composers ever."

"Right. People would be listening to all that beautiful music, and outside somebody would be having his intestines torn out."

Mick nodded his head in bitter acknowledgement, then left her to it and went into the restaurant to greet two groups of tourists, one from Poland, the other from Hungary. It was early April, and he was glad to see them. He sat down and chatted with them — and with their interpreters — for a while, giving them some tips on sightseeing and entertainment. Then he stepped outside where his former son-in-law was kicking a football around with his children. The effort was lacklustre; it was plain to see that his heart wasn't in it. Róisín came out after him and stood against the wall of the hotel.

"He'll never get signed on to manage the Gaels with that attitude," Mick said. The Gaels were Enniskillen's long-standing Gaelic Athletic Association football club.

"Daddy!" Rory called out. "We'll make those bushes down there the goal, 'cause I can kick it that far, all the way from here!

Watch this!" Rory drew back his right foot and booted the ball almost to the bushes. He turned to his father in triumph, but Brayden had missed it. Too busy staring down at his mobile phone. Mick thought there was a jittery, nervous look about him. Something on his mind and it wasn't his children. "Dad, look!"

But it wasn't long before the players came off the pitch, and one of them demanded compensation. "Daddy," Ciara said, "you told us you'd be bringing us a kit to make a playhouse. And we'd be building it ourselves. But you didn't bring it!"

Brayden walked towards Mick and Róisín, lighting up a smoke and muttering, "Can hardly be buying playhouses after being sacked, can I?"

"Daddy!" Ciara tried again. "You said!"

But he didn't seem to have heard.

"What?" Róisín asked. "You got sacked?" Mick could hear the exasperation in her voice. He also intuited an unspoken "again?" at the end of her question.

"You heard me."

He directed a curt nod in Mick's direction.

Brayden had tried several avenues of employment. He had somehow managed to buy a gymnasium full of exercise equipment, but the business tanked not long after he opened it, and he was left with a load of debt as a result. Lately, he had been working on a building site. Now, apparently, he was out on his arse once again.

"They didn't need all the fellas they had on the site. So I can't be buying luxury toys for the kids, as much as I'd like to." He cast his eyes in the direction of the two tour buses parked outside the hotel, and said, "But there's no reason they can't have a play-house if they want it." No reason the Tierneys couldn't provide the luxuries, was the less-than-subtle message.

And the message made it as far as the ears that most wanted to hear it. "We're getting the playhouse!" Ciara called out to her brother.

"Will there be a barn with it? We'll get toy animals for it!"

"A barn and a house! And we'll put it right between those two big trees in the back, won't we, Mummy?"

"Not in the back, sweetheart, no. That's where they're going to be digging."

"Who's going to be digging?" Ciara came up beside her mother.

"A team of scientists to see if there's an old, old house down there under the ground! Where members of our family lived hundreds of years ago."

"Did they have weans like me and Rory? Maybe there's an old playhouse, too! And dolls and toy dishes, like we saw on that show about the old places on the telly!"

Róisín ruffled her daughter's ginger hair. "Maybe so."

"So the old gran has come round to agree with the plan, has she?" Brayden had rejoined the conversation.

"Aye, she has, but she's still not happy about it."

"What do you really think you're going to find out there under the ground?"

"We're hoping for anything that might be considered a monument or an object of historical or archaeological interest."

"Is there stuff like that down there?"

"Very likely, given that the old guesthouse was there. But even if there isn't, what we want is an archaeological team here, taking all the time in the world to dig around."

"Because of that Yank and his building plans."

"Right. We want all this commotion and delay to put him off the plan and go elsewhere."

Brayden took a last drag of his cigarette, threw it down, and ground it out with his heel. He caught his former wife's disapproving look, sighed, and picked up the butt. He gave his children a distracted wave and walked away.

CHAPTER XIII

Stars, hide your fires; let not light see my black and deep desires.

— Shakespeare, *Macbeth*

1595

Marcus stopped in at the infirmary before bedtime to see how Colm was faring. The man seemed to be sleeping peacefully, so Marcus retired to his bed. But no sooner was he asleep than he was awakened by Brother Bartholomew. "I am sorry to wake you, Father Abbot, but Brother Aidan is not well at all!"

Marcus struggled to shake off his sleep. "What has happened? Was he out wandering again?"

"Not wandering, Father, he was in the dormitory. I heard him coughing. And raving—"

Marcus sat up and swung his legs over the side of his bed. "Raving? What do you mean, Bartholomew?"

"You'll see for yourself. We took him to the infirmary. The physician is with him."

Marcus got up and followed Bartholomew to the infirmary, and there was Brother Aidan, lying on his back, his eyes wild, and his hands flying up into the air as if to push away an unseen assailant. Marcus laid a hand on his forehead, which was hot with fever. "Aidan," he said, but there was no recognition in the eyes.

Marcus felt a spike of fear; his worries over Brother Aidan were never far from the surface. He had brought Aidan home to Ireland so Aidan could spend his last years with his own people, after the harrowing events he had experienced in England. Marcus felt that he had a sacred duty to watch over the beloved old man. Had Marcus failed to keep him safe?

"Dragged them up there, up to the Tor!" It was a cracked voice that emerged from the old man's throat.

"What do you mean, Aidan?" Marcus asked. He looked to Brother Dominic, the physician.

Dominic moved closer to the abbot and said, "I think this is a result of him seeing that man brought in with the wound. Colm the watchman. There was so much moaning and groaning out of him, and the blood seeping through his bandage, I think that's what is working on Aidan's mind. Violent thoughts, or memories, coming to him."

"Up the hill, put ropes around their necks," Aidan shouted. "Hanged them by their necks!"

Marcus turned then to Brother Bartholomew. "What is this? Has his mind gone back to—"

"He's been rambling on about Glastonbury Abbey, the abbot murdered there."

Marcus was aware of the outrage that had been perpetrated on the abbot of Glastonbury, that being Richard Whiting, and two other monks.

"Was Brother Aidan there when it happened?" Bartholomew asked.

"I believe he was. That was the story when he came back here to Fermanagh. He fled Glastonbury and joined another abbey and then, a couple of years later, it suffered the same fate. Plundered, destroyed, the way it was done to so many of our holy places." Aidan was still deeply affected by what he had witnessed. It nearly broke Marcus's heart to see him like this. He made the sign of the cross on Aidan's forehead; it was still burning hot. He began to pray over him, even as Aidan relived the butchery visited upon the men he had known.

"Ripping their bodies apart!" Aidan shouted. "Pulled the guts right out of them! The bodies God gave us for our earthly life, torn open by the king's savages. And the brothers' heads cut off them!"

Brother Dominic checked his heart and his breathing and assured Marcus that Aidan would recover, physically, from this episode.

⚇

Brigid heard someone knocking at the door and she went down to find Father Fiach O'Moylan standing there, looking none too well. There was a smell of ale coming off him. He was carrying a large rectangular bag made of calf skin.

"Fiach, welcome! Come in." They went upstairs, and she said, "Have something to eat, have a cup of something to drink."

"I'd take a cup of ale, Brigid."

"Certainly. We'll all have some."

Shane got up and offered to get the drinks. There were plates of oatcakes on the banquet table, and soon they were all seated with the cakes and tankards of ale before them. They made conversation about little things, avoiding the subject uppermost in their minds.

Then Fiach said, "There was someone else there."

Nobody pretended not to know where he meant, or when. "Tell us," Brigid said.

Fiach took a good, long swig from his tankard and said, "Of course, we all know someone else was there eventually and we know it was not you, Shane. I never believed it was. But I am saying there was someone hidden in the trees — as I was myself — whilst Sorcha was uttering her prophecies. I know this because of what she said."

"What was it?" Shane asked.

Fiach reached down, and from his bag, he drew out a small package wrapped in parchment and removed the wrapping. Inside were a few pages of vellum, and Brigid could see letters marking the surface of the top page.

"Are these . . . ?" Brigid began.

"The prophecies of Sorcha. 'I see the great harbour. I see a ship. And I see women weeping and sons and daughters left behind. Our men step off the land of Ireland for the last time. They climb aboard the ship and the ship sails out against the sky. And it carries our greatest men, the lords of Ireland, away to sea. And we are without defences. And they shall never, ever return.'"

Brigid felt chills running down her spine.

"If you could have seen her eyes!" Fiach said. "She looked as if she was seeing hell come to earth."

"Perhaps she was," muttered Shane.

"And then she said, 'And a lonely lamp burns in the castle for Cúchonnacht Óg.'"

"Cúchonnacht! But it's his brother Hugh who is the Maguire. If she saw our chieftains leaving . . ."

"I don't know, Shane. All I can do is tell you what she said, as best I can remember it. Then she said invaders would come and take the lands of Ulster from our own people. And, after that, 'A great heretic will come and claim that he is doing the work of God, and he will slaughter our warriors and our priests, our women and our innocents. And he will drive our people from our lands and out to the far ends of our island. And after many more years have passed, our people will starve on the land.'"

"They starved in my land," said Shane, "or died of the diseases that come with it, thousands of people in Munster. Children, mothers, fathers. I was riding by and saw a young woman lying dead at the edge of a field, and her little girl on top of her, silent. They looked like skeletons. I got down and lifted the girl. She may have been two years old. She was still alive, but barely. She felt like a little handful of sticks in my arms. I carried her on the horse with me; she gave out little cries like the mewling of a kitten. I brought her into the town to a woman I knew who would try to take care of her. She . . ." It was one of the rare times Brigid had ever seen Shane lost for words. He looked away and said in a quiet voice, "The little girl died two days later. And all of this was deliberate! The English, this was their plan! And now we have Sorcha saying it will happen again!"

"This heretic will have no success here, Fiach. Not as long as there are Irish warriors living and breathing in this country!"

"I know, Shane. I pray that our warriors will be able to alter the course of the future Sorcha foretold. Though without our chieftains—"

"They'd never leave," Shane declared with the confidence of one saying the sun would never fail to rise.

"'Our Holy Mass will be forbidden. Our sacraments will be given in secret, furtively, like sins. Our priests will be hunted down, expelled, or battered to death.'" Fiach looked up. "I've heard from the abbot and from poor old Brother Aidan what the queen's men do to their own people in England if they do not attest that the queen is the supreme authority of the Church as well as the country. I cannot bear to think what they would do to *us*, if they succeed in their efforts to overrun us!"

Brigid sat there, absorbing the terrifying prophecies. She felt as if she was staring into the mouth of hell.

"When I returned to the abbey, I wrote as if the furies were after me, trying to get all her words down on my pages."

The three of them sat in silence. Finally, Shane said, "The two of you knew Sorcha much longer than I did. She was known to be a wise woman, a seer. Do you know of prophecies that were fulfilled? Things that were out of the ordinary, not the regular occurrences that any of us might have predicted?"

"She could indeed predict future events," Fiach confirmed.

"Many times," said Brigid. "Only recently, she gave Domhnall the blacksmith a prediction of some kind. I saw him leaving her house looking as if he had stared death in the face. And it was not long after that that his brother and the brother's little boy were drowned in Lough Erne. And mind you the time little Nessa McElroy was lost? She'd wandered off, fallen, and injured herself. The McElroys didn't go to Sorcha to help find her; Sorcha called down to their house and told them she was lying in the forest, over a mile from their house. She had hurt her foot, but she would recover her health. And they found her exactly where Sorcha told them. Remember that? Those were only two of many instances of her foresight."

Sorcha's visions were never to be dismissed. Brigid did not want to follow the course of thought that suggested itself to her. But she could not shut out the thoughts once they were formed in her mind: that the prophecy of Ireland's leading men abandoning their people would, if believed, cause fear and unrest among the people, and suspicions that their leaders were not to be trusted. This could give rival factions all the encouragement they needed to make a move against the chieftains, bringing on yet another round of bloodshed and destruction. It was chilling to contemplate an increase in discord between the families when what was needed, more than ever before, was unity in the face of the English ambitions to rule the entire country. From the perspective of the great clans themselves, this prophecy would be such a slanderous accusation that it must not be repeated. And the only way to make sure of that would be to silence the visionary for all time.

Brigid looked at Shane and knew that he would have reached the same disturbing conclusions. But she knew that neither of them would give voice to the question: did someone from the Maguire castle kill Sorcha to ensure that the slander did not spread?

But this was not the end of it.

Fiach looked mortified. "There was one more thing she said, and I have told no one until now. She was speaking to the person hidden in the dark. I know this because she said 'your.' 'Your family is cursed and shall be cursed down the generations. All of this for your tangling in the family bed. If any child be born of your unnatural unions, he shall leave as your descendants a line of idiots and evil-doers until the end of time.'"

Shane's face reflected the revulsion Brigid felt hearing such a curse pronounced.

"But," said Shane, "we know all the families here. I have seen nothing like that in all my time in this part of Fermanagh. And I never heard anything about this from you, Brigid, and you have lived here all your life."

"There is no one of that sort here, no close family relations coming together in that manner. Not that I have ever seen or heard."

The priest looked even more distressed as he gave voice to

his thoughts. "I do not like to say this, but with just the three of us here I'll speak of it: could this be about one of the Maguires? Chieftains, leading families, it is no secret that men like that are able to have, well, a selection of ladies . . . and if one of them were a close relation . . ."

Shane was shaking his head, as was Brigid. She said, "Nothing like that with the Maguire men. And the very idea of one of them entering the room of a daughter or anything of that nature . . . and then committing a secret killing of Sorcha? That would never happen."

"And, of course," said Shane, "if we ever did think of someone and name that man, someone with improper relations within, well, within the family bed, whoever we name for sins like that we are also naming as a killer. Of Sorcha and maybe of Murrough. And it could be that same man who tried to kill Colm as well. That kind of accusation . . ."

"It doesn't bear thinking about," said Fiach. "If we were correct in our suspicions, any of us might be the next to feel the point of a sword or arrow. And if we were wrong, well, we might suffer the same fate. I am tempted, of course, to destroy these pages and try to forget I ever heard what I heard that night. But I think that would be wrong. I believe that Sorcha's prophecies, as dreadful as they are, should be preserved. No one can predict when I might want to bring them to light one day. Memories fade, and if someone is found for the murders, and there is another hearing on judgment day, it may be wise to have these documents to show what Sorcha foretold. What someone overheard. And there's another reason. I'm afraid that they might well come true, and if so, it should be noted that our prophetess was wise even beyond what we knew her to be. That sometime in a future none of us can foresee, she will be honoured for her wisdom and her ability to foretell what is to come. So, my hope is that they will be preserved, but not in the scriptorium or the dormitory of the abbey. Somewhere out of sight."

Brigid and Shane nodded in acquiescence.

"Because," Fiach said with a laugh in his voice, "it must be said that I do not want anyone finding such inflammatory material in my possession! I guess that makes me a coward."

Shane leapt to his defence. "You are being wise, not cowardly."

"What I have in mind," the priest said, "is to keep these pages securely wrapped in parchment and bury them. Do you remember some years ago the men digging a trench in an area of bog, and they found an old manuscript that had been lost there many generations before? They marvelled at the sight, and it was in fairly good condition. At least, at first. For some reason it deteriorated after they brought it out and took it around to show everyone. But my only interest here is getting it buried. Now here is where I become a supplicant. A mendicant friar, you might say!"

They laughed along with him, and he said, "There are too many eyes at Drumlyon. I do not want any of my brothers at the abbey to see me burying these scandalous documents, where they would be tempted to dig up what I have hidden. So, here is my request: would you allow me to find a secluded place on the property of your home and bury the pages here? I believe I could carry out this work and not be seen by anyone."

"I have no objection to that, Fiach," Brigid assured him. Shane immediately agreed and offered to assist him.

So, under cover of night, with the wind whipping their hair and clothing, and clouds scudding across the stars, Brigid stood with Shane and the priest as the two men cut into the earth with spade and pitchfork. Brigid kept a lookout as the secret work went on. They were in the boggiest part of the lands outside the guesthouse, and they dug and cut and threw the brown-black turf and the green stems of moss aside until they had a burial plot for the documents. Brigid made sure the pages were securely wrapped in the parchment, then lowered them into the ground. Shane and Fiach restored the plot as best they could, and to Brigid's eyes, there was nothing about the site that would catch the eye of anyone passing by. Nothing to alert anyone to the predictions of their dismal future buried beneath their feet.

CHAPTER XIV

Loss of our learning brought darkness, weakness, and woe
on me and mine, amid these unrighteous hordes.
Oafs have entered the places of the poets
and taken the light of the schools from everyone.

— Eoghan Rua Ó Súilleabháin, in *An Duanaire 1600–1900:*
Poems of the Dispossessed, presented by Seán Ó Tuama,
translated by Thomas Kinsella

Who sees these dismal Heaps, but would demand
What barbarous Invader sack'd the Land?
But when he hears, no Goth, no Turk did bring
This desolation, but a Christian King . . .

— Sir John Denham, "Coopers-Hill"

O ver at the abbey, the gravediggers had done their work, and the wet, muddy ground was open to receive the body of Murrough the pikeman. Two of his fellow soldiers carried the shrouded body and lowered it into its final resting place, as his parents, sisters, and brother looked on, silent in their grief.

Marcus the abbot and his priests and brothers stood around the grave, chanting their prayers, as their habits and scapulars dripped from the grey mist hanging over the graveyard. When Murrough was finally commended to his Lord, the gravediggers stepped forward with their shovels and cast the dirt down upon him, until he was buried six feet below.

Earlier that morning, before the funeral, Marcus and Brother Aidan and some others were in the refectory for their morning meal. Fiach came in and greeted them, and took modest servings of the milk and curds, bread and porridge that constituted the meal.

"A sad day for the castle," Aidan remarked. The others nodded their agreement.

Marcus noted the steadiness of the old monk's voice and of his hands. It was a relief to see him in better form now.

"To lose a warrior," Aidan was saying, "and him not a victim of a skirmish but of murder, it would put tears of grief on you."

"It would," a couple of the monks agreed.

"And the other man, the fellow who was wounded, where is he now? He was in the infirmary and now there he is — gone!"

"Oh, is that so?" Marcus asked. "Our physician must have declared him fit and ready to leave his sick bed. That is good news."

"Good news indeed, and our chieftain's brother so fond of him, the watchman. When I saw them they were deep in conversation. Out for a walk in the wood, they must have been. A man of the people is Cúchonnacht Maguire to give his time and attention to a lowly watchman."

Fiach said, "But that wasn't Cúchonnacht you'd have seen with the watchman that time, Brother Aidan. I remember you saying the man with Colm had a crooked arm. It wasn't Cúchonnacht who injured his arm."

"Ah, I had it wrong then. But there was a resemblance there. Another member of the family perhaps."

"Another branch of the family, the Maguires in Magheraste-phena. It was Connor Óg Maguire who had the injured arm. Son of Connor Roe, the son also called Connor Roe. But there's another name that's been put on the son. They call him the 'English Maguire.'"

"The English Maguire! I don't like the sound of that."

"And well you shouldn't. He's allied with the English forces here, and against the Maguires of Enniskillen Castle."

"Do you tell me so?!" The old monk appeared ready to take up a sword and go off to fight.

"I do. And I'm asking myself what a watchman from the castle would be doing with the English Maguire, off in the wood with him."

"I tell you, Fiach, they looked as if they had serious matters to discuss. I saw Colm the watchman looking about him as if he was afraid someone might come upon them."

Marcus put this down to the old man's active imagination; there had been no word of this furtiveness when Aidan was in the infirmary and first mentioned the meeting. Of course, he would not likely have mentioned that when he was talking to Cúchonnacht Maguire, thinking at the time that it was Cúchonnacht he had seen with the watchman.

"No Irishman should have any business taking up with the Saxons! If you had seen what I saw in England, what the English did to their own people! What, then, would they do to *us*? Well, I'll tell you. I saw this with my own two eyes!" Aidan thrust himself forward at the table, his meal forgotten. And he had the full attention of the other men around him; they leaned forward to hear what the old brother had to say.

"How well I remember the day they came to our abbey in England. I was vain about my work that day. Was I guilty of the sin of pride? I believe so. Young and proud. But I was transcribing Paul's letter to the Corinthians, and in one of the verses Paul refers to a pipe and a harp. I knew a bit of decoration was called for there. What would please God more than the image of the harp of Brian Boru, the Ard Rí, the high king of Ireland? Brian was a highly educated man, who studied Julius Caesar, studied Xenophon, Brian being a thinker and a soldier. Anyway, on that day I began to paint the harp, ever so delicately, in gold. The shining golden harp in the strong white hands of Brian. A fitting tribute to our ancient king, dead for all these ages. And a fitting tribute, of course, to the great Apostle Paul.

"I had been working on that manuscript for two years. Surely it is no sin to admire the beauty of the manuscripts, the brilliant colours on the vellum, put there over the long years by myself and our brothers in the abbeys. So, there I was one evening, singing the office of Compline with the other monks. Oh, our voices had never been more beautiful. There's that vanity again. The evening light shone in on us through the coloured glass of our windows. As we began to sing in unison, Marcus, I felt as if I had transcended the stone of the abbey, the chanting of my brothers, the good green fields outside, and had risen to the heavens. After the other monks departed, I stayed behind, still entranced. It was as if, at last, I would see no more through a glass darkly, but be face to face with the loving—

"But then I heard the sound of horses. A clatter of hoofs, the rude shouts of men, the clanging of metal. What was happening? Before I could compose my thoughts, a clump of men burst into the abbey. I, a coward, hid myself in the shadows just inside the chapel door. We all knew of monks who had been hanged by the king's men. The king being the eighth Henry of England. This was the monks' punishment for *treason*, which was simply remaining true to the Church of Rome! The very Church the king himself had been defending — Pope Leo X had bestowed on him the title 'Defender of the Faith' — but he tossed all that aside when he got the urge to exchange his marriage bed for another.

"What I saw next was nearly as atrocious as the foul murders of my brothers. One of the bandits — again, agents of the king — one of these destroyers grabbed the golden chalice from the tabernacle and secreted it inside his clothing. Another snatched the monstrance with the Holy Sacrament inside and banged it against the stone wall so the sacred host fell out. The sacrilege against the host was unforgivable. Then he stole the monstrance. But theft was a small thing beside the destruction that came next. I saw the unholy mob raise their axes and swords and smash the beautiful Saint Aldhelm window into splinters. They roared with laughter as they stomped on the fragments. They went at all the coloured glass windows. Pulverized them. The light flashed off the splinters as they flew, and the cracking sound was so loud it pained my ears. Suddenly, after all the ages that had passed, these images were 'idolatrous'! And these barbarous louts went all through the abbey. I crept along in the shadows behind them. They went into the scriptorium. I knew that my lovely manuscript was the only one in there that day. And one of the oafs came out again with a manuscript — mine, that was, the Word of God, the work of my own two years, the bright illustrations, my lovely king's harp. And do you know what that barbarian did with it? He used the precious thing to wipe the muck from his boots! And then he proceeded to rip it to shreds. That took the heart right out of me."

The old man had a haunted look about him, as if he had lived through the whole, ghastly event all over again. The other monks were horrified at the tale.

"And, of course, they came back and tore off our roof to present the lead metal to their greedy king for its value. And came back again with torches and set our abbey on fire. What kind of hellhounds would do such a thing?"

It was time to leave the refectory and prepare for the funeral, but Marcus's mind was not on the day's events. In his own time in England, he had seen the crumbling ruins of once-magnificent houses of God. Some of the greatest feats of architects and builders were now nothing but gaping horrors. Steeples and pinnacles, arches and walls, were now jagged spears of stone pointing upwards at the empty sky. Henry and Edward's new *civilization* was built upon the destruction of their country's past. It was the Sack of Rome all over again.

As he vested for the funeral, he asked himself how many people had suffered hideous deaths under the monarchs of England. Marcus knew that Queen Mary was responsible for many deaths herself during the five years of her reign, as she tried to restore the Catholic faith in England; there was no denying the murders orchestrated by "Bloody Mary." But how many people had been slaughtered during the thirty-seven years of Henry VIII, a man who had caused two of his six wives to be beheaded? Some said many thousands had been put to death during his reign. And what about the current queen, now persecuting the Irish with such grim determination? How many people had "Good Queen Bess" caused to be executed?

There wasn't room in the abbey church to hold all the people who had come to mourn the fallen soldier, a soldier who had died not in battle but at the hands of a murderer. The Maguires, of course, along with Murrough's family, had pride of place in the front of the church. Many others stood outside in the cloister under lowering skies. Among those arriving early enough for a place inside were Brigid Tierney and Shane O'Callaghan. A couple of times during the funeral Mass, Marcus noticed O'Callaghan casting his eyes around at the mourners. The dead man, after all, had given false testimony against O'Callaghan. And someone else had killed him. Did O'Callaghan now hope to see suspicious behaviour, or a guilty look in the eyes of one or more in the crowd?

After the funeral and burial, when the brothers were back inside the abbey, Aidan came up to Marcus and put a hand on his arm to draw him aside. The hand was shaking.

"That man has me wondering."

"Whom do you mean, Aidan?"

"Colm the watchman. I didn't see him in the church, and him well enough to get up on the two legs God gave him and walk out of our infirmary! What was he up to? Was he in league with the English against us? Is he still?"

"Now, Aidan, you can't draw any conclusions just from seeing two men talking."

"But they shouldn't have been talking at all! I'm of a mind to go there."

"Go where?"

"To the English Maguire." He laughed then, and said in a whisper, "To spy on him!"

"Aidan, settle down now. It's nearly time for Sext. The prayers will calm you."

"You may be right, Father Abbot." He smiled then. "Or the Lord may have other plans for me."

Marcus was kept busy for the rest of the day and evening, and he noticed that Aidan appeared for the afternoon prayers but was not present later on for Vespers. As soon as the service concluded, Marcus went to the dormitory. Aidan wasn't there. Marcus told himself not to be alarmed; he would look around the abbey for the restless old brother and would no doubt find him bending the ear of one of the other monks about the English Maguire, the funeral, or whatever else might be occupying his thoughts this evening. And in fact he found him in the scriptorium, holding up a manuscript and peering at it in the candlelight. Another of his monks writing in the night; Marcus wondered if he should declare the scriptorium off limits at nighttime, but immediately rejected the thought. Whenever a man was inspired to write, he should write. It was not as if eerie prophecies were going to be the subject of their work every night!

"Good evening, Aidan."

"Good evening, Abbot. See what I've done here." He pointed to his piece of vellum. "These are people I knew in England, the Crawford family, a man and wife and their four children." Marcus saw the family drawn with long faces and mouths gaping open, eyes wide with horror. They were dressed in rags. "They were among the many who were left paupers when the churches and monasteries were shut down." The old man's eyes blazed at Marcus. "We must resist the Saxons and their determination to conquer this country!"

"The chiefs of clans, the warriors here, are doing their best to prevent that, Brother Aidan."

"I should be at their side, not sitting on my arse here in the abbey."

⁂

Brigid had a crowd from Armagh as guests the day after Murrough's funeral, and the evening turned into a céilí. One of the men was a piper, and he opened with a couple of laments. Once again, it struck Brigid what a plaintive sound it was when a lament was played on the pipes. Shane announced to the visitors then that Brigid was not only the best-loved hospitaller in this part of Fermanagh, but a talented harper as well, and the guests demanded that she play for them. This being so soon after the pikeman's funeral, she played a few laments, and the guests caught the mood and were solemn. Brigid, too, felt the solemnity and gave thanks to God for the gift of her music, thanks that she could bring this feeling to life through the strings of her instrument.

But then it was time for livelier tunes, and she started those and the piper joined in. And that got everyone up dancing, including Eileen and Owny and the other children in the party. Brigid's own mood lifted with the tempo of her playing. Father Fiach O'Moylan was visiting as well, and he had a fine set of feet for the dancing, so he and Shane had the women guests up and stepping lightly all over the floor. The bright colours of the swirling dresses, the rich tapestries on the walls, the warm golden light of the candles, it all made Brigid thankful yet again that her family was, by long tradition, able to provide such enjoyable accommodation for any travellers who stopped by.

When it was time for a rest and a drink, Shane poured Spanish wine into the goblets, and stood up and gave them all a story about his boyhood in Cork. "I fancied myself a poet in those days. Well, I still do. But as a young lad, I knew about the claim that a poet could 'rhyme to death' both men and animals. Rats were said to be particularly susceptible. I always liked to roam the quays when I was young, and I came upon a ship and heard that rats were annoying the sailors day and night. So I came up with a plan. I obtained — I stole — a block of cheese and hid it on the shore, and in time the rats sniffed it out. When I saw this, I stood

tall and straight on the quay and recited a brilliant poem that
I composed on the spot. And the sailors saw the rats scurrying
from the ship and gave me a silver coin! A silver coin was a rare
sight, as I'm sure you know. And I was the toast of the crew of
that ship. Until the cheese was gone. And the rats were running
back towards the ship, and the crew were running up towards me
to get their coin back, and I turned and got my arse out of there
just in time!"

Brigid couldn't miss the admiring glances that rested on her
man, and when he finished, to great applause, she herself got
up to speak. Emboldened perhaps by the wine, she recited a
poem she had learned in the past. Learned in the past, fitting for
tonight. "I'll give to you a poem called 'A Glance.'

> Black of brow, with cheeks aglow,
> blue of eye, with hair so smooth,
> wind rowing through your parted locks —
> fine women at the fair are watching!
>
> Wives, pretending not to look,
> plait their hair in front of you.
> With fingers through her lovely hair
> one of them is studying you."

The recital was well received. Brigid sat down, smiling, and
took up her goblet again. Fiach O'Moylan rose to thank Brigid
and Shane for their recitals and for their hospitality. "I pray to the
Almighty God that such gatherings as this continue for all our
lives and those of our children — and I do have children myself! —
and for all the descendants of our loins! Remember all of ye,
that the Saxon passed laws to stop the adoption of our customs

and laws by those English, those Normans, who landed on our shores four hundred years ago. The kings and queens of England have not been pleased with how well those settlers have blended in with us Irish and taken up our language, intermarried with us, and have become some of our most faithful neighbours. So, to prevent the old English from becoming any more Irish, they passed laws in a so-called *parliament* at Kilkenny. They made it unlawful for our English neighbours to speak our language; in fact, I believe the laws stated that we Irishmen ourselves could not use our own language when talking to the English! The English could not sell us a horse in time of war or peace, nor food in time of war. That was considered treason. Marriage between Irish and English or Anglo-Normans was forbidden, and Irish names for children were forbidden as well. The law even stated that a man — at least a man of the better sort, with a certain value in lands — must ride a horse with a saddle in the English fashion! No bareback riding. I hear they even took offence to 'our' women looking to the right when they are sitting on a horse behind a man, whilst the English women look to the left!" This met with great merriment, and Fiach bowed to acknowledge the crowd's response.

"*And*," said Shane, rising to his feet, "the English were not permitted to have any enjoyment of the kind we are having here tonight; they were not allowed any contact with Irish pipers, story-tellers, rhymers, or babblers! Because we're all a crowd of spies!"

"Rhyme on, O'Callaghan!" someone shouted. "Babble away!"

"Here in Ulster we are Irishmen! The same cannot be said for many other parts of our country, such as Dublin and Galway, and some of you have seen the vain parade of English fashions, even on our own people. And so I quote lines from a poem I heard in my wanderings:

These fashions on the plain of Éibhear make me sick —
beggarwomen's sons with curling locks,
white cuffs around their wrists, and fancy rings,
like Ireland's one-time princes of Dál gCais,

Slaveys and their sons starched to the chin,
garters upon them and their scarves thrown back,
tobacco pipe in jaw, at full blow,
and bracelets on their claws at every joint.

A trick of this false world has laid me low:
servants in every home with grimy English
but no regard for one of the poet class
save 'Out! and take your precious Gaelic with you!'"

The poem brought on roars of delight but also "Go dtachtadh
an diabhal iad!" May the devil choke them! That was just one of
several curses directed at those who would eject the poet and his
Irish tongue from society.

The piper spoke up then and asked Shane, "What kind of
pipe was it the men in the poem had in imitation of the English?"

"Ah now, it wasn't a musical pipe at all. There's some sort of
leaf they brought back from one of their far colonies a few short
years ago, and they say a man rolls up these leaves in a pipe, sets
them aflame, puts the pipe to his mouth, and breathes in the
smoke." This improbable picture was met with mocking laughter.
"I've never seen it myself."

"Wouldn't I love to see the idiot with his face on fire!"

Others in the crowd gave suggestions as to what they would
like to see befall the fire-breathing fop, and then someone began
a long and lonesome song. Brigid looked around the room and

noticed that the old monk from Drumlyon had come in. He was sitting near the back of the hall with a cup in his hand. Good, Shane had seen him arrive and poured ale into his cup. Brigid walked over to greet him.

"Good evening, Brother Aidan. Welcome!"

"Good evening, Brigid. This is a fine gathering, and there was some fine poetry being recited when I came in. And well we should mock those who have no regard for our poet class or our ancient language! Were we not the first people in this part of the world to have a written language, us after the Greeks and the Romans?"

"Don't be sitting here by yourself now, Aidan. You'll come and join us." She took him by the hand and was surprised at how agile he was in his walking. He brought his cup and joined Shane and Fiach at their table.

"How did you get yourself here, Aidan?" Fiach asked him. "If I'd known you were coming, I'd have ridden over to collect you."

"I've been walking much of the day, Fiach, stopping to eat some fruit from the trees and then bathing in a lovely rain pool to get the heat off me. Your lovely house was my destination, Brigid, because I have something to ask of you. Wasn't I fortunate to arrive in the midst of such a celebration here!"

"And we are fortunate that you are here with us." On a side table were chewits, pies containing meat and fruit, and Brigid walked over and put a couple on a plate for her latest guest. His eyes lit up and he said a quick prayer of thanks before enjoying the meal. "Ah, these are lovely! And now, Brigid, I must get on to the reason for my visit. And there's no getting around the fact that I am begging a kindness from you if you might be kindly disposed to grant it." He looked all around him before leaning towards them and saying, "I would like to go to Magherastephena!"

Shane looked at him, startled. And Fiach said, "Aidan! Why are you wanting to go there?"

"To spend some time in Killygullan Monastery."

"What put this in your mind?"

"I'll tell you." The old monk leaned in even closer, an intense look in his light-green eyes, and said, "I don't like what I've been hearing about that place! Not the monastery, but the area around there, the men and the master they serve."

"That branch of the family has its eyes turned to the east," said Shane.

"The English Maguire! And those who ally themselves with him."

"What is it you hope to do there, Aidan?" That was Fiach.

"Accept the hospitality of the monastery and go about spreading the word. I'll be telling the people there about the destruction the English will bring, and their cruel laws and punishments, so the men will turn away from their errors and fight with, not against, the Gaelic lords of Ireland."

Shane's expression was one of disbelief, Fiach's of pity. The priest said, "Aidan, they'll not listen to you. Don't go ahead with this plan."

"They'll hang you," said Shane.

"Shane!" Brigid was shocked at the brutal words. She turned to Aidan then and said, "No good can come of this, Aidan. Why don't you stay with us for a few days instead, and we'll—"

"I have set my course. I am going. And this is where I come back to the favour I have to ask of you. More than one favour. Would your horseboy or one of your other men be able to take me there? And may I have your word that you will not tell Father Abbot where I have gone?"

Fiach's answer was immediate. "I cannot lie to the abbot, Aidan."

Nor would Brigid want to lie to the abbot. If Aidan carried through with this outrageous plan, what could she say when next she saw Father Marcus? She could not imagine herself pretending she hadn't seen Aidan, saying she had no idea where he might be.

No one had a solution. The merriment and singing went on around them. Fiach was deep in thought. Then he said, "I shall arrange transportation for you and I'll come along for the journey, to see you safely arrived at Killygullan. Then, when I return to Drumlyon, I'll confess all to Father Marcus. Well, not all. I'll tell him you got it into your head to see how some of our other monastic communities are faring, that I could not dissuade you" — everyone smiled at that, including Aidan — "and so I left you there for a few days of contemplation and rest."

It was clear from his expression that Shane O'Callaghan did not see anything good coming out of the elderly monk's mission to the misguided souls of Magherastephena.

CHAPTER XV

We have thought good by this to acquaint your Lordships with the present condition of Connor Roe Maguire, and with our purpose to make use of him for Her Majesty's service, as well in Fermanagh as in other Irish countries.

— The Lord Deputy Mountjoy to the Privy Council, *Calendar of the State Papers Relating to Ireland, during the Reigns of Henry VIII, Edward VI, Mary, and Elizabeth*

Morrison makes some curious remarks, showing the estimation in which the lives of the mere Irish were held, and it appears it was considered that the more of these miserable mercenaries fell the better. In giving an account of some Irish soldiers who were killed in Mountjoy's expedition to Ulster, in 1600, he says, "the death of these unpeaceable swordsmen, though falling on our side, yet was rather a gain than loss to the commonwealth." . . . again, in reference to 50 of the Irish kerns, in the queen's service, who were killed in a conflict at the fort of Lisgannon, he says, "and 50 of our side were slain, but we cannot learn that any

*English were among them, so we account our loss to
be no more than the taking of Captain Esmond, who
was with them.*"

— trans. Owen Connellan, *Annals of the Four Masters*

M arcus was not at all pleased when Fiach had come to
him the week before and told him he had, without even
seeking, let alone obtaining, Marcus's permission, travelled with
Brother Aidan to Killygullan Monastery in Magherastephena,
ten or twelve miles from the abbey, and left him there. Why,
if Aidan was hoping to broaden his spiritual horizons, had he
not come to Marcus for guidance? Was the old man dissatisfied
with Drumlyon Abbey? With Marcus as abbot? Was his mind
wandering as his legs were wont to do? Or was it simply that,
home at last from England, he wanted to see as much of his
beloved land as he could in the time left to him?

But those ruminations were swept aside a week later when
a monk from the Killygullan Monastery arrived at Drumlyon
with a pale, weak-looking Aidan leaning on him for support. The
abbey's groom had tied up their horse, and the monks entered
the abbey.

"Dia anseo isteach," said Aidan's companion as he entered the
abbey. He hastily introduced himself as Brother Petrus and then
ceded the conversation to the two Cistercians.

"Aidan, what happened to you?"

Aidan pointed to his right side and said, "A man came out of
the woods at me, and fired an arrow into me, readied himself to
fire another, and then he heard horses and he fled!"

"Did they treat your wound at Killygullan?"

"We did, Father Abbot," Brother Petrus said. "Our physician treated and dressed it. Brother Aidan lost much blood, and was weak and in pain, but we are told he will recover, thanks be to God."

"We'll get him into the infirmary, and inform our physician here."

Aidan draped an arm over the shoulder of each of the two men, and they took him into the infirmary. Marcus left to fetch Brother Dominic, who came immediately and undressed the injured man and examined the wound. It was at the outer edge of the right flank and looked painful, but had not affected any vital areas of the body.

Marcus and Petrus left Aidan in expert hands and walked to the church in order to pray for him. Marcus offered the visitor a meal, a drink, and a bed for however long he would like one.

"I'll stay this one night, Father Abbot, and then be on my way."

"What did he say about the man who did this?"

"He wouldn't say anything about him. Only said he didn't know who it was. But I know this much: before this injury, age had not slowed Brother Aidan down. He was out more often than he was in. He'd say his morning prayers with us, have his morning meal, and then he'd be off. He had me concerned so I followed after him one day. I saw him making his way towards the Maguire stronghold there. I caught him up and made no secret of my interest in what he was doing. And he told me about his time in England, about the destruction and plunder, the people hanged, drawn and quartered, and he got himself all worked up — who wouldn't be worked up over such horrors? — and he said he wanted to meet with 'the English Maguire' and do what? Warn him, plead with him to change his allegiance? I don't think Aidan was clear himself. But on one of those days out, he met with this misfortune. This attempt on his life."

"He offended the men of Magherastephena so grievously with his talk that they tried to kill him?"

"I don't know, Father, but I do not think that is very likely. An old man like that in the habit of a monk. It's difficult to imagine that they'd think of him as a threat to them."

"Well, somebody did."

⊛

Later that day, when Marcus had one of the other monks showing Brother Petrus around Drumlyon, Marcus went to the infirmary to see Aidan. In contrast to his usual cheerful and restless ways, he was subdued. Frightened. As well he might be after a close call with death. Marcus said a prayer over him and then asked how he was feeling.

"The wound is painful, but it will get better. I hope and pray the fear goes away, so I won't be cowering in here like a frightened rabbit."

"It's no wonder you're afraid, Aidan, after what happened. But you're safe in here."

"Do you say so?"

"Of course I do."

"The man who tried to kill me knows he did not succeed. There were horses coming; he heard them and he took his bow and arrows and fled back into the woods. I want you to get the aigne for me. What is his name, that lawyer?"

"Do you mean Terence Blake?"

"I do. I want him to find the man who attacked me and bring him to law."

238

"I shall send a message to him for you. Now, where were you when this happened? What woods?"

"Not far from the stronghold of Connor Roe the younger, Connor Óg."

Marcus restrained himself from asking what Aidan thought he could accomplish at the home of the Magherastephena Maguires. In a way, he had his answer. Instead, he asked, "Who do you think it was who tried to kill you?"

Aidan's wary green eyes surveyed the room, as if there might be a spy concealed in the shadows. "I don't know him. Don't know his name. I saw him only for a quick, fleeting moment. But I can tell you this: his face was familiar."

"How could that be, Aidan? That place is miles away. You wouldn't know anyone there."

"I don't know his name. I don't know anyone there. But I know I have seen that man here in these parts."

❧

Terence Blake visited the abbey and listened to Brother Aidan's story. The old monk was in pain, but that did not stop him from talking, and repeating over and over the events of the ill-starred trip to Magherastephena. All he could say about the man who shot him was that he had seen him in this part of Fermanagh.

"Did you, em, have many conversations with the men there?" Terence asked him. "Did you perhaps give out to the people you saw there, offering your opinions on the various branches of the Maguire clan?" In other words, did he make it almost inevitable that someone would string a bow and shoot an arrow into him?

Aidan's reply did not quite address the question. "I spoke to a few people I met there but never got to the home of the Maguires."

Terence knew there was no point in tiring the old man out with more questioning. He wished Aidan well, and assured him that he would do his best to find the aggressor, then went away with many questions in his mind. The man who had shot an arrow at Brother Aidan was a man who had been seen here. Did that man happen to see Aidan on the lands of the English Maguire and form the motive right then and there to kill him? Why? There is a monastery in Magherastephena, and Aidan is a monk; why could he not be in the area? But the grounds of the Maguire stronghold would be something else. Aidan was known to go off on rambles of his own. Did the man recognize Aidan but not know that about him? What was the shooter doing there himself? Did he suspect that Aidan was there to confront Connor Óg Maguire about his alliance with the invaders? Or had the man known in advance that the monk would be going there? Had somebody told him of Aidan's plan? If so, there was more than one man behind this attempt at killing.

If Aidan had seen his assailant in this area, had anyone else noticed an unfamiliar face? Terence questioned the monks at Drumlyon Abbey, but none of them remembered seeing a stranger around the abbey or the lands nearby. Once more, in service of a client, Terence presented himself at the alehouse. But there again, he came away with nothing. Nothing but a stomach full of ale. So, the following morning, he went to the home of Brigid Tierney. She knew just about everyone who lived in the area, and many who visited from other places. Perhaps there would be no one who could help him there, any more than there had been at the abbey or the alehouse, but he would give it a try.

A maid spotted him at the door and brought him in and up the stairs. In the main hall he found Brigid, her brother Diarmait, Shane O'Callaghan, and the two children. They all greeted him, and Brigid asked him, "Wine or ale or whiskey, Terence?"

"Ah now, a glass of wine would be nice."

She went for the wine and came back with a goblet brimming with the fine red liquid.

"Thank you."

"Perhaps you can assist us here, Terence," said Shane. "*Again*, I mean. Your assistance to me recently was most heartily appreciated. We have two little ones here who are learning their Roman history. And today's lesson is about Cicero. A great statesman, orator, and, like yourself, a lawyer. Who would not want to learn about him?"

"Who indeed?"

"Well, as difficult as it is to believe, there is a young boy in this room who does not seem concerned about his class at school and is not inclined to commit to memory the first of Cicero's great Catiline orations." He looked at his son, and said in mock frustration, "O tempore! O mores! At the same time, we have a young girl who can recite the words of Cicero in perfect Latin and appears to take great enjoyment in doing so."

Terence looked at the little girl and saw her face blush a bright pink.

Her brother Owny delivered himself of an oration then. "Eileen doesn't have to go to school, so she thinks it's entertaining to memorize all these words and make the speeches of all those old men who stood around arguing and talking into the wind."

Shane spoke up again, this time in verse. "I cannot claim to be the author of this poem but it fits the occasion:

Every morning, my young lad,
pray guidance from the Trinity.
Wash well, and take your book
in clean hands without a mark.

Study each line clearly, wisely,
get things often off by heart
— a short lesson, a sharp mind.
Study every word, my child.

Don't stare around at everyone.
Attend to your assigned work.
Root it deeply in your head.
Stay at it, though the fight is hard."

Everyone but Owny was appreciative of the recital. The young lad compressed his lips together and said, "I know all about the Romans. I want to dress like a centurion and wear his helmet and carry a gladius! That's his double-edged sword, and I'll frighten away all the foreigners or run them through with my gladius! Nobody told them they had to talk or sit and write things down."

"Cicero *was* a soldier," Eileen said, "but then he studied the law and he liked that better."

"He defended a man who was accused of killing his own father, and Cicero won for the man." Young Owny pleaded his own case. "I know all that. He lived from 106 to 43 BC. I was listening to Father Valerius in the class."

"Very good, Owny," his mother said.

"Perhaps there is hope here after all, Terence," said Shane. "Now, what can we do for you?"

"As you may have heard, one of the brothers at the abbey was attacked during a visit to Magherastephena. He was staying at the monastery. He went out for a walk, as he often does, and a man shot him with an arrow. The wound was not serious, but the intent was all too serious."

Diarmait, whom Terence knew to be one of Hugh Maguire's musketeers, said, "We'll not let them get away with this. What did he say the man looked like? We know some of the men from Magherastephena." He looked over at Shane. "And if we know who he is, we'll be after him with our muskets. We won't waste our time with arrows. A belly full of lead is what that fellow has coming to him if we find him."

"That's right," Shane agreed. "Between the two of us, there won't be a patch of skin on his body that won't be full of holes."

"I'm coming with you," Owny declared.

Terence laughed. "Well, I've come to the right place to find people sympathetic to my client. But I'm more in mind of a court than a revenge killing. Find the man who did it, have him acknowledge his deed, and pay the fine and the honour price. And no more spilling of blood."

"If we had a description," Shane said, "we could get some men together and go look for him."

"Shane," Brigid asked, "how would you ever know you had the right man?"

"I suppose we could tie him up and bring him to the abbey here. Get Brother Aidan to have a look at him."

"I suppose," Terence replied, "but here is the strange thing about it. Aidan said he had caught sight of the man in the lands around us here."

This brought stunned looks to all their faces.

"Is he saying," asked Diarmait, "that the man is from here, lives here? If so, how can he not know who he is? Or is he saying the man is a stranger who appeared in these parts?"

"Just that he has seen him here."

"So," said Shane, "the would-be assassin is still out there, and now we learn he is from this area, or at least has been here. If the man is intent on killing him, the brother won't be safe until we hunt down the attacker."

"You must keep the poor monk within the walls of the abbey," Diarmait said, "until the danger is past. Shane, we have work to do here!"

❀

Shane arranged for several of his fellow musketeers and marksmen to come to the Tierney house the day after Terence Blake had come by on behalf of Brother Aidan. Brigid smiled at the group of able-bodied men sitting at her tables with plates of honey cake and cups of ale. Some had their muskets with them.

"If ever I wanted to raise an army and wage a battle against an enemy of my family," one man said, "this would be the time to do it!"

"Only say the word," Diarmait replied, "and we are at your service! Now, I want to thank you for coming here today. Shane would have told you what we are hoping to do."

"I told them that one of the monks was wounded by an arrow and that Terence Blake is acting on his behalf. And that we are looking for any information we can get, which might lead to the man who did this. And now I shall tell you a bit more about the shooting, which is not very much, I'm sorry to say. Brother Aidan had taken a notion to travel to Magherastephena. One reason he gave for the journey was to spend some time in the monastery there, called Killygullan. The other reason would be obvious to anyone who has met Aidan on his wanderings, or heard the slew of words he emits on the subject of the Saxon invader. And the Saxons' allies among the Maguires of Magherastephena."

"Don't be telling us he went off there to confront Connor Óg Maguire!" one of the soldiers exclaimed. "Little wonder someone took a shot at him."

"That may be what he intended to do. From what Terence told us, though, it seems he did a bit of gabbling with people there but not with the leading family."

"Gabbling in the wrong places, in the wrong ears."

"Perhaps so. Now what he claims is that a man standing in the wood took aim and shot at him and then was frightened off by the approach of horses. It was only a brief glimpse he had but he said he recognized the fellow's face. Can't put a name to him, but he's someone Aidan had seen *here*."

"A man from here, standing in the trees in Magherastephena, trying to kill one of our monks?! That makes little sense to me."

"I understand. But it may not have been one of our people; it may have been one of theirs, sneaking around here for some reason. We don't know. Has any one of you seen a stranger lurking about the place here?"

There was some laughter at this, and one of the musketeers said, "If I'd seen such a fellow, he'd have been in no condition to go back to Magherastephena and take a shot at a poor old wandering monk."

"I'm sure of that!"

"And," the man continued, "the same goes for whoever got hold of Murrough the pikeman and ran him through with a sword. And attempted to kill Colm the lookout. Have you heard anything that would put us on the trail of whoever struck out at those friends of ours? We'd be willing to expend some lead in their direction whenever they are found."

"I know. I haven't heard anything that would make any sense of those attacks."

In the end, nobody had any information or suggestions to offer. It was the same the following day when Shane brought together another group of Hugh Maguire's soldiers, these being pikemen and also some kerns who carried swords and arrows or darts (feathered spears) as their weaponry. Their reactions were much like those of the musketeers. They, too, were much more concerned with the attempt on the watchman and the murder of their fellow warrior, and there was nothing anyone could offer in relation to those offences either. Shane and Brigid were none the wiser when they departed.

And they were still none the wiser about whoever had committed the unacknowledged and secret killing of Sorcha the physician and seer.

☙

Terence had just said goodbye to a man, Síoda, who had allowed his neighbour to take his supply of malt for beer making, on the understanding that the malt would be replaced well in time for a feast Síoda was planning to host. But the neighbour had not replaced the malt in time, which resulted in great embarrassment to Síoda, who had failed in his duty to provide hospitality. Terence had secured payment of Síoda's honour price, and the matter was put to rest, with Terence receiving his customary one-third of the award. After that, he had a client who needed nothing more than reassurance. He was a man with an extensive property and a large herd of cattle. One of his cows had escaped the enclosure and trampled on his neighbour's field, destroying some of the crop and setting his animals running about in panic. The client described the way his cow had been behaving lately, strange and wild-eyed and easily startled. Terence reassured the cattle owner that the law was on his side, that there is no fine or compensation payable by the owner of "a bovine which has parted from its sense." The man thanked Terence and walked away, relieved.

It had been raining steadily for hours but now the sun had made an appearance. Terence was considering going outside for a short walk. But before he could start off, Aoife came upstairs and told him he had a visitor. Terence got up to see that it was Diarmait Tierney. They greeted one another, and Diarmait said, "I'm only just back from Magherastephena, and that is where you'll have to go to find out who tried to kill the old man."

"Come in, Diarmait, and tell me what you learned." He signalled to his guest to have a seat while he poured out two cups of ale.

When they were seated across from one another, Diarmait said, "I met with a man there. What I'm telling you, Terence, cannot be spoken about anywhere. No one besides the two of us must know."

"What are you saying, Diarmait? Whoever committed this offence will be brought before the brehon on judgment day, and—"

"There will be no judgment day for this."

"It is not for us to set aside the law and procedure that we have been living by since the ancient times."

"I'll explain it all to you, and you'll understand. There is a man in Magherastephena who is working against his own people, working for us and against the English Maguire."

"Oh! A spy, you mean."

"A spy."

"Has this man been, however one would say it, reporting to you? Telling you about the activities and plans of Connor Óg Maguire?"

Diarmait laughed. "He does not report to me. This is far above my head! But I've been let in on it, on the secret, and I'm no cowardly little hare, but this has me terrified. That I might blunder somehow and destroy the trust this man, this spy, has in the men of Enniskillen. It cannot be spoken of in low or high places."

In the marketplace, the alehouse, or the castle, Terence said to himself. He could well understand why no one was to breathe a word of it.

"But," Diarmait said, "I can take you to meet this fellow, and he will tell you what he knows about the shooting of Aidan the monk."

"Why would he speak to me if his dealings with us are so secret?"

Diarmait smiled. "Because he knows that we know. And he does not want to disappoint or anger us, which might upset the delicate position he is in."

And that is how it came about that Terence Blake and one of Hugh Maguire's musketeers rode along the muddy and barely passable trails through the woods to Magherastephena and waited in the shadows for the man who was betraying the English Maguire to Maguire's cousins in Enniskillen Castle.

Along the way, Terence had caught glimpses of Sgiath Gabhra, the hill which had been the inauguration mound for the Maguire chieftains for three hundred years. Hugh Maguire had been inaugurated there six years ago, in 1589. But people said it went back thousands of years. Diarmait led Terence to a thick wood where they would wait for the spy to meet them in the shadows. Soon enough Terence heard the sound of a horse's hoofs, and shortly afterwards, he saw a man dressed in a long, shaggy woollen mantle. His hair was long and the glib hung down over his eyes in the typical Irish fashion, so that it would be quite difficult from a distance to describe his face. He directed a nervous glance to Diarmait and then to Terence.

Diarmait immediately sought to reassure him. "You are safe with us here. No one knows of this parley except the three of us. You may tell the aigne here what you know of the shooting of the monk."

"It wasn't I who shot at him!"

"But you know who did."

"I know."

"Why did someone want to shoot this monk?"

The man looked at Diarmait before speaking. Then, "He knew the monk had been spreading slander about Connor Óg and his family."

From Terence's understanding of Brother Aidan, he was concerned about the loyalties of the English Maguire here in Magherastephena and was not a man for keeping his opinions to himself. As far as Aidan was concerned, the horrors he had seen in England compelled him to warn the men here against any further encroachments by the invaders.

"The man who shot the arrow that day believed he was doing his duty to protect Connor Óg Maguire and his people. Something happened to frighten him off, though, and so no more arrows were shot and the monk escaped with his life."

Terence spoke up then. "So, this is the man who should be brought to justice for the injury to Brother Aidan."

The man standing before Terence said, "This cannot happen. If he is taken to Enniskillen for judgment, it may be revealed how you came to know of him, and I will be revealed as . . . revealed for my assistance to the junior Maguires."

Terence knew this meant the branch of the family in Enniskillen. The Magherastephena Maguires were the senior line, senior in time and genealogy. "But this way, the attempt on Aidan goes unacknowledged, and he receives no compensation for his injury."

"There is another way. The honour price and the fine can be paid. The value raised here by means of . . ."

"There may be raids coming up," Diarmait put in. Raids by one family against the cattle and other wealth of another family, the suggestion being that some of the gains could be set aside for payment for the injury caused by the arrow in Aidan's side.

The man was anxious to get away, and so they thanked him and watched him depart.

Terence's mind went back to Aidan's words, that he had seen the man who shot the arrow, had seen him previously in the area around Enniskillen and the abbey. When had the attacker become aware of Aidan and his mission to convert the English Maguire's men back to the true faith, to the Irish Maguires? Or had he been in the area for some other reason? Or, Terence wondered then — twenty years spent working as a lawyer in Galway and Fermanagh having planted a suspicious seed in his mind — had the spy he'd just met, the spy who was working for the Enniskillen Maguires against his own people, had he been in the Enniskillen area himself as part of his service to the powerful lord and his retinue at Enniskillen Castle? Was it possible that there was no other man out there at all? Was this man himself the shooter, motivated by the fear that Aidan would recognize his face and let it slip that he was in touch with the Maguires of Enniskillen? Had Terence just met the man who had tried to kill Brother Aidan?

CHAPTER XVI

*War, plundering and burning, want and famine,
lamentation and desolation, prevailed in their time
in the country; rent and tribute were levied for each
of them . . .*

— Connellan, *Annals of the Four Masters*

2018

The first shovel was driven into the earth outside Tierney's Hotel on the twenty-first of April, 2018. Aisling, a tall, fair-haired young woman, was the principal archaeologist. She and Róisín had struck up a friendly relationship right away. Aisling explained to Mick that all objects found on his land would belong to him, except in the case of treasure. Anything like that would have to be offered for sale to a museum. He assured her that the museums could have everything that was found, treasure or not. Other than that, they did not have much time to chat. Aisling was busy directing a team of three men and one woman, all of them in hard hats, as they dug into the earth with picks and shovels. And when the top layers of grass and soil had been removed, Róisín had to hold her wee boy, Rory, back from jumping into the square-shaped hole. His sister, Ciara, looked ready to follow him in. Mick had stood out in the bright spring sun and watched the first stage of the dig, and then returned to his work inside the hotel. Later in the day he came out to have a look again. The four-person team had widened the excavation and gone deeper into the earth. The equipment was more delicate now; two of the archaeologists were digging slowly and carefully with trowels. Another was crouched on the grass using a sieve to catch anything that might be found in the soil. A fourth member of the team was using a brush to clean off what looked like rock but, in Mick's imagination, might have been a nugget of gold. It was a rock.

This first assault on the ground had come after a months-long process of red tape and regulations, paperwork and approvals, and then geophysical and topographical surveys, health and safety assessments, environmental assessments, and other preparatory work. Mick hoped and prayed that some significant historical artifacts would be found, priceless emblems of history that would be at risk if the Vegas-Disney-Prule outrage was permitted to be built. There was no loud, heavy equipment on the site, and the dig prompted more fascination than complaints on the part of Mick's guests. But he did not want to picture the expression on his grandmother's face when she realized what was going on. He saw it soon enough, though, when he hoofed it over to Cait's house, and her face was like a thundercloud when she met him at the door. She gave him a shelling as expected but she knew that the project was on, and that whatever was under the earth was going to be resurrected.

And then, late in the afternoon: "We've found something!" Aisling was standing beside the excavation, her long blond hair streaming out from under her hard hat. She said, "It's a section of wall, nearly three feet thick. And you can see a stone hearth there."

The dig had begun just behind the nineteenth-century addition to the present hotel, and now it seemed possible that the centuries-old guesthouse was being exhumed.

Róisín certainly thought so. "This is brilliant!" she exclaimed. "The museums will be bidding against each other to get bits of the Tierney guesthouse for their collections. Don't you think so, Aisling?"

The archaeologist laughed. "For definite, Róisín!"

❧

Over the next few days, the team found shards of decorated pottery, part of a wooden bowl, a couple of nearly intact drinking cups, a short string of colourful beads that Aisling believed had been a bracelet, and a golden crucifix with a chain through it, likely worn as a necklace. The archaeologists took great care with each item, and Róisín looked forward to the day when they would be put on display to be viewed and admired.

It was time for another visit to Grandma's house. Cait began giving out to Mick before he'd even finished his report on the findings. "Baubles and old crumbling walls are one thing," the old lady said, "and fair dues to Róisín, I can understand her interest in them. But you just wait." A trembling finger was pointed at Mick's heart. "Wait till they dig up something that will put the whole crowd of us out of business and into the workhouse!"

"There've been no skeletons uncovered yet, Gran."

"Ach, would you catch yourself on, Michael! 'Yet,' says he, as if 'yet' stands for all time. I told you and that father of yours that no good can come of this."

"That all happened a hundred and seventy years ago."

"And what do you suppose happened over four hundred years ago? Did ye never give any thought to how it was we held on to the old guesthouse?"

He knew where she was headed now. In the early 1600s, the province of Ulster was planted with English and Scottish settlers. The Irish of the most Irish part of the island were booted off their lands so the colony could be filled with good industrious farmers and burghers loyal to the English crown. But Mick had never lost any sleep wondering how the Tierneys back in the day had managed to hang on to the property, or get it back. He had always assumed that some wily ancestor had married the right person, greased the right palm, charmed somebody during a night of heroic drinking, or had done whatever else might have been necessary at the time to retain or regain the Tierney house. All he said was "Gran, to the extent that anybody wonders about that, you can be sure they're glad our ancestors outfoxed the colonizers and kept the place in native Irish hands."

"Aye, a better result than losing the place."

She poured them each a cup of tea, and they sat down at the kitchen table.

"Now, Gran, you know why we're doing this. The alternative is to be surrounded by fake-stone, out-of-proportion holiday homes got up to look like the castle watergate, and a massive casino with the name of yer man the Yank glaring out in great gold letters: PRULE! Do ye want to be looking at that out your window? A feckin' theme park is what it will be! Not even to mention that all this shite will destroy our view. This is the only way to sabotage that plan."

It was a sly look she gave him then. "Use yer head, big lad. D'ye really think the boys destroyed everything they had during the decommissioning process?" She meant the process of destroying all the guns and ammunition and explosives in the possession of the paramilitaries when the peace agreement was signed twenty years ago. "What was the name of that man, the legendary fella from Africa?"

Mick had no idea where the conversation was headed now.

"You know," she said, "he fought against the system down there that kept the Black people separated from the White."

"Apartheid, you mean, in South Africa?"

"Of course that's what I mean. He was a rebel and he fought against whatever you called it, the segregation, and they banged him up in prison but he ended up being president of the country! Mandela, that's his name."

"Right. Nelson Mandela."

"Well, do you remember what he said when he came to this island and visited Dublin?"

"I think he gave a speech, or a lecture at the university. Trinity College. It was quite a few years ago."

"Yes, years ago. And he gave a speech. But it's what he said at lunch with a bunch of news reporters that I'm getting at here. We read about it in the *Tele*."

The *Belfast Telegraph*. The story was coming back to him now.

"The reporters or editors, whatever they were," said Cait, "a few of them were invited to have lunch with Mandela. I still have the news cutting somewhere. I saw it a couple of years ago when I was clearing out some things. So they had lunch with him, and somebody mentioned the decommissioning of the weapons here in the North, and asked Mandela what he thought of it. What advice he'd give to young Gerry." Gerry Adams, she meant, the very well-known republican and Sinn Féin man. "Mr. Mandela said his advice would be 'You don't hand over your weapons until you get what you want.'"

"Yes, that's what he said."

"Can't you imagine the faces on them around the table that day?" Cait's old face lit up at the thought of it. "It's not as if those news editors were a crowd of republican rabble-rousers!"

"No, indeed. And now that I think of it, didn't the editor of the *Tele* come back here to the North, to Belfast, for a meeting with some official types and tell them about it?"

"Now, I don't remember that part of it. But I still have the cutting. It'd be in my old cedar chest."

"It was some high-level Brit he spoke to at the meeting in Belfast. A politician, a member of the cabinet, I don't recall now. But the man asked what Mandela had to say about the situation here in Ireland, and the man wasn't best pleased when he heard it!"

"I'm sure he wasn't. Nor would he have been pleased when Gerry Adams was asked about the 'RA during the peace negotiations. There'd been some commotion between the loyalists and the republicans again, and Gerry was giving a speech and somebody shouted, 'Bring back the IRA.' And Ger says, 'They haven't gone away, you know.'"

"Sure, that's one of his most famous lines."

"Well, there you are. That's my point."

"Your point, Gran?"

She leaned towards him, with a mischievous look on her face. "Maybe the bombs haven't gone away either." She waited, and when he made no reply, she said, "We'll have some of the lads come back out of the shadows and blow Mr. Prule's feckin' theme park to smithereens."

But Mick decided to stick to the legally acceptable course of searching underground for discoveries that would keep Prule and his fantasies away from the Tierney lands. By the middle of May, the archaeologists had extended their explorations beyond the site of the old guesthouse. There were new holes now, deep in the boggy area on the southern part of the property. All the better, as Mick saw it.

⚛

Saturday the second of June was Ciara's fifth birthday, and the family decided to give her a little trip out of town. They wanted to make a long weekend of it, so they left their staff in charge of the hotel and headed off for a motoring holiday in County Donegal. Liam went along with Mick, Róisín, and the children in a hired van that comfortably held them all, and they had a fun, relaxing time away.

But the peace and tranquillity were short-lived. When Mick and Liam arrived at Cait's place Monday night, they found the dear old soul pushing herself up from her chair, quaking with fear.

"What is it, Ma?"

"What is it, Gran?"

"Your precious *dig* was ransacked!"

"What?!"

Mick hadn't even glanced at the excavation site when he arrived back at the hotel; he had come straight to Cait's to bring Liam home.

"Come here till I tell you. I was frightened half out of my wits! I've the kettle boiling but I haven't had a cup yet. I meant to but . . ."

Liam wrapped his arms around his mother, then eased her back into her favourite chair and went to the kitchen and poured the cups of tea.

When they were all seated, she said, "I had a visitor."

"Oh?" Liam asked.

"He was hiding in the trees and jumped out when he saw me coming back from Mass on Sunday. Old Anne O'Rourke gave me a spin there and back — she's still driving! As soon as she pulled away, he was up behind me, and he told me to keep quiet or I'd get hurt, and to go straight into the house. And he came in on my heels and shut the door behind me."

Liam let out a string of curses in Irish and threats against whoever it was who had the gall to accost his mother.

Her hand was shaking so badly she had to put her teacup back on the saucer. Mick's heart went out to her, and he shared his father's rage. But he kept his voice even. "Take your time, Gran. Tell us what happened."

"He was big and tall, and he had dark glasses on and a black wool hat pulled down over his hair and ears, and there was nothing about him I could recognize. He was young, I could tell that much from his mouth and his hands. And he said to me — I warned you this would happen, Michael!"

Whatever this was, she hadn't warned him it would happen but he kept his silence and waited for the rest.

"He said he'd been down in the hole. The excavation, he meant. He'd gone down there in the night with a shovel, or a tool of some kind, and he got down below where the archaeologists had got to, and he found something!"

Mick took a deep breath. He glanced over at his father, who had a look on his face that said, *There'll be blood spilt.* "What did he find, Gran?"

"Exactly what I told you would be down there!"

"You mean something about—"

"He said this place — Tierney's Hotel, he meant — was built on the backs of poor, starving people during the Famine.

And us making a profit off the place all these years. And he had the proof!"

"What kind of proof?"

"All he said was 'Everybody will know what old Roddo Tierney did to his tenants, and him after lying about it. Everybody will know.'"

Oh, Christ, had his grandmother's fears really come true after all? That there would be a scandal arising out of whatever old Tierney had done back in 1847, and it would be used against the family and the business? But that was almost beside the point now; the point now was this outrageous treatment of an old lady alone in her house. He pictured his gran, her thin, frail body trembling with fear as this lout loomed over her. He couldn't bear the thought of it. Whatever it took, Mick and his father would track down this fucker and . . .

"And then he got down to brass tacks. He would make all this public if I didn't come up with ten thousand quid!"

"Ten thousand quid!"

Cait sat forward in her chair and said, "That's right, Michael. And he had some complicated plan for me delivering the money or stashing it to be collected by somebody. But I was too terror-ized to keep track of what he said. And he got right up in my face and warned me not to go to the peelers or to tell you fellas or anybody else because — and here he laughed, and he spoke like somebody in the gangster fillums — 'I know where you live!' And if he got lifted and sent to jail, his pals would know where I live! It's not safe for me here now, my own home!"

Mick said, "You'll both be spending the night at the hotel, and the nights after that until we track this scumbag down."

"I'll not be put out of my own house!"

"But, Gran—"

"I will not leave my house, Michael."

"We'll find this blackmailing bastard, Ma," Liam said in a voice low and dangerous. "And he'll not be bothering you or anyone else in this family ever again."

CHAPTER XVII

There were some very pretty girls there, with whom
I was on friendly terms, and I used to go into their
houses sometimes to chat . . .

— Captain Francisco de Cuellar, *A letter written on*
October 4, 1589, by Captain Cuellar, of the Spanish
Armada, to His Majesty King Philip II, recounting his
misadventures in Ireland and elsewhere after the wreck of
his ship, trans. H. D. Sedgwick Jr.

1595

B rigid and Shane rode across their land on horseback, looking
at the wild flowers and the view below them, the blue sky
reflected in the shining waters of the River Erne. And the
Maguire castle, a sentinel at the edge of the land. But they
were not out there to enjoy the view. They were on their way to
the home of Tomás MacMahon, first husband of Sorcha, father
of Peadar. Their decision had come after a conversation earlier in
the day, when they were sitting at the table after their meal and
trying once again to figure out who had the motive to kill Sorcha.
Brigid knew that the brehon was still questioning people about

the killing, but she felt compelled to follow up any information she could uncover.

"How can it be that we have no idea who wanted her dead?" Shane had asked.

"Perhaps it's because we loved and admired her so, and therefore cannot imagine who would be so vile as to take her life," Brigid replied. "But it's because we loved and admired her so that we have to keep looking for the answer."

"I keep coming back to the prophecies. Except that this raises the question: what was the man doing on her land in the dead of night whilst the prophecies were being uttered? Surely no one knows in advance when a seer is going to see the future. Unless he's a seer himself and foresees that she is going to see . . . Well, I don't think either of us believes that!"

"No. So was the man there for a benign reason, wanting to speak with her that night? Or was he there to do her harm?"

Brigid got up from the table to clear away the plates and cups. She put them aside for the maid to wash and thought once again about the people in Sorcha's life. Her parents were long dead, and she had only one sister, who was married and living far away. Her little daughter Ónora was living with her foster family. Her son, Peadar, was home that night, and Brigid had seen his genuine grief the morning after. Sorcha had only one maid, and she was not there that night or the day after. She had gone to her own family for the week because her daughter had just given birth.

"Peadar was there," Shane said.

"Peadar would never have hurt her."

"So, we are left with the husbands, the most recent being Father O'Moylan."

"Fiach didn't kill her."

"I certainly hope you're right! The first husband was the cavalry man, Tomás MacMahon. I haven't seen any sign of him trying to find the killer."

"You'd think he would, for his son's sake."

"You'd think so."

They looked at each other, and Brigid said, "Let's pay him a visit."

And so they were on their horses, riding towards the home of Tomás MacMahon. They carried on their discussion when the pathways allowed them to ride close to one another.

"He wasn't at the banquet, was he, Shane? I'd have expected any of the Maguire's horsemen to be on hand for that, given that Hugh Maguire is a cavalry man himself. Do you know him well at all? You'd have fought with him."

"Been in battle with him, but I don't know him all that well. He wasn't at the banquet, and he wasn't there with Peadar on judgment day."

"Now that I think of it, I believe someone told me he'd been wounded. So he may not have been able for judgment day at all."

"Wounded, and his wife the physician! Do you suppose—"

"Former wife, and—" A fox came running out from the wood, and Muirisc, Brigid's mare, shied away from it. Brigid held on tight and spoke calming words to the horse, got her settled down, and resumed the conversation. "Former wife, and the marriage was a long time ago. And I do not suppose she failed to cure his wound and he killed her as a result! From what I recall of Tomás, he would have taken her to law himself to recover his honour price! He comes from a family who own a great amount of land, and they . . . well . . . their wealth and their honour are important to them."

"Did he divorce Sorcha, or she him?"

"She divorced him."

"Why?"

"I don't know what the official grounds were, but it was really because she had fallen for Fiach O'Moylan."

"So MacMahon may have felt that his honour had been sullied by her divorcing him for another man."

"He would have been hurt by it, and shamed by it, there's no denying it, but it was many years ago, Shane. They have seen each other countless times since then, and she never spoke ill of him at any time. Never said a word about him being angry or resentful. They were amiable with one another, as far as I know, as she was with Fiach."

"They had a life together; they have a son together. Tomás may well have some information about her life that we don't have."

The MacMahon house was to the west and on lower land than the Tierney place; it took nearly an hour for Brigid and Shane to ride there. Cows grazed in the pastures, and there were a couple of men working the fields. The two-storey house was well kept, as were the outbuildings. A horseboy emerged from behind the house; they greeted him and dismounted, leaving him to tie up their horses. As Brigid was about to walk up to the door, she looked to the side and saw Peadar, with a magnificent bird of prey on his left wrist. This part of Ireland was renowned for the quality of its goshawks. The bird sighted the new arrivals before the young man did; Peadar followed the bird's line of vision and saw them. Shane signalled that he and Brigid would go to the house, so as not to disturb the communion between man and hawk.

The door was answered by a young woman, who said that Tomás was out but was expected back for his evening meal. She invited them inside and offered them a glass of wine and some oatcakes. They expressed their thanks and sat at a table at the side of the room.

A few minutes later, Peadar came in and greeted them. The alert posture Brigid had noticed in him when he was with his hawk had given way to a slackness in the young man. He slumped into a chair opposite his guests. Brigid felt regret for taking him away from an activity he enjoyed to sit inside with people who, without doubt, served as reminders of his mother's death.

"Do you have news?" he asked them.

"No news, I'm sorry, Peadar," Brigid replied.

"Why has the priest not been brought to judgment?" Brigid tried to form her answer, but the boy bent forward and interrupted her, his face an angry red. "It wouldn't have happened if she had taken my father back into her life!"

Before she could respond to this, Tomás himself walked into the room. He was a tall muscular man with grey hair; his eyes were a slightly darker grey. It took a couple of seconds before Brigid noticed that he did not appear to be injured. Perhaps whatever wound he had suffered was now healed.

"Welcome," he said to them and sat next to his son.

Brigid said, "We haven't had the opportunity before now to tell you how sorry we are for the loss of Sorcha. Ar dheis Dé go raibh a hanam." May her soul be on God's right hand. "I know that you and she remained on very good terms, and that she took a great interest in your son." She looked at Peadar, whose face retained its angry hue.

"She did," Tomás replied. "We are filled with sorrow. No one has been called to account for this dreadful deed." He said to

Shane, "You were accused by a man who turned out to be a liar. That accusation never made sense; I never believed it."

Shane bowed his head in acknowledgement.

"So," Tomás repeated, "Nobody has been made to pay for her death."

"That is right," Brigid said, "as painful as it is to think of it. We were wondering whether you might have any idea who would have wished her harm."

The former husband looked into her eyes and held her gaze, but did not speak.

"Tomás?" she prompted him.

Finally, he spoke. "She never admitted to me that anyone hated her or wished harm upon her."

Admitted? "Is this something you and she spoke about? She was worried or afraid but would not say why, or who had her concerned?"

"How could she not have known, Brigid?"

"I'm sorry, Tomás, I don't know what you mean."

"She was a seer, a wise woman, descendant of Druids! In addition to her skills as a physician, she was able to see into the future. Able to see into the hearts of men. How could she not have known that someone harboured a desire to hurt her? How could she not have known who that man was?"

"Do you know yourself, Tomás?"

"I do not possess the strange and terrible gifts that were bestowed by God upon my wife."

※

Terence Blake was restless and anxious to get away from his everyday work, and particularly to get away from a man named

Torna who, not for the first time, had prevailed upon Terence to challenge on his behalf a contract he had made with another man whilst they were drunk. Torna seemed to have made a habit of forming contracts over cups of ale in the alehouse and then trying to renege on them the next day.

"Torna, you cannot escape the responsibilities of this contract you made."

"But, Terence, you've told me yourself that the law defines drunkenness as not being able to remember in the morning what you did the night before. And that lowest of men took advantage of me by trying to hold me to whatever I said to him that night."

"Torna, it was a contract relating to joint ploughing. We have been over this before. Drunkenness does not invalidate that kind of contract; the law recognizes that contracts like that are regularly made in the alehouse or at feasts when men are enjoying good times together. In other words, the contracts are made between neighbours who are drinking — or drunk — together."

It took a while to get Torna out of the house and on his way. And then Terence was able to concentrate on what was uppermost in his mind. And his plan, like so many of Torna's ill-fated plans, involved a trip to the alehouse. Terence had not been called upon to represent the families of the two men stabbed following the judgment in favour of Shane O'Callaghan. This, of course, came as no surprise. At least one of them, Murrough, had been party to a plan to have O'Callaghan judged guilty of killing Sorcha O'Cassidy. If another lawyer or lawyers had been consulted, he didn't know about it. Nor had Terence been called upon to do any investigating after O'Callaghan was declared to be innocent on judgment day. But he was haunted by the fact that someone had tried to cast the blame on O'Callaghan. For what reason? And who had decided that the pair of them, Murrough and Colm, had to be punished? Or silenced? Again, for what reason? Terence knew that the brehon, O'Breslin, was conducting an investigation into the death of Murrough, the wounding of Colm, and the unsolved killing of Sorcha herself. But the questions made Terence restless. It was natural for him to wonder who had tried to make Shane out to be a killer, and who had attacked the two men involved in that plot.

Murrough had testified that someone sent him from where the soldiers were encamped to Enniskillen Castle with a message for Colm the watchman. Who had sent the man on that errand? Maguire's warriors were not encamped anywhere now, so they were scattered all around Fermanagh. Terence could not see himself spending days travelling around the area, hoping someone might remember who sent Murrough out on that night more than a month ago. Would any of them remember? Would they tell Terence if they did? Well, he asked Shane if he could suggest one or two of the men who lived nearby, and Terence spoke to them. But he was no further ahead after those conversations. The men professed to know nothing. They could not remember anything about Murrough that night, one way or another. And that was understandable, Terence had to admit; it was not until much later that Murrough's actions that night were found to be significant. Terence also made the assumption that if the men were all in the camp together at night, there would be drink taken, and memories would not be reliable.

Then Shane had another idea for Terence. Shane knew of someone who was well aware of the soldiers' movements when encamped or on the move. And when there were no military operations going on, she could be found most nights of the week in the alehouse. She was well known as a camp follower, known by the nickname Síle Shalach, Dirty Sheila. When an army is on the move, it is not just the horsemen, the foot, the marksmen who go off to the camps. There are also family members and others who go along: to cook the meals, tend to the wounded, and provide "other services" to the warriors. One of those most noted for providing other services was Síle.

It took a couple of trips to the alehouse, not at all an unpleasant assignment for Terence, but he found his quarry on a windy, rainy night when the place was full to the rafters. Sheltered from the weather, the crowd was merry. Candle flames were reflected in the shine of the cups and goblets, and a piper played lively tunes in the corner of the room. Men and women were up dancing, and the others watched and cheered them on from the benches. Síle was sitting with two other women, all of them pleasing to the eye. The two had long yellow hair and they were well in their cups. One crooked her finger at Terence and indicated the place across from her. He decided that was his way in, so he walked forward and took a seat. One of the golden-haired beauties began regaling him with stories of some recent adventures in a soldiers' camp, and he could not keep himself from laughing. Síle herself did not appear to be sotted with drink. Nor did her appearance accord with the unfriendly nickname that had attached itself to her. She looked as if she had just emerged from the bath. Her long dark curls hung loose around her shoulders, and the upper regions of her bright-green dress were loosely laced. A crucifix hung on a long chain and Terence remarked to himself that the place-ment of the cross on Síle gave rise to thoughts not at all related to the crucifixion of our Lord. He admonished himself for getting distracted; he was there to work, not to goggle at the women. He put his lips to her ear and asked if he might have a word alone with her. This was met with winks and lewd remarks from the men, and the women as well, but she got up and followed him to the quietest corner of the room. There were a couple of places to sit, and he offered to get her a cup of ale. She thanked him, and when they were seated, he asked after her health and family, and then got to the point of his encounter with her.

It turned out to be a brief encounter. He introduced the subject and asked her, "Were you at the camp that night, Síle?"

"I was."

"Now, can you tell me whether you remember the pikeman Murrough arriving at the camp, rather late in the night, and then being sent away with a message for a watchman at the castle?"

"He said that on judgment day."

"He did."

She was silent for a moment and then said, "I didn't see him."

Not everyone would be delicate in his dealings with Síle Shalach, but Terence had no desire to be crude with the woman, no matter what she got up to with the men in the camps. So he phrased his question carefully. "Were you with the group of people there who would have seen a rider approach, or might you have been in private conversation with someone and missed a person's arrival?"

"I was sitting with a crowd of them there. No one came late to the camp."

"No one? You didn't see Murrough ride up to the encampment?"

"Murrough didn't come."

"Ar chor ar bith?" At all?

"Ar chor ar bith." At all.

Terence was the object of some amused glances, the odd wink, and a few salacious remarks as he parted from Síle and left the alehouse. He believed that the woman was telling the truth, and that Murrough therefore had lied: he had not been to the camp. So where was he that night, and why did he try to have Shane O'Callaghan judged guilty of a secret and unacknowledged killing? Murrough's story was that he delivered a message to Colm the lookout. Colm had not been on the hill on judgment day. And then he himself was wounded. But he had survived. Had he returned to his work for the Maguire? It was time — it was past time — for Terence to have a word with the watchman.

He knew Colm to see him, but their paths rarely crossed, Terence being a lawyer working from his home and Colm being on duty at Enniskillen Castle. Well, tomorrow morning Terence would present himself at the river's edge and have the boatman take him across to the castle, see what Colm had to say about the night of Sorcha's death, and the morning after.

But his time within the castle walls left him not with the answer but with questions. None of the Maguire's men had seen Colm since he walked away from the infirmary at Drumlyon Abbey nearly two weeks ago. Nobody knew where he was; he had simply disappeared.

CHAPTER XVIII

Then is it sin to rush into the secret house of death . . . ?

— Shakespeare, *Antony and Cleopatra*

The first week of July brought glorious weather to Fermanagh, and Brigid took advantage of those sunny days, stepping out to enjoy the view of Enniskillen Castle below, and to admire the bright pink roses and the lilies that grew at the edge of the wood behind her house. The scent was lovely. She thought about planting more of each flower, and perhaps some others as well. As she was bending over to pluck the head of a fading rose, she was startled by a noise behind her and whirled around to face it. This happened to her sometimes, reacting with a jolt of fear when she was outside alone and heard a sound. It had been happening, from time to time, ever since the man attacked her in the wood. On this occasion she saw a horse approaching and stood up and squinted into the sun to see who was coming. The rider stopped a few feet away and dismounted. No reason to be afraid: it was Sorcha's son, Peadar.

She greeted him, and he said, "May I speak to you and . . . ?" He looked around.

"Shane?" she asked. "He's not here today." Shane had been called to duty and had gone off with some of the Maguire's other marksmen, confident as always that he would not fall in battle, if there was a battle, insisting that there was no need for Brigid to worry as she always did for his safety. She could not predict when he would return. Now she gave her attention to the young visitor. "But can I be of assistance to you, Peadar?"

The young fellow took a deep breath; he looked ill at ease.

"Come into the house and have a cup of ale."

"I'd like that."

So she directed him to tie up his horse, and he followed her into the house. She poured him a cup of ale and placed a plate of biscuits before him on the table. Then she sat down, smiled, and asked him what was on his mind.

"I . . . I found something."

"Oh? What is it you found?"

"I never looked around the house before. After, I mean. After her death. I left and went to my father's place. Took her dog with me. Goldie. I spend some of my time at my father's house, and some at my mother's. I mean, I did spend . . . before it happened, I meant to say."

"Of course. Take your time, Peadar. There is no rush here."

He took a good mouthful of ale and resumed his story. "So I never saw it before. Never saw it right after she died. Until now. I returned from my father's place last night. You know my mother had only one servant at the house and she was away with her family. And she's not been back; well, why would she be? So I went to the house last night, but before the sun went down.

And I saw that something was broken. Something like this." He held up the drinking cup. "It was on the floor, and I could not remember whether it was I who . . . whether I broke it, or threw it down after I found her body, or I dropped it. I don't remember doing that but I may have. I wasn't thinking clearly."

"Of course not, Peadar. Nobody would have been. So, you may have dropped a cup and broken it." She smiled at him again. "Not a great loss."

"It was not a great loss indeed. But when I bent to pick up the pieces, that's when I found something."

"What did you find?"

She saw then that he had a small leather bag with him. He reached inside and drew out a crumpled piece of vellum and laid it on the table. He opened it and there, wrapped within it, was a brilliant gold ring, elaborately carved, inset with a red stone. Brigid recognized it instantly. Fiach O'Moylan had given it to Sorcha a few years after they were married.

"This lovely ring," she said. "I remember when he came home with it after travelling to Galway. He bought it from a Spanish trader who had sailed into Galway with his cargo of jewels and wine."

"Bought it!" The young man's mouth was twisted in scorn.

"He bought it for her from the Spaniard."

"Took it off one of the sailors that floated ashore after that armada was wrecked on the coast!"

"Peadar, that is not true. It was the year 1588 when the armada was wrecked. Your mother had the ring well before that."

The young man looked unconvinced, but Brigid let it go. He wasn't much more than a boy, and he had suffered the loss of his mother.

The document was familiar as well. Fiach was far from being a priest in those days, but his family were wrights, craftsmen skilled in working with wood and other materials, and he had been trained in their skills, trained to do beautiful work. Brigid knew that he admired the lovely manuscripts made by the monks at the abbey and that he had made this one for her himself when they were married. It was a passage from Holy Scripture, Mark 10:9. It had beautifully scrolled and decorated letters and was written in Latin, but Brigid knew the meaning:

God made them male and female.
For this reason, a man shall leave his father and
    mother and be joined to his wife,
And the two shall become one. So they are no longer
    two but one.
What therefore God has joined together, let not
    man put asunder.

It was the Church's — the Lord's — law against divorce.

"Where did you find these, Peadar?"

"They were in a corner of the front room, behind the leg of a bench she had there. I saw it when I crouched down to pick up the shards of the broken cup."

This was disturbing to Brigid. The precious ring and the marriage verse were both gifts from Fiach. What were they doing on the floor behind the leg of a bench?

"Where were the ring and vellum usually kept, Peadar?"

"They were not in the house. I know I had never seen them since she divorced him."

"Divorced Fiach."

"Right. He took them back from her!"

Or had she given them back to him, the valuable gold ring and the verse that she had defied? Did she want Fiach to have the value of the ring, perhaps to sell? Could she not bear to see the verse again?

"What do you think happened, Peadar? How would the ring and manuscript have ended up on the floor of your mother's house?"

He looked at her as if to say, *Is it not obvious?* "He came in that night. He started a row with her. He threw the ring and the page at her in anger. Threw the cup as well, or it got broken in the midst of all that."

"Oh, Peadar, Fiach is not that kind of man. He would not have acted like that. He didn't go into the house. He left after she uttered her prophecies, didn't even speak to her."

The look again. "He wanted her back. He didn't want the divorce!"

"But he became a priest of the Church. He knew that a wife is entitled to divorce a man who takes Holy Orders. He never gave any indication that he wanted to leave the priesthood and return to—"

"He wouldn't, would he? Give any indication. But it was inside him, the lust for her. He wanted her, and she turned him away! Men have killed for less."

They had, she knew. But that wasn't Fiach; that wasn't the man, the priest, she knew.

Now, after talking to Peadar, Brigid steeled herself for a conversation she did not want to have. She was going to see Father O'Moylan. She rode to the abbey, where she waited until Fiach was free to come and speak with her. He gave her a friendly greeting and invited her to sit. There were several other monks within the abbey's walls, so she suggested they walk outside. When they were alone, she recounted the story as Peadar MacMahon had told it to her.

The priest's eyes narrowed, and she saw that his fists were clenched by his sides. After a moment, he spoke. "Brigid, you know me. You know I would never have hurt Sorcha. I loved her." He raised a hand as if he anticipated a protest. "I loved her, but I was not trying to win her back. I'm a priest now, and I intend to devote my life to my vocation. I loved her but I understood that we could never be together that way again."

Brigid felt a certain shame in questioning him further, but she had to ask, "What about the ring and the manuscript, Fiach? They were found on the floor of her house."

"I haven't seen the ring or the manuscript since we parted all those years ago. She did not return them to me, and I certainly did not take them back from her. If anyone threw them to the floor, perhaps in a fit of rage or jealousy, it certainly was not me."

"I believe you, Fiach. I just felt I had to ask."

"I know. I understand." They walked for a while in silence, and she wondered what he was thinking. Then he turned to face her and said, "Don't you find it strange that the ring and manuscript were suddenly found on the floor of her house after all these weeks?"

She remembered something then: the brehon had gone into the house while Sorcha's body was still lying in the oak leaves. If there had been a broken cup on the floor, he would have seen it and wondered whether it was evidence of a violent dispute. All the more so if he had seen the ring and the quote from scripture.

Fiach said, "Surely Peadar has been in the house since the killing. And" — his light brown eyes looked into hers — "perhaps Tomás MacMahon has as well. He's a greedy fellow. If I were

Peadar, I'd be searching the house to see what might have disappeared, not what suddenly appeared out of nowhere. And, Brigid, I happen to know from what Sorcha told me over the years: Tomás was the bitter man after being divorced. Not me."

"You're saying it was Tomás who killed her!"

"I can't say that. I don't know. But whether he did it or not, he would not be above putting evidence in place that would make it look as if the guilty man was me."

⸭

To Brigid's great relief, Shane returned to the guesthouse two weeks later, weary but not wounded, after engaging the enemy in a series of brief skirmishes. The Maguire's company lost only two men; the casualties were higher amongst the English. After hearing all the details, or at least those that Shane cared to report, Brigid relayed to him the conversations she'd had with Peadar and with Fiach.

Once again, as they sat side by side in the guesthouse, Shane's arm around her shoulders, they were left to wonder what was eluding them about the murder of their friend. Who was it that hid in the trees and fired two arrows into Sorcha? Was it a personal grievance at play there? Was it an act carried out to make sure she did not repeat the frightening things she said that night, her prophecies of a dismal future for Ireland, for Fermanagh, someone outraged at the insinuation that the country's chieftains would abandon the country to its fate? Who could predict what men would do if they believed those things would happen? Some would conspire to take power for themselves. Others might try to agree to terms with the enemy to have a strong position in case the prophecies might someday be fulfilled. And what of Sorcha's

curse on an incestuous family here in Fermanagh? Brigid remembered learning that back in the days of ancient Greece, Socrates
said there was an unwritten law against incest, because it increases
the chances of defective offspring. Someone would certainly want
that curse buried. Or was there some other secret that accounted
for the murder of the physician and seer?

PART II

CHAPTER XIX

Sad it is to me that Hugh Maguire, tonight in a strange land, lies under the lurid glow of showering, flashing thunderbolts, beneath the fury of armed savage clouds. . . .

Grievous to me — it has wounded my heart — that the soft slope of his smooth comely side should be crushed in the wild sullen night, in a chilly suit of complete steel.

Gentle hand versed in ungentle strife, icy weather welding it tight against the slender shaft of a cold-pointed spear — bitter it is for Hugh tonight!

— Eochaidh Ó hEoghusa (O'Hussey), "A Winter Campaign," or "O'Hussey's Ode to the Maguire," in *Irish Bardic Poetry*, ed. Osborn Bergin, Fergus Kelly, David Greene

1600

I n the year 1600, in the month of March, Enniskillen Castle
— all of Fermanagh — was rocked by a catastrophic event
in the south of the country. A messenger brought the shocking
news from the castle to Drumlyon Abbey. Marcus Valerius stood
in the locutory of his abbey and listened to what the man had to
say, and he felt a chill that had nothing to do with the cool spring
day. The news came from Cork. Hugh Maguire, the Lord of
Fermanagh, had gone off to fight with Hugh the Great O'Neill,
the Earl of Tyrone — a man known far and wide for his valour
and his wit — against the English tyrants who had supplanted
the native population of Munster with people of their own. Now
Marcus was told that the Maguire had been killed in a skirmish
with an English soldier by the name of Sir Warham St. Leger.
The two had engaged each other in single combat. The story was
that Maguire charged towards the Englishman, brandishing his
spear, but St. Leger managed to shoot Maguire with his pistol.
Even so, Maguire was able to pierce St. Leger's helmet with his
spear and leave it hanging from his head. Maguire never made it
back to O'Neill at the Irishmen's camp. He got down from his
horse and — Marcus thanked God for this — was expiated by
his priest and died there on the spot. St. Leger died of his head
wound sometime later.

The messenger also relayed a message from the castle that the
chieftain's family would like a Mass said for the chieftain, and that
every man, woman, and child in this part of Fermanagh would
almost certainly be in attendance. Marcus knew that even the
local population might exceed the confines of the abbey church,
but he assured the envoy that he would make all the necessary
arrangements.

Marcus may have been committing the sin of pride, as he looked out over the congregation attending the Mass for the slain Lord of Fermanagh. Cúchonnacht Maguire led the members of the noble family into the church, with their cavalry men, foot soldiers, and others from the castle. Wives and children, members of the population both high and humble, and all the brothers and priests of the abbey were on hand for the solemn occasion. Never had the light blazed so beautifully through the richly coloured glass of the windows; never had the chanting of the monks resonated so magnificently throughout the building. Even the monks who were old and infirm had insisted on being present, and their younger brethren assisted or carried them into the church and stayed beside them to support their weakened bodies.

When it was time for Holy Communion, Marcus and two other priests distributed the sacred hosts to the communicants kneeling at the altar rail. When he had placed the host on the tongue of the last person to receive, Marcus looked out to see if there were any stragglers. There were not. Father Fiach O'Moylan walked to the ailing brothers and gave them the sacrament. But there was one man who showed no interest in or awareness of the approaching priest. Brother Aidan, who had come close to death several times over the past few years but had survived into his eighty-eighth year, was staring intently at the congregation on the other side of the aisle. Marcus saw in the old man's face a mixture of anger and fear. Father O'Moylan prompted him gently, and Aidan looked up at him with the same disturbed expression on his face. But he took the host in his mouth and seemed to settle down after he received the sacrament.

·The monks of Drumlyon Abbey had offered hospitality to any and all who wished to stay on after Mass. The brewers and cooks had been hard at work; food was plentiful and the ale flowed freely. The members of Hugh's family stayed for a short time, mixing with the people, before returning to the castle. Those who remained at the abbey spoke of Hugh Maguire's illustrious deeds, and poems were recited, songs sung, and vengeance vowed. The death of the chieftain had sent Maguire's country into yet another spiral of crisis and uncertainty.

Marcus limited himself to one cup of ale and stood off to the side, watching as the people of Fermanagh celebrated their lost leader, and grieved for him, and did their best to hide their fears for the future. All this brought to mind the prophecies of Sorcha, her visions of a desolate future for Ireland. As his thoughts veered from one frightful prognostication to the next — the loss of Ireland's leaders, the weeping of the women, the persecution of the priests, the tyranny to come — Marcus saw Fiach O'Moylan crossing the room towards him.

"Marcus. Did you see Aidan in the church?"

"I did."

"The look in his eyes?"

"What had him disturbed?"

"He said he saw the man who shot the arrow into him all those years ago!"

"In the church today?"

"With the Maguire's men."

"God save us! The man must have thought old Aidan would not be able to recognize him after all these years have passed."

"Or thought he wouldn't be able to rise from his bed for the Mass."

"I know this: the warriors who were here today were here under orders from the castle. To honour Hugh, of course, but also to protect the family. Others were to remain on duty to defend the castle."

"Does Aidan know the man's name?"

"He does not. I don't know which man he meant, but whoever he is, Aidan recognized him. I'm convinced of that."

࿇

With all the commotion and grief over the death of Hugh Maguire, Terence Blake had not heard that the father of Colm the watchman had recently died and been buried. Or that the family had dispersed after gathering for the burial; if Colm was still alive, he almost certainly would have retreated to wherever he had gone after being wounded back in 1595. But when Terence finally heard news of the family's loss, it brought to the front of his mind the murders of Sorcha and Murrough the pikeman, and the attempt on Colm's life. Terence had always felt that the attack on Colm was related to the false accusations against his client, Shane O'Callaghan, and it still disturbed Terence five years later that nobody had been brought to justice for those attacks. As far as Terence knew, the watchman was the only person who might have an idea who was behind the series of violent acts. So the lawyer decided to make some casual inquiries of family members living in the area of Enniskillen: condolences over the death, nosy little questions about the wake and funeral, how was the health of this or that person, where is such-and-such a man now? It took a few days, but someone finally let it slip that Colm was living a good distance away in Belleek. And Terence knew that before the week was out he would be packing some food and supplies, getting up on his horse and heading northwest to Belleek, at the outer edge of Fermanagh.

He invented a story to tell to the people around Belleek; he pretended he had travelled there to settle a property dispute between two landowners and, of course, had to deflect the curious questions about which land and what dispute. He made up some answers on the fly and, oh, by the way, I know someone who lives in these parts, a man by the name of Colm. In the end, finally, he located Colm working with a herd of pigs on the property of a prosperous landowner who, to Terence's knowledge, had no dispute with any of his neighbours. Terence came face to face with the former castle watchman at the fence at the edge of the field.

The man's face was pale and thin, his posture weak; he was obviously exhausted. Terence considered ways to work up to the real reason for his being there but decided, after inquiring about the man's health and expressing his condolences for the loss of his father, to get directly to the point.

"Why did you leave the castle, Colm? What happened, that you left the infirmary after your injury and you were never seen again?"

Colm's eyes darted around the countryside as if he feared that someone would come riding in and do him harm all over again.

"Colm?"

"They would have killed me! They would have made sure they succeeded the next time they tried it."

"Who?"

He did not answer the question. Instead, he said, "They threatened me."

"They shot you, Colm!"

"I mean back when it all started."

Terence reminded himself that the real story was more likely to emerge if not directed by the questioner. He stayed silent and waited.

"Murrough, he took payment. Costly items, jewels for the women, a plot of land in the territory of the English Maguire. He was one of their spies. And then after judgment day, when he gave evidence about the killing of the wise woman, he was killed."

This was hard to follow. Murrough was a spy in the pay of the English Maguire? And his death came after his testimony about the death of Sorcha O'Cassidy, his testimony against Shane O'Callaghan.

Colm said, "He told the brehon that he had been sent by the soldiers at the camp to deliver a message to me at the castle."

"That's what he said, I know."

"But it was a lie."

That came as no surprise. After all, Murrough's claim that he saw a man who looked like Shane hiding in Sorcha's trees was contradicted by the evidence discovered at the home of the Dowds. The court had declared that Murrough's statement to that effect was false.

"And that's why Murrough was killed?" Terence asked. "Because of the lie?"

"Because the man who killed him could not take the chance that the true story would be revealed. And that's why he tried to kill me."

"What was the true story, Colm?"

Terence detected in Colm's expression an effort to appear crafty. His effort was not at all convincing. Nevertheless, Terence heard him out.

"The truth is that it must have been another one of the English Maguire's spies who killed the prophetess."

"Why would the English Maguire want the prophetess dead?"

Colm continued his tale as if he hadn't heard the question. "And that man commanded Murrough to say he went by the O'Cassidy place on the way to deliver his message and saw O'Callaghan there."

"Why did this man want the blame put on O'Callaghan?" Why did he drag Terence's client before the brehon and have him accused of a secret and unacknowledged killing?

Colm looked like a man who did not want the truth pulled out of him. "What does it matter why? He needed someone to point to as the killer."

"Why O'Callaghan?" Terence asked again.

"I don't know!"

"Who was the man behind all this, Colm? Who killed Sorcha?"

"I don't know!"

He did know, but he was petrified with fear. Terence knew he would get no more information from the former watchman. No information supplied voluntarily. But the revelation that Murrough had taken jewels and a gift of land and other favours was not only a revelation about Murrough; it also told a tale on Colm. How likely was it that Colm would know the secret behind that unless he, Colm, was in league with Murrough as another of the English Maguire's spies? Whoever was behind the killings, Colm felt that his reach could extend all the way to Belleek five years after the blood was shed.

CHAPTER XX

I do not think, but know, that they [the mere Irish]
will never be reformed in religion, manners and
constant obedience to our laws but by the awe of the
sword and by a strong hand . . .

— Fynes Moryson, principal secretary to Lord
Mountjoy, Queen Elizabeth's Lord Deputy in Ireland,
An Itinerary, 1617-c 1626

Let us but remember our late, gracious Queen
[Elizabeth], with what mildness and with what
mercy she ruled and governed forty-and-odd years,
and with what disloyalty was she still requited . . .
I think the ingratitude of the Irish (considering
how mildly they have been and are yet governed)
deserveth no less to be condemned than their treasons
and rebellions. . . . I hope there is no man that will
accuse me of partiality . . .

— Barnabe Rich, *A New Description of Ireland,* 1610

Five years had passed and no one had been brought to law for the secret killing of Sorcha O'Cassidy. Brigid and Shane had followed every lead they could think of to find the killer, to no avail. To this day, Brigid still found herself thinking, *I'll talk to Sorcha about this or that event, or bit of foolishness; she'd have a laugh about it or I've a new tune on the harp that Sorcha will like; let's invite her over for a night of music and conversation.* Brigid felt a pang every time these thoughts came to her and she remembered that she would never see her friend again. Nobody would ever fill the void Sorcha's death had left in Brigid's life.

So she was thankful for the opportunity to get away from Fermanagh. Brigid had not spent any time in the company of her older sister, Mary, since they were girls together in the guesthouse. Her sister had married Cormac Dougherty, who had grown up in the area of Ballyshannon and worked for the O'Donnells at their castle there. Brigid recalled the excitement of attending the wedding; she remembered Mary as a shy bride, Cormac as a beaming groom, the two families celebrating in their brightly coloured, festive clothing. Then Cormac and Mary had moved away to Dublin not long after their marriage. They had never made it back to Fermanagh since then. But in the year 1598 in August, Shane had fought with Hugh Maguire in what turned out to be Ireland's greatest victory over the English in hundreds of years, England's greatest loss on Irish soil. It was in Armagh and it was known as the Battle of the Yellow Ford. The English commander, whose name was Bagenal, brought with him four thousand men, infantry and cavalry, to relieve a fort that the Irish had under siege. But Bagenal had not foreseen what Hugh Maguire, Hugh O'Neill, the Earl of Tyrone, and Red Hugh O'Donnell and their men could do. They dug a series of ditches criss-crossing each other and trapped the English warriors in them. And then the English were shot by Irish marksmen, marksmen like Shane himself, leaving hundreds of the English dead. Bagenal himself was shot to death.

When Shane was fighting in Armagh, he met a man from Dublin who knew another man in Dublin, and somewhere in this chain of acquaintances was Cormac, Mary's husband. Cormac was now working on the Dublin quays, loading and unloading merchandise on and off the ships. Messages were sent and received along this chain of acquaintances and out of this a plan emerged. Brigid and her family were going to Dublin. She didn't know how Shane and Cormac set this up — didn't know what favours might have been promised or paid — but it was arranged that the family would travel to Dublin by ship. Owny nearly burst his skin with excitement when he heard it. "A pirate ship?!" He was brought down to earth when told they'd be travelling with a cargo of fish. It was a ship out of Bordeaux in France, bringing wine to the port of Ballyshannon and returning to France with a load of salmon. Ballyshannon, at the mouth of the Erne, was a frequent port of call for ships bringing the highly prized wine to the Irish shores. Everyone knew that wine was the biggest import into Ireland. And salmon from the north of Ireland was highly valued in France. The ship would put in at Dublin before sailing to France. Brigid suspected that Dublin was where the favours would be collected and loaded onto the ship: Uisce beatha? Hides? Brigid had often heard of the beautiful leather goods that were made on the continent; Irish hides were greatly admired there. Or was there another explanation for the ship stopping in at Dublin? Was somebody fleeing from there to the continent? But Shane laughed her questions away. All she had to know was that they would disembark at Dublin, and Cormac would meet them on the quay.

The plan was initiated a year and a half ago, and now in March 1600, Brigid, Shane, Owny, and Eileen were at the threshold of the great city, after an exhausting and at times sickening journey halfway around the island of Ireland. It was not the voyage on a gently rolling sea that she and Sorcha had long imagined, the voyage to sun-baked foreign shores with their fantastic people and customs and languages melodious as music to the ears. But it was an adventure, no question. To be at sea, to view the coast of their country from the water, to see the starry skies above them was an experience Brigid would not have missed. But they sailed into a storm and the seas were rough, and it took the better part of a week to reach the mouth of the River Liffey. The end couldn't come soon enough for Eileen. She said she never wanted to see a salmon again for the rest of her life. Fortunately, the seas and winds were calm when they made the east coast, and although this slowed the journey down again, it provided the opportunity for much-needed sleep. Now all Brigid could think of, as they stepped onto the shore, was a much-needed bath. She tried to put out of her mind what kind of a picture she and her family would present to her sister when they arrived at her house. For now, the only member of the family in sight was Cormac. He was tall and broad, with wavy light-brown hair. His face was lined, which it hadn't been the last time Brigid had seen him, but that was sixteen years ago at the wedding. He greeted Shane and then the rest of the family. Brigid introduced him to her children. He had another man with him, and they had two horses and carts to transport the family and their belongings to Cormac and Mary's home.

"It's not the way the Lord Deputy travels," Cormac said, "but if you don't mind the discomfort, these will get us to the house."

They assured him they didn't mind and thanked him for arranging their journey.

"So now we'll head for home," Cormac said. "We live in Irishtown and you will be comfortable there."

"Irishtown?" Shane asked.

Cormac laughed but there was little humour in it. "You don't think we'd have been permitted to live in Dublin, do you? They packed all us Irish off to Irishtown."

"But," Brigid protested, "this is Ireland!"

"That isn't," Cormac replied, pointing in the direction of the walled city. "You'd think it was England itself, to hear them talk. This is, after all, the seat of government for the Pale." That was the area around Dublin and some ways beyond, controlled by the English. "We'll come back into the city tomorrow, and you'll see how they make a show of themselves. Now, on to Irishtown!"

Brigid and the children gaped at what they could see of the city above the great stone wall with its towers. In some places could be seen the stone tops of buildings, so many of them in one walled space. Brigid had never been to a city before. The walls muffled the noise coming out of it, but she could hear the clattering of carts carrying goods along the streets and the banging of hammers. People must be constructing and repairing things here every day. She looked forward to seeing more of Dublin tomorrow. But nothing could top the anticipation she felt about seeing her sister after all these years.

Mary and Cormac's house was a modest one, a cottage, but its white walls were bright and clean. There was a chimney in the middle of the newly thatched roof. Mary appeared at the door when the horses stopped in front of the house. Brigid started to call out to her sister, but her voice caught in her throat. She was seized with a feeling of joy, but it was joy mixed with regret. She was elated to see her sister for the first time in sixteen years, but she understood instantly what a gap had been carved out of their lives. Mary was fairly tall and slim like Brigid, and her hair was of a similar coppery tone but lighter. Her dress was a quiet brown in contrast with Brigid's bright blue. They embraced each other, and smiles soon turned to tears as they realized how much they had missed, growing to adulthood and raising their children without a sister close by. Without the company and comfort of each for the other.

Owny was now fourteen and Eileen a year younger. Mary's three boys, Art, Cian, and Pádraig, were fifteen, twelve and ten, and the daughter, Nuala, was nine. The children had varying degrees of Cormac's features, combined with Mary's reddish hair and pale skin. The cousins were shy with each other at first but it didn't last, and they were soon bubbling over about the games they would play together and the sights they would see. The two men got into a conversation straight away, talking about ships, travel, and, of course, warriors and war. Mary had curtained off an area at the back of the house and filled a large tub with warm water. She had put out lovely Castile soap, finer than the soap Brigid had at home, and Brigid jumped at the chance to be the first to bathe. More pots of water were being heated over the fire, for the rest of the baths. Not only that, but Mary had provided a change of clothing for every one of the visitors, so their own clothing could be washed and made presentable again. The house offered sufficient room for both families to sleep comfortably, but it was a long time before anyone fell asleep, with food and drink to be consumed and one and a half decades of talk to catch up on.

The next day, the two families walked to the city centre. Cormac identified some of the sights as they moved along. He pointed to a striking complex of stone buildings ranged around a square in the eastern area of the city. He said it was a new college built on the grounds of the old All Hallows monastery. "You'd be well familiar with the dissolution and suppression of the monasteries under the English King Henry, and now Elizabeth. Not as bad up where you live."

"They don't have the stranglehold on us in the North," Shane declared. "They never will."

"May it please God," Brigid prayed quietly.

She looked at Shane, who smiled at her and said, in a voice only she could hear, "It didn't happen." He was referring to the old prophecy uttered by Sorcha, God rest her, five years before. Thanks be to God, the Gaelic lords had not in fact left the country and abandoned their people to be conquered by the foreigner. But the English under Queen Elizabeth were relentless, Brigid knew. She hoped and prayed that the northern part of the country, where the Saxon invaders had enjoyed the least success, would remain unconquered.

They walked through Dublin, inside and outside the walls. Brigid looked about her at the big grey city. She didn't quite know what she'd been expecting: towers of gold? It came as a surprise to see that many of the buildings seemed decrepit, their stonework crumbling and in need of repair. Some streets outside the walls were lined with thatched cottages.

Mary said, "We'll circle about and save the castle to the last. It's a sight to behold."

"Let me know if you get tired of the walking," said Cormac. "We've a good many taverns here in Dublin!"

"Don't be telling him that," Brigid replied, pointing to Shane. "We'll not see another thing but the inside of an alehouse!"

"No, no, I'll resist the temptation," said Shane, laughing. "I want to look around the city, not into a tankard of ale."

As they moved along, Brigid was distressed to see poor, thin people in raggedy clothes; beggars they were, and in great number.

By way of contrast, the richer class of Dublin people strutted along the streets in their English finery: silks and taffeta, velvet and lace. Many wore garments that were pinked — cut in such a way as to display the luxurious fabrics beneath the outer layers.

"*Those* people," Cormac said in a quiet voice, nodding towards the lavishly dressed, "have no regard for *those* people." This time he indicated the beggars. "They wish that the beggars would simply vanish into the air, or that they'd be pushed into the river. They're an ugly stain on the city of Dublin, is the way they think. And, God forgive me, I thought that way myself when I first arrived here, me fresh from my years working for the O'Donnells in their fine castle in Ballyshannon! But then one day, not long after I arrived and started my work on the quays, I came out of a tavern after swallowing a good quantity of ale, and there was a beggar standing outside, and he started to talk to me and I to him. He said he used to work repairing horse carts but he'd had a bad injury to his right arm and couldn't find work. And I thought, *That could just as easily have been me.* And who was I to look down on this unfortunate man and others like him? And I brought him into the tavern and got a drink for him and had another myself. And I came out, unsteady on my legs, and thought how I could have a fall and be injured and be unable to work."

"I remember that," Mary said.

"So even if we someday become grand ourselves, eh Mary, we'll give a beggar what we can give, and thank the heavens we have it to give."

She nodded in agreement. "That's the way it should be."

Brigid enjoyed the story of the beggar, and Cormac's affinity for the man. Prior to this visit, Brigid had met Cormac only briefly, at his and Mary's wedding. She remembered being favourably impressed by the young husband; it was gratifying to know that his early promise had been fulfilled. Mary had a wonderful man in her life.

They passed a fine-looking stone church, and Cormac said, "A great many churches and monasteries here were shut down and looted. Places in Tipperary, too, Kilkenny, all over this part of the country, and as far away as Waterford. Never mind that the monasteries had the custom of providing hospitality and education, caring for orphans and the poor and the sick. The Saxons claim we worship idols, so those idols have to be destroyed. But more often, it's the king and his men stealing treasures, gold and silver, sacred vessels, jewels and plate, church bells, and also glass and lead for buildings of their own. Some of them take the friaries over as grand houses for themselves. Grabbing everything to make themselves rich. Merchants here tell me they heard that there were so many bells and other objects stolen and so much lead stripped off the roofs of the holy buildings in England that the prices for metals fell in the European markets!"

"Thieves and destroyers!"

"And that's when they weren't cutting the heads off us and putting them up on spikes," Cormac said.

"Not heads!" Brigid cried out.

"They did. They put them on spikes at the castle to display them, the heads of our men who dared to rebel against English tyranny. We're coming up to the castle. Who knows, you may see some today!"

The massive stone fortress that was Dublin Castle loomed ahead of them. They walked all around it and peered in at the parts they could see, but fortune was smiling on them that day; there were no heads on spikes. Brigid sensed that even Owny was relieved that all the craning of his neck and standing on the tips of his toes brought him no sightings of severed heads.

But Cormac was not quite finished with the subject. "And it's not just here in Dublin. The queen's men in other parts of the country have done the same. I was in Munster and I heard horrifying stories. The governor she imposed on our people there liked to have a line of heads on display in front of his quarters. And he didn't stop at killing men; women and children fell victim to him as well. Gilbert was his name, Humphrey Gilbert. And again, he was not by any count the only one of the queen's valiant men chopping off Irish heads to bring our country into submission!

"And," Cormac lowered his voice even further, and said to Shane and Brigid, "they seem to enjoy inventing ghastly tortures for their enemies. You may have heard of the fate that befell the Archbishop of Cashel."

"I have heard of it," said Shane, though whatever he knew he had not passed on to Brigid.

Cormac told the story. "Dermot O'Hurley was his name. He was born near Limerick and when grown he went to study in Paris and Louvain and was superior in many areas of study: rhetoric, theology, and the law. He spent some years in Rome as well and was consecrated Archbishop of Cashel. He was hunted by the English, but managed to elude capture for two years, because the people in Cashel protected him. But he eventually fell into the hands of his enemies, who brought him here to Dublin and presented him to the authorities. They prevailed upon him to renounce his faith, which he refused to do. You'll think I've gone mad when I relate what they did to him then, but it's the truth. They encased his feet in boots filled with tallow and pitch, oil, salt, and water, and lit a fire beneath them, and boiled his feet until the bones were exposed. And still he refused to betray his faith or acknowledge Queen Elizabeth's supremacy in the matter of religion."

Brigid looked at Cormac in horror, but she knew all too well that he was recounting what had really happened.

"Maybe he refused to acknowledge her gentleness and mercy," Shane remarked.

"O'Hurley not only endured this but, witnesses said, endured it cheerfully and with serenity and still did not give in. Thereafter they took him to a place outside the city and hanged him. There was also the man I saw, the Abbot O'Culenan. Did you ever have a dream that has you crying out in the night? Because you can feel the pains the dream is showing you? That's what happened to me after I saw the body of the abbot hanged here in Dublin! O'Culenan was like O'Hurley, a great man for learning. He had studied abroad, at Louvain and Rome. He, too, suffered tortures at the hands of the Saxons; they crushed his fingers and his limbs with a mallet, and yet he refused to yield. And then they hanged him, here in Dublin, and his body was displayed for all to see, hanging from the battlements of the castle. I saw O'Culenan's body with my own eyes, and the sight of it haunted my dreams for weeks. It still does sometimes, and I see the heads on the spikes, and I'm startled and I wake up and think it was a dream. And it was, but it was a reflection of what I really saw. And these English invaders are the people who want to make gentlemen out of *us*!"

Brigid said, "We have heard dismal stories about the Catholic queen, too, though. People were executed in ferocious ways under her rule as well. I've heard her called Bloody Mary!"

"That shows you, then," Cormac replied. "They breed vicious tyrants over there. Mary was a daughter of King Henry the Eighth. Now it's another daughter, Bloody Bess. Queen Elizabeth, and she's been on the throne for over forty years now, so try to imagine how many deaths she's been responsible for. Men boiled in oil, and heads on spikes, to prove how worthy a person she is to rule over us. These are the people who banished the likes of *us* to *Irishtown!*"

Brigid felt weak at the hearing of it. She looked over at the children. They were cheerfully ignoring their parents and talking excitedly about the sights all around them. Even though some of them were nearly grown now, Brigid did not want their ears, or their souls, sullied by what the governors of much of their country had done to the native population here.

⁂

When they were back in the house in Irishtown with a meal and goblets of red wine in front of them, Cormac said, "If it weren't for my work here, I'd want to take my Mary back to Fermanagh. The English have failed in their attempts to establish themselves there; your chiefs are strong."

"They must stay strong," Brigid said, "and they must cease fighting amongst themselves, which allows our enemies to divide us. Sometimes our men submit to the English, often just as a deception or to use the alliance for their own purposes, but still it weakens us."

Shane rose to Ireland's defence. "We are a country with one language, one faith, across all the land. Except where the invaders pushed us out and installed their own customs and foreign tongue, *planted* their own people on our soil. Like weeds. God save us from Dublin! And Galway, where they won't even allow an 'O' in a name, or a 'Mac.' A society like the one they're trying to impose on us will never last! Thanks be to God and Mary and Saint Patrick that we live in Ulster. We have the O'Neill, we have the Maguire, the O'Donnell. The three Hughs! And other great chieftains and warriors. There will be no 'plantation' of Ulster!"

Brigid took a sip of the brilliant French wine and prayed that Shane was right, that their men in Ulster would continue to prevail against the relentless invaders.

But this was a family occasion, and they celebrated their reunion, feasted well, and drank modest quantities of ale and wine and uisce beatha, and talked and sang and told stories and enjoyed themselves mightily. Eileen and Owny got on well with their cousins and they all had their own tales to tell, some of them prompting shrieks of laughter.

Two weeks after their arrival, however, they received terrible news. Hugh Maguire had been killed fighting against the English in Cork. Brigid and Mary and their husbands fell to their knees in prayer and then drank a toast to their courageous chieftain. Shane immediately began talking about returning to Fermanagh. With their beloved chief slain, his territory would be vulnerable to attack. And there could be conflict about the succession as well. Who would be inaugurated the Maguire now?

Shane took Brigid aside and said to her, "I will go to Fermanagh and take Owny with me. Cormac will arrange horses and packs. It will be a long, arduous journey. You and Eileen will stay here." She protested but to no avail. "I'll send for you and make arrangements when the wine ship will be coming from Bordeaux. But first I'll wait to see how things are at home. It will be a dangerous time."

"Dangerous for you and Owny!"

"I'm a soldier, my love."

"Owny is not!"

"You know that is all he's ever wanted to be. But I . . . Brigid, I'm telling you, if I could talk him out of it, I would. If I don't take him with me now, you know he will run away and join the fighting somewhere. I'll have my men keep an eye out for him as best they can." That did not sound like Shane, not like the Shane she had known so long, blithely heading off to battle with a confidence she could never have matched. He had been a more serious man in the last few years, brooding over the death and wounding of people who had been part of their lives in Fermanagh, and over the calamities that had been visited upon their country. And he would now give voice to worries for the children, something he had kept to himself in the early years, always making a point to reassure her that Eileen would grow out of her timidity and Owny would be careful whenever he came of age and took up sword or musket. Nowadays, Shane shared his worries with Brigid. Oh, there was still a comical side to him, and he was still the bard of foolish rhymes and slanders. But life — life and death and loss — had changed him, as it changes all of us.

The two families had a final meal together the night before Shane and Owny started out for Fermanagh. After they had eaten, Cormac and Shane took themselves off and left the house. Brigid peered out the window and saw them deep in conversation. Brigid was about to turn away to clean up the cups and glasses and plates when she noticed an abrupt change in the expression on Shane's face. He stared at Cormac in horror and then he glanced at the house. He caught sight of Brigid, then quickly looked away.

What are they talking about? Brigid wondered. What has Shane just learned from Cormac?

It was a tearful scene as Brigid and Eileen said goodbye to Shane and young Owny. Brigid could tell that her son was practically hopping with excitement about the journey back with his father. But it was a journey to a land almost certainly fated to endure a period of strife. And Shane now knew something he hadn't known before. She had asked him whether something was wrong. He brushed off her question, but she could tell he was preoccupied. Was it a warning Cormac had given him? Had some other catastrophe unfolded in the battle against Ireland's determined invaders? Finally, she got it out of him. He told her that there was news that several of the Fermanagh pikemen and musketeers had never returned from fighting in Munster. And that her brother, Diarmait, may have been among them. Please, God, no!

When Shane and Owny had gone, and Eileen was chatting and laughing with her cousins, Brigid went out with her sister for a walk to the seaside. She decided not to relay to Mary the uncertainty over the fate of their brother. It was not known yet that he had been killed; it had happened more times than Brigid could count that rumours of catastrophe had come from embattled regions of the country, and then the men had returned and all was well. By the time Brigid was back home in Fermanagh, Diarmait would probably appear at the door as usual with his rowdy companions. She kept telling herself that it would happen; she would not give in to grief when there was no proof that he had died. She would not give in to grief and fear when she had a young son who was longing to get onto the field of battle.

Resolutely turning her mind to the present, she felt a thrill to be standing on the shore and looking out at the boundless sea, and felt this way even after her long, at times turbulent voyage on the French ship to Dublin. She loved her view at home of the River Erne and the lough, but this was the sea, beyond which lay lands she could scarcely imagine. What must it be like to sail far from Ireland and see strange cities and foreign peoples? What would they look like, sound like? What would they wear? She expressed her thoughts to Mary who, in turn, entertained her with tales of the strange people she had seen right here on Irish soil. She described the lordly ways of Dubliners who had taken on the styles and manners of the English occupiers, and they shared a laugh.

Then Brigid asked, "Mary, do you ever think of coming home to Fermanagh?"

Mary's eyes left Brigid's. She looked down at the ground. Then her gaze returned to her sister and she said, "I wish . . . Well, we're settled here, with the children. Cormac's work is here." She looked to the ground again.

Brigid moved towards her, put her arms around her, and they stood in each other's embrace while their tears flowed and the waters of the sea lapped the shore beside them. Then Mary said, "Would you ever think of coming here to stay?"

Brigid shook her head. Her heart ached with the thought of parting from her sister again. They would have to visit each other before too many more years had passed. But Brigid knew she could not move her family to the English Pale. And she didn't even want to imagine Shane in this place. They'd be here two weeks, and his head would be displayed outside Dublin Castle, on a spike.

CHAPTER XXI

*A faint wailing sound, so wild and indescribable
that it seemed almost something unearthly, came
floating on the light morning breeze . . . The effect
of the whole was most striking, and had something
even grand in it . . . it certainly struck me as the
most singularly plaintive and mournful expression of
excessive grief that could well be imagined.*

— O'G., "The Irish Funeral Cry," *Dublin Penny
Journal* (1833)

2018

Mick's father and grandmother were adamant in their refusal to leave their home after the blackmailer's threat to Cait. Mick had been reluctant to leave them there, but finally he returned to the hotel. It wasn't long, however, before something occurred to him, and he hoofed it back to the house. On the way by, he cast an eye on the now-unprotected excavation. Not surprisingly, when he arrived at the house, Liam was wide awake.

"I'm wondering if this struck you the way it did me, Da. The fella who did this must have known we were away for the weekend. And he knew when Cait would be coming home from Mass on Sunday."

"You may be sure I took note of that."

"And do you recall what Gran said, how she said it? According to her, the fucker put it this way: 'Everybody will know what old Roddo Tierney did to his tenants and him after lying about it.' Something close to that anyway."

"Aye. *Roddo*."

"Right. Anyone looking through old records would see the man listed as Roderick. It was only the family that referred to him as Roddo."

"The family. But Ma would have recognized the wee bastard."

"He didn't come himself. He sent one of his drug-pushing scumbag mates to do the job."

"All right, Mick, we're off. Time to let Brayden know that *we know where you live*."

"We should have the peelers on him, have him lifted, and charged with extortion."

Liam gave him a look, which conveyed a lifetime of history, a lifetime of avoiding any cooperation with the police, be they the Royal Ulster Constabulary of old or the Police Service of Northern Ireland of today.

"It's time for an exception, Da. There's nothing I'd like better than seeing Brayden Waring banged up in jail for this or for anything else we could pin on him."

"Michael. We'll handle this ourselves."

"But—"

"I take it you really do know where he lives?"

"I do."

"Let's go. Get your car and come back for me."

"Why don't we just walk over and get it?"

Liam's only reply was a gesture of his head in the direction of the door. Mick went off to get the car.

⊛

Brayden Waring had the basement flat in a house that was sorely in need of repair. Mick wouldn't want to see his grandchildren in such a place; good thing the courts had taken care of that. Visiting rights were permitted only in the company of Róisín and her family. There was a light on in the sitting room, but no movement that Mick could see as he peered in through the grimy window. It wasn't midnight yet; Brayden was likely still out partying in one of the clubs.

"He's not there, Da."

"So we'll go in and make ourselves comfortable while we wait for him. If we can bear the stink of the place. It looks like a fucking kip."

"It does. But how do you propose we gain entry?"

Another look from his father's dark-blue eyes, which this time suggested there would be no problem gaining entry to this place. But then there was a sound inside, and Mick and Liam both eased themselves away from the window. The light dimmed. Waring was home.

Liam immediately rapped on the door. No response. Rapped louder. And this time Mick could hear footsteps. The footsteps stopped, and Liam hammered on the door. Finally, there was a creak and the door opened a crack. Liam stepped forward, somebody stumbled, and then they were in.

Brayden Waring pushed himself upright and stared at the two men who had forced their way into his home. The sitting room was dimly lit and filled with shabby, worn furniture. There was a stale smell about the place. Brayden's oiled hair was dishevelled and he was in need of a shave. *Might be the fashion this week*, Mick thought. The expression on his ex-son-in-law's face seemed to vary between belligerence and fear, both of those being appropriate reactions under the circumstances.

"What the—"

"You." Liam took a step towards him. "You. Threatened. My. Mother." Mick had never heard his father sound so menacing, his voice low, calm, lethal. Mick could now imagine the cold, shivering terror he must have induced in anyone who crossed him, or crossed the republican cause, during the recent dirty war in this country.

"What are you talking about, you crazy old bastard?" Brayden thrust his hands out and lurched towards Liam. Liam, as quick as a flash, reached into his pocket and pulled out a gun, pointed it at Brayden.

Oh, Christ, Mick thought. That's how fast these things can escalate. He now knew why Liam hadn't immediately left with Mick to get the car.

"Sit down," Liam commanded. "Now."

Brayden backed away, his terrified eyes on the weapon, his hands held up to ward off the older man. He dropped into an armchair and stared. Just then there was a loud bang to the right of Liam and someone burst into the room. Someone in dark clothing, coming in low to the ground. Liam's reaction was immediate; his gun hand swivelled to meet the new threat. There was an ear-splitting scream and the sound of a gunshot.

The scream intensified and was joined by the sound of someone crying. Mick stood there, shocked into immobility, trying to sort out what had just occurred. He turned to his father, who was standing there poleaxed, a look of horror on his face. The gun was now pointing to the floor. Mick turned then to the source of the screaming. Something glinted in the low light, something metal. What he saw was a skateboard with metal wheels. And he remembered Brayden boasting of finding a "vintage board." But . . . then he saw her. A little girl, no older than eight or nine, on her knees on the skateboard. She was all in black. Costume for a play? Black raincoat? A woman in her late twenties was now bent over the child, clinging to her and crying. She looked up and stared in disbelief at Mick's father. Brayden Waring sat, shell-shocked, in his chair.

Mick moved towards the woman and child, and both shrank away from him in terror. He raised his hands in an effort to convey that he meant no harm. "Are you hurt?" he managed to say, to both of them at once. But it was immediately apparent that no one had been hurt; the bullet had gone into the door frame above their heads. It seemed that Liam's hand had jerked upwards at the sound of the scream, and the gun had fired, and — thanks be to God — no one had been hit.

Finally, Mick found his voice again. "Nobody's going to hurt you." Hard to make that sound convincing, after what had just happened in the room.

Then it was Liam, his tone gentle but firm. He put the gun back in his pocket and said to the woman, "We'll not be hurting you. Take the wee girl into the bedroom and shut the door. Our quarrel is with him." He nodded in the direction of Brayden. "Go."

The woman turned her frightened glance from Liam to Mick and to Brayden. Brayden said, "Get back into the room. I'll deal with this."

When the woman and child had backed away and closed the door, Brayden said, "What kind of a man are you, terrorizing a wee woman and her child? If you—"

Liam cut him off. "Save it. What kind of a man are *you*, sending some great lump of a bastard to terrorize an old lady and try to extort money out of her?"

"I don't know what the fuck you're on about."

"Yeah, you do. We know it was you behind it." And he pulled out the gun again. Pointed it at Brayden's face.

"Da," Mick began. He had a sudden image of the woman in the back room, ringing the Police Service of Northern Ireland, sirens and flashing lights hurtling towards the house. But he could not, absolutely could not, bring himself to go into that room and see those two terrified faces, and terrify them further by warning them not to call the peelers. Or else. Or else what?

Liam was speaking. "If this is the only language this wee get understands, this is the language he's going to hear." Liam moved closer, the gun held steady in his hand.

"Brayden," Mick said, "what did you do at the excavation?"

"I didn't do nothing."

Liam moved in even closer and pointed the gun in the direction of Brayden's kneecap. There was no missing the fear in the younger man's face; whatever he saw in Liam Tierney, he believed in it and recognized it for the threat it was.

"I didn't do it!"

"Don't you even—"

"No! It wasn't my idea. Some fellas I know. They . . ." His eyes raked the room as if the fellas might be lurking in the shadows. "They know about the hotel, the money yous are making off it. And they heard me talking one night about the bloke back in the Famine times, and the old . . . your mother being scared something would be dug up out of the hole about what happened to those tenants back then. And they put the pressure on me about it."

"What do you mean, they put pressure on you?"

"They decided that . . . one of them was going to sneak into that dig in the nighttime and mess it up, and then go to the old . . . to the lady's house after she came home from church, and he'd tell her that he found something really bad about old Roddo Tierney, and she had to pay up or the story would get out."

Mick spoke up then. "That sounds more like you than some other shithead, Brayden. You're the one who heard all of that old history from Róisín, and how Cait was worried about it."

"I knew it, and I ended up telling them one night when I was . . . I had some drink in me. But it was them!"

"And they put pressure on you, you're telling us. How could they do that? Are these mates of yours? Who are they?"

"I can't fucking tell you that! What am I, a tout?"

"You're a useless, scheming—" That was Liam.

Mick overrode him. "Tell us now, or we'll have the peelers on you for extortion." Which, of course, wasn't going to happen. Liam Tierney would never shop anyone to the peelers, and Mick was not about to bring that kind of attention to his family. And, if that had ever been his intention, the bullet in the wall had put paid to that idea. He wondered again when he'd be hearing sirens. It was time to get to the bottom of this and get out.

"Tell us now, or you're not even going to recognize your life from this night on."

There was no doubt about the fact that Brayden was badly shaken. The defiant tone was gone. "I'm into them for . . . I owe them money. A few thousand quid. They said they'd write off the debt if they could get money out of the old lady."

"How did you run up a debt like that?"

Silence.

"Brayden! How did you—"

"I've been selling stuff for them. Not really heavy stuff, just, you know, hash and disco biscuits, like—"

"Disco biscuits?!" Liam barked at him.

"Ecstasy pills."

Liam turned to Mick. "The father of your two wee grandchildren is a drug dealer, Mick. What are we going to do about that?"

"I won't do it anymore!" It came out almost as a sob.

"You're fucking right you won't."

Mick thought of something then. "What did you mean, mess up the dig?"

"Make it look like something got taken out of it."

"And was something taken out? If anything was removed from that excavation—"

"Nothing was! He . . . I didn't take nothing."

So it was Brayden himself who broke into the site. "What did you fucking take, Brayden?"

"I told you, nothing!"

"You're lying. Who went to Cait's house? Was it you?"

"No! They wanted me to do it myself, but I told them she'd know my voice. She might recognize me somehow."

"So, who was it?"

"I don't know. One of them. They didn't tell me who was going to do it."

That may or may not have been true, but Mick believed that it wasn't Brayden at Cait's house, for the very reason he'd stated: Cait might have noticed something familiar about him. "Who was it, Brayden, who put an old lady in fear of her life?"

But Liam brought the discussion back to Brayden's brief career as a drug dealer. "It's not just weed and disco biscuits, or whatever you called them, is it? Not for long. It's all this shite that people are dying of, overdosing on. Here we are with the war behind us.

But now that the shooting is over, you — the peacetime generation — are poisoning each other with drugs and killing each other over the profits! Well, that career is over for you. As of this minute. Because you know what's going to happen if you keep at it? You may have heard that a number of republicans have taken up another cause, in addition to insisting on a united Ireland. Do you know that?"

Brayden's eyes were wide as he acknowledged that he knew. There were republicans on both sides of the border who were taking the law into their own hands when it came to drug dealers in their communities. If the peelers didn't get to you first, anti-drug vigilantes might show up at your door. And a bullet fired by one of those lads wouldn't be lodged in a door frame.

By the time Liam and Mick left the premises of Mick's former son-in-law, they knew they would not be having any more trouble from that quarter.

When they got into Mick's car, Liam did not look at all well. In a quiet voice, with none of the steel Mick had heard in it earlier, Liam said, "The expression on that wee girl's face. She thought I was going to shoot her. As if I would ever hurt a woman or a child. But she couldn't have known that. And the gun going off. What if it had . . . ? Michael, I'll never forget the look in her eyes. And it was me who had her petrified. It was me . . . I never would have hurt her."

Mick was in his bed late that night, fast asleep, until his sleep was disturbed by an unearthly sound out behind the hotel. What was happening? Was it some shower of shites he'd booked in, and them now making a racket and waking every living soul with their noise? Everyone in the hotel would be yanked awake and cross with Mick in the morning. But, no, it was a Monday night, and there were only a few guests in the place. Only two old couples, and they were staying in the front of the building. He was so tired that the idea of getting up and putting an end to the ruckus was almost too much for him to contemplate. But Jesus, Mary, and Joseph, what kind of singing was that? As he swung his legs over the side of the bed, and started to push himself upright, a chill ran through him from head to toe. The sound now was terrifying, yet in some way beautiful. It sounded as if somebody was wailing the end of all life as we know it. It would put the hair standing straight up on your head, and so it was with Mick. Well, he'd put an end to whatever life was out there bawling in the midst of his garden.

He rose from his bed, took a step to his window, and pulled the curtains aside. He peered out. The stars were brilliant and the land was illuminated by a three-quarter moon. The lamentation went on and on. But there was nobody there, nothing on two legs, nothing on four. It seemed to be coming from the area of the old family home, but his view of the property was limited. Was somebody out there on the other side of the house causing all this carry-on? The last thing he wanted to do at three o'clock in the morning was get dressed and leave the hotel, but he was determined to put an end to the disruption. So he went to the sink, splashed water on his face to get him good and wakened up, dressed, and left the hotel for the house where he'd been raised.

The sound grew louder as he approached the house. When he reached the Tierney family home, he stopped in his tracks. There was his grandmother in the open front doorway in her white night-dress and a black shawl, on her knees and rocking back and forth. It was her keening, her wailing cries, that were filling the skies.

He couldn't bear what he saw in her, the grief and the loss. She didn't interrupt her grieving, just pointed a shaky finger to her left, to the side of the house. Mick walked over, and there lay his father, her son. Liam. He was sprawled on his back, on the flagstones of the path, his sightless eyes wide open to the stars. It was plain that there was no life left in him, but Mick dropped to his knees and took his father's left hand in his. It was stone cold. Mick touched his neck for a pulse but, of course, there was nothing. Mick stayed there, kneeling, helpless.

It seemed like hours but it was likely only seconds when he realized that the crying had stopped. His grandmother came towards him, and he got up. She stumbled into his arms, trembling. They held each other in a prolonged embrace before Mick gently released her and took her hand, leading her towards the house.

She halted in her tracks. "We can't be leaving him out here!"

"We'll not be leaving him out, Gran. I'm calling the ambulance, even though . . . I'm calling the ambulance." Mick was surprised at himself, that he could speak so calmly while standing over his father's body. He knew that calmness would be shattered when it all sank in.

"I heard him up," she said. "I heard him. I think he fell against the dresser in his room. Something happened that woke me. And I went in, and he looked like death already, and he said he was going to drive himself to the hospital.

"And I said, 'Liam, what's wrong? What happened?' And do you know what he said to me? He said, 'I would never have hurt her. She thought I was going to hurt her, but I never would have.' He was rambling like that, Michael. He wasn't making any sense at all."

Mick said nothing. He turned to look at his father, lifeless there on the ground. Then they went inside and he rang 999, though he knew there was nothing the paramedics could do. The night unfolded as these awful nights do. The ear-splitting sound of the siren, the flashing blue lights, as the emergency services rushed to the house for Liam. The flying trip to the hospital, Cait and Mick with the body of the man who had long ago survived a bullet but could not survive a stricken conscience.

The following morning, Mick and his gran met with Liam's doctor. "His heart gave out on him," the doctor said. "As you know, we've seen him here several times over the past couple of years, for his long-standing congestive heart failure." The doctor peered at them. "Did he never tell you?"

Mick was shaking his head. "He never let on."

That night, sitting across from Cait in the silent house, Mick remembered the stories which he hadn't thought of for years, stories about his grandmother back in the day. She had been one of the last professional keeners, professional mourners, the women who attended funerals and raised their cries of grief to the very heavens.

CHAPTER XXII

This was a distinguished crew for one ship; for it is indeed certain that the sea had not supported, and the winds had not wafted from Ireland, in modern times, a party of one ship who would have been more illustrious or noble, in point of genealogy, or more renowned for deeds, valour, prowess, or high achievements, than they . . . woe to the council that decided on the project of their setting out on this voyage, without knowing whether they should ever return to their native principalities or patrimonies to the end of the world.

— O'Donovan, *Annals of the Kingdom of Ireland, by the Four Masters*

1607

It was late September. Brigid sat at her harp and tried to play. Nothing would come but the most sorrowful of laments. The Irish had been defeated at the Battle of Kinsale. That was six years ago, and the country had experienced nothing but devastation ever since. The rebellion — the long war — begun by Hugh

Maguire and the other Gaelic lords against the foreign invaders was over. The conquest of Ireland was all but complete in 1603, with the submission of Hugh O'Neill, the Earl of Tyrone, to the English crown. Fermanagh's own lord, Cúchonnacht Maguire, was the last to submit. Insincere submissions, Brigid knew, as they so often had been, accommodations to allow them time to regroup. Following Cúchonnacht's submission, Fermanagh was divided between himself and his rival, the English Maguire.

In the years before that, the queen's man in Ireland, Mountjoy, had committed such depredations across the land that Brigid had for a long time refused to believe the stories she had heard. Mountjoy and his men swept through the country from south to north and into Ulster, scorching the earth, burning the crops, burning the houses, killing or stealing the animals, and murdering the men, children, and women young and old. Those who were not slaughtered did not long survive. The planned and deliberate famine made sure of that. Shane had seen with his own eyes people lying dead on the ground, thin as skeletons, their mouths stained green from eating whatever plants they could find. He had witnessed these horrors in Munster, and now again in Ulster. He saw many of the dead lying unburied, and he'd heard that there were over three thousand people who had starved to death in Tyrone.

Shane was away again now, in Tirconnell she thought. Whenever he came home, he busied himself with managing the Tierney lands and herds. He avoided Brigid's questions about what he'd been doing. Fighting with a few of the Maguire's men who had refused to acknowledge the submission? Fighting on his own, a lone marksman picking off the occasional representative of the dominant power? She was never sure. She missed him painfully; she always did when he was away for any length of time, but it was worse now, knowing that he was facing an enemy that could not be vanquished. She thought, as she so often did, of Sorcha and her frightful prophecies. A kingdom divided would be brought to desolation. The enemy would get its hold on Ulster and take over the Irish people's lands. Sorcha was right; she always had been. Brigid's dear friend had been gone for a dozen years now, and Brigid still felt the emptiness of her loss. She had tried and failed to find the man who had killed her. Brigid and Shane, Terence and the brehon all had worked for years to uncover the secret of her killing, and all had failed. Someone had taken her life and was still out there enjoying his own.

Brigid was terrified of what the future might bring. She knew it would not bring the fulfillment of the dreams she had shared with Sorcha, the dreams of travelling to foreign lands, seeing the sights, the flowers, the animals, the people she imagined so different from herself in their appearance and their speech. And what about Mary, so far away in Dublin? Would she ever see Mary again? Brigid felt she would be fortunate just to survive here in Ireland. She didn't know how long she could hold out, how long she could keep the old Tierney house for herself and Shane, their children and the coming generations. And if she lost the house, where would she go?

She abandoned her efforts to call up music for the harp, and walked through the dark, silent house to her room. This was the way of it now, an empty guesthouse. There had been no guests for weeks. The rooms were cold and dark, the cauldron often dry. She found herself unable to settle; she was haunted by the images of her people lying starved on the parched ground. She twisted and turned about, until at last she fell into an uneasy sleep. Then, at the darkest hour of the night, she was jolted awake by an eerie sound. It was a heart-tearing cry, the pitch rising and falling, a long, sustained wailing coming from outside the house. Was it the children? Brigid rose from her bed and then her mind cleared. The children? Eileen was married now, to a Maguire, and living with her husband. They had a little girl, and Eileen was expecting her second baby soon. Owny hadn't married yet; he devoted much of his time to drinking and carousing. He was off somewhere, as he often was for days on end. Like so many others, he was waiting and hoping for the day when the O'Neill, the O'Donnell, and the Maguire would decide the time was right to rise and fight again. Though there was another side to Owny now; he was expressing a great interest in carrying on the family tradition of providing hospitality in the house "someday." She shook away the thoughts; her children were grown and not at home. Something else accounted for the sounds she was hearing.

She lit a taper from her fireplace and descended the spiral stairs. Was it one of the servants making an outlandish din? Animals? Perhaps a pair of mating foxes; she knew they had a cry that sounded almost human. She stood at the door and looked out in the direction whence came the lament. She saw nothing on the ground, no person, no animal. And no living thing could wail incessantly without stopping for breath. She walked out into the night and looked all around again and up into the trees. Nothing. The sound was coming from above her, above and also from the direction of the River Erne and Enniskillen Castle. But when she turned in that direction, it was behind her, too. It was everywhere. She had never heard a more lonesome sound; it was a sound of sorrow, of absolute desolation, like the sound of keening women mourning the dead at a funeral. But magnified a hundredfold. The night was black, the stars remote in their cold heaven. The cry continued to pierce the sky. Brigid knew that whoever, whatever, was rending the night with her lamentation was beyond the earthly realm.

The Banshee. Brigid remembered a conversation she had had with Sorcha many years ago, after an old woman had run along the banks of the Erne, waving her spindly arms and shouting that she had heard the Banshee cry. Brigid had looked at Sorcha. She well knew that the physician believed that some of the ailments people reported were really caused by their minds, worrying and fretting and causing upset in their stomachs. Brigid asked the doctor then, "Is the Banshee something that exists only in people's minds?" Came the doctor's, the seer's, reply: "It is not. I have heard the Banshee cry. And so will you."

The wailing cry continued unabated, rising and falling in pitch and volume, a desperate keening that seemed to fill the vault of the heavens, to fill the entire world.

It was four days later that Shane came riding up to the house, man and horse exhausted, and delivered the dreadful news. "They're gone! The lords of all of Ulster!"

"What are you saying, Shane, they're gone?"

"I heard news from Rathmullan, and I travelled there myself. The Maguire, Cúchonnacht, arrived in the harbour of the Great Swilly with a ship. He was able to hire a ship on the continent and he rigged it up with fishing nets and claimed it was for fishing. He was in disguise as a mariner. They say he could disguise himself so well his own friends wouldn't recognize him!"

Brigid almost smiled in spite of it all; she could well imagine Cúchonnacht getting into the spirit of the thing and donning the costume and manners of someone quite different from himself.

Shane continued the story. "The captain was a man named John Rath from Drogheda. There was an O'Brien and a Tully with them, and they sailed into the harbour. And our lords boarded the ship and sailed out of the lough on the fourteenth of September! Try to imagine what was in their minds as they watched the beautiful coast of Tirconnell recede behind them."

"Shane, please slow down. Come inside. What you're saying is beyond sense." She took him by the hand and led him inside and up the stairs, poured them both a cup of ale, and sat down with him in the main hall.

"Brigid, listen to me. Our nobles have left the country for Spain. The Earl of Tyrone, Hugh O'Neill; Rory O'Donnell, who as you know is now the Earl of Tirconnell; and our own Lord of Fermanagh. Members of other great families as well. There are nearly a hundred people on board, including some priests and students who will be studying in Europe. And Tadhg Ó'Cianáin. Isn't he related to the Maguires?"

"His family have been chroniclers of the Maguires for hundreds of years."

"Well, he is on the ship. The families of some of the men are making the voyage. The O'Neill's current wife, Catherine, and two of their sons. But their other boy, Conn — he's only five years old — he's in fosterage and could not be found before the ship sailed out. They had to leave the little boy behind!"

"This is horrible." Brigid's eyes filled with tears, for the young son of the O'Neills, for the Gaelic princes of Ireland, for the people left to endure whatever outrages the English would visit upon them now.

"But," said Shane, "their plan is to get up a force to return here and drive the English out."

"Hoping for Spanish help again!" She well knew what had

happened in the past. Spanish ships wrecked on the Irish coast, Spanish soldiers landing at Kinsale, at the very southern tip of the island, so the Irish warriors had to march the entire length of the country in the mud and bog and cold of November and December in order to join the battle. It was no wonder that the Irish had been so utterly defeated.

And this had been foretold. Brigid knew the legend. The Earl of Thomond, the O'Brien, had seen an old book in which it had been written that a battle would be fought near Kinsale, and the Irish would be defeated by the English. And it had also been prophesied — in that same ancient book? Brigid did not know — that when the three Hughs were conquered in Munster, Ireland would be lost. Hugh O'Neill and Red Hugh O'Donnell were defeated at Kinsale in Munster. And the greatly mourned Hugh Maguire had been slain in a skirmish in Munster before that, in the year 1600.

And here was the proof that the chieftains had not truly submitted to the invader: once again, they were attempting to engage England's old enemy, Spain, in the Irish cause against the English. "But that will be years away," she said to Shane, "if the Spanish king even agrees. And what will happen to us in the meantime, with all our leaders gone out of the country? Will our last remaining lands be taken from us? Will our people be banished to the far reaches of our island? What will it be, more heads on spikes?"

Brigid felt her stomach seize up, felt herself growing weak; the old prophecies about the three Hughs and the defeat at Kinsale were not the only prophecies that spoke of the events of these agonizing years. Brigid saw in her mind's eye the pages on which Father Fiach O'Moylan had inscribed the predictions uttered by Sorcha the night she was killed.

"And, Shane, I heard the Banshee cry."

"Brigid, she cries only for the dead: to announce that a death is coming or that someone has just died. She was heard here when Hugh Maguire was in battle."

"She is crying for the death of Gaelic Ireland. And of our princes who will die on foreign shores. That's what Sorcha saw in the future. She saw our nobles leaving our shores. Forever. They will not be coming back."

CHAPTER XXIII

Melodious lyre of Inisfail, strike mournful notes.
The heroes who delighted in thy festive strains, and
cherished thy muse, are hastening to the last act of the
fatal tragedy, which closes with their utter overthrow,
saddened by calamities unequalled, by desolation and
ruin. A nation patriarchal in its recorded antiquity,
in its constitution, laws, manners, and customs, is
on the point of extermination; or, if a remnant is to
survive slaughter and famine, 'tis only to irretrievable
degradation.

— Capt. William Taafe, in Connellan, *Annals of the*
Four Masters

2018

After the nighttime incursion into the dig site, Mick had
been required to invent a story about "kids" sneaking
onto the site at night and "doing a bit of messing." Aisling
and the rest of the crew were understandably distressed when
they saw that someone had gone in under cover of darkness
and rooted around in the excavation. It was one of the more

recent sites, farther out on the property. The "intruder" hadn't even bothered to replace the plastic sheeting that had covered the hole. This all could have spelled disaster, allowing further damage to the excavation. The archaeologists, of course, could not tell whether anything had been taken from a depth they had not yet examined. Mick at least knew that there had been nothing pulled up that related to old Roddo Tierney; Brayden and his lowlife associates had made that story up for the extortion attempt. If they'd had something, they'd have brandished it in Cait Tierney's face.

Now, standing with the archaeologists at the scene of the crime, Mick called upon his storytelling skills — which weren't a patch on those of his father — as he tried to offer reassurances to the team. It was unlikely, he told them, that "the kids" would return to the site again. How did he know that? Oh, he had a fairly good idea. He accepted condolences over his father's sudden death and gave no hint that the events were linked.

Mick missed his father ferociously, as, of course, did Cait and Róisín and the rest of the family, and they were making plans for his funeral. And Mick had to speak to his daughter and have a conversation he dreaded. She'd hear the story eventually, and Mick wanted it to be his version she heard, not that of Brayden Waring.

He called her into the conference room and closed the door. He told her how Cait's description of the extortion incident, specifically the use of the nickname Roddo, had tipped Mick and his father off about Brayden Waring's likely involvement in the scheme.

Her face bespoke anger. Anger but not surprise. "I was afraid of that, Dad. That it was Brayden. I'd never have thought he could stoop *that* low, but as soon as I heard it, I pictured him and those maggots he goes around with, pictured them planning this. Messing with the dig, that was bad enough, but threatening Gran! Threatening anyone's gran!"

"Did you ask him about it?"

"Not bloody likely. I've not heard from him at all."

"Right. So, we went to confront him." She merely nodded at that. "Liam didn't know what we'd be facing, who else might be there, so he . . . he brought a gun."

"Oh!"

"We got into the flat, and Liam started giving out to Brayden about threatening Gran, and Brayden came lunging towards Liam. And Liam pulled out the gun."

"Jesus, Mary, and Joseph!"

Then Mick told her about the sudden noise, someone bursting into the room, a child and her mother. Róisín did not ask who they were; Mick assumed she had no interest in Waring's post-divorce relationships. And then he told her about Liam's gun hand jolting up and the gun firing. And that it was the sudden arrival of the little girl that had startled Liam.

"Oh, God! Did anyone get—"

"Nobody was hurt, buíochas le Dia."

"But to think what could have happened to that child!"

"I know, love, and that's what haunted Liam. He kept talking about it over and over in the car as we drove away. 'I never would have hurt her.'"

Mick told her then what accounted for Brayden's role in the extortion, the pressure from his so-called mates.

"That pathetic wee glipe," she said. "He'd fall for any line they'd feed him. Thank God in heaven my children don't take after the likes of him!"

"They don't, for definite. They're all you, Rosie." Then, "Poor Liam. I'll be hearing his words forever: 'I never would have hurt her.'"

Róisín was in tears, and Mick put his arms around her. "That poor wee girl," she said. "And poor Grandda. And it's all Brayden's fault! Grandda couldn't get over what might have happened to the child. And he . . . His heart gave out on him."

Mick and the family got through the funeral. Somehow. He could not conceive of his life here in Enniskillen without Liam. He would hear something said or reported in the newspaper and he'd think, *Wait till the old fella hears this.* Or *Next time we're down the pub, me and Liam, I'll get him to tell the story of* . . . The ache over the loss of his father was physical; he felt it in his gut as well as in his mind. The two of them had been so close it was as if Mick had lost a part of himself.

Then, after a couple of days cutting through the bog, Aisling came flying into the lobby of the hotel. "Mr. Tierney!"

"No need to be formal, now, Aisling. Just call me Mick."

"Mick, we've found something. Is Róisín around?"

"She's just behind in the office. Go right in."

"Oh, I . . ." Only then did she realize she was covered in turf. "I'd better not go in. I'll get the place dirty."

"No, no, you go ahead. Anything that falls off you, we'll save for the fire." Turf was a traditional heat source in Ireland.

She laughed and went around to the office, Mick following on her heels. Róisín looked up from the desk and greeted the other young woman.

"We've found something. And it's marvellous! An old manuscript, wrapped in parchment."

"You're joking me!"

"Not at all. One of the fellas is down there safeguarding it. Would yous like to come see it?"

"Just try and stop me!" Róisín got up from the desk, and the three of them hurried out to the bog.

A young lad stood in the excavation, pointing down. "There it is." All Mick could see was something brown and rectangular resting in the soggy earth.

"Now, we have procedures as you might expect," Aisling said. "We've called in a team of experts to come and examine the scene, then remove the manuscript and take it to the conservation lab. It's at the Ulster Museum in Belfast. Sorry we can't give you any more than the glimpse you're getting from up here. Until the team arrives, it has to be kept in the waterlogged peat. Can't let it dry out or it could quickly start to deteriorate."

"How old is it, any idea?"

"Too soon to tell but likely medieval or early modern. All we know otherwise is that it's smaller than, say, a biblical manuscript, and the package is thin, only a few pages."

"How did something from those times survive being buried in there?" Mick pointed to the bog.

"Same way the bogmen were preserved," Aisling said, referring to the mummified bodies that had been found in Ireland. "Cashel Man was discovered a few years ago, the oldest body ever found with flesh still attached. He's four thousand years old! A bog is anaerobic, that is, it has no oxygen. The micro-organisms that would have caused decay and decomposition can't live in that environment without oxygen. We've had a quick look. The vellum — vellum is calf skin, as you probably know — the vellum of this wee manuscript has been preserved in this waterlogged environment, and it will be stored in peat in a cold room until we can safely begin the process of separating the pages."

Aisling went on to describe some of the scientific procedures that would be used to conserve the manuscript; it would be encased in "cellocast resin bandages" for transportation to the lab in Belfast, then stored in a cold room. There was something about "vacuum packing," "blottings," "ethanol," and a lot of other scientific terminology, all in the service of ensuring the survival of the object. "Now, I know the two of you are curious, but it will be a while before we can safely separate the pages. It's all just one big clump now. Separation of larger books has sometimes taken months or even years."

"Ah, no!" Róisín exclaimed, then, "Sorry, sorry, I know you're doing everything right. I just, well, I'm dying to know what it says!"

"I understand, Róisín, entirely. I'm anxious to see it, too! Now, obviously, we won't be able to return the original to you. But eventually, if all works out, it will be housed and displayed for people to see. And we'll be making digital photos of it, and we'll provide you with copies. But, as I say, it could take a long time to separate the pages."

❦

As the months passed after the discovery of the manuscript, it began to look as if Mick would not have to call on nominally retired paramilitaries to blow the Vegas-Disney development to smithereens. In fact, it all seemed to be going according to Mick and Róisín's original plan: there had been no sign of Jebb Prule in

County Fermanagh, and Jimmy over in America had not heard any more about the development project, since the earth was opened up and the proverbial red tape started to spool around the site. In fact, Jimmy reported that Prule had recently been talking up other plans for the North of Ireland and had made no mention at all of Enniskillen.

Then, at the end of August, Aisling was standing at the reception desk of Tierney's Hotel with a manila envelope.

"Digital photos of the pages," she told Mick, and he had to resist the urge to tear them out of Aisling's hand and start looking them over. But he would do no such thing. A lovely family from Newfoundland had just checked in and, to his delight, asked well-informed questions about the town and surrounding countryside. As soon as they went up to their room, Mick gave his full attention to Aisling, who described how the pages had been separated successfully with some loss of quality, but readable nonetheless.

Mick gave her an effusive thanks and picked up the phone to call Róisín. She was there in seconds. "Is it the pages?!" Róisín had gone back to her childhood, bouncing on her feet with impatience to see what Santy had brought her for the Christmas.

The three of them went into the hotel's conference room, and Aisling opened the envelope. "You'll remember that the pages were smaller than what we'd see if it was an illuminated manuscript of Bible verses, or something like that. Vellum was valuable, and it appears that this scribe may have used half-sized pages for his work. There are only four pages." She laid the copies on the table. Aisling couldn't stay, but she had brought along a knapsack full of what she called supplementary reading that she would lend them in order to put the information in context. "And these books are all online, too." She told them that the photocopied pages were theirs to keep and display in any way they chose.

"D'yous read Irish?" she asked.

"We do," Róisín answered.

"In the old script?"

"Well, I could work my way through it. I wish they still used the old Gaelic script, to be honest with you. Dots over the letters instead of all those Hs. Words are twice as long as they need to be, the way it is now."

"Right you are. Well, I have to leave you now. Happy reading!"

They thanked Aisling and directed their attention to the manuscript. Unlike the majority of the population, Mick and Róisín could truthfully say they had enough of the old language, their native Irish tongue, to translate as they read along.

And what a read it was.

In the middle of the first page were the words "The Prophecies of Sorcha O'Cassidy, physician and seer."

"Do we even want to know?" Mick asked.

"Oh yes, we do," his daughter replied. "I remember reading that the O'Cassidy family were physicians going back centuries. And look at this." She pointed to something written in small letters below the title. It was the old-script equivalent of "Transcribed by An tAth F. O M., 1595."

"An tAthair. Father somebody, O'M, and he's given us the date, God bless him. Now let's see what the seer foretold. You read it out, Róisín."

"Every kingdom divided against itself is brought to desolation, and every city or house divided against itself will not stand."

"An apt warning but far too late by 1595. Our clans had been brawling for centuries, and the English took advantage of it. Divide and conquer."

"You say it was too late, Dad, but isn't it from the Bible?"

"You're right, love. I should be paying more attention to

the Holy Word. If our lads had been listening in Mass, they'd have heeded this warning even before the invaders got a foot on our shores."

"Then on the next page it says, 'I see the great harbour. I see a ship. Our men step off the land of Ireland for the last time. They climb aboard the ship and the ship sails out against the sky. Our beloved prince is upon it, the last of our princes. Our greatest men, the lords of Ireland, are away to sea. And women are weeping, and sons and daughters are left behind. And we are without defences. They shall never, ever return. Our world has ended."

They looked at each other. Mick saw tears forming in his daughter's eyes. She said, "The woman saw this, twelve years before it happened. The Flight of the Earls."

"Aye, she did."

"Then it says, 'And a lonely lamp burns in the castle for Cúchonnacht Óg.'"

"He was a Maguire," said Mick. "Well, you probably know this. He was the brother, or I guess half-brother, of Hugh Maguire, the great cavalry commander and Lord of Fermanagh. Hugh was killed in County Cork in the year 1600."

"Right. And after some strife with a rival faction of the clan, Cúchonnacht was named the Maguire. That's who she must have meant by 'the last of our princes.'"

"Right, and, of course, we all know the story."

They did. At the end of the Nine Years' War, in 1603, Hugh O'Neill signed the Treaty of Mellifont, apparently making peace with England. O'Neill was the head of the oldest royal family in all of Europe. He had never given up his loyalty to Ireland, but the only thing he could do at that point was submit. His time would come later. But it wasn't long before he sensed which way the wind was blowing, and it was an ill wind indeed. The English were hammering away at the prerogatives of the earls — the Ulster chieftains — and were replacing the old Irish system of governance and laws. O'Neill and Rory O'Donnell (who had become the Earl of Tirconnell with the signing of the treaty) had the feeling that they'd eventually wind up in the Tower of London.

"Cúchonnacht Maguire was the last to give in to the inevitable," Mick said, "and he was granted half his lands back, the other half held by the rival branch of the Maguires. That didn't suit Cúchonnacht."

Mick had learned the story at his father's knee. He thought back to the days of his childhood when he would sit on Liam's lap. Liam would have his left hand wrapped around a can of beer, and his right arm around his wee lad, and the stories would be flowing. And one of the most dramatic of all was the Flight of the Earls. The chiefs of the clans in the north of Ireland, the princes of the Gaelic nobility, boarded a ship at the northern tip of the island and headed for Spain, apparently in the hope — yet again — of obtaining Spanish aid to defeat the English invaders. But it didn't work out. Right from the start, the winds were against them. A storm blew up and made it impossible to sail to Spain. Storm, rough seas, sickness, and diminishing stores of food and drink forced them to go ashore in northern France. The political winds had turned against them, too, and Spain didn't want them. By this time, the Spanish were having trouble with their own colonies, specifically the Spanish Netherlands, and they very much desired England's cooperation. The Spanish king wanted nothing to do with these Irish chieftains and their plan to overthrow English rule. So the Irishmen set out on foot for the trek from the north of Europe to the south, to a new destination. Rome.

To his daughter, Mick said, "They never set foot on Irish soil again."

"Every one of them died over there," said Róisín in a voice Mick could barely hear.

"That's right."

"So what Sorcha saw in her vision was the end of the Gaelic order." She was silent for a long moment, then she pulled her phone out of her back pocket and poked and swiped at it. "Worst fears realized. Many members of the chieftains' families did end up in the Tower of London. Including Hugh O'Neill's wee son Conn. He was in fosterage, and they weren't able to find him when it was time to board the ship! I can't bear to think about it!"

"It breaks your heart to read about, to be sure."

"But," she looked up at Mick, "in the midst of all this I can't help but think that Grandda would be over the moon to see what we have here. I mean, he'd be giving out about our tragic history and the Brits and all, but the fact that this document has survived for us to read! And the fact that we're not going to be surrounded by all those shite holiday homes. I wish to God he could be here with us!"

"Me, too, acushla. For him to be taken from us like that . . ." His father's absence was a dark void in the fabric of their lives. "But I'm sure he's smiling on us wherever he is now."

"I'm sure of it! You know what I'm going to do, Dad? I'm going to do a mural of him from one of our photos, and I'll put a pint in his hand, and have him giving one of his recitals. It'll be in our bar."

"Beautiful idea, Róisín." They observed a moment of silence, then Mick said, "What other bad tidings did Sorcha announce?"

"'Soon invaders will come and take for themselves the lands of the families of Ulster.' Well, she was bang on there. Everyone knows our people were pushed off their land when this province was planted with Scots and English."

"Pushed off their land and lived to tell about it, if they were lucky!"

"Lucky?"

"Well, only compared to the fate of thousands of others. I did some internet searching myself. I remembered hearing one of Da's recitals at the pub, and he mentioned a fella by the name of Moryson."

"I remember that name from school."

"Look him up, see what he said about his burning exploits."

She did her search and said, "Oh, God. Listen to this. 'We burned a town in O'Kane's country, together with many women and children in it, and killed also forty kernes and churls.' I can't believe all this stuff, Dad. Or at least I wish I couldn't believe it. Makes me want to pack up and emigrate!"

"That's what they *want* you to think!" He affected a snooty British accent. "Be off with you, you mere Irish."

"Yes, you mere *mick*, you *wilde Irishman*," she replied in the same accent. "Be gone. This land is ours now." In her real voice, she said, "And to think this used to be the least colonized part of the country."

"It's been a long time since we could make that claim, but that was true of the past. Ulster hadn't even been 'Normanized.' It remained the most Irish of all the provinces and was known as 'the fountainhead of rebellion.' And look at us now!"

"Ah, we've had our moments of rebellion, Dad."

They had indeed. All through history, and most recently through their own Thirty Years' War. And yet the country remained divided because the descendants of the planters refused to unite with the *mere Irish* south of the border.

"What does she say next, Rosie?"

"Things don't go any better for us. 'A great heretic will come and claim that he is doing the work of God, and he will slaughter our warriors and our priests, our women and our innocents. And he will drive our people from our lands and out to the far ends of our island.'"

"God help us, she predicted Cromwell. And that's exactly what he and his men did, slaughtered all those people, especially in Drogheda and Wexford. And any of us that were left standing were packed off to the west."

"To Hell or Connacht." The two of them recited the well-known phrase in chorus.

"But it was only right, after all," said Mick. "Cromwell, the *Lord Protector*, was carrying out 'the righteous judgment of God on these barbarous wretches.' That's us, the barbarous wretches."

"Well, it's me, without question," said Róisín. "Surely not your good self, though, Daddy."

"I don't think he discriminated, did old Cromwell. We were all equal under God, barbarous wretches each and every one of us Irish."

"And as if that wasn't enough, Sorcha foresaw that 'after many more years have passed, our people will starve on the land.' The Great Famine of the 1800s!"

"And, as we know all too well, it wasn't the first."

"I miss Grandda so much!" There were tears in Róisín's eyes again, and Mick could feel them starting in his own. "I can still see him that day, reciting lines from the *Faerie Queene*. Even though, if that horrid man Spenser were alive today, after writing that stuff in favour of starving the Irish people to death, Grandda would have . . . well . . ."

"Yeah, he would have."

"Dad, did you ever record him, you know, when he was down the pub and singing his songs or reciting his poems about Spenser and those other old war criminals? Record him on your phone?"

Mick shook his head. He had a mobile phone but didn't do much with it, aside from using it as a phone. It had never occurred to him to take it out and place it on the bar and capture his da in full flight singing or doing a recital. Never thought about the obvious: that his father wouldn't always be with him. "I only wish . . ."

His daughter came over to him, and they put their arms around one another. They stood there for a while, then Mick said, "Now, what else did the prophetess have to say?"

Róisín made an obvious effort to shake off her sorrow, at least for the present. "Our Holy Mass will be forbidden. Our sacraments will be given in secret, furtively, like sins. Our priests will be hunted down and expelled or battered to death."

"Old Sorcha was right on the money again. Penal laws were in place from the end of the 1600s through to the early 1800s. Catholics couldn't practise their religion. That's why there were hedge schools, secret schools out in the fields and hedgerows. And they weren't allowed to buy land or own a horse worth over a certain amount."

"So now I know why you and Mum only got me that wee pony when I was little, instead of the racehorse I was demanding! Ach, I shouldn't be making jokes about it, all that discrimination against our people."

"It's either laugh or cry, darlin'. And if you think all this discrimination is a thing of the distant past . . . I can tell you that when I was born, we didn't even have equal voting rights or access to jobs and housing here in the Six Counties. My oul fella" — he looked heavenward — "was out on the street demonstrating for equal rights in the time leading up to the Troubles here."

"Our Liam carried more than a picket sign in those times, amn't I right, Dad?"

Mick merely nodded his head. Róisín worked away at her phone again.

"Oh! I've found something here about the last of our chieftains."

"You like that fella, do you?"

"I do! This is what the Masters say about Cúchonnacht Óg Maguire: he was an 'intelligent, comely, courageous, magnanimous, rapid-marching, adventurous man, endowed with wisdom and personal beauty, and all the other good qualifications.' I've noticed a lot of references in the old writings to how good-looking our people were! Not only our own bards but foreigners remarked on it in their reports."

"Of course they did! How could they not? Are we not a fine-looking race of people?"

"We are. And Cúchonnacht Óg Maguire is singled out for special mention in this regard."

"That means he fit the mould of an Irish king. No wonder he got special recognition in the wise woman's prophecies. A king had to have a perfect body, without blemish, or he would not be inaugurated as the king. Setting the bar high in those days."

"Maybe I'll suss out where the Maguire descendants do their drinking, and I'll start showing up at whatever bar it is."

"You could do worse."

"And have done. Sorcha must have been heart-scalded seeing him in her mind, stepping onto that ship and sailing away forever."

"She must have been. He died less than a year after leaving this country." Mick picked up one of the books left by the archaeologist and thumbed through it. "Says here he came down with a 'raging fever' in Naples and later travelled to Genoa. That's where he died. You can imagine an Irishman trying to survive in a hot, steamy climate the likes of that! And to think we complain about the weather here. Maguire could not survive the conditions in Italy."

"You barely survived that trip we took to Spain, Dad."

Mick thought for a minute and said, "Sorcha didn't foresee everything in our dismal history, though, did she? Nothing about King Billy and the Battle of the Boyne. That was only a hundred years after her lifetime. The Orangemen are still crowing about that victory! And there was nothing in the prophecies about our more recent history: our War of Independence, partition, the recent Troubles . . ."

"But it's amazing what she did see."

"And we have to keep in mind that this is what was written down by the priest, Father O'M. She may have had a lifetime of other visions that were never recorded."

"Oh, the thought of that! That there was more and it's lost to us."

She and Mick stood facing each other. They were both silent for a few seconds and then Róisín said, "This is incredible, Dad! Sorcha O'Cassidy really was a seer, a prophetess. I wonder how many people really have that gift."

"Most people who claim to have that gift are making it up or imagining it, but not our Sorcha. I wouldn't want it, I can tell you that. I'd never have a moment's rest if I had the kinds of visions she had. Given the history of the world so far, and the history of this country, we can be sure there are catastrophes coming to us that we can't even imagine. And I don't want to know! But you're right about Sorcha: her abilities were astounding!"

"And her prophecies were buried right here on Tierney land!"

Over the next few weeks, the archaeological team continued to uncover structures and artifacts on the Tierney land, and so the project was further extended. And that was fine with Mick. Because Prule and his ghastly development had faded into the mists. So, fine with Mick. Not so with his grandmother, but she was so subdued by grief for her son that her protests against the digging were only half-hearted. Mick had her over for lunch at the hotel on a mild cloudy day in mid-September, and she barely gave a glance out the window to the work going on outside. Mick almost missed the fiery opposition she had maintained before Liam's death. And he missed his father even more than he would have thought possible.

So he welcomed the distraction when Aisling arrived at the hotel. She saw him sitting with his grandmother and hesitated to enter the restaurant. Mick got up and went over to her.

And she announced another find. "We're in the boggy area again, Mick, and we found a bone."

"Oh?! What sort of a bone is it?"

"Human heel bone. So we kept excavating, with great care as you can imagine. And we've uncovered a body."

CHAPTER XXIV

He does not win who plays with Sin
In the secret House of Shame.

— Oscar Wilde, *The Ballad of Reading Gaol*

Mick was stunned at the news of a body being found on his land. Aisling told him it was wrapped in a woollen cloak. "In the way you'd wrap someone in a shroud."

"Jaysus. Any idea — no, you wouldn't know yet how long it's been there, how old it is."

"I'll have more information for you as soon as I can. You and Róisín will be the first to know. I have to get back out there. Now you can imagine the care we take when we're dealing with human remains. First to be called are the police; they're on their way. We've called in medical experts, a pathologist, people from the museum, conservation experts; the priority is to conserve the body. It should be handled as little as possible; deterioration can be rapid once it's removed from the find spot, so everybody works together to avoid that."

"We can come out and see it, me and Róisín?"

"Of course. You won't see much at this point, just the cloak and the heel bone."

"We'll be out in a jiffy; I'll just break the news to my grandmother."

"All right, so. See you out there."

He returned to the table and faced his grandmother's curiosity. "Who's that one, now?"

"She's the lead archaeologist on the dig out there."

His grandmother's lips clamped together, and she emitted a short sigh.

Mick took a deep breath. "Gran, they think they've found a body."

She stared at him as if her gaze alone could force him to take back the words.

Then she got started. "Scientists know how to measure how old things are. If that body turns out to be from the 1840s, then it will prove all the old rumours true. What that blackmailer, the blaggard that had me terrorized half to death that night, what he failed to do will now be done. It will be a public scandal that Roderick Tierney did not provide safe passage for the tenants he pushed off his land. That they died right here of starvation, right under the nose of old Roddo. Or worse. Thank God and all his angels that your grandfather and his line were the *good* Tierneys." She was silent again, a pointed silence that was meant to resurrect the old libel that Roderick Tierney had killed his tenants after they became a liability to him in the straitened times of the Famine.

"Wee Róisín loves this place almost as much as she'd love a third child. What is she going to do if the Tierney reputation suffers a final blow with this skeleton being dug up out of the bog?"

Mick wished he could vanish in thin air, maybe jump into the bog himself, rather than look any longer at the anguish in his grandmother's face. The woman was mourning her beloved son Liam, and now she believed that the family was in for disgrace and ruin. It was small comfort in that moment that the casino and the grotesque parody of Enniskillen architecture and history, as interpreted by the vulgar and toothy Jebb Prule, had no more chance of going ahead than Edmund Spenser, Oliver Cromwell, or Ian Paisley had of a rosary being said for the repose of their souls.

Mick coaxed his grandmother into leaving the hotel with him, and after seeing her safely if not quietly home, he returned to the hotel and picked up the phone. He knew Róisín was working on a room on the second floor, so he rang the room and said, "Drop whatever you're doing and come down. They've found a body."

"They haven't!"

"They have."

She appeared in the lobby seconds later, wide-eyed, and they headed out. The police were there, in conference with the archaeologists. Mick noticed that they were standing by the same hole that had been damaged by Brayden Waring. Aisling raised her index finger to Mick and Róisín, signalling "Wait." After a couple of minutes, she came over and said, "We're waiting for the doctors. They'll have a look, and then the body will be taken to the hospital. Until then we're keeping it encased in the peat. We have to keep to a minimum the exposure to air and warm temperatures until we can get it in proper storage."

Róisín said, "Police, doctors, hospitals. It's as if the fellow just died last night. It's good, though, isn't it? That they treat someone, even someone who's been buried for years — centuries, maybe — with such care. I hope we can get a look at him. Or her."

"You won't see much, I'm afraid. Just a quick glance when it's raised from the excavation, and it will still be in the cloak."

"Any idea how long the body has been there?" Mick asked. "How old it is?"

She shook her head. "We don't know yet."

They didn't see anything more that day than a bundle quickly transferred into protective custody, so to speak, but Aisling assured them that she would keep them informed. "We've been taking digital photographs of everything, and will continue to do so. I'll make sure you get to see his picture when he's unwrapped. I can't promise that he or she will be presentable, though; don't get your hopes up!"

And two days later, she kept her word. She came by with photos. "Meet the 'Enniskillen Bogman.' Adult male, thirty-five to perhaps forty-five years old."

First, she showed the body wrapped in the cloak, and then unwrapped when it was about to undergo examination. And it was a body, not merely a skeleton. A mummified body with leathery flesh still on most parts of the face and frame, though some places were exposed bone. Where there was skin, it was now a dark brown. He still had the hair on one side of his head, and it was long and wavy, light brown in colour. Mick could even see his eyebrows and lashes. There was bare skull on the other side, and it was damaged. There was damage to the chest as well. Mick stared down at him, more fascinated than horrified.

"What happened to him? Look at his head, and his chest there."

"He came to a violent end, Mick. The autopsy showed that he'd been shot in the chest and head."

"Oh!" Róisín cried out. "A victim of murder, and him buried on our land!"

"The police will know we had nothing to do with it, Rosie!"

"And there's something else. More reading for you. Again, it's a manuscript. Wrapped in parchment like the earlier find containing the prophecies of Sorcha. This one looks thin, maybe only a page or two, and it will have to undergo the same procedures at the lab for conservation and separation of the pages. And, of course, there are stringent protocols for conserving the body. I would expect that eventually he'll be displayed in Belfast at the Ulster Museum, but that's a ways off yet."

"So what do you do, Aisling?" Róisín asked. "Write up a report?"

"Oh yes, I've kept a record of everything, and I'll be writing a paper for one of the journals. This is a major find. I have to say I'm glad you called us in!"

"So am I, Aisling," said Mick, "so am I. Imagine if he'd stayed buried, forever, beneath the parking lot of a casino."

🝲

Three weeks later, Róisín came into the hotel lobby with a problem that had nothing to do with ancient history. A problem that was all too current. And one look at her white face and red-rimmed eyes told Mick it was serious.

"What is it, Rosie?"

"It's Brayden, Dad. He's in trouble."

Mick stopped himself from making the obvious reply, "When has he not been in trouble?" He took her by the hand and headed for the conference room. When they were seated at the table, he said, "Tell me."

"I rang him on his mobile to ask why he didn't stop by to see the kids yesterday. Those fellas are after him, Dad! The crowd of lousers he was going around with, the guys who tried to extort the money out of Gran. They say he owes them four thousand pounds, and they're threatening to break his legs! We've got to help him, Dad!"

We've got to help him after him being useless to his family all these years. "Is this what he asked you to do, Rosie? Come to me for help? For the four thousand quid maybe?"

"No! He told me not to tell you. He doesn't want you to know. He knows you think he's good for nothing. He only wanted me to understand why he won't be able to see Ciara and Rory for a while, because he has to go into hiding. He was in tears, Dad. There was nothing phony about it. It all came spilling out of him, how he's messed up his life, ruined things between him and me and the kids. He was sincere. And you know I've been cynical about him for the last couple of years, and then raging over what him and those fellas did to Gran, so I wasn't going to fall for a line. But, no, this is real: he's devastated."

"Where does he think he can go, where that shower of shites won't find him?"

"He doesn't know. He talked about trying to rent a place in Belfast, but, of course, he doesn't have the money for that."

Mick was surprised by his own reaction, that he was not thinking, *Serves him right if they catch him.* No, Brayden was the father of Mick's grandchildren. He wasn't a bad young fella when he first came into their lives. Immature, yes; not ready to be a husband and father, true. But not deserving of being crippled by this other pack of gougers who were obviously much worse than he'd ever been.

Mick reached across the table for his daughter's hand. "I'll go talk to him."

"Dad, no! He told me not to let on to you."

Because he knew Mick would probably say, "The hell with him."

What was coming over Mick these days? He was on his way to becoming the smiling innkeeper, after saving the hotel he now knew he cherished. And today he might be offering assistance to his ne'er-do-well former son-in-law?

⚇

Once again, Mick found himself in Brayden Waring's flat, this time without the paterfamilias, armed and dangerous, at his side. And this time no threats were needed. There was none of the defiant bluster Brayden had displayed so often in the past. He sat on his grimy sofa, dressed in a grey track suit.

"I know I've fucked up royally, okay? I'm sorry. I told Rosie I'm sorry for acting the maggot all this time. Any time I'd be with the kids, I was so distracted by all this aggravation hanging over my head. The need for money, these guys having something over me. I know she's not going to have me back, too late for that now. But I don't want to lose contact with my kids. It's just that . . ."

Mick saw no sign of the other woman and child who had been here on the last visit, no sign of their belongings. That mother must have given up on him, too. And there was no doubt in Mick's mind that Brayden was contrite — and terrified. If Mick had come with any intention of blasting the kid for his stupidity, that was not going to happen. He had a better idea.

"There's a house, south of the border. County Cavan. I used to use it when . . . Well, it's still there." It was an IRA safe house, for when the lads were on the run across the border, the border they did not officially recognize. When things were too hot to hide the fellas in Tierney's Hotel, Mick had arranged for them to stay in the Cavan house. He was still in touch with the owner. And he would call upon him again now. "Whatever you do, Brayden, don't mention fucking drugs! A little dissident republican activity gone wrong, that would go over much better."

Brayden was almost tearful in his gratitude, and Mick's heart went out to him. *What's happening to me?* Mick asked himself. *Have I become an old softie in my latter years?* Well, if so, that was all right. He could live with it. And now he'd get on with seeking shelter for Brayden Waring. After all, Mick came from a long line of hospitallers.

With the threat hanging over Brayden's head, there was no time to lose in getting him out of Enniskillen. Mick put a finger to his lips as a signal for Brayden to stay quiet, and then he searched his phone for the number of the man in Cavan. It took a few minutes, but Mick got through to him. They had traded favours over the years, and Mick knew the drill. There was no need for small talk before getting to the point. So Mick told him he had a young lad who would be most grateful if he could enjoy some Cavan hospitality for a while. Mick would provide more details if and when they arrived in Cavan. Both parties to the call knew it would not be wise to say any more over the phone. Yes, the man said, he could accommodate the lad. Come any time. Mick ended the call and gave Brayden the welcome news. Brayden looked nearly faint with relief.

"Here's what you're going to tell Ciara and Rory. You are going away for a while to work. You'll tell them the job is in Derry."

Brayden nodded in agreement.

Mick leaned forward in his seat. "And now," he said, and Brayden tensed at the change in tone, "you are going to tell me exactly what you did that night at the dig site."

Mick could see him searching his mind for a way out, but there wasn't a way out, and he knew it. So he cast his eyes downward and said, "Those guys I owe the money to, they came up with the plan to scare the old gran about something we found in the dig. It wasn't me that went to her house that night!"

Mick knew that. "Go on."

"But it was me that had to go to the dig and mess it up. So it was late the night before — Saturday night, it was — and I brought a trowel with me and I pulled off the covering over the hole. And I thought I'd just throw the dirt around a bit, the turf or whatever it is. But then I thought, *Why not have a look and see if there's anything valuable down there.* I looked around and there was nobody in sight. So I started digging into it. And I found something metal, looked like the base of a cup of some kind. And then a few pieces of pottery, broken, but if it's old, maybe it's worth something, right?"

Mick told himself to maintain his patience and his temper and let the story unfold.

"Then I found this round metal thing on a chain, like a necklace. And there was this leathery thing, just thin. I figured it was papers or something. So I grabbed the things and took off. Just left the covering off the hole because that was the plan: to show that the dig had been opened up. And I started across the field and there were other excavations. And I was almost away when I saw a car coming towards the property and it was late and its lights were on, and I got scared and thought he might have spotted me. And I didn't want to be caught with those things, stolen goods, like. So I saw a hole close to me, covered over, and I flattened myself on the ground beside it till the car lights went away. Then I opened it up and pushed the things way down in the earth, and patted turf down all over them, and replaced the cover on the surface, and I thought I'd come back another time and get the things. But then . . ."

But then Mick and his father had showed up and confronted

Brayden in his flat. And a gun was produced, and a shot was fired. And that, apparently, was sufficient to discourage Brayden from undertaking any further archaeological expeditions. He never returned to the site.

"All right. Pack your things."

Brayden's eyes widened. "We're going now?"

"You'd rather wait till your former pals arrive to take their pound of flesh?"

The young fellow whirled towards the door, as if Mick's words alone were sufficient to summon his demons. Then he looked around the flat and said in a plaintive voice, "But I can't take all this stuff."

"Did ye never hear the expression 'You made your bed, now lie in it'?"

"Yeah."

"Well, you've made your bed, and you'll not be lying in it. Pack whatever you can in a couple of cases, and get your arse in gear."

He scrabbled about the place, banging drawers and cabinets, and finally had three cases packed. He picked up two of the cases, took a last look at his former home, and headed for the door. Mick lifted the third bag and followed him out.

And then they hit the road, Mick and his fugitive former son-in-law driving through the night and crossing the Irish border into County Cavan. The trip took less than an hour, and there wasn't much in the way of conversation. Mick could practically feel the tension emanating from his young passenger, and he could certainly understand it. It was well warranted. Mick reminded him, in case a reminder was necessary, that he was a dissident republican, not a failed dope dealer. The Cavan man greeted the two of them when they pulled up at his house, and

Brayden again expressed his gratitude, which Mick knew was heartfelt. And then Mick got into his car and headed back across the border to County Fermanagh.

⚛

It was later in the autumn when Aisling came back to Mick with news about the body. "The man we found in your bog died in the year 1600."

"As old as that!" So, no Famine-era scandal to upset Cait Tierney. "I didn't know you could date things so precisely."

She laughed. "We can't. The pages found with his body give the date and details of his death." She handed him an envelope. "Digital copies of the original vellum. There are two pages that are quite readable, just a few gaps and smudges on them. There was a first page, though, maybe a title page. And we could not get it separated from the parchment in which it was wrapped. But the remaining pages tell the story."

"Do I want to hear the story?"

"It's pretty grim. But I'll leave you to it."

Mick thanked her and hurried off to fetch his daughter. Her eyes fastened on the envelope and she reached out to take it.

"Patience now, love. There's a crowd using the conference room, but there's a vacant room on the second floor."

She turned on her heel and ran to the stairs. He stopped at the reception desk to get the key for room 213, then walked upstairs and entered the room. They sat cross-legged, facing each other on the bed, and Mick opened the envelope. He drew out two pages, copies of the originals, written in the old Gaelic script. Róisín pulled her phone out of her back pocket. "In case we have to translate any of the words. All right. Let's get to it."

What they had was two large pages of writing. They began to read.

Judgment against the Killer of Sorcha O'Cassidy

I am not the brehon. I am Shane O'Callaghan, and this is the just judgment made out by me on the 27th April, 1600.

How many reasons are there for the execution of this judgment? Not difficult, seven:

1. He committed the secret and unlawful killing of our physician and wise woman.

2. He did not acknowledge the killing.

3. He forced the pikeman Murrough to give evidence on Judgment Day, to deceive the court into thinking it was I who killed the physician.

4. He killed Murrough. He did this for two reasons: to hide the truth about Sorcha's death and to hide from the Irish Maguire, that being the great Hugh Maguire, that he himself was betraying him.

5. He was a spy for Connor Óg, the English Maguire, and pretended that he had a nest of spies working for Hugh Maguire, when the opposite was true. He wounded two other men as well to hide his treachery, those being Colm the lookout and Brother Aidan.

6. The reason he began working as a spy for the English Maguire was that the English Maguire knew a dreadful truth and threatened to reveal

it to Hugh, who had been a great friend of this man's father. I do not know how the English Maguire acquired this knowledge about the man, but I know he had spies in many places.

How did this one man end up committing so many vile acts?

7.   He was under a curse put on him by Sorcha because of something he had done years before, and he could not have anyone learn what Sorcha knew.

"My God! Sorcha's curse?" Róisín looked at Mick. "Was that in the prophecies we read?"

He stared at the manuscript. "Well, our entire history was cursed, and she predicted many of our worst catastrophes. But there wasn't a curse spelt out as such."

"Whatever it was, it seems to have fallen on this fella's head," she said, "our Enniskillen Bogman. Who was he, I wonder."

Mick shrugged. And then he said, "I keep thinking of Liam. What would he have to say about all this? I wish to Christ he hadn't missed it all! And he wouldn't have, if not for—"

"That fecking ex-husband of mine!" If not for Brayden and the scene in his flat, certainly. "I don't know what to think, Dad. If not for him, Grandda would still be with us. I can't imagine I'll ever forgive him for that. But he's . . . it's more that he's weak than bad. He's not evil. And despite all he's done, I'd never want that *drug cartel* or whatever those bastards fancy themselves to be, I'd never want them to hurt him. Or worse. I guess we'll only hope he's keeping his nose clean over there in Cavan."

"The fact that his arse hasn't been booted out of there and back here to Fermanagh suggests that he has been. The man who runs the safe house wouldn't put up with any aggravation from young Waring."

"You've saved his life, Dad, I've little doubt."

"Ah now," Mick replied in a parody of a humble man accepting his due.

"But it's Liam we're missing here today. I'd give anything to see his reaction to what's been dug up round our place. It's heart-scalding that he's not here to see it!"

"It is." Mick stood up and said, "Let's go to his room, Liam's. I always feel close to him somehow, seeing his books and his republican posters and all that."

"Aye, let's do that."

They left the hotel and walked over to Cait's house and chatted with her for a few minutes, then told her they wanted to go up to Liam's room. She didn't see anything unusual about that and told them to go ahead. The room hadn't been touched since his death, except for Cait's occasional bouts of dusting. There was an old-fashioned record player and a stack of albums, mostly Celtic music and republican rebel songs, but also some American country. Mick stood in front of his father's bookcase, where books stood and leaned and looked ready to slide off the shelves. "Would you look at all his books on Spenser and Milton, and all those other Saxons. You'd think Liam was an English scholar!"

"Only until you opened the books and saw all the sticky notes and comical comments he pencilled in! It's up to you now, Dad, to carry on the tradition. Go down the pub, and do your father's recitations."

"Oh, I could never live up to him. Now look at the fella pointing the Armalite directly at the English poets. D'ye think that's a coincidence?" He was looking at a poster on the wall across the room. The poster, dating from the Troubles, showed an

357

IRA man in a balaclava, aiming his rifle at the enemy. There were other republican items and books and newspaper clippings. But there were softer touches to the room's décor, including framed pictures of his grandchildren, those being Róisín and her sister, Bríd. And a picture Liam had taken of Ciara and Rory working on their mural in the hotel. Above it was Róisín's mural of the Tierneys and Maguires at their lavish banquet.

"Liam," Mick said, "wherever you are now, if you meet a woman named Sorcha, be sure to tell her that she truly had the sight. Her prophecies were all too prophetic."

"She knows that, Dad."

"Ah, you're right, love. She knows."

CHAPTER XXV

Yet each man kills the thing he loves. By each let this
   be heard.
Some do it with a bitter look; some with a flattering
   word.
The coward does it with a kiss; the brave man with
   a sword.

— Oscar Wilde, *The Ballad of Reading Gaol*

1607

B rigid sat by her window playing her harp. It was a tune she had composed — or, to be more accurate, a tune which had come to her unbidden two months before — after she heard about the Lord of Fermanagh and the other men leaving Ireland on the ship. But she was roused from her grim preoccupations by the arrival of a messenger, and he bore news of a most welcome kind: a letter from her sister Mary, announcing that she and Cormac had sailed from Dublin to Ballyshannon to visit Cormac's family. And they would be coming to Fermanagh later this month, November, to see Brigid at the guesthouse. Brigid was beside herself with anticipation.

Shane, too, was looking forward to the visit. And he made the comment that Cormac, with his long years of experience in the English Pale, might be well placed to negotiate with the English occupiers he would be meeting along the pathways and waterways of the northwest of Ireland. Their control extended much farther than that, now that Ulster's Gaelic lords had left the country. And worst of all, Enniskillen Castle was in English hands. Five years earlier, Cúchonnacht Maguire had gone so far as to demolish the castle! This was to prevent the English from using it as a strategic base in Fermanagh. Well, the English had it now and were building and rebuilding it to meet their requirements. Every time Brigid looked from her house down to the castle, she was filled with sorrow. And trepidation. How could the Maguire castle, which had been the family's stronghold, in one form or another, for nearly two hundred years, now be the seat of English power? How was that power going to be used here in Fermanagh? And how long would she and her family retain their ancestral home high above the river? The situation was so unthinkable, so perilous, that Shane and Owny spent all their time managing the guesthouse and the servants, the lands and the herds, and keeping watch over the family property. They were determined to keep alive the hope that the house would soon again be filled with guests.

As much as it galled them to do so, they were putting on a show of loyalty to the English crown. Shane and Owny, laying down their weapons! But only for now, only to keep themselves alive and in good form for the next rebellion against foreign rule.

The whole family was at the door when Mary and Cormac arrived at the Tierney guesthouse. Owny was there with a lovely girl, Sinead; they were to be married soon. Eileen and her husband, Donnacha Maguire, stood beaming with their little girl and her new baby sister. Eileen and Owny asked all about their Dublin cousins, and Mary told them they hoped to accompany their parents on another voyage north someday. Owny said he would beat them to it; he would take a trip to Dublin and surprise them in their beds. There was feasting and drinking and never a moment of silence, as they celebrated their reunion well into the night.

The following morning, Brigid invited Mary out for a walk around the property. It was a cold, bright day with a gusty wind, and they donned their cloaks and headed out. They strolled along, looking at the expanses of pasture, the leafless trees, the view of the *English* castle. The conversation turned, inevitably, to the loss of Cúchonnacht Maguire, Rory O'Donnell, Hugh O'Neill, and the other men who had until so recently ruled this part of Ireland.

And then, "Mary, I imagine Cormac told you that day in Dublin — Shane's last day there — that a number of our men did not return from the battles in Munster." Mary stopped and faced Brigid. "And that Diarmait was amongst those . . . Shane has since confirmed that Diarmait fell in battle." Mary was stone-still and didn't speak. "I'm sorry. I've had time to mourn, and maybe you have as well, if you'd already received the news . . ."

Brigid reached out and put her arms around her sister. But Mary pulled away. Brigid was shocked at the look on her face. Mary was in tears, but her expression was one of anger, not grief. "I don't mourn him! If he were alive and here in Fermanagh, I would not have come. As much as I have longed to see you, Brigid, I would not have come."

"Why, Mary? What do you mean?"

She stayed quiet for a long few seconds, then spoke in a voice Brigid could barely hear, "You remember that I warned you about men, a certain kind of man, I mean."

"You were right, Mary. A man forced himself on me. I don't know who he was." Brigid felt the old terror, the old shame, of the attack she had endured. But why was Mary thinking of this now?

"Brigid, it was our brother who did it to me!"

Brigid reared back. "No! That can't be! Did you see his face? I didn't see—"

"It is the truth, Brigid. And if he did it to me, he would do it to you."

Brigid was overcome with weakness; she reached out and grasped the trunk of a tree to keep herself upright. "Why would he do such a terrible thing to us?"

Mary shook her head. "There is no *why*. There is no explanation for a man who would violate his own sisters in such a way."

A blast of wind came up from the water, causing bare branches of the trees to clack against each other. The wind whipped the sisters' cloaks out from their bodies, and they both clutched at their garments and pulled them tight.

Brigid stood shivering, trying to collect her thoughts. She started to speak, but her voice failed her. She cleared her throat and tried again. "How . . . how do you know this, Mary? The man who attacked me was disguised. He was in the robes of a monk from the abbey, and he had a mask over his face."

"That's the way it was for me. If he had been an unknown man, passing through Fermanagh, he would have had no need to hide his face."

"How do you know it was him?" Brigid asked again.

"I didn't know when I gave you that warning, or I'd have told you. I didn't know for years. At the time of my marriage to Cormac, the night before the wedding, some of the young men got into the ale and drank a great quantity of it. Then they went swimming in the river. He was swimming with Diarmait, and he noticed a strange mark on Diarmait's leg, high up on the leg. It looked something like a crown. Cormac pointed to it and asked Diarmait how he got it. And our brother said something like, 'It's the mark of the crown. All Tierney men have it; it's a sign that we are destined for greatness!' He said it in jest. How the mark really got there, Cormac didn't know. Diarmait had fallen on an oddly shaped stone? A friend had jabbed him with something whilst playing the fool?" Mary shrugged her shoulders. "I don't know. I never saw any mark when we were children, so it must have happened when he was older. Anyway, it was years later when Cormac told me this. He never thought to mention it to me until many years later when we were swimming with our children. Our son Art stumbled and fell on a rock and cut his arm. It was bleeding. And this brought back the memory to Cormac; he said something to Art like, 'Don't worry. You may be left with the mark of a crown. And that means you are destined for great things.' And we all laughed a bit. And that's when he told me about the scar on Diarmait's leg."

Mary looked into Brigid's eyes then and said, "I saw that mark — a mark shaped something like a crown — on the leg of the man who raped me."

"Oh, God! I didn't see his leg, but it seems to me now that Diarmait was acting strangely the day after . . . it happened to me in the wood. Avoiding my eyes? I can't remember it in any specific way now. And then he went away and I didn't see him for several weeks. But never, never did it enter my mind that he was the one who . . ."

Mary stepped forward and took Brigid in her arms, and the two of them began to weep over what they had endured, how they had been betrayed.

After a few minutes, Mary gently pulled away and said, "I had a child from it."

Brigid stared at her in horror. "No!"

"Yes. The rape left me pregnant." When Brigid started to speak again, Mary raised a hand. "That's why I left Fermanagh, even though I did not know at the time who had done it to me."

The pain was so raw in Mary's face that Brigid had to turn away. She looked out at the river, at the castle where she would never again enjoy a feast, never again hear the harp played and the praise poems recited. The seat of power no longer of the Lords of Fermanagh but of the rapacious English conquerors.

Mary was looking in the same direction, seeing the same symbol of Irish defeat. But she spoke of the tragedy closer to the family home. "You remember old Eimear."

"I do," Brigid replied. She was an old woman who had close ties to the Tierney family.

"I confided in her, and she made arrangements for me to leave Fermanagh. I gave birth but did not keep the child. I think she took the baby to a friary in Tirconnell, and someone else would be raising him. It sounds heartless for me to say this: I was his mother, but I didn't even want to look at him, him being the product of that man. And I met Cormac soon after that. And thanks be to God, I was able to begin a new life with him. I wonder sometimes about the . . . my son from that time, wonder where he is, how he's getting along, but I force it out of my mind. The circumstances are far too painful for me to think of. I told Cormac all about it when we met, that I had been violated by a stranger, and, of course, he wanted to find the man and kill him. But we left for Dublin and started our life together. And then when he told me the story of the crown mark, he saw that I reacted to it. But we were out with the children, so I put off his questions. I broke down, though, and told him that night. Oh, he was in a rage against that brother."

Once again, the two sisters embraced. Then Mary shocked Brigid again. She said, "Shane knows."

"Eh?"

"I know Cormac told Shane when you were in Dublin."

"Oh!"

Brigid thought back to the joyous reunion with Mary seven years before, and the good times they had, exploring the city and watching the young cousins getting to know one another. And she remembered, too, the look on Shane's face when she saw him and Cormac through the window. Shane had reacted strongly to whatever he had heard. He had told Brigid there was disturbing news out of Munster, that several of the Maguire's musketeers and pikemen had not come home to Fermanagh after Hugh Maguire himself had been killed. And that Diarmait was amongst those still missing. Was that what Shane had just heard? Or had he learned the truth from Cormac about Diarmait's attack on his sister? If so, why had he not told Brigid? She felt a flash of anger at Shane. Didn't she have a right to know? But she understood why he had kept silent: he thought the knowledge would be too painful for her to bear. Well, one thing had been confirmed now, according to Shane: Diarmait was no longer amongst the living.

Somehow, on the hill above the river, Mary and Brigid were able to turn their minds to other things, their children, their grandchildren, the fear for Ireland's future. They returned to the house and had their noonday meal. Then someone began to sing, and Shane asked Brigid to play a tune on the harp. She intended to play a joyful piece but her fingers, as if of their own accord, played out one of her laments. Everyone in the room knew it was a lament for Gaelic Ireland, the death of the Gaelic order. And there were several in the room who knew of another kind of loss, another kind of betrayal. Brigid tried to shake off the mood and switched to some lively tunes that had everyone up dancing.

When she and Shane were alone in their room, she told him what she had learned from Mary. And Shane admitted that, yes, he had heard about Diarmait's monstrous actions, had heard the story from Cormac that day in Dublin. But he had not wanted to subject Brigid to the pain of knowing. Something struck Brigid then: she remembered the expression on Shane's face that day. She pictured the scene again. Shane had looked horrified; he turned to the window, saw Brigid watching him, and he turned away. Now, for the first time, she asked herself, *Did Diarmait really die on the battlefield in Munster?*

Her mind was racing. Her next memory was of Fiach O'Moylan coming to the house with the sheaf of prophecies Sorcha O'Cassidy had uttered the night of her death. The prophecies that had come true with devastating effect. And the curse she had put upon someone for *tangling in the family bed.*

To Shane, she said, "It was Diarmait she was talking to. Sorcha. It was Diarmait standing in the shadows, hearing the curse against him."

"It was."

"It was Diarmait who killed her! My brother murdered my dearest friend! So it must have been Diarmait who got Murrough to give false testimony against you? And then . . ." The look in Shane's eyes was all the confirmation she needed. She lowered her voice and said, "Shane, does Fiach know? Terence Blake? The brehon?"

"I have no reason to think they ever learned the truth of it, after all this time. The brehon is old and weak now, but still, he and the others—"

She raised a hand to stop him. It was clear to her that Shane had kept silent all these years to protect her from the appalling truth. But now he believed that the priest, the lawyer, and the brehon should be told. But Brigid knew she could not bear the disgrace of it, the shameful family secret out in the open, the people of Fermanagh knowing what a member of the Tierney family had done.

"No. Let it stay buried."

CHAPTER XXVI

It is a wise father that knows his own child.

— Shakespeare, *The Merchant of Venice*

2018

Two days after receiving the judgment rendered in 1600 by Shane O'Callaghan, Aisling came rushing into Tierney's hotel lobby again. She said, "You'll be wanting to call Róisín in for this."

Mick picked up the phone and rang the room where he knew Róisín was applying wallpaper and painting the trim. "Rosie, Aisling is here and she has something for us."

"On my way!" And she appeared in the lobby a few seconds later, with nary a drop of paint on her person. "'Bout ye, Aisling?"

"Hi ye, Róisín. I've something here. Two more pages of vellum. And photos of a piece of jewellery." Róisín's eyes lit up. "But I don't think you'll be wanting to wear it. There were a couple of fragments of pottery in the same place, and the base of what may have been a goblet. But I've just brought you the significant items."

"Come on in here," Mick said and led them to the conference room with its long table and chairs. When they were seated, he said, "Let's have it."

"Well, this is strange," Aisling said. "These items weren't there, weren't in the excavation, any time we were working down there. I mean, in the grave — the excavation where we found the body. If they'd been there, we'd have spotted them! We found them in another hole, some distance away. But they clearly relate to the body. Some of the organic matter we found on them matched what was in the grave. We are very fortunate that whoever . . . however they got into that second hole, they were shoved deep enough into the bog and covered, so the vellum did not deteriorate."

Mick and Róisín were silent. The grave where the body was found was the hole that Brayden Waring had invaded. The second hole was where he had reburied the items in a panic after seeing a car approaching.

"These things were not buried down as deeply as the body, as I say, not found *with* our bogman," Aislin said, "so my thinking is that the man who buried the body back in 1600 — and I think we can assume it was the man who authored the 'judgment,' Shane O'Callaghan — put these in later. Maybe he had second thoughts. At first he wasn't going to reveal the whole sordid tale; then he decided, yes, he would. So the pages and the piece of jewellery would have been put into the grave later, above the peat that had been shovelled over the corpse. A layer or two above the body, in other words. So we know they were removed from the excavation before our team got down as far as the body."

That would fit with the timing, Mick knew. The dig had been ransacked the first weekend in June, before the body was discovered.

Aisling reached into her bag and drew out two papers, photocopies of the recovered vellum, and gently slid them across the table. "Once again, you'll be calling upon your skills in reading the Irish language. And I warn you: it doesn't make pleasant reading." And indeed it did not.

> Sorcha, the night she was murdered, uttered prophecies. Transcribed by Father Fiach O'Moylan. And she put a curse upon this man who lies here: "Your family is cursed, and shall be cursed down the generations. All of this for your tangling in the family bed. If any child be born of your unnatural unions, he shall leave as your descendants a line of idiots and evil-doers until the end of time."

"Oh God!" Róisín exclaimed.

> This man was the father of the first-born child of his own sister. The child was left unnamed at a friary in Tirconnell. I learned this from that sister's husband in Dublin. The vile man also raped his other sister. (Owny, if this is unearthed in your lifetime, be assured that you are my son, not the son of this wicked man, your uncle. You resemble me in every way, black curls, blue eyes, your fighting spirit. And you, too, my lovely Eileen, are mine.)

"His own sisters! What a revolting, evil man he was!"

> This man saw Sorcha's knowing eyes on him and his innocent sister at a banquet at the castle. He went to Sorcha's home and heard the curse proclaimed against him and he killed her that same night. This he confessed to me as I stood over him with my musket, before I shot him. My beloved Brigid does not know

I have done this. I deceived her by saying her brother had not returned from a distant battle.

If he had acknowledged his deeds to the brehon, and paid restitution, he would be alive today. But he withheld the truth and attacked many people to keep the truth from being revealed. He might have succeeded in killing Colm and Aidan if he had used his musket, but that would have revealed him as a musketeer. So his weapons were swords and arrows.

Shane O'Callaghan

Mick and his daughter sat at the table without speaking, trying to take in all they had learned. Then Aisling reached into her bag again and produced two photographs. She slid them across the table to Róisín. They showed two sides of an iron disc attached to a chain.

"Ah, the jewellery," Róisín said.

Another item Brayden had snatched from the dig and then returned. Fortunately, in a rare instance of good judgment, he'd had enough sense to cover it up.

"There are words scratched onto one side of the disc," said Róisín, squinting at the photo. "It looks like . . . oh God, it says Tierney."

"Of course it does, Rosie."

"And the first name. It looks like a D. I can't . . ."

Aisling replied, "The man, Shane, must have tossed this in some time after the burial, to leave no doubt about the identity of the body for whoever might find it later. The name looks to me like Diarmait."

Afterwards, when Aisling had gone, Mick and Róisín were sitting in the hotel bar with glasses of whiskey. The two of them were gobsmacked by what they had learned about the Tierneys who preceded them by four hundred years.

"That baby," Róisín began, "the product of incest between brother and sister, could he be the ancestor of what Gran always talked about as the bad Tierneys? Ancestor of old Roddo who disgraced the family name during the Famine?"

"Unlikely, Rosie. The baby was left on the doorstep of a friary, maybe raised there or given to a man and his wife to raise. Those pages say the child was left there 'unnamed.' The mother may have left her wee bundle there and scooted away. However it happened, I doubt that the child was brought up with the name Tierney. And the write-up refers to the sister's husband in Dublin, so she married and moved south. Probably had other children, with the husband. And if this murderous bastard Diarmait went on to have a family, it wasn't with his sisters!"

"So Roddo . . ."

"Was probably just a bad apple. Nothing to do with those horrific incidents in the 1500s."

"Aye, Dad, you're probably right." She took a sip of her whiskey, then raised her glass and clinked it against her father's. "But our own ancestor was Brigid. We've always known that, and she was named on one of those pages. And now we know somebody else: Shane O'Callaghan!"

"Right. Our great-great-, how many greats, grandfather!"

"Of course, now it's going to be known that he killed a man, shot this Diarmait with his musket. I wonder how Gran will react to that."

"She'll react the same way I would, and Liam would have: that incestuous, murdering thug *needed killing*! He violated his own sisters, and then killed the prophetess, and some other fella, and attacked others as well. Sure, we'd bring him to trial if it happened today, but, well, old Shane took care of things — avenged Brigid and her sister and Sorcha — in his own way."

"True enough."

"And," Mick said, leaning towards her over the table, "you'll have noted that the name Tierney does not appear anywhere in that document about the curse. We'll see if we can persuade Aisling to put off displaying the locket, or maybe display only the side with no writing, until . . . Well, Cait, God bless her, won't be with us forever. She's in her nineties now."

"Poor Gran! But you're right; she'd not want to have it on public view in the museum, with our family name there for all to see."

They finished off their whiskeys, and Mick took hold of the two glasses and stood up. He said, "Shane makes it clear that Brigid's son, Owny, was not the product of the . . . was not Diarmait's son. Black curls, blue eyes. That's Liam, *was* Liam, and it's myself. This fellow Shane is our ancestor."

"So are we Tierneys, Dad?"

"Sure we are. Descendants of a Tierney woman."

"Right. And Shane doesn't say 'my wife Brigid.' It's 'my beloved Brigid.' But either way, I know that the women in Gaelic Ireland kept their own names. The way I did myself!"

"Good on you, Róisín Tierney! Another thing we know is that the tower house was always in the Tierney name. We kept it for ourselves and our hotel. And there's no need to have it emblazoned in big gold letters. There will be no gaudy displays of gold here now."

"But maybe another mural."

"For definite, another mural."

POSTSCRIPT

The plantation of Ulster began in earnest after the Flight of the Earls. The Irish were driven off their lands; the lands were given to English and Scottish settlers. The effects continue to reverberate to this day.

I have taken the liberty of using a few of the wonderful poems that were written some years after the date of my story, when they accurately reflected the situation I have described. Credits are in the notes below.

It should be noted that in a story set this far back in history, there are some matters that are, simply, unknown, and I have done my best with those. Brehon law experts differ in their interpretations of some of the legal principles, including those relating to honour price in the case of murder. Following my reading and discussions with various scholars, I have taken the approach that the honour price to be paid by the killer here was the victim's honour price. For my court scene, I have simplified matters, leaving out some of the technical procedures that might have been used. With respect to names, I have seen documents showing that Hugh Maguire's wife was Margaret. There is some uncertainty amongst historians about this, but I decided to use that name. The physical descriptions of some historical figures are not available, so I added some details of my own.

This is a work of fiction. Any liberties taken in the interests of the story, or any errors committed, are mine alone.

NOTES

Chapter I

"The boast of the Irish": John O'Donovan, *The Tribes of Ireland: A Satire by Aenghus O'Daly with Poetical Translation by the Late James Clarence Mangan* (Dublin: John O'Daly, 1852), 23.

"The inhabitants": J. (or T.) Dolan, 1719, in Father P. Ó Maolagáin, "An Early History of Fermanagh," *Clogher Record* (1955), 113.

"Bastards had their portion": Sir John Davies, 1610, in Sir Charles Coote, *Statistical Survey of the County of Cavan* (Graisberry & Campbell, 1802), xvii.

"Rhymers": Fynes Moryson, "The Manners and Customs of Ireland," in *Illustrations of Irish History and Topography, Mainly of the Seventeenth Century*, ed. C. Litton Falkiner (New York: Longmans, Green, and Co., 1904), 311.

Chapter II

"Strains of music": Cú Choigcríche Ó Cléirigh, Maguire praise poem XX, in *Duanaire Mhéig Uidhir*, ed. and trans. David

Greene (Dublin: The School of Celtic Studies of the Dublin Institute for Advanced Studies, 1972, 1991).

"Ships are not sufficient": Iollann Ó Domhnallán, Maguire praise poem XXIV, in *Duanaire Mhéig Uidhir*.

Chapter III
"Something sacred": Tacitus, c. 98 AD, in Peter Berresford Ellis, *The Druids* (London: Constable and Company Ltd., 1994), 97.

Chapter IV
"Would to God": Gwalchmai ap Meilyr, twelfth-century Welsh bard, in Ellis, *The Druids*, 87.

Chapter V
"Shame is an ornament": Aristotle, d. 322 BC.

Chapter VI
"The people are thus inclined": Edmund Campion, *A History of Ireland*, 1571, in *Elizabethan Ireland: A Selection of Writings by Elizabethan Writers on Ireland*, ed. James P. Myers (Hamden: Archon Books, 1983), 24.

Chapter VII
"Under Lionel Duke": William Blackstone, *Commentary on the Laws of England, Vol 1, Introduction, Section iv* (Oxford: Clarendon Press, 1768), 100.

Chapter VIII
"She resided in the summit": Tacitus, c. 98 AD, in Ellis, *The Druids*, 96.

Chapter IX

"Chains of gold": Unknown poet, "Mallacht ort, a Shuaitheantais" ("Curse on you, Emblem"), in Máiréad Dunlevy, *Dress in Ireland* (London: Batsford, 1989), 70.

Chapter X

"How many kinds of court": *Airecht* text, appendix 1, no. 71, in Fergus Kelly, *A Guide to Early Irish Law* (Dublin: The School of Celtic Studies of the Dublin Institute for Advanced Studies, 2015), 362–3.

Chapter XI

"Cúchonnacht Maguire": trans. John O'Donovan, *Annals of the Kingdom of Ireland, by the Four Masters* (Dublin: Hodges, Smith & Co., 1856), 2367.

"Blessings on your head": Pádraigín Haicéad, "For Robert Óg Carrún," in *An Duanaire 1600–1900: Poems of the Dispossessed,* ed./presenter Seán Ó Tuama and trans. Thomas Kinsella (Portlaoise: The Dolmen Press/Bord na Gaeilge, 1981, 1985), 95.

"Granuaile story": Anne Chambers, *Granuaile: Grace O'Malley, Ireland's Pirate Queen* (Dublin: Gill & Macmillan, 2009).

Chapter XII

"None shall wear": *Statutes of Apparel* (6 May 1562) 4 Elizabeth I and (June 15, 1574) 16 Elizabeth I, Elizabethan Sumptuary Statutes, http://elizabethan.org/sumptuary/.

"Spenser, advocating famine": Edmund Spenser, *A View of the Present State of Ireland* (1596), in Myers, *Elizabethan Ireland*, 115–6.

"Great Queene of glory bright": Edmund Spenser, *The Faerie Queene*, Book I, Canto I (1596), 29–30.

"Killed for wrong clothing": Dunlevy, *Dress in Ireland*, 80.

Chapter XIII
"Stars, hide your fires": William Shakespeare, *Macbeth* (I.iv.51–52), in *Shakespeare: The Complete Works*, ed. G.B. Harrison (New York: Harcourt, Brace & World, Inc., 1968).

Chapter XIV
"Loss of our learning": Eoghan Rua Ó Súilleabháin, in Ó Tuama and Kinsella, *An Duanaire*, 195.

"Dismal heaps": Sir John Denham, "Coopers-Hill," in *Sir John Denham Poems and Translations with The Sophy* (London: Henry Herringman, 1668), 149–152.

"A Glance": Anonymous, "A Glance," in Ó Tuama and Kinsella, *An Duanaire*, 15.

"These fashions": Brian Mac Giolla Phádraig, "These Fashions on the Plain of Éibhear," in Ó Tuama and Kinsella, *An Duanaire*, 91.

Chapter XV
"Make use of Connor Roe": The Lord Deputy Mountjoy to the Privy Council, *Calendar of the State Papers Relating to Ireland, during the Reigns of Henry VIII, Edward VI, Mary, and Elizabeth*, vol. 10, 55.

"Morrison re the Mere Irish": trans. Owen Connellan, *Annals of the Four Masters* (Dublin: Bryan Geraghty, 1846), 658.

"Every morning": Anonymous, "Every Morning, My Young Lad," in Ó Tuama and Kinsella, *An Duanaire*, 19.

Chapter XVI
"War, plundering": Connellan, *Annals,* 423.

Chapter XVII
"Pretty girls": Captain Francisco de Cuellar, *A letter written on October 4, 1589, by Captain Cuellar, of the Spanish Armada, to His Majesty King Philip II, recounting his misadventures in Ireland and elsewhere after the wreck of his ship*, trans. H. D. Sedgwick Jr. (New York: G.H. Richmond, 1895), 92.

Chapter XVIII
"Then is it sin": William Shakespeare, *Antony and Cleopatra* (IV. xv. 80–81), in Harrison, *Shakespeare*.

Chapter XIX
"Ode to the Maguire": Eochaidh Ó hEoghusa (O'Hussey), "A Winter Campaign," or "O'Hussey's Ode to the Maguire," in *Irish Bardic Poetry*, ed. Osborn Bergin, Fergus Kelly, David Greene (Dublin: The School of Celtic Studies of the Dublin Institute for Advanced Studies, 1970), 269.

Chapter XX
"Mere Irish will never be reformed": Fynes Moryson, principal secretary to Lord Mountjoy, Queen Elizabeth's Lord Deputy

in Ireland, *An Itinerary*, 1617- c.1626, in Myers, *Elizabethan Ireland*, 199.

"Ingratitude of the Irish": Barnabe Rich, *A New Description of Ireland*, 1610, in Myers, *Elizabethan Ireland*, 135-6, 143.

Chapter XXI
"Faint wailing sound": O'G., "The Irish Funeral Cry," *Dublin Penny Journal* 1, no. 3 (January 26, 1833).

Chapter XXII
"Distinguished crew": O'Donovan, *Annals*, 2359.

Chapter XXIII
"Melodious lyre": Capt. William Taafe, in Connellan, *Annals*, 699.

"Killing in O'Kane's country": Fynes Moryson, in Connellan, *Annals*, 714.

"Cúchonnacht Maguire": O'Donovan, *Annals*, 2367.

Chapter XXIV
"He does not win": Oscar Wilde, *The Ballad of Reading Gaol*, in *The Poems of Oscar Wilde*, intro by Temple Scott (New York: Brentano's, 1910), 3.137–138.

Chapter XXV
"Each man kills": Oscar Wilde, *The Ballad of Reading Gaol*, in Scott, 1.37–42

Chapter XXVI

"A wise father": Shakespeare, *The Merchant of Venice* (II. ii. 79–80), in Harrison, *Shakespeare*.

SELECTED SOURCES CITED
AND CONSULTED

Bergin, Osborn, Fergus Kelly, and David Greene, eds. *Irish Bardic Poetry*. Dublin: The School of Celtic Studies of the Dublin Institute for Advanced Studies, 1970.

Blackstone, William, 1723–1780. *Commentaries on the Laws of England*. Oxford: Clarendon Press, 1768.

Brady, Conor. *The Guarding of Ireland: The Garda Síochána & the Irish State 1960–2014*. Dublin: Gill & Macmillan, 2014.

Cahill, Thomas. *How the Irish Saved Civilization*. New York: Nan Talese/Doubleday, 1995.

Campbell, Eve, Elizabeth FitzPatrick, and Audrey Horning, eds. *Becoming and Belonging in Ireland AD c. 1200–1600: Essays in Identity and Cultural Practice*. Cork: Cork University Press, 2018.

Campion, Edmund. *A History of Ireland (1571)*. In *Elizabethan Ireland: A Selection of Writings by Elizabethan Writers on Ireland*, edited by James P. Myers, 22–35. Hamden: Archon Books, 1983.

Chambers, Anne. *Granuaile: Grace O'Malley, Ireland's Pirate Queen*. Dublin: Gill & Macmillan, 2009.

Connellan, Owen, translator. *Annals of the Four Masters*. Dublin: Bryan Geraghty, 1846.

De Cuellar, Capt. Francisco. *A letter written on October 4, 1589, by Captain Cuellar, of the Spanish Armada, to His Majesty King Philip II, Recounting His Misadventures in Ireland and Elsewhere after the Wreck of his Ship*. Translated by H.D. Sedgwick Jr. New York: G.H. Richmond, 1895.

Delaney, M. and R. O Floinn. "A Bog Body from Meenybraddan Bog, County Donegal, Ireland." In *Bog Bodies*, edited by R. Turner and R. Scaife, 123–132. London: British Museum Press, 1995.

Denham, Sir John. "Coopers-Hill." In *Sir John Denham Poems and Translations with The Sophy*. London: Henry Herringman, 1668.

Dunlevy, Máiréad. *Dress in Ireland*. London: Batsford, 1989.

Flavin, Susan. *Consumption and Culture in Sixteenth-Century Ireland: Saffron, Stockings and Silk*. Woodbridge: The Boydell Press, 2014.

Ginnell, Lawrence. *The Brehon Laws: A Legal Handbook*. 1894. London: Forgotten Books, 2012.

Great Britain. Public Record Office. *Calendar of the State Papers Relating to Ireland, of the Reigns of Henry VIII, Edward VI, Mary, and Elizabeth*, edited by Robert Pentland Mahaffy, Ernest George Atkinson, and Hans Claude Hamilton. London: Longman, Green, Longman, & Roberts, 1860–1912.

Greene, David, ed. *Duanaire Mhéig Uidhir: The Poembook of Cú Chonnacht Mág Uidhir, Lord of Fermanagh 1566–1589*. Dublin: The School of Celtic Studies of the Dublin Institute for Advanced Studies, 1991.

Johnson, Gordon. *Maguire's House Party*, a model of a 1586 banquet at Enniskillen Castle.

Kelly, Fergus. *A Guide to Early Irish Law*. Dublin: The School of

Celtic Studies of the Dublin Institute for Advanced Studies, 2015.

Lawrence, Richard. *The Interest of Ireland in its Trade and Wealth*. Dublin, 1682. Cited in *Dress in Ireland*, by Máiréad Dunlevy, 83. London: Batsford, 1989.

Lysaght, Patricia. *The Banshee: The Irish Supernatural Death Messenger*. Dublin: The O'Brien Press, 1986.

McGowan, Brendan. "By-Laws of Medieval Galway." National Museum of Ireland, October 1, 2012. http://www. ouririshheritage.org/content/archive/place/mo-ghaillimh-fein-my-own-galway/within-the-walls-of-medieval-galway/by-laws-of-medieval-galway.

Moryson, Fynes. *An Itinerary, 1617–c. 1626*. In *Elizabethan Ireland: A Selection of Writings by Elizabethan Writers on Ireland*, edited by James P. Myers, 185–240. Hamden: Archon Books, 1983.

Moryson, Fynes, "The Manners and Customs of Ireland." In *Illustrations of Irish History and Topography, Mainly of the Seventeenth Century*, edited by C. Litton Falkiner, 310–325. New York: Longmans, Green, and Co., 1904.

Moss, Rachel. "Continuity and Change: The Material Setting of Public Worship in the Sixteenth-Century." In *Dublin and the Pale in the Renaissance, 1494–1660*, edited by M. Potterton and T. Herron, 182–206. Dublin: Four Courts Press, 2011.

Moss, Rachel. "Reduce, Re-use, Re-cycle: Irish Monastic Architecture c. 1540–1640." In *Irish Gothic Architecture: Construction, Decay and Reinvention*, edited by R. Stalley, 115–160. Dublin: Wordwell, 2012.

Myers, James P., ed. *Elizabethan Ireland: A Selection of Writings by Elizabethan Writers on Ireland*. Hamden: Archon Books, 1983.

Ó Corráin, Donnchadh. "Women and the Law in Early Ireland." In *Chattel, Servant or Citizen: Women's Status in Church, State and Society*, edited by Mary O'Dowd and Sabine Wichert, 45–57. Belfast: Institute of Irish Studies, Queen's University, 1995.

O'Donovan, John, trans. *Annals of the Kingdom of Ireland, by the Four Masters from the Earliest Period to the Year 1616* (seven volumes). Dublin: Hodges, Smith, & Co., 1856.

O'Donovan, John. "The Maguires of Fermanagh." *Duffy's Hibernian Magazine* 2, no. 10, (1861).

O'Donovan, John. *The Tribes of Ireland: A Satire by Aenghus O'Daly with Poetical Translation by the Late James Clarence Mangan*, 23. Dublin: John O'Daly, 1852.

O'G. "The Irish Funeral Cry." *Dublin Penny Journal* 1, no. 31 (January 26, 1833).

Ó Maolagáin, Father P. "An Early History of Fermanagh." *Clogher Record* 1, no. 3 (1955): 131.

O'Sullivan Beare, Philip. 1621. *Ireland Under Elizabeth: Chapters Towards a History of Ireland in the Reign of Elizabeth*. Translated by Matthew J. Byrne. Dublin: Sealy, Bryers, & Walker, 1903.

O'Sullivan, Catherine Marie. *Hospitality in Medieval Ireland 900–1500*. Dublin: Four Courts Press, 2004.

Ó Tuama, Seán, ed. and presenter, and Thomas Kinsella, trans. *An Duanaire 1600–1900: Poems of the Dispossessed*. Portlaoise: The Dolmen Press i gcomhar le Bord na Gaeilge, 1981, 1985.

Rich, Barnabe. 1610. *A New Description of Ireland, Together with the Manners, Customs, and Dispositions of the People*. In *Elizabethan Ireland: A Selection of Writings by Elizabethan Writers on Ireland*, edited by James P. Myers, 126–145. Hamden: Archon Books, 1983.

Shakespeare, William. *Shakespeare: The Complete Works*, edited by G. B. Harrison, 579–612, *Merchant of Venice*; 1184–1218, *Macbeth*; 1219–1264, *Antony and Cleopatra*. New York: Harcourt, Brace & World, Inc., 1968.

Simms, Katharine. "Guesting and Feasting in Gaelic Ireland." In *The Journal of the Royal Society of Antiquaries of Ireland* 108 (1978): 67–100.

Spenser, Edmund. *A View of the Present State of Ireland*. 1596. In *Elizabethan Ireland: A Selection of Writings by Elizabethan Writers on Ireland*, edited by James P. Myers. Hamden: Archon Books, 1983.

Spenser, Edmund. *The Faerie Queene*. Book I, Canto I, 1596.

Statutes of Apparel, (6 May 1562) 4 Elizabeth I and (15 June 1574) 16 Elizabeth I. Elizabethan Sumptuary Statutes. http://elizabethan .org/sumptuary/.

Swords, Liam. *The Flight of the Earls: A Popular History*. Dublin: The Columba Press, 2007.

Walsh, Rev. Paul. "The Chieftains of Fermanagh." *The Irish Ecclesiastical Record*. c. 1922. https://archive.org/stream/ s5p1irishecclesi19dubluoft/s5p1irishecclesi19dubluoft_djvu.txt.

Wilde, Oscar. *The Ballad of Reading Gaol*, 1898. In *The Poems of Oscar Wilde*, introduction by Temple Scott, 255–85. New York: Brentano's, 1910.

ACKNOWLEDGEMENTS

I would like to thank the following people for their kind assistance and expertise. Rhea McGarva, who found a copy of *An Duanaire 1600–1900: Poems of the Dispossessed* in a charity shop in Nova Scotia; the volunteer at the shop did not want any payment because it was considered to be of little value! This priceless volume was one of the main inspirations for the novel. Heartfelt thanks as well to Joan Butcher, Joe A. Cameron, and the following professors, authors, museum curators, and other experts: Fergus Kelly, Martin Kelly, Liam Breatnach, Eibhlin Nic Dhonnca, The School of Celtic Studies of the Dublin Institute for Advanced Studies, Thomas Kinsella, Pádraig Ó Siadhail, Paul Mullarkey, Rachel Moss, Susan Flavin, Sparky Booker, Liam Corry, Peter McElhinney, Fergus Britton, Colm Lennon, Viola Wiggins, Caoimhe Ní Ghormáin, Fred Ternan, Kevin Flanagan Coombes. The people at the Enniskillen Library: Melanie Ward, Margaret Kane, Seán Corr, and Fiona. Thanks as well to Ursula and Tim Fernée, Mary Turley-McGrath, and Jim and Angela Chestnutt. And Ranke de Vries, the Celtic Studies Department, St. F.X. University (Antigonish), Lorena Brothers, and Susan Cameron.

And, as always, thanks to my very astute editors, Cat London and Crissy Calhoun.

ENVIRONMENTAL BENEFITS STATEMENT

ECW Press Ltd saved the following resources by printing the pages of this book on chlorine free paper made with 100% post-consumer waste.

TREES	WATER	ENERGY	SOLID WASTE	GREENHOUSE GASES
25	2,000	10	90	10,650
FULLY GROWN	GALLONS	MILLION BTUs	POUNDS	POUNDS

Environmental impact estimates were made using the Environmental Paper Network Paper Calculator 4.0. For more information visit www.papercalculator.org

This book is also available as a Global Certified Accessible™ (GCA) ebook. ECW Press's ebooks are screen reader friendly and are built to meet the needs of those who are unable to read standard print due to blindness, low vision, dyslexia, or a physical disability.

Purchase the print edition and receive the eBook free!
Just send an email to ebook@ecwpress.com and include:

- the book title
- the name of the store where you purchased it
- your receipt number
- your preference of file type: PDF or ePub

A real person will respond to your email with your eBook attached.
And thanks for supporting an independently owned Canadian publisher with your purchase!